Modernization of Korean Theatre in the 20th Century

Lee provides a comprehensive guide that traces the transformation of Korean theatre from traditional to modern theatre and examines the impact of the introduction of Western plays to Korean society.

Important changes in Korean theatre are discussed chronologically from the beginning of the modernization: *Sinpa* Theatre, *Singeuk* Theatre, Theatre of Ideology, The Little Theatre Movement, *Madanggeuk*, experiments for modernizing traditional Korean theatrical arts, and transitions to postmodern theatre. These changes happened rapidly and coupled with Eurocentric globalization. By the end of the century, the reinterpretations of Western drama like Shakespeare's plays had reached a point where they received attention from the Western world. Today, Korean theatre keeps pace with the world theatre and strives to contribute as a member of it.

This book is a vital resource for scholars and students pursuing Korean studies and East Asian theatres with an authentic Korean perspective from a Korean scholar who has lived and researched in Korea.

Meewon Lee is Professor Emerita of Korea National University of Arts in Seoul, Korea. Her publications include *Korean Traditions and Performances in the Postmodern Era*. She is focused on esthetics of Korean theatre, related to its traditions and world theatre.

Recent Advances in Korean Studies

53. South Korea's foreign aid
The domestic politics of middle power diplomacy
Hyo-sook Kim

54. Commons Perspectives in South Korea
Contexts, Fields, and Alternatives
Edited by Hyun Choe, Ja-Kyung Kim, Hun-Gyo Jang, Yea-Yl Yoon and Suh-Hyun Park

55. Confucian Reform in Chosun Korea
Yu Hyŏngwŏn's Pan'gye surok
Authored by Yu Hyŏngwŏn and edited by Woosung Bae

56. Social Policy Dynamics in South Korea
Soon-Yang Kim

57. Korean Film and Festivals
Global Transcultural Flows
Soon-Yang Kim

58. Power and the Elite in North Korea
Paektu and Kanbu
Jae-Cheon Lim

59. State, Rural Women, and Domestication in Korea
The Aspiring Middle Class
Jaok Kwon

60. Innovations of Modern Korean Theatre in the 20th Century
Meewon Lee

For more information about this series, please visit:
www.routledge.com/asianstudies/series/SE0505

Modernization of Korean Theatre in the 20th Century

Meewon Lee

Routledge
Taylor & Francis Group
LONDON AND NEW YORK

First published 2025
by Routledge
4 Park Square, Milton Park, Abingdon, Oxon OX14 4RN

and by Routledge
605 Third Avenue, New York, NY 10158

Routledge is an imprint of the Taylor & Francis Group, an informa business

British Library Cataloguing-in-Publication Data
A catalogue record for this book is available from the British Library

ISBN: 9781032791418 (hbk)
ISBN: 9781032791425 (pbk)
ISBN: 9781003490708 (ebk)

DOI: 10.4324/9781003490708

Typeset in Galliard
by Deanta Global Publishing Services, Chennai, India

This work was supported by the Ministry of Education of the Republic of Korea and the National Research Foundation of Korea (NRF-2020S1A5A2A01044030).

To my father, Dr. Duhyun Lee, who himself was a great scholar in Korean theatre and inspired me throughout my life.

Contents

List of Figures

Preface

This book, *Modernization of Korean Theatre in the 20th Century,* intends to be a comprehensive guide to 20th-century Korean theatre, especially for scholars and students pursuing Korean studies as well as those studying East Asian theatres. This book emerged from the necessity to fill gaps in Korean theatre research in English. Based on the concept of theatre historiography, a Korean theatre history is written from the perspective of an indigenous Korean scholar. It contains the greatest amount of data and research materials regarding Korean theatre ever written in English, collected and written by a Korean scholar who has conducted research for years while residing in Korea. It not only helps to delineate the history of Korean theatre from Korean's authentic perspective, but it also provides contexts for Korean theatre within the larger domain of world theatre.

The 20th century was the period when Western modernization began in earnest in Korea, bringing more changes than ever before. Korean theatre transformed from traditional theatre to modern realism theatre. This book addresses the modernization of Korean theatre during the colonial period and after, i.e., the process of incorporating realism theatre, and examines the impact of the introduction of Western plays to Korean society. In short, it is a detailed discussion of the modernization and innovation of Korean theatre in the 20th century. Cultural and political debates are also discussed here. The scope is encyclopedic and aims to cover key terms, genres, movements, plays, and artists in the Korean theatre as expressions of Korean modernity. The major changes in theatre are discussed from the beginning of the modernization of Korean theatre: such as *Sinpa Theatre, Singeuk* Theatre, Theatre of Ideology, The Little Theatre Movement, *Madanggeuk,* the experiments to modernize traditional Korean theatrical arts, and the transitions to the postmodern theatre. These changes were rapid and were parts of a process that kept pace with Westernized globalization. By the end of the century, the reinterpretations of Western drama like Shakespeare matured enough to draw attention from the West. Today, Korean theatre keeps pace with world theater and strives to contribute as a member of it.

Due to its bulky volume, it is divided into two books: the first book, *Modernization of Korean Theatre in the 20th Century* is about the history of

20th-century Korean theatre divided according to the major transitions, and the second book, *Innovation of Modern Korean Theare in the 20th Century*, is about the selection of topics that require in-depth evaluation for their importance within Korean theatre throughout the 20th century. The chronological history and significant subjects among the history complement each other and describe 20th-century Korean theatre in detail. It can be read as a conversation between the linear official history of theatre in Korea and the moments of rupture and innovation.

The romanization followed the current romanization system of The National Institute of the Korean Language of the Ministry of Culture, Sports, and Tourism[1] instead of the McCune-Reischauer system, which is most often used in the West. The current Korean romanization is more convenient since it does not need to use diacritics on vowels. Korean names usually consist of a family name, followed by a given name; thus, I used the last name first. Among the last names, many of them do not fit the current romanization system but have been used conventionally. For example, Lee or Park are often used instead of Yi or Bak. If English names are known, I follow them instead of following the current romanization system. The writer apologizes to readers who may be confused by the differences between the two translation systems, but there is no significant difference if you pay a little attention.

Hardly anyone can write a book of this scope without great debt to many scholars. I express my deep gratitude and respect for their achievements. Their contributions are duly recognized in the notes and bibliography since they

vowel				consonant			
한글	영문	한글	영문	한글	영문	한글	영문
ㅏ	a	ㅕ	yeo	ㄱ	g, k	ㅌ	t
ㅓ	eo	ㅛ	yo	ㄴ	n	ㅍ	p
ㅗ	o	ㅠ	yu	ㄷ	d, t	ㅎ	h
ㅜ	u	ㅒ	yae	ㄹ	r, l	ㄲ	kk
ㅡ	eu	ㅖ	yeo	ㅁ	m	ㄸ	tt
ㅣ	i	ㅘ	wa	ㅂ	b, p	ㅃ	pp
ㅐ	ae	ㅙ	wae	ㅅ	s	ㅆ	ss
ㅔ	e	ㅝ	wo	ㅇ	ng	ㅉ	jj
ㅚ	oe	ㅞ	we	ㅈ	j		
ㅟ	wi	ㅢ	ui	ㅊ	ch		
ㅑ	ya			ㅋ	k		

Figure 0.1 The Chart That Shows the Romanization Rules of Korean Words According to The National Institute of the Korean Language of the Ministry of Culture, Sports, and Tourism.

are too many to name one by one. I send my special thanks to Ms. Jennifer Schaupp, Ms. Bona Choi, and Ms. Jiyoung Kim for their proofreading and assistance. I am also grateful to my husband Soonchul Jo for his encouragement. However, my deepest gratitude goes to the memory of my parents, Dr. Duhyun Lee and Ms. Gyebong Hwang. Especially, from the bottom of my heart, I must dedicate this book to my father Dr. Duhyun Lee, who himself was a great scholar in Korean theatre history, guided me to be a theatre scholar, asked me to write Korean theatre history in English to let the world know Korean theatre, and above all inspired me throughout my life.

Introduction: What is Modernization in Korea?

Historical Background

What is modernization in Korea? It is necessary to discuss the concept of modernization in order to understand consider the modernization of Korean theatre. Indeed, what is modernization? Modern age is one of the three large periods in Western history, which includes ancient, medieval, and modern ages. Modernization in the Western world is commonly deemed to have started after the French Revolution and the Industrial Revolution in the 18th century. In other words, it happened after the achievement of social equality and the accumulation of capital. The French Revolution eventually destroyed the aristocratic social hierarchy and achieved equality and freedom for the people, while the Industrial Revolution changed the basis of the economy. Agricultural society consisted of aristocrats and common farmers was transformed into an industrial ones. Mechanical innovations, such as the steam engine, made mass industrial productions possible, which sped up the accumulation of capital. Thus, strong nations were politically built, and reasoning and scientific thought prevailed in culture. Along with these cultural trends, Western imperialism emerged. Imperialism was a way to meet the needs of industrial materials and markets to sell mass produced industrial goods. Therefore, Western imperialism expanded, and the accumulation of capital accelerated as modernization ensued.

In Asia, modernization began with Western imperialism. To most Asian countries, including Korea, modern mostly meant Western. The beginning of modernization differed depending on when Western imperialism started in each country. Since the mid-19th century of Joseon, the last royal dynasty of Korea, periods of multiple rapid social and political changes had emerged. Daewongun (大院君), a major political figure and the father of King Gojong, banned all foreign trades and any cultural interaction in the 19th century. He was afraid of foreign powers' invasions. However, upon losing the battle of Ganghwa Island with Japan, a compulsory trade treaty with Japan was ratified in 1876. Japan, learning from Western civilizations, was quick to imitate the imperialism of the West. Japan, therefore, made an unequal treaty that paved a path toward colonizing Joseon. After this trade agreement, many Western powers, such as England, U.S.A., and Russia, sought the same benefits from Korea, and, from there on, Westernization rapidly spread.

DOI: 10.4324/9781003490708-1

Korean society soon realized the power of Westernization and the need to learn the West's political, social, and economic systems. Thus, the Western modernization of Korea began. The biggest reformation of the Joseon government was initiated from Gabogeongjang (甲午更張:The Joseon's Modern Reformation) in 1894. It declared the abolishment of social classes and slavery, executing a new government-hiring scheme based on individual talent. It also included prohibition of early marriages, legalization of remarriage of widows, tax payments in cash, standardization of weights and measures, establishment of banks and companies, and many others. Although nowadays there are conflicting views on the success of this reformation, Gabogeongjang at least served as momentum for the modernization in Korea. In other words, it was the official beginning of Westernized modernization of Korea.[1]

Indeed, scholars have different opinions about the beginning period of Korean modernization; there are mainly three opinions that coincide with the literary views on Korean modernization.[2] The first and the most prevailing opinion is that the beginning of Korean Westernization was the beginning of modernization in Korea. As mentioned above, Gabogeongjang was considered to be the first step of modernization. Westernization and modernization went hand in hand in Korea throughout the 20th century.

The other opinions about the beginning period of Korean modernization were suggested after post-colonial thoughts in the 1970s. Among them, two are most dominant; one views the beginning of modernization around the 18th century, and the other views it after 1945, when Korea was liberated from Japan. The former opinion sees modernization from the same perspective as the West: i.e., the beginning of accumulation of capital and the abolition of caste system. After the two invasions from Japan (1592-98) and China (1636-37), Joseon dynasty began to change around the 18th century; the agricultural society based on farming became destabilized, and the peddler (i.e., merchant) class was rising accumulating wealth (the signs of capital accumulations). The Yangban, aristocrats of Joseon Dynasty, was weakened after the 18th century due to the two wars. There was even a case of marriage between a rich peddler's daughter and a poor Yangban's son, which was not possible before the 18th century. In addition, although the official letters were still in Chinese characters, vernacular Korean letters, Hangeul, were widely used. In writing prose style prevailed over that of poetic. Scholars with this point of view consider the modernization in Korea to be independent of imperialism and Westernization since the economic, social, and cultural signs indicated the modernization of Korea in the 18th century.[3] Other scholars who believe that Korean modernization began after the independence consider civic consciousness to be essential for true modernization. No civic consciousness, freedom, or equality existed under colonial Korea, and limitations on economic activities for capital accumulation were enforced. Therefore, these scholars believe true modernization could not have proceeded under the colonial society and also consider independence to be an important factor for modernization. In other words, self-developed modernization is vital to post-colonial scholars.

However, these two ideas on the beginning of modernization in Korea are minor opinions, and, in general, the reception of Westernization in Joseon is believed to be the beginning of modernization in Korea.

The Westernization of Korea was strongly concentrated on the cultural aspect while economic and political aspects were very neglected. It was because korea lost its diplomatic rights in 1905 and finally was colonized in 1910 by Japan. Korea did not exist as a nation until 1945 when Japan lost World War II. Modernization was limited to imitating rational and scientific Western thoughts and systems, such as the abolition of the caste system. Though cultural resistance against Western culture existed, most of the intelligentsia of the time was very eager to be westernized since the West had superior military power. In order to overcome the imperial interference in their domestic affairs, they believed it was important to learn and imitate the Western powers and science of that time. Even so, under the colonial occupation, it was difficult to do any political action and economically prosper for Korea. The economic conditions worsened as Japanese colonial policies became severe. Freedom of thought, especially in politics, was extremely restricted in contrast to other colonial nations of Japan and the West. In fact, only the social caste system ended up getting abolished. That, too, was relatively easy to overturn since Korea's government collapsed. Most intelligentsia of the time were concerned about gaining independence; thus, some members refused modernization since it came with colonialism.

Various historical events led to Joseon's colonization. In the process of modernization, all of the events described below arose for the independence of Joseon, but as a result, they drew in the armed forces of China and Japan, and this led Joseon on the path of colonization. Before the official colonial rule of Japan, severe social conflicts developed between the Confucian conservatives and the modern progressives, the two main factions of the Joseon dynasty. The conservatives hoped to keep the tradition and nationality amid overwhelming foreign powers, while the progressives wanted to utilize Western science and powers. The conflicts began right after the compulsory trade treaty with Japan in 1876. After losing the battle of Ganghwa Island against Japan, Daewongun, a major conservative political figure and the father of King Gojong, lost his political power while Queen Min, the wife of King Gojong, emerged as the progressive political power in the royal family. These two people were the heads of the conservative and the progressive powers and were hostile to each other, whereas King Gojong tended to remain neutral amid the power struggles. The progressive Queen Min's cabinet treated the old military army poorly in contrast to being supportive of the new modern military army. For instance, soldiers of the old army did not receive salaries for more than a year. And when they finally received a month's worth of salary, half of their salary rice was mingled with grits. The old army rebelled against Queen Min's cabinet and asked for the help of Daewongun. Although Daewongun officially asked for the restraint of the old army, he still supported the old army. He even attempted to kill Queen Min and, at the same time, mowed down the Japanese army as well as overthrew Queen Min's cabinet in 1882. Queen Min soon after fled and asked for the help from China. As a result, China sent its army, kidnapped, brought Daewongun to China, and overthrew his cabinet. The conservative power lasted only briefly, and, consequently, China expanded its power over Korea. This 1882 event became known as Imogunran(壬午軍亂).

As the Chinese interference in Korean domestic affairs grew, young progressive intellectuals, including Kim OkGyun and Park YoungHo, gathered. They aimed to be independent from any foreign powers and to build a modern nation. They even raised a private military for this purpose. The Japanese diplomatic minister approached them and offered assistance to expand their power in Korea. In order to expel the Chinese army, the progressive—or enlightenment—party accepted this offer. When China withdrew half of its army to the war against France in Vietnam, the progressive party decided to act. They chose the opening ceremony of the postal office in 1884 and overthrew the pro-Chinese cabinet. But, Queen Min secretly allied with China and insisted that King Gojong should move back to Changdeok palace, where it was difficult to defend the intruders from the outside. Ultimately, the Chinese army succeeded in seizing the king. The progressive party's revolt only lasted three days. Japan did not keep its promise to help. This 1884 event was called Gapsin-Jongbyun(甲申政變).

In addition to the events above, the Donghak Revolution(東學革命), the uprising of the peasants in 1894, provided a good excuse for China and Japan to dispatch their armies. They sent their armies to suppress the farmers' uprising in Korea under the guise of protection. However, even when the Donghak Revolution ended, Japan refused to retreat its army. Japan suggested the co-reformation of the Korean government with the Chinese government, but China refused. Then, Japan declared war against China, and China against Japan. Quite easily, Japan won the war with China in 1895 and ended the Sino-centric world order in Asia. Even though Korea resisted Japan, Japanese supervision over the Korean cabinet became stronger as time went by. Japan had another war between 1904 and 1905 with Russia for the control of Korea and Manchuria. Japan also won this war and gained control over Korea. Japan deprived Korea of its diplomatic rights in 1905 and finally colonized Korea in 1910. During this period of rapid changes, the progressives gained more power over the conservatives.[4]

Both sides had their advantages, but the progressives had to compromise with Japanese colonial policies in order to be modernized. In spite of their goodwill at the beginning, the progressives became a pro-Japanese party and betrayers to the independence movement. Contemporary Koreans at that time had mixed feelings toward the modernization in Korea. Therefore, a large number of people, especially among the conservatives, were against Korean modernization even though they agreed on Western science and ideals. Eventually, Western culture arrived in Korea at least by the 1920s via Japan. Regardless of whether various aspects of modernization were fully established, refused, or not welcomed, the importance of time should be considered when discussing modernization. Ultimately, modernization, along with Westernization, in Korea was achieved at least by the second decade of the 20th century. Modernization brought many changes to Korean social system, ideology, and culture. Korean theatre was influenced by these changes. Modern realism drama from the West made its first appearance at the turn of the 20th century and found permanence in the 1920s. Thus, the 20th century was the time of theatrical modernization and innovation along with other cultural changes in Korea.

Notes

1 On the history of this period, many Korean history books are referenced, such as the following:
Lee, GiBaek. *HangukSa Sango.* Seoul, Iljogak, 2005.
Lee, GwangRin. *Hanguk GaeWhaSa YeonGu.* Seoul, Iljogak, 1984.
Yang, DongHyun. *GaeHwaGi Minjung GyohwaSa.* Seoul, CahngJoGak, 1988.
2 The discussion of Korean modernity in literature is best represented in the following book:
Formation process of modern literature. Korean Association of Traditional Literature Ed., Seoul, Munhak gwa Jiseongsa, 1983.
3 Kim, Yunsik, and Kim Hyun. *Korean Literary History.* Seoul, Minumsa, 1973.
4 Refer to the history books above.

1 The Beginning of Modern Theatre and Cultural Resistance

The modernization of Korean theatre began at the turn of the 20th century with the reception and incorporation of Western realist theatre. The reformation of Korean theatre started amidst larger social reformations. The reception of Western culture and modernization was controversial in Korea at the time. The society understood the advantages of Westernization but feared the loss of tradition threatened by the hostility of imperialism. This chapter explores first the possible forms of autochthonous modern Korean theatre and then the influx of Western culture and the introduction of Western theatre, showcasing the transition from traditional theatre to Western theatre.

1.1 The Possible Autochthonous Modern Korean Theatre

Some scholars assert that Korean modernization was independent of imperialism and Westernization because of the economic, social, and cultural signs indicating the modernization of Korea. The evidence of modernization appeared as early as the mid-17th century. Theatre needed change since the *Sandae* governmental office (called *Sandae-* or *Narye-Dogam* 山臺都監), which presided over court theatrical arts, was abolished in 1635 during the regime of King Injo. It was abolished due to the financial shortages that resulted from the two massive wars with Japan and China.[1] The transition of the Chinese kingdom from Ming to Qing also resulted in a lesser need for official performances that welcomed Chinese envoys, which the Joseon government had been providing because Joseon thought itself as a brother country of the Ming. The performers dismissed from the government had to find new patrons and wandered around the country. It is assumed that they allied with local performers and created new genres, such as Mask-Dance theatres (*Talnori, Talchum, Gamyeongeuk, or Kamyeongeuk*[2]) and *Pansori.*

These new genres indicated that Korean modernization started independently from Westernization and imperialism since the cultural signs as well as the social and economic directions already suggested the modernization of Korea in the 18th century. These two genres, Mask-Dance theatres and *Pansori,* were quite different from the earlier forms of *Sandae* Hundred Entertainments. While *Sandae* Hundred Entertainments largely comprised

DOI: 10.4324/9781003490708-2

dances, acrobatics, and short skits, Mask-Dance theatre had many language-based storytelling scenes, and *Pansori* mostly depended on narrations delivered through singing. These are the aspects of self-sustaining theatrical genres of Korean modern theatre. Although their forms were quite different from Westernized genres, they will be introduced as examples that show the signs of Korean modernization.

1.1.1 Mask-Dance Theatres

Mask-Dance theatres (*Talnori, Talchum, or 假面劇)* stemmed from folk theatres and gradually became a mixture of folk and professional theatres. Mask-Dance theatres were popular among the public; they were originally performed at village rituals, festivals, and religious celebrations, such as Buddha's birthday. After the abolition of *Sandae-Dogam*, the governmental office that presided over court theatrical arts, folk Mask-Dance theatres accepted professional performers of *Sandae-Dogam* and became semi-professional by the 18th century. Mask-Dance theatres had regional variations and were spread out throughout the Korean peninsula. It is necessary to identify their regional variations and to characterize their typical examples to fully understand Mask-Dance theatres.

Two types of extant Korean Mask-Dance theatres are worth noting; one is the 13th-century folk version performed in farming villages, and the other is the 18th-century semi-professional version performed in developing cities at the time.[3] Pyolsin Kut-Nori of Hahoe and Byeongsan Mask-Dance theatre are the remnants of the earlier forms, while the later forms include *Talchum* of Bongsan and Enyeul in the Hwanghae Province, *Sandae-Nori* of Yangju and Songpa in the Gyunggi Province, *Yaryu* of Suyong and DongRae on the eastern side of Nakdong River, and *Okwangdae* of Tongyong, Gosong, and Gasan on the western side in the Gyeongsang Province. The earlier and the later types of Mask-Dance theatres have substantial differences. Table 1.1 shows the episodes of each representative Mask-Dance theatres. In this table, the columns further to the left include more episodes of theatres than those on the right, indicating that the theatres on the further left were developed later (Table 1.1).

The general structure of Korean Mask-Dance theatres was episodic; they had a series of episodes within the ritualistic frame. There were no linear plot connections among episodes, but each episode reflected the ordinary people's lives at the time. The opening and closing of Mask-Dance theatres included ritual ceremonies, and, in between them, the story episodes unfolded. Overall, Korean Mask-Dance theatres have a ritualistic frame similar to the old Greek tragedy and comedy, with parodos and exodus at the beginning and the end of the performance. Episodes could be divided into two groups: one is the episodes of song and dance, and the other is the episodes of stories. The song and dance episodes are Monk Dance, Sadang Dance, Lion Dance, and Leper Dance. Among these dances, only

Table 1.1 Table of Korean Mask-Dance Episodes

Type Various FormsRegional Area	*Town-Type Mask-Dance Theatre*					*Village-Type*
	Talchum	*Sandae Nori*	*Okwang-dae*	*Yaryu*	*Lion Dance*	*Pyosin Kut-Nori*
	Pongsan	*Yangju*	*Gasan*	*Suyong*	*Pukchong*	*Hohoe*
Exorcising Dance	0	0	0	X	0	0
The Buddhist Monk	0	0	X	X	X	X
Omjung/Sangchwa	X	0				
Mokjung/Omjung	X	0				
Yonip/Nunkkum- joki	X	0				
Yombul-Nori	0	0				
Pupko-Nori	▵	0				
Acupuncture Play	X	0				
Sadang Dance	0	X	X	X	X	X
The Old Priest	0	0	0	X	X	0
The Priest	0	0	0			0
The Shoe Seller	0	0	X			X
The Prodigal	0	0	X			X
The Lion Dance	0	X	X	0	0	X
The Noblemen	0	0	0	0	▵	0
Umak-Nori	0	0	0	0		0
Podobujang	▵	0	X	X		X
The Leper Play	X	X	0	X	X	X
The Old Man &Wife	0	0	0	0	X	▵
The Man & Wife	0	0	0	0		▵
The Concubine	0	X	0	0		X
The Ritual for the Dead	0	0	0	X	X	X

Key: 0—Episode or Scene is present.
X—Episode or Scene is not present.
▵ —Episode or Scene was probably present in the past or has a similar variation.

the episode of Monk Dance includes a few lines of witticism and satire. However, these lines do not aim for any development of the story. Thus, the song and dance episodes mainly contribute to the merriment and the festivity of the performance.

Figure 1.1 Monk Dance. Photo by *Bongsan* Mask-Dance Preservation Group

Figure 1.2 The Lion Dance. Photo by *Bongsan* Mask-Dance Preservation Group

Except for the ritualistic beginning and ending and the episodes of songs and dances, three episodes remain. They are the episode of the Old Priest, the episode of the Noblemen, and the episode of the Old Man and Wife. These three pieces contain stories and are the main episodes of Korean Mask-Dance theatres. They are different from the acrobatic traditions of *Sandae* Hundred Entertainments, showing signs of Korean theatrical modernization. First of all, they use colloquial everyday language and reflect the lives of common people. They satirize the aristocrats and Buddhist priests and depict the tyrannies of men and the contradictions of patriarchy even in a common family. The ongoing story is drawn from the point of common people, reflecting their plights and satirizing the ruling class. The detailed episodes are as follows.[4]

The episode of the Old Priest is a satire of Buddhism. Instead of praying to the Buddha, an old priest comes to a town and falls in love with a shaman-concubine. This episode combines a linear plot, a parallel plot, and a repetitious plot. There are three scenes: the Old Priest falling in love with the shaman-concubine; a shoe seller with a monkey selling a shoe for the concubine to the priest; and Chwibari, a prodigal in town, fighting for the concubine and getting a son from her. The love triangle among the priest, the prodigal, and the concubine is a linear plot, but the story of the shoe seller and the monkey is inserted in between the love triangle story. Because of its irrelevance to the main plot, the scene of the shoe seller creates a parallel structure to the main plot. The scene of the shoe seller is a retrogressive motif in the progressive plot of the love triangle. This parallel insertion can also be found in the prodigal's long-winded talks; his love story with eight ladies is, in fact, from the famous *Old Novel* of *Guunmon* (九雲夢). The repetitious plot is evidently shown when the priest flirts with the concubine. He repeats his dances, and so does the concubine.

The episode of the Noblemen mainly is a satire of the noble class. It clearly shows a circular plot. It satirizes the noble class by repeating the following structures: the pretending of the noblemen's dignity, the disobedience of the servant named Malttugi, the scolding of the noblemen, the excuse of the servant, the satisfaction of the noblemen, and a merry dance among the noblemen and the servant.[5] The repetition of this circular structure sharply accentuates the satire toward the noblemen. In addition, since the long-winded talks of the servant Malttugi insert many unrelated stories, the main circular plot includes a parallel plot in addition to the repetitious plot as well.

The episode of the Old Man and Wife is a satire of patriarchal society. Its plot shows a strong combination of a linear and circular plot. Again, many repetitions are employed. An old wife looks for her old husband since she lost him in the war. The old husband of hers is also looking for his old wife, and eventually, they meet. After their bold sexual intercourse, the wife tells him about the death of their son. When the husband declares divorce because the son died, a concubine comes to the husband. The love triangle ends when the wife dies while fighting with the concubine. A shamanistic ceremony is held for the dead wife. In short, the episode is repetitious and makes a circular structure; the way of searching for the lost husband is identical to that of the lost wife. Then, the linear plot of the love triangle follows. The parallel plot insertion is also found in the dialogue between the husband and wife. Through the family life of common people, the contradiction of patriarchal society is well demonstrated.

As far as its formal characteristics, Korean Mask-Dance theatres, first of all, stand out for their openness of plots. Texts were flexible, and any episodes could be inserted. The structure of repetitious and parallel plots was closely related to this openness. The acting was also strongly connected with this open structure. The improvisations of master actors were often considered to be the highlight of the performance. Master actors improvised new parallel stories and created variations of repetitions. Thus, the structure remained open for the actors' improvisations. While enjoying food and drink, the audiences were welcomed to join the performance with their supportive shouting, called *Chuimsae*. In other words, the performance could be adjusted according to the reaction of the audience. The mutual sympathy between actors and the audience was essential to the performance of Mask-Dance theatres. All of these factors added up to make the open structure of Mask-Dance theatres. Korean Mask-Dance theatres aimed at festivity and community while satirizing the upper class rather than offering philosophical or literary statements. The performative aspects of Mask-Dance theatres overwhelm the stories they contain. The thing which breathed life into Mask-Dance theatres was its performance, sparked by improvisation rooted in skillful art practices. Performance, thus, required experienced dancing and gesturing only acquired through years of

Figure 1.3 A Scene from NoJang GwaJang—the Old Priest's Episode. In Fertility Rites, Black Symbolizes Old Age and Barrenness, and Red Symbolizes Youth and Abundance. Photo by *Bongsan* Mask-Dance Preservation Group

Figure 1.4 A Scene from Noblemen Episode. Photo by *Bongsan* Mask-Dance Preservation Group.

Figure 1.5 A Scene from AeSaDang BeopGo Nori, *Yangju* Mask-Dance Theatre. Photo by the *Yangju* Mask-Dance Preservation Group.

Figure 1.6 The Old Wife Miyal. Photo by *Bongsan* Mask-Dance Preservation Group.

training. Moreover, music is a necessity from the beginning to the end of the performance. In other words, performativity from the postmodern sense governed the performance of Mask-Dance theatres.

There is no special stage for Mask-Dance theatre performances. Any large space that could accommodate the audience was sufficient. Mask-Dance theatre stages were diverse, ranging from a slope on the hill to a temporary stage constructed for the performance. Older forms of Mask-Dance theatres utilized wooden masks, while later ones utilized paper or gourd for masks. Masks highlighted the personalities of characters. They are not used as one-dimensional decorations but as compositional elements steering the plot, symbolizing characters.

These performances did not focus on causality, which can be found in Aristotelian drama. Therefore, the modern realism of Mask-Dance theatres can be questioned. However, Mask-Dance theatres were clearly connected to it in that they basically reflected the lives of ordinary people and their emotions in everyday language. The exaggerations in the above stories of Mask-Dance theatres challenged the authority of religion, the noble class, and patriarchy, all of which were symbols of power at the time. The themes reflected the awakening of common people's consciousness and the desire for an equal society.

Unlike the early village ritual Mask-Dance theatres, the performing context of the town-type Mask-Dance theatres detached itself from ritual: they were performed to meet the entertainment needs of emerging cities, and the performance occasions and actors' sacred statuses were flexible (i.e., not confined to ritual performance or the god's nomination). Unlike the masks which had been considered sacred in the village ritual/festival-type Mask-Dance theatres, masks of the town-type were not regarded as subjects to worship. For town-type Mask-Dance theatres, though many actors came from shaman families, they did not possess god-entrusted powers. During the 1920s, the taboo of female actors was broken as *Gisaeng* (female entertainer)appeared in women's roles. The introduction of female actresses coincided with the arrival of the modern age. All of the above were signs of modernization.

Like many folk theatres, there are no accurate records of their origins or history, as written records of the sort were not kept until the 20th century. As with Western Commedia dell'Arte, the performances contained substantial improvisation and relied less on literary techniques, thereby making the confirmation of fixed text unreliable. However, since Mask-Dance theatres were recorded after the 20th century, they could be said to gain modernity because the transition from oral literature to recorded literature was another characteristic of modernity. As a theatre form that combined first-rate acrobatic feats with literature and reflected the life of the times, it was the most beloved folk style of Korean traditional theatre, performed until the early 20th century in the villages.[6]

1.1.2 Pansori

Pansori is an indigenous genre of musical storytelling by a singing performer and a drummer.[7] The performer called *Gwangdae* sings a story using a fan and gestures, which express various emotions, accompanied by *Gosu*, the drummer. Originally, *Pansori* was a form of folk entertainment that gradually received the support of the upper class, Yangban, and became professional. It seems to have originated in the late 17th century and was also supported by the upper class in the mid-18th century. The 19th century was the golden age of *Pansori* when Shin JaeHyo recorded the orally handed-down texts of *Pansori* and encouraged *Pansori* to become more professional overall. He also trained the first female *Pansori* actresses, like Jin ChaeSeon, in the late 19th century.[8] The popularity of *Pansori* declined as modernization progressed in the first half of the 20th century, but it was also the first genre which actively embraced Western modernization.

The plot of *Pansori* is linear and progresses as a single story. It is closer to a Western-style plot than Mask-Dance theatres. Although it is sung rather than spoken in everyday language, the plot is what connects *Pansori* to modern drama. Thus, it is relatively easy to adapt to the Western style of theatre. Some *Pansori* traditions are transformed into *Changgeuk*, where various characters act out the story instead of one person singing the narration. *Pansori* gradually recovered its popularity as a traditional performing art in the 20th century, and it is probably the only traditional genre that is still often seen in contemporary Korean theatre. UNESCO recognized *Pansori* as a Masterpiece of Oral and Intangible Heritage of Humanity in 2003.

1.1.2.1 Performing Pansori

Gosu, the drummer, sits on the side of the performance space, and *Gwangdae*, the performer, comes out, which signals the start of the performance. The word *Pansori* is composed of two words, i.e., *Pan* meaning "ground," where things happen, and *Sori* meaning "singing." So, *Pansori* suggests "singing stage." The stage could be anywhere a rectangular or square carpet could fit, surrounded by audiences on three sides of the carpet. The performance space used to be usually inside a large guest room of a nobleman, but it could also be an open field outside, such as a pavilion. There is no scenery or special costumes. A fan is the only prop, and the performer can express different situations and emotions by opening and closing the fan.

Gwangdae sings and narrates stories from the repertories of *Pansori*. Singing is called Sori, narration is Aniri, and the performer's gestures and acting are Neorumsae. The audience joins the performance by encouragement shouting, which is called Chuimsae. There are several Chuimsaes, such as "Ulsu,"[9] "Cheering," "Good," and "Well done." Originally, the whole performance could last up to eight or nine hours, but practitioners began to choose the best parts, thereby gradually lessening the performance runtime to two or three hours.

Figure 1.7 A Typical *Pansori* Performance. A Man in a Korean Traditional Coat Is Standing and Singing. Photo from *National Theatre of Korea 70th Anniversary*, Seoul, Gemunsa, vol. History, 2020. p.189.

Figure 1.8 A *Pansori* Scene, Performers Sat Close. Photo from *National Theatre of Korea 70th Anniversary,* Seoul, Gemunsa, vol. History, 2020. p.243.

1.1.2.2 Text of Pansori

There are five extant traditional *Pansori* texts: *Chunhyang-Ga*, *Simchong-Ga*, *Heungbo-Ga*, *Sugung-Ga*, and *Jokbeok-Ga*. Ga means "song." These stories are very similar to those of Shin JaeHyo, with the exception of *Byongangsoe-Ga*. Shin JaeHyo was a nobleman who wrote down the oral *Pansori* in the mid-19th century. In addition to these six *Pansori* texts, he recorded over 20 Dan-Jap-Ga, short and various songs which are considered to be the sources of *Pansori*. There are also novel versions of these five texts, and it is still a scholarly argument which versions, novels or *Pansori*, came first. There are two opposing theories concerning this controversy: some argue old tales developed into novels and then into songs, while others argue that old tales were sung first and then written down as novels. *Pansori* and novels were developed around the same time.

ChunHyang-Ga is a love story between the son of a nobleman and the daughter of a Korean geisha, but it also deals with the morality of Confucianism: a woman's chastity. A boy and a girl of 16 years old first meet at GwangHanRu, the pavilion of the Namwon area still in existence in the southern part of Korea, during the Dano festival, the spring festival, in May. They fall in love at first sight. That evening, the boy, Myongryong, who happens to be the only son of the official chief in the region, visits Chunhyang's house and persuades her mother to allow his marriage with Chunhyang, whose name means "the fragrance of spring." Though it is not a legal marriage, her mother believes it's a good match for her daughter. Myongryong swears to Chunhyang that he will love her forever. Due to the caste system at that time, their legal marriage is impossible and Chunhyang could become a concubine at best. Soon after their secret marriage, Myongryong has to depart from the town, leaving Chunhyang alone, since his father receives an order of transference to Seoul. In spite of their sorrow, they have to part. Myongryong promises Chunhyang that he will come back when he passes the national examination for officials. When the new official chief comes to town, he wants to see Chunhyang since he heard about her beauty. Since her mother is a retired geisha in the government office, Chunhyang's caste is unstable. Though her father was a noble officer, she legally has to take over her mother's caste. Chunhyang's mother already redeemed Chunhyang by offering her ransom to the office. However, the new chief officer Byun asks Chunhyang to do bed service. Chunhyang firmly refuses to become his mistress, not because she is disobedient, but because she is already married. In the Confucian society of Joseon dynasty, any woman, even geishas, could maintain chastity for one man. In fact, Confucian society encourages the virtue of women's chastity no matter what. The chief officer Byun arrests Chunhyang, tortures her, and puts her in jail. Even after harsh times pass, Chunhyang refuses to be his mistress and waits for the day to be killed, i.e., the birthday of the chief officer Byun. Meanwhile, Myongryong wins first place in the national examination to be an official and becomes a secret royal inspector. On his way to Chunhyang, he meets the former servant who tells him about Chunhyang's situation. Disguised as a beggar among peers, Myongryong visits the jail and meets Chunhyang. Though she is surprised by his look, her love for him is firm, and she chooses to die rather than become the mistress of the current chief. On the day of the chief officer's birthday, a big party is held, and Chunhyang awaits her death. Then, the secret royal inspector Myongryong busts the party and accuses the chief officer Byun of his corrupt politics. Finally, Chunhyang and Myongryong reunite.

The story of Chunhyang has been very popular since its inception in the 17th century. The young lovers' relationship could never have been possible without the dilapidation of the caste system since their birth statuses as a nobleman and a geisha were too different. But thanks to the two great wars with Japan and China in the 16th and 17th centuries, the original caste system was loosened. Thus, with the geisha mother's financial support, Chunhyang could have received an education as a nobleman's daughter. The aristocratic society began to crumble and capital became important. However, the story still pleads its justification to the morals of Confucianism. Whenever the chief officer Byun orders her to attend at night as mistress, she insists a woman should only serve one man, a very important moral belief in Joseon patriarchal society. In spite of a life-threatening situation, Chunhyang's love and purity, along with her beauty, allow her to win the true love of Myongryong. It is still not clear in the story whether Chunhyang becomes a wife or a mistress. However, the audience loved the story owing to the young lovers and their sweet first love. The song of *Sarang-Ga* (Love Song) is famous and popular even nowadays.

SimCheong-Ga deals with another aspect of Confucian morality: filial duty. A blind man, Sim, raises his dutiful daughter, Sim Cheong, alone since his wife died giving birth. One day, Sim goes out to greet his daughter, who is returning home from work, but falls into the stream by mistake. A Buddhist monk nearby helps him out and tells him that he could make him see if he donates 300 bundles of rice to the temple. Sim promises to donate the rice without thinking because he is so happy to hear that he might see. When he arrives home, he begins to worry about the large sum of donation money. Since he made an oath to God, he cannot break it. When Sim Cheong hears about her father's worry, she tries to find the donation money in vain. Then, at a nearby village, InDangSu is known as the notorious sea where waves and winds are so high that ships often break down. When Sim Cheong is working hard to prepare the donation money, she happens to encounter a sailor who tries to buy a young maiden as a sacrifice to the sea for his safe journey. Sim Cheong volunteers to be sold in exchange for the donation money to the temple. When the day comes, Sim Cheong bows to her father and follows the sailors. The blind man, Sim, cries out in vain when he gets to know the truth. He cannot see in spite of the donation money to the temple. When the ship arrives at InDangSu, Sim Cheong is thrown into the stormy sea as a scapegoat, and the sea calms down. Sim Cheong falls into the deep sea and reaches the palace of the undersea world where she meets her dead mother. The king of the sea world thinks highly of her filial duty and decides to send her back to the world. She is seated in a big lotus, and the sailors who are returning back home from the trip find the lotus. They dredge the lotus and dedicate it to the king, who is pleased with the lotus and leaves it near him. One evening, when he feels lonely, Sim Cheong appears from the lotus. The king falls in love with her and marries Sim Cheong. Even though she becomes the queen, she thinks of her blind father all the time. The king orders for a national party which all blind men in the country have to attend. Meanwhile, the blind man, Sim, remarries a woman who has eyes on all the money he has. Having lost all his fortunes, he departs to Seoul, where the national party for blind men is held. Finally, Sim Cheong and her father are reunited at the party and live happily ever after.

This story has many popular elements, such as a dutiful daughter, death and resurrection reversal motif, and a happy ending. Plus, it has many famous songs, such as Sim Cheong's song on the day of departure for death, in which she laments her hard fate and prays for her father's well-being. In addition, some songs describe the undersea world and the king's palace. *SimCheong-Ga* also expands the imagination of audiences.

HeungBo-Ga is a story about brothers. The elder, Nolbo, is very greedy and stingy, while the younger, Heungbo, is good-hearted and generous. While the elder one knows his own interests, the younger one is slower to see his benefits. Thus, the household of the younger one is very poor with many children, while the elder one is rich. One spring day, Heungbo finds a swallow with a broken leg, so he treats it carefully and takes care of it until it recovers. When fall comes, the swallow flies off to the South and returns the next spring. It drops a pumpkin seed, and Heungbo plants it in the ground. The next fall, Heungbo harvests the pumpkin and cuts it in half. To Heungbo's surprise, gold and silver come out of the pumpkin. Heungbo becomes rich. When the elder brother hears about Heungbo's fortune, he comes to Heungbo to see what happened to him. Heungbo tells him the story of the cured swallow. When the next spring comes, Nolbo looks for a swallow with a broken leg but couldn't, so he breaks the leg of a swallow and treats it. In the following spring, the swallow also brings Nolbo a pumpkin seed. Nolbo is very glad and plants it with care. When Nolbo harvests and cuts the pumpkin, garbage and scraps come out endlessly. He is punished.

The story is about the promotion of virtue and reproval of vice and also emphasizes a virtue of Confucianism—brotherly love. The presentation of the story is very comic. When Heungbo asks for a scoop of rice from his brother's wife, she slaps his cheek with a rice paddle. Heungbo is happy to eat the leftover pieces of rice on his cheek. The song of cutting the pumpkin is also very humorous.

SuGung-Ga is a story about tricks. When the undersea king gets sick, the doctor says the liver of a rabbit would make him recover. A turtle called ByolJubu volunteers to seek the liver of a rabbit. Finally, he finds a rabbit and entices the rabbit with fair words, saying that the rabbit will have a good life in the kingdom under the sea. When ByolJubu and the rabbit go under the sea, the rabbit is told that she has to give her liver for the ill king. The rabbit whimsically says that her liver is left on earth with the bright sun because the liver needs to be dried from time to time. Though ByolJubu is unwilling, he guides the rabbit back to land. As soon as they reach the surface, the rabbit runs away.

It is said that this Machiavellian trick story originated from the flight of one general of Silla from Goguryo in the Three Kingdoms period, i.e., around AD 600. However, no one is sure of it. The reversals of tactful tricks were fun for the audience. Many songs, such as *Drawing Portrait of a Rabbit*, *The Beautiful Earth World*, and *The Rabbit's Escape*, became popular.

JokByeok-Ga is part of the story from the Chinese *Samgukgi Yeonui*(三國志演義), "The Old Three Countries Contest." *JokByeok-Ga* begins at the scene where Liu Bei personally visits Zhuge Liang's house three times to recruit him. Zhuge Liang foresees the wind from the East-South, which is the opposite direction of the wind at that time, and shoots fire arrows with the wind, winning against Jojo's army. When Jojo retreats from the battlefield, he is caught by Gwanwu, the generous general of Han. Gwanwu lets Jojo go because he once owed his life to Jojo.

Though the story of *JokByeok-Ga* is about loyalty to the throne, an important virtue of Confucianism, it also tells of the resentment of common soldiers' agony in the war. The commoners' protests and satire play an important part in *JokByeok-Ga*. Since there are many war scenes, the tempo of songs is fast and masculine. This *Pansori* was popular among the noblemen and nowadays is difficult to recreate due to the feminization of *Pansori* singers.

In addition to these five representative five Pansori, there are seven more, such as *ByonGangSoe-Ga, BaebiJang-Ga, OnGoJip-Ga, GangReung*

MaeHwa-Ga, *MuSuGi-Ga*, *JangGgi-Ga*, and *SugYoungNangJa-Ga*. *Though* *ByonGangSoe-Ga* is included in Shin JaeHyo's recorded six *Pansori* and is rarely performed, it seems to be almost lost. In the story, Byongangsoe is introduced as a sexually active man, while Ongneo is a lecherous woman. They are poor nomads with no land and home. One day, Byongangsoe pulls out a *Jangseung*, a traditional Korean totem pole at the village entrance, to sell it as firewood, but he suddenly dies due to the wrath of the earth gods. His dead body is not only detached from the earth, but it also makes the person who tried to clear away his corpse die. At last, a shamanic ritual is held to console his soul. This *Pansori* is not only notorious for filthy talk and dirty sexual stories but also for criticizing the social problems of the poor wandering people. The performance was almost lost during the enlightenment period as it was not considered appropriate for noblemen and women. The other six *Pansori* were handed down only by name, but most of the stories are well-known through old novels.

1.1.2.3 The Style of Pansori

There are three styles of songs in *Pansori*: *Dongpyeonje*, *Seopueonje*, and *Junggoje*.

Dongpyeonje is sung in the eastern part of the Seomjin River, including Gurye and Namwon. These songs could be metaphorically compared to the moon rising stealthily over the hill. The songs are cheerful with short rhythmic beats and powerful high tones. The songs do not require showing off vocal techniques. Therefore, the songs are known for their clean and light tones, and the feeling of masculinity feels strong thanks to the blandness and avoidance of finesse.

Seopyeonje is sung in the western part of the Seomjin River, including Bosong, Kwangju, and Naju. The songs of *Seopyeonje* sound like spring in full bloom. This style uses many techniques, such as screeching the last note. Most songs are in minor; thus, the sounds are sad and feminine. Most *Pansori* today is *Seopyeonje*.

Junggoje is not as popular as the other two styles of *Pansori*. It is said that its techniques of song are neither *Dongpungje* nor *Seopunje*. Its style is sung in the Chungcheong area, the middle part of South Korea. It is a minor style of *Pansori*.

1.1.1.4 The Development of Changgeuk from Pansori

Changgeuk was developed from *Pansori* at the turn of the 20th century. Ever since Western theatre was imported into Korea in the late 19th century, its influences grew because of Western imperialism. *Pansori Gwangdae* began to divide its roles and singing according to each character. In other words, instead of one performer narrating the story, different performers portrayed each character, allowing more room for acting. *Dochang*, the narrator, encompasses the whole narration. In a way, *Changgeuk* was Westernized *Pansori*. It employed a realistically painted backdrop as the scenery.

Changgeuk began at the turn of the 20th century when *Hepyulsa* was opened in 1902, the first royal indoor theatre. It flourished with *Wongaksa*, the first civilian indoor theatre that was started in 1908. *Changgeuk* was performed with Japanese style *Sinpa* theatre in the 1910s. Its scenery developed from backdrops to three-dimensional houses and employed many props and costumes. Yet, it gradually declined since *Sinpa* and *Singeuk*, new realistic Western theater styles, gained popularity among people. In 1933, all famous *Changgeuk* Gwangdaes gathered together and formed "Joseon Songak Yeonguhoe" to promote the development of *Changgeuk*. The opening of *Oriental (Dongyang) Theatre* in 1935 also helped *Changuk* to flourish again. The directors of *Oriental Theatre* directed *Changgeuk* with famous Gwangdaes and Western techniques. Moreover, since *Oriental Theatre* aimed at commercial theatre, the profit for a performance of *Changgeuk* was far larger than that of other companies. *Changgeuk* gradually gained popularity again and flourished in the 1940s.

National *Changgeuk* Company was founded in 1962 under the *National Theater*. The company served as an opportunity to gather *Pansori* masters and managed to continue its tradition. *Changgeuk* was renovated when Heo Gyu became the chief of National *Cahnggeuk* company in the late 1970s. Heo Gyu directed *Changgeuk* with various fringe folk arts. He restored the old repertory of *Gangreung Maehwa-Ga* (which was handed down only by title) with old performers and even created a new *Pansori* repertory called *Gwangdae-Ga*, which dealt with the story of Shin JaeHyo, the first documenter of *Pansori*. After him, the succeeding chiefs steadily tried to renovate *Changgeuk*; Sugung-Ga in 2011, directed by Achim Freyer, is a good example of innovation of *Changgeuk*.[10]

In conclusion, the Mask-Dance theatres and *Pansori* were widely spread among people in the 18th century, which was considered to be the earliest period of Korean modernization. These two genres are quite different from the earlier forms of *Sandae* Hundred Entertainments. While *Sandae* Hundred Entertainments were largely composed of dances, acrobatics, and short skits, Mask-Dance theatres and *Pansori* instead had storytelling. In other words, they used common language reflecting the prose style of modern arts and included many satires of the everyday lives of the time, reflecting the gradual enlightenment of commoners' consciousness. Their episodes and stories reflected the so-called modern thoughts, such as equality awareness, protests for suppressed women, the power of capital, and so on. In short, they had many characteristics of modern styles and Western thoughts. Mask-Dance theatres and *Pansori* both flourished in the 19th century and lasted until the first half of the 20th century. While performances of Mask-Dance theatres are rare nowadays,[11] *Pansori* and *Changgeuk*, their Westernized counterparts, are often performed at national theatres.

Figure 1.9 A Scene from Achim Freyer's *Changgeuk Sugung-Ga*. The Chorus is Coming Out from Dochang—the Narrator's Skirt. Photo taken by National *Changgeuk* Company.

1.2 Records of Western Theatres, Influx of Western Culture, and New Literary Genres

The first record of Western theatre in Korean text is shown in *The Record of Western Travelog* (*Soyu Geonmun* 西遊見聞) by Yu Giljun in 1895. Yu went to the United States and stayed there for about 18 months and wrote about his experience.[12] This book, selected as some schools' textbook of the time, exerted its influence around the 1900s. The Western theatre was described in chapter 16 as follows: "theatre has the stage with various equipment and an inclined auditorium, surrounded by windowed walls," "there is an orchestra in front of the stage," "the contents of the performance on stage are a tragedy or a comedy," and "each play is divided into several acts, and the curtain is closed at the end of each act."[13] This explanation tells not only the theatre building and its shape but also the content and form of narrated stories. Since Korea did not have theatres or plays in the Western sense at the time, Yu's descriptions were valuable for the understanding of Western theatre.

Another record of the Western theatre is *Advance towards the Broad World* (海天秋帆) by Min YoungHwan in 1896. He led the delegation to the coronation of Nicholas II in Russia. He went on an around-the-world trip to Russia, China, Japan, America, Great Britain, the Netherlands, Germany, Poland, and then back to Korea via Siberia. The trip took about six months with careful observations of the unfamiliar Western civilizations. The book also recorded the Russian theatre building. It had seven stories with about 500–600 booths altogether, and each booth had eight seats. The emperor and the empress attended the performances, which included spectacles of a wedding or a war.[14]

Cultural Westernization appeared in Korean society around the turn of the 20th century. Newspapers were published: *Hansong Sunbo* (漢城旬報, the ten-day Newspaper of Seoul) was published in 1883, *Dokrip Sinmun* (獨立新聞 Independent Newspaper) in 1896, *Jeguk Sinmun* (帝國新聞, Empire Newspaper) and *Hwangseong Sinmun* (皇城新聞, Emperor's Castle Newspaper) in 1898, and *Daehan Maeil Sinbo* (大韓每日申報, Korea Daily Newspaper) in 1904. The first newspaper in Korea, *Hansong Sunbo*, published by the royal court, lasted for only around a year, while *Dokrip Sinmun* was the first civilian newspaper that lasted for about three years. All three other papers were published by civilians and lasted until 1910 when Korea was annexed by Japan. They all aimed for the independence of Korea and encouraged people's enlightenment, free from foreign influences. Additionally, they promoted thoughts of nationalism, democracy, and modern science to the common people. These newspapers were abolished by the Japanese Government General of Korea after Japan annexed Korea in 1910. Since most of these newspapers also had English editions as well as Korean, they sped up the Westernization of Korean society.[15]

The first appearance of Western literature in Korea was the Bible in the late 19th century. By the turn of the 20th century, *Gaewha Gasa* (開化歌辭) and *Changga* (唱歌) were popular. *Gasa* was a literary form between poetry and prose from the Joseon dynasty, composed of repeating arithmetic words, while *Gaewha* means enlightenment period. This old form preached patriotism, independent nationalism, and enlightenment. *Changga* included lyrics set to Western songs. The contents of *Changga* are almost the same as *Gaewha Gasa* but more influential than *Gaewha Gasa* since *Changga* was actually possible to be sung by people or even by audiences. Some of *Changga* was developed into long epic poetry, such as *Gyongbu Railroad Song* (京府鐵道歌) and *Trip Around the World* (世界一周歌). They both lasted until the early 1910s and are representative of early modern literary forms.

Soon, *Sinche Poetry* (新體詩) and *New Novel* (新小說) succeeded *Gaewha Gasa* and *Changga* in the 1910s. New intelligentsia of the time, including Choi NamSeon, Lee GwangSu, and Ahn ChangHo, wrote *Sinche Poetry*, which preached cultural enlightenment and social reformations in forms of seven and five lyrical tones, an indigenous Korean lyrical form. *New Novel* (新小說) also came into being, mostly as serial stories in the newspapers.

Gaewha Gasa, *Changga*, *Sinche Poetry*, and *New Novel* were new literary forms at the time of enlightenment, co-existed until the 1910s, and all preached ① Independence, ② Freedom and Civil Rights, ③ New Westernized Education, ④ Breaking of Superstition and Dissemination of Western Science, ⑤ Freedom of Free Love and Love Marriage, and ⑥ Egalitarianism. These were transitional forms, which bridged Joseon's poetry and novels to Westernized literary forms. Chinese letters, often used for the language of the

Joseon Dynasty, were stopped being used, and Hangeul finally became the unified language of speech and writing in these forms.[16]

This circumstance of new Western literature was also reflected in the theatre of the time. Mask-Dance theatres, which still reflected much of the medieval *Sandae* Hundred Entertainments tradition, started to decline after the 20th century. In contrast to Mask-Dance theatres, *Pansori*, which had a unified storyline largely depending on language, began to accommodate the Western theatrical style and was developed into *Changgeuk*. Instead of one person singing the entire narrative, it divided the song according to the characters in the storyline and performed only selected interesting parts of *Pansori* in order to shorten the runtime. It also added new repertories along with the six repertories of Shin JaeHyo in the 19th century.

1.3 The First Western-Style Indoor Theatres: *Heopyeulsa* (協律社) and the Private Indoor Theatres

The first indoor theatre in Western style, called *Heopyeulsa* (協律社),[17] opened in 1902 at the royal court and became the official royal theatre. *Heopyeulsa* had a stage building called *Hidae* (戲臺) and an office at the court. In order to celebrate the 40th jubilee of King Gojeong's coronation, the *Heopyeulsa* office was made in the court and prepared the gala celebration on *Hidae*.[18] The advisors of Korean diplomats who had been in Western countries worked to build Western-style theatre to entertain and foster interaction among foreign diplomatic envoys. Thus, the first indoor theatre *Hidae* came into being on the outskirts of royal palaces. However, *Heopyeulsa*'s official opening ceremony was postponed due to national difficulties, such as severe drought, a serious illness of the King's son, and a bad harvest. The gala was finally held in an informal way in 1903. At that ceremony, it was said that *Changgeuk*, *Pansori* whose each character is performed by its designated singer, was presented. After the gala celebration, *Heopyeulsa* became a business theatre rather than a royal court theatre as originally intended. It became a social club for rich citizens instead of foreign diplomats.

Traditional performances, including *Pansori* and traditional dances, were performed on stage. The first performance was *Sochundaeyoohee* (笑春臺遊戲), which was composed of dances by Korean Geisha and employed singers of *Pansori* in 1902. Although the indoor Western proscenium stage was provided, Western theatrical forms were not performed due to the absence of Western-style plays. Since *Pansori* was popular among the royal and noble classes at the beginning of the 19th century, it was preferred to be performed. In addition, *Pansori* was also the best fit for the proscenium stage among the traditional theatrical arts. While most traditional theatres had actors moving around the entire playground, including the spectators' in various ways, *Pansori* had the drummer and the singer who were mostly stationary, and adapted easily to the proscenium stage.

The performers of *Pansori* soon adapted to the Westernization of the time. A new genre called *Changgeuk*(唱劇) based on *Pansori* was developed at *Heopyeulsa*. Each actor played a role alongside the main narrator. In the beginning, the prototype of *Changgeuk* was likely performed by only two singer-actors at *Heopyeulsa*. It was made up of a few scenes in which the hero and heroine appeared. It meant an actress was on the stage when a heroine role was needed. The appearance of female actors (in fact, geishas) was well received by the audience. *ChunHyangGa*, a love story of two young lovers, was likely the first *Pansori*, which was played in the *Changgeuk* style.[19]

The social situations in the 1900s were serious because of the threat of imperialism; therefore, learning was encouraged. According to the intellectual reformists at that time, the content of the performances of *Heopyeulsa* was considered obscene, lewd, and filthy for the age of enlightenment. Instead of expressing new ideas of modernization, their content was mainly from old *Pansori* and acrobatics, only serving for entertainment. Furthermore, the audiences of *Heopyeulsa* were mainly the rich or geishas rather than diplomatic envoys. Many officials who were Confucian scholars and believers in social betterment appealed to the court to close down *Heopyeulsa*, blaming its offenses toward public morals. Eventually, the court decided to close down *Heopyeulsa* in 1906, even before its formal opening ceremony. The performances at *Heopyeulsa* remained traditional, and realistic productions were still many years off.

In addition to *Heopyeulsa*, private theatres, such as *Gwangmudae* (光武臺), *Danseongsa* (團成社), *Yeonheungsa* (演興社) in 1907, and *Jangansa* (長安社) in 1908, appeared. *Danseongsa* and *Jangansa* played motion pictures along with some traditional theatrical arts, while Gwangmudae and Yeonheungsa mainly performed traditional theatrical arts. The civilian owners of these theatres tried to reconstruct traditional *Pansori* into *Changgeuk* with many *Pansori* singers and geishas. For example, *Gwangmudae* had pre-*Changgeuk ChunHyangGa* with songs sung alternately and adjusting the tone and pitch. It is recorded that *Yeonheungsa* also hired 30 *Pansori* singers to perform the repertoires of *Pansori*.[20] This change shows that *Pansori* singers were very popular at the time and often performed acting roles as *Changgeuk* emerged. The newspapers assumed critical attitudes since the repertoires repeated old *Pansori*, unlike other new literary forms. However, these indoor Western-style theatres showcasing traditional arts were very popular at the time.

1.4 The Development of *Changgeuk*

Changgeuk was the most important theatrical genre in this enlightenment period. As mentioned above, it was a type of *Pansori* with roles divided among the performers in the beginning, and new repertoires were developed along with increasing popularity. When *Pansori* was performed at indoor Westernized theatres, the performance time tended to be shorter compared with the old *Pansori*, which was usually performed in the men's part of the house without a time limit, according to the reactions of the audience. Since the new audience, mostly men about town and geisha, who had to go back to their homes, the selected number of highlighted or famous songs were often sung instead of the complete *Pansori*, Soon, producers of *Pansori* realized the need for limits in order to anticipate ending time. These effects appeared in private theatres after 1907. Plus, suppressions of Korean traditional arts from the Japanese Police Agency made the shortened time more necessary after the Eulsa treaty in 1905, which was a treaty that deprived Joseon's diplomatic rights. For example, Korea Daily Newspapers said that any traditional performance after 12 o'clock would be banned and punished.[21]

Foreign theatrical influences were also important to the development of *Changgeuk*. *Pansori* needed to adapt to foreign-style productions, such as Chinese Opera, Japanese Kabuki, and Western opera, which were occasionally performed in foreign dwellings in Seoul by foreigners. Many foreign powers and foreigners at that time tried to gain financial benefits from Korea. *Pansori* singers, such as Kang YongHwan, attended Chinese Opera performances, which featured multiple characters at that time. Kang YongHwan was impressed by what he saw and ended up playing an important role in developing *Changgeuk* from *Pansori*.[22] Plus, traditional theatrical arts received pressure to change due to the social needs of enlightenment. Thus, *Pansori* began to employ multiple actors playing each character from *Pansori*. Since one man's song was divided into characters, the power of singing became less important than acting skills. Some theatres used cotton cloth as a backdrop and painted illusionary scenery. Ultimately, theatres cautiously applied Western realistic techniques to *Changgeuk*.

Another possible reason for the divided roles was the overflow of *Pansori* singers, who were trained extensively in the 19th century, the golden age of *Pansori*. Since only a few singers could have a chance to be sponsored by the royal family or rich noblemen, most young *Pansori* singers were looking for opportunities to perform. "Considering the availability of artists, the vast majority of underemployed singer-actors must have welcomed the new idea [of dividing roles] and saw it as another opportunity to engage in their profession."[23]

Changgeuk became popular and was widely performed in *Heopyeulsa* and private theatres, such as *Gwangmudae*, by 1907. Many famous masters of *Pansori* singing performed *Changgeuk*. Indeed, *Changgeuk* was the leading theatrical genre in the decade of the 1900s. Partly because of its popularity, the debates of *The Silver World* also erupted.

1.5 *Wongaksa (圓覺社)* and the Arguments of *The Silver World*

The private theatre *Wongaksa (圓覺社)* opened in 1908 at the same place where *Heopyeulsa* closed in 1906. Unlike the developers of private theatres, the people related to *Wongaksa* were pro-Japanese and experts in new culture. They gained political power, especially after Joseon had lost its diplomatic rights in 1905. Lee Injik (李人稙: 1862–1916),[24] a major supporter of theatre, was a high official at the court and had studied in Japan at the turn of the century. Using his influence and interest, he rented the first indoor theatre, where traditional theatrical performances were held, and opened it with a new name, *Wongaksa*. This opening of *Wongaksa* initiated the Westernized reformation of Korean theatre. He tried a new theatre with his play *The Silver World* (銀世界: 1908), which was inspired by a corrupt local governor at the time. The novel *The Silver World* was published almost simultaneously with its performance.[25] Though the script was lost, the remaining novel implies the story on stage.

The Silver World was not a completely original story. It borrowed some storylines from the popular *Changgeuk* called *the Song of Choi Byongdo*. In order to distinguish *The Silver World* from *The Song of Choi Byongdo*, the detailed stories need to be described. A popular new repertory of *Changgeuk* called *the Song of Choi Byongdo* was developed at the turn of the 20th century. This *Changgeuk*, based on the real story from the Gangwon province, portrays the tyranny of the county magistrate. The magistrate puts a false charge on Choi Byongdo, a rich man of the village, in order to steal his fortune. After collecting a fine, he releases Choi Byongdo, who dies within a month due to the tortures in jail. Since the corruption of officials prevailed in the early 20th century, this story of social satire was very popular. Lee Injik added the latter part to the story: Choi's wife goes crazy and his friend takes care of his son and daughter. The guardian is an enlightened man and sends the children to the United States to learn Western culture. When the guardian also dies because of the corrupt officials, the disappointed children, now in Washington, D.C., try committing suicide, but they are rescued by a kind American couple, who sponsor the children to finish their studies. The children finally return to Korea with the will to reform Korean society. When they visit their mother at a temple, they get killed by a mob supporting a conservative party after a dispute.

When *The Silver World* was performed, a *Changgeuk*, *The Song of Choi Byongdo*, won fame from the public. This seemed to be why some witnesses of actual corruption claimed that *The Silver World* was *The Song of Choi Byongdo*. Actually, this is the basis of some scholars' argument that *The Silver World* is also a *Changgeuk*. They think that *The Silver World* is, in fact, *The Song of Choi Byongdo*. But the audience of the time never called the play *The Silver World* but called it *The Song of Choi Byongdo*. Furthermore, not only were the stories of the two plays quite different, but also Lee Injik, a civilized leading intellect of the time, would not have allowed the performance with his name being called the same title as a *Changgeuk* piece based on an old theatrical form. Lee Injik dreamed of introducing Western theatre to Korea. Since no Korean actors at the time were trained in the Western style of acting, it is possible that the acting style remained similar to that of *Changgeuk*. In other words, actors' dialogues were often delivered in *Pansori* songs and included many folk songs. Plus, Lee Injik, a high government officer who visited Japan many times

Figure 1.10 A Black and White Image of *Wongaksa*.

during the rehearsal period, could not spend much time in person to direct the performance. Thus, the production possibly showed many characteristics as a transitional form of theatre between the traditional and *Sinpa*, the new Western-based style.

In spite of its transitional characteristics, *The Silver World* aimed to perform in a form of *Sinpa*, which was based on Japanese *Sinpa* and was the first Westernized form of theatre that was delivered using only everyday language. Along with accusations against the governor in *The Silver World*, Lee Injik included new ideas of modernization on the side of social progressivism. Advanced Western technologies, such as steamships, which the main characters boarded to go to the U.S., were introduced, and the Westerners were portrayed as generous and kind, as evidenced by their American guardians who helped them complete their education. Meanwhile, the conservatives were described as mobs who killed a well-educated hero without clear reasons. Furthermore, Lee Injik borrowed the title of *The Silver World* from the Japanese *Sinpa* theatre (新派劇). Due to its transitional characteristics, the production style of *The Silver World* was seen by a minority as similar to that of *Changgeuk* rather than that of the new *Sinpa* theatre. However, due to Lee Injik's revolutionary and pro-Western tendencies, *The Silver World* is commonly credited as a new form of theatre, i.e., *Sinpa*.[26]

At the center of this argument was the issue of the first Westernized theatre in Korea. *Changgeuk*, though modernized from *Pansori*, cannot be considered a Westernized theatre since its root is in *Pansori*. *Sinpa (新派)* theatre, in contrast to the traditional theatre (舊派), was the real beginning of modern Westernized theatre. Though the acting style of *The Silver World* was dubious, the play was performed in an indoor theatre with the visible intention of enlightenment and even included Western steamers and many Western places, such as Washington, D.C. Thus, *The Silver World* is considered to be the first production of Westernized theatre, i.e., the beginning of modern Western theatre.

1.6 Three Social Stances toward Theatre in the 1900s

Three stances toward theatrical arts existed in the 1900s. The first one was based on the traditional Confucianism of Joseon and was held by the noble class, *Yangban*. It basically considered theatrical arts as obscene, lewd, filthy, and against public morals. It thought lowly of popular arts. This was why the social status of actors was of the lowest class during the Joseon dynasty. To explain further, Lee Pilwha, a Confucian officer whose theatrical stance was based on traditional Confucianism, appealed to the court to abolish *Hyeoprulsa*, where only filthy performances took place.[27] In his public appeal to the king, he insisted on its abolishment since it undermined the morality of the common people. The traditional Confucians did not realize the possible social influences of theatrical arts; they only saw the entertainment and immoral aspects.

The second stance was of the group of new conservative intellectuals, such as Jang Jiyeon, Shin Caeho, and Park Ensik, who insisted on nationalism and enlightenment. They emphasized heroes of the period and tried to reform old literature. Shin Caeho wrote a hero novel about General Elgimundeok and General Lee Sunsin, the saviors of their kingdom in the old days of Korea. In fact, this group did not contribute much to theatre but criticized the traditional theatrical arts performed in private theatres of the time. This group insisted on theatrical improvements and believed that theatre would be useful for mass enlightenment if it dealt with saviors and patriotic martyrs of the nation.[28] Their nationalism, in contrast to the pro-Japanese intellect, supported traditional actors who were against Japanese cultural invasion. Existing traditional actors called *Gwangdae* were reluctant to perform in Western style partly because they did not know the new Western theatre but also because they had pride in their traditional theatrical skills. They rather wandered around the country and gradually faded out of popularity. Therefore, only a few *Pansori* singers survived among the traditional arts, and the new intellectual actors, who were educated in Western style, came into being after the 1910s. Despite the old *Gwangdae's* resistances, traditional performances, such as Mask-Dance theatres and shaman performances, were oppressed, and new Western-style entertainments were encouraged.

The third stance was that of the progressive group from the new theatre movement, which sought Western modernization through Japan. Despite their goodwill of enlightenment through Westernization for the people, the members were apt to be pro-Japanese, including Lee Injik. This group ignored the traditional actors and theatrical arts. When they spoke of modernization and enlightenment, they meant Westernization.

All three stances did not help much to improve or reform traditional theatrical arts. They all insisted on the utilitarianism of theatre; theatre should serve to enlighten the people. But the theatre of the time still mostly dealt with old popular stories, dances, and songs without many new topics of the changing period. Since there were no playwrights and directors, not to speak of intellectual supporters, it was difficult to reform traditional theatre.

Korea was colonized by Japan in 1910, accelerating the Western modernization in Korea. Theatre was not an exception. Since the modernization of Korean theatre underwent along with the colonization, there were some definite limits. It could never discuss independence, imperialism, and total freedom. Modernization was mainly focused on scientific reformations and accepting efficient Western social systems. In other words, modernization was achieved not in its deep cultural basis but only in techniques. So-called scientific reformations of traditional customs were imposed to oppress Korean traditions and theatrical arts. All aspects of society began to change rapidly, and so did the theatre in this period of enlightenment. Finally, the new theatrical form, *Sinpa*, which Injik Lee tried in 1908, came into being and flourished in the 1910s.

Notes

1 Lee, Duhyun. *Korean Theatre History*. Seoul, Hankyeonsa. 1985, p. 168.
2 Mask-Dance theaters are sometimes called *Talnori or Talchum* in Korean and are also spelled 假面劇 in traditional Chinese characters, pronounced as *Gamyeongeuk* or *Kamyeongeuk* according to the different ways of romanization.
3 Lee, Duhyun. *Korean Mask-Dance Theatre*. Seoul, The Association of Korean Mask-Dance Theatre, 1969.
4 Most information on detailed episodes of Mask-Dance theatre is based on Lee, Op .cit.
5 Jo, DongIl. *The Esthetics of Korean Mask-Dance Theatre*. Seoul, Hanguk Daily Newspaper, 1975, pp. 168–186.
6 For further detailed information, consult
Lee, Meewon. *Kamyeongeuk: The Mask-Dance Theatre of Korea*. 1983. University of Pittsburgh, PhD dissertation.
7 For general information on *Pansori*, references are from the below and others.
Jin, Bonggyu. *Pansori: Theory and Practice*. Seoul, Suseowon, 1989.
Kang, Hanyoung. *Pansori*. Seoul, Sejong Daewang Giyeomsayeophoe, 2000.
Kim, Heunggyu. *Pansori*. Seoul, Jeonbuk Aeyang Bonbu, 1988.
A Study on Shin JaeHyo's Pansori. The Association of *Pansori* Studies, ed. Seoul, The Association of Pansori Studies, 1990.
8 The appearance of a female actor can be considered as the arrival of the modern period.
9 A kind of cheering sound
10 Further detailed information, refer
Kim, Woo-Ok. *P'ansori: An Indigenous Theatre of Korea*. 1980. New York University, Ph.D. dissertation.
Um, Haekyung. *Korean Musical Drama: P'ansori and the Making of Tradition in Modernity*. London & New York, Routledge, 2013.

11 Most Mask-Dance theatres were nominated as National Cultural Intangible Properties in the 1960s and the 1970s. Nowadays their performances are hard to see at regular theatres. The definite occasions for performances are the annual evaluations of their preservation of cultural values by the Ministry of Culture and Tourism. Otherwise, each regional group rarely performs. One cannot see the performances whenever one wants.
12 Lee, Hansup, ed. *The Record of Western Travelog*(*Soyu Geonmun*): *Complete Texts.* Seoul, Parkeejung, 2000.
13 Ibid.
14 Min, Younghwan. *The posthumous Work of Patriot Min* (*Min Chungjunggong Yugo*). Trans. Lee Minsu. Seoul, Ilsogak, 2000, p. 89.
15 Referenced from Danguk University's Dongyanghak Yeonguso. *Anthology of Dongyanghak 38: Newspapers.* Seoul, Minsokwon, 2010.
16 Referenced from
Lee, Jaeseon, et al. *Literature of the Enlightenment Period (Gaehwagi Munhankron).* Seoul, Hanguk Haksul Jeongbo, 2002.
Kim, Hakdong. *A Study on Korean Poetry of the Enlightenment Period.* Seoul, Simunhaksa, 1981.
17 *Sa* (社) means a company or an organization. Though there were temporary stages or modified indoor stages as parts of buildings, there were no indoor permanent theatres before *Heopyeulsa.*
18 Yu, Minyoung. *Modern Korean His*tory(韓國近代演劇史). Seoul, Danguk University Press, 1996, p. 34.
19 Park, Hwang. *A Study of Cahnggeuk History* (唱劇史 硏究). Seoul, Peknoksa, 1976, p. 20.
20 *Korea Daily Newspapers (Daehan Maeil Sinbo),* 1908. 5.6.
21 Korea Daily Newspapers (Daehan Maeil Sinbo), 1908. 6.23.
22 Park, Hwang. *A Study of Changgeuk History.* Seoul, Peknoksa, 1976, p. 17.
23 Cho, Oh-Kon. *Korean Theatre: From Rituals to the Avant-Garde.* Fremont, Jain Publishing Company, 2015, p. 110.
24 He is the pioneer in the modernization of Korean theatre but was the secretary of Lee Wan-Yong, who played a major role in the signing of the treaty of Japanese annexation of Korea. *The Silver World* was the only theatrical production.
25 *The Silver World* followed Western style in the following aspects: it tries to keep the causality of the plot, to pick up the issues of society, and employs everyday language. Because of the story's pro-Japanese attitudes, its insistence on modern reformations is devalued nowadays.
26 This is assumed just from the fact that the Korean theatre community held an event in 2008 to commemorate the 100th anniversary of modern Western-style theatre.
27 Lee, Duhyun. *Korean Theatre History.* Seoul, Hankyeonsa, 1985, p. 249.
28 Yu, Minyoung. *A Study on the Theatre of Enlightenment (Gaewhagi Yeonguk SahoeSa).* Seoul, Samoonsa, 1987, p. 56.

2 *Sinpa Theatre*

Transitional Melodrama from Westernized Japan and Its Influences on Commercial Theatre

2.1 The Influx of *Sinpa* Theatre and Its Historical Meaning

Sinpa theatre (新派劇) flourished in the 1910s when traditional performances were rapidly decreasing. Lee InJik first attempted this form of theatre in 1908 with *The Silver World*. However, since there were no Korean actors trained in the new *Sinpa* style acting at that time, the acting style was similar to that of traditional *Changgeuk*; the actors' dialogues were often delivered in *Pansori* songs and included many folk songs.[1] The further development of *Sinpa* theatre was contributed by the foreign residents in Seoul at that time. Around 1907 in Seoul, there were 16,643 Japanese residents compared to 199,000 Koreans.[2] However, in 1910, the Japanese population increased to 34,468.[3] Thus, many Japanese performance groups visiting from Japan, and Japanese private theatres, such as Kabugi-jwa and Gyeongseong-jwa, arrived in Seoul between 1908 and 1910 to meet their needs for entertainment. Japanese private theatres also existed in Incheon and Busan, port cities that had round-trip ships to Japan.[4] The best ten repertoires of Japanese *Sinpa* at that time were performed.[5] There is also a record of performances of Western playwrights; for example, Shakespeare's *Hamlet* was produced in 1907.[6] In the midst of all these, the popularity of traditional Korean theatrical arts, such as *Pansori*, Changgeuk, and folk dances were still in existence. The Japanese Governor-General of Korea encouraged *Sinpa* theatre while oppressing the traditional arts in order to minimize the differences between Koreans and Japanese through cultural elements. Under the pretense of improving theatre quality, the Japanese government insisted on the utilitarianism of theatre, and since Westernized theatre intellectuals also agreed with this opinion, it was hard for Korean traditional theatrical arts to survive. Modernization was made compulsory by the Japanese imperial government, and it affected every corner of society; theatre was not an exception.

When *Sinpa* theatre was first presented to the public, it was considered light fare with sentimentality. It was often evaluated as an overemotional melodrama for entertainment purposes, which was far from enlightenment. Furthermore, it was a completely transplanted genre from colonial Japan, incurring anti-nationalistic sentiments and disconnection from the traditional

DOI: 10.4324/9781003490708-3

theatrical arts.[7] Recently, scholars wonder how *Sinpa* theatre could have been enormously popular if it was transplanted from Japan. Therefore, they started to see *Sinpa* theatre as the transitional theatrical form between the traditional arts and Western theatre.[8] The stories of *Sinpa* came from the New Novels (新小說) of the time as well as from the *Old Novels* of the Joseon dynasty. Although in Japan it was common to produce *Sinpa* theatre with New Novels, especially those from the serial stories in newspapers, *Sinpa* theatre of Korea came from not only New Novels but also from the *Old Novels*, such as *The Story of Janghwa and Hongnyeon* (薔花紅蓮傳), *The Southern Trip of Mrs. Sa* (謝氏南征記), and traditional *Pansori* songs, including *The Song of the Undersea Palace* (水宮歌) and *The Song of ChunHyang* (春香歌).[9]

Sinpa theatre's transitional characteristics seem parallel to those of New Novels. New Novels are commonly acknowledged as a transitional form from the old novels to modern realism novels. New Novels inherited the complicated development of stories, not necessarily satisfying causality, to arouse interest from the old novels and made them more sensuous and effective, while some modern realism novels adapted the structure of the New Novels in serial stories.[10] In spite of the Westernization, the modern novel still shows its roots in old traditional novels through the intermediary role of the New Novels.[11]

Sinpa theatre also plays a similar intermediary role in theatrical arts. Like traditional arts, it uses story development to arouse interest even if it has nothing to do with realism and also deals with the *Old Novels*' story motives, such as conflicts between wife and concubine, between mother-in-law and daughter-in-law, and between half-brothers and a step-mother. The plot structures of the *Sinpa* theatre are often similar to those of the *Old Novels*: a wife, who is in conflict with the concubine, suffers with her young child. Her husband also ends up entrapped. Finally, with a sudden turn of fortune, the family is saved and gets a happy ending. The frequent changes in the plot to intensify dramatic tensions make the plot sentimental and melodramatic.

In addition to the characteristics above, *Sinpa* theatre also affected the modern realism theatre, including emotional exaggerations and the recurring theme of family sufferings. The early realism plays, such as *The Resentment in the Wife's Bedroom* (閨恨),[12] *Fate* (運命), and *The Death of Kim Yeongil* (金英一ui 死), developed their plots relying on luck, emotional exaggeration (extreme apparent madness), and family trouble motives, including a sick mother and a young sister who needs care. Also, the directors of modern theatres at the time, such as Hong Haesung, Lee Seohyang, and Han Nodan, directed the *Sinpa* theatre as well. In other words, modern realism theatre owes its plot partly to *Sinpa* theatre.

In short, Korean *Sinpa* theatre as a popular theatre has characteristics of melodrama as follows. Its plot is dominated by situations rather than causality, characters are often typical such as good and evil, and it supports conservative moral standards. Although it tries to teach and give lessons, it is ultimately a commercial theatre with sensationalism. Thus, acting is often exaggerated, but it is a stage of pre-realism since it uses everyday language. Intellectuals joined even its writing and directing as time went by. Since it emphazised sensibility, music and other sensuous devices were used. It is not surprising that *Yeonswaegeuk* (連鎖劇) and *Akgeuk* (樂劇), which employed motion picture and music, were spun off from it. In short, Korean *Sinpa* theatre was such a popular theatre that its melodramatic legacy even found its way to present-day theatre and television drama. It also contributed to the spread of everyday language-based theatre. Additionally, modern realistic theatre could not have settled down so fast if *Sinpa* theatre had not become popular. Just like how melodrama was re-evaluated in the postmodern world because of pop culture's importance, *Sinpa* theatre has been re-evaluated as the stepping stone to modern realistic theatre from traditional theatre.

As examined, *Sinpa* theatre was not completely transferred from Japan, nor did it extend solely from the traditional arts. It cleverly took elements from the narrative traditions of the old novel and *Pansori*, except for the performative skills of the traditional Mask-Dance theatre. Essentially, Korean *Sinpa* theatre adopted the structures and motives of the *Old Novel* and combined those with the new Japanese *Sinpa* theatre, and, in turn, influenced the development of realism theatre in Korea. Korean *Sinpa* theatre was so popular that its legacy can even be found in present-day theatre and television drama. It also contributed to the spread of everyday language-based theatres. Additionally, modern realism theatre could not have settled down so fast if *Sinpa* theatre had not become popular. Just like how melodrama was re-evaluated in the postmodern world thanks to pop culture's importance, *Sinpa* theatre has been re-evaluated as the stepping stone to modern realism theatre from traditional theatre.

2.2 Early Troupes and Their Productions

Though Lee InJik made the first step in *Sinpa* Theatre in 1908 with *The Silver World,* Ihm SeongGu (林聖九) (1887–1921) opened a new era of *Sinpa* theatre (新派劇) in the 1910s. He started the theatre company "*Renovation* (革新團)" and produced a play titled *An Undutiful Son Must Be Punished* (不孝天罰)[13] in 1911 according to the new Japanese *Sinpa* theatre form. This became the first Korean production of Westernized theatre. Ihm did not get a proper education, but he enjoyed Japanese *Sinpa* in Japanese theatres for the Japanese residents in Seoul. Ihm did not have formal education in *Sinpa* theatre; it is said that he was either a shoe-keeper of the audience or a helper at a backstage of Japanese theatre in Seoul.[14] He self-taught stagecraft and performance skills along with other backstage activities. He finally produced an imitation of a Japanese *Sinpa* production he had seen in Seoul. *An Undutiful Son Must Be Punished* is a story of a prodigal son whose wretched behavior leads his mother to death. The son receives punishment from heaven by having a snake wound around his body, but with his repentance, he is finally forgiven. The content of the play emphasizes filial duty, a traditional theatre element. Many repertories of Japanese *Sinpa* were adapted into Korean *Sinpa*, including *An Undutiful Son Must Be Punished*, which adapted the Japanese *Obsessiveness of the Snake* (蛇之執念). *An Undutiful Son Must Be Punished* was not successful. It closed after only one night of performance due to a small audience number. There was no advertisement—only a few banners around the theatre—and almost every aspect of the performance was amateur. Unlike Lee InJik, nobody knew Ihm SeongGu or his company. That was why Ihm SeongGu decided to close the show after just one night.

Ihm SeongGu realized a more cautious preparation was needed for the next performance. He recruited a Japanese actor, who taught his company Japanese *Sinpa* makeup and advertised the performances in the newspapers. In 1912, Ihm SeongGu led the subsequent repertory, *A Robber with a Six-Chambered Revolver* (六穴砲 ┌盜), more related to the new age of modernization than the previous show. This time, *A Robber with a Six-Chambered Revolver* (六穴砲 ┌盜) was very successful. An adaptation of the Japanese *Pistol Robber Shimizu Sadakichi* (清水定吉), *A Robber with a Six-Chambered Revolver* is the story of a policeman who risks his life arresting a robber with a revolver for social order. The appearance of the new cultural product, a pistol, and the theme of social justice matched *Sinpa* format. The third repertory, *Tears(Nunmeul)*, also a great success; this play was based on a family novel originally published as a serial novel in newspapers at the time. The narrative involves the twists and turns of a feudal family, which moved the audience to tears. From this work, domestic *Sinpa* began, and "tears" became the representative characteristic of *Sinpa* theatre thereafter. The audience would weep, and through shedding tears, they would find unconditional comfort under the hardship of Japanese colonial rule.

The objectives of *Sinpa* theatre were 1) to encourage good and to punish evil, 2) to improve the old customs, 3) to develop the people's intellect, and 4) to be loyal to the nation and King Gojeong.[15] These aims were the same as the Japanese Sinpa except for the last one, consequently supporting social enlightenment and supporting the utilitarianism of theatre. Korean Sinpa Theatre's famous repertories were mostly adaptations from Japanese Sinpa. Initially, the plays dealt with political and social topics, like in *The Silber World* and *A Robber with a Six-chambered Revolver*, but soon they started to deal with domestic issues under colonial rule.

The early *Sinpa* theatre in Korea did not have a full script; there was only a synopsis, so the actors had to make up their lines. For this reason, a star system was applied to *Sinpa* productions. This was because proficient star actors were more capable of turning the synopsis into a complete script. As a result, the performances were built for the star actors, resulting in performances far from realistic. For example, Ihm SeongGu, who gained more popularity than anybody else, was so popular that he wore silk clothes even when he played a beggar, which the audience applauded. His tendency to appeal to emotions seemed effective for the *Sinpa* theatre. The opening was announced with the tapping of a crackle—,the influence of Japanese *Sinpa*. Then a director of the group came out to greet the audience. The director, male at that time, would outline the plot, and at the end of the play, he would close his speech with thanks. Like Japanese *Sinpa*, male actors sometimes played female roles in women's robes because of the insufficient number of actresses. The play was promoted in the traditional Korean way; a flag was set in front of the theatre, and drums, gongs, and pipes were played altogether to attract the audiences.[16] Even though Korean *Sinpa* theatre was deeply influenced by Japanese *Sinpa*, it was a little different from it because Korea did not have the same Japanese theatrical traditions, such as *Kabuki,* whose stereotypical vocalization method influenced the exaggerated accents of Japanese *Sinpa* theatre. Thus, the vocal tone or the accents of Japanese *Sinpa* were significantly different from those of Korean *Sinpa* theatre.

In addition to Ihm SeongGu, Yun BaekNam (尹白南: 1888–1954) and Lee GiSae (李基世: 1888–1945) were also established directors of *Sinpa* theatre. While *Gwangdae*, or traditional actors, were outcasts of society, Yun's and Lee's appearances made the status of actors respectable. They were theatre people who received higher education abroad. They both studied theatre at Japanese universities and understood Japanese *Sinpa* better than Ihm SeongGu, though their efforts to identically imitate Japanese *Sinpa* without Korean adaptation made them unpopular.

Yun BaekNam, along with Jo IlJae—a well-known expert in adaptation at that period—created a company called *MunSuSeong* in 1912 and performed *Bulyeogui* (不如歸) a month and a half after the company Renovation's second performance of *A Robber with a Six-Chambered Revolver*. *Bulyeogui* was the representative domestic tragedy of Japanese *Sinpa* theatre. Yun BaekNam and Jo IlJae criticized Ihm SeongGu's *Sinpa* for being a perverse theatre, while they called their *Sinpa* a legitimate theatre. Therefore, Yun BaekNam's repertories were mostly chosen from classic family tragedies of Japanese *Sinpa* theatre, including the opening show, and tried to be true to the Japanese *Sinpa*. However, in the face of Japanese imperialism, the *Sinpa* theatre of Yun BaekNam, especially its acting style, which was similar to Japanese *Kabuki*, made Korean audiences uncomfortable. Nevertheless, the overall productions of Yun BaekNam were said to be not much different from those of Ihm SeongGu.

Lee GiSae organized *The Only Theatre (*唯一團*)* in his home city, Gaesong, right after he came back from Japan in 1912. He studied under Sizuma Goziro (靜問 小次郎), who was renowned as one of the nine representatives of the Japanese *Sinpa* theatres and was the leader of the Tokyo *Sinpa* group. While Lee GiSae was studying for two years, his main job was to recopy scripts, and when he returned home, he arrived with theatre materials in his trunk. The opening repertory of *The Only Theatre* was *Wife* (*Cheo*), and the company produced adaptations of the classic Japanese *Sinpa* repertories such as *Bulyeogui, Jagi ui Joe* (自己 罪), and *JangHanMong* (長恨夢), an adaptation of the classic Japanese *Sinpa* repertory, *Bulyeogui, Jagijoe* (自己 *ui* 罪), and *JangHanMong* (長恨夢).[17] The company closed due to financial difficulties in 1914. The Only Theatre had a strong flavor of Japanese *Sinpa* and showed what *Sinpa* theatre was like.[18] Eventually, Lee GiSae and Yun BaekNam organized another *Sinpa* theatre company called YeSung-Jwa in 1916, which also did not last long. However, its performance of *Katyusha* (Катюша), an adaptation of Tolstoy's *Resurrection*, was a popular repertory of realism theatre in the 1920s.

The repertories of Korean *Sinpa* theatre came from many sources. The first source was adaptations from the Japanese *Sinpa* theatre. Famous Japanese *Sinpa was* rapidly adapted to Korean *Sinpa*. The second source was the adaptations of the New Novels of Japan and Korea. When a director or a manager of a company read a novel and decided it was suitable for performance, they made the novel into a script in a short period of time. The third source was to make a current compositional drama based on what happened in society or newspaper articles. In addition, some other sources were traditional *Old Novels*, *Pansori*, and, very rarely, original plays. Since a play was usually performed for two or three days, and a couple of plays were performed at the same time, there was always a need for scripts.

The audience of those days was not as courteous as the audience of today. They often ate and drank during the shows and agitated others by shouting during the performances. These habits originated from the customs of traditional theatre, where the participation of the audience was encouraged and the food and drinks were allowed.

Korean *Sinpa* theatre had many characteristics of Western melodrama. It appealed to emotions, often allowing for sensual exaggerations, and it focused on the promotion of virtues and the reproof of vice. In addition, Korean *Sinpa* theatre pursued ideas of Korean wealth and armament in the beginning, but it soon became a theatre of domestic affairs because the imperial Japanese government forbade any imposition of social ideas. The acting style was based on everyday language (though exaggerated), star systems, and improvisations from story outlines. Detailed scripts were not written, and actors had to ad-lib after learning the outline of the story, which was similar to the improvisations of Commedia dell'Arte.

Under the excuse of modernization, *Sinpa* theatre was encouraged by the Japanese governor-general, who was trying to suppress Korean traditional performances. Although *Sinpa* theatre's style was different from the traditional one, its repertories often borrowed stories from traditional novels and *Pansori*. In other words, *Sinpa* theatre tried to adjust to Korean culture and audiences in the middle of Westernization. Although *Sinpa* theatre failed to become a modern realism theatre, it popularized the concept of everyday-language theatre.

2.3 Improved *Sinpa*

After the Samil Independence Revolution in 1919, where not only Korean intelligentsia but also the general Korean public protested against Japanese imperialism, the Japanese governor-general switched policy rules from oppression to appeasement. Korean newspapers, such as *Donga* and *Joseon,* were published, and many other journals were allowed to be issued as well. This culturally more unbinding atmosphere allowed university students to offer enlightenment lectures to the public. Along with these lectures, new forms of theatre and music were introduced to the public. Realism theatre came about with the students' productions. Original modern realism plays were performed, and the first academy for actors was also opened in 1920 by Hyun Chul. All these changes brought about the improvement of *Sinpa* theatre.

The *Sinpa* theatre of the early 1920s was led by Yun BaekNam, Lee GiSae, and Kim SoRang after Ihm SeongGu's death in 1921. Stimulated by realism theatre, *Sinpa* theatre sought transformations to attract audiences. *The Arts Association Group (藝術協會, 1921)*, led by Lee GiSae, declared the theatre of everyday lives. It refused far-fetched stories and found new semi-realistic plays to produce. Lee insisted on the importance of creative plays; he produced many new original plays, such as *Fate* (運命*)* by Yun BaekNam, *Tears of the Hope* (希望*ui Nunmul*) by himself, and *The Poet's Family* (詩人*ui* 家庭*)* by Kim YoungBo. His insistence on creative plays laid the foundation for new playwrights in the 1920s. Yun BaekNam also established The People's Theatre (民衆劇團) in 1922. He recruited Kim UnJeong, who studied under Simamura Hogecheu (島村抱月), a forerunner of Japanese realism theatre. Kim UnJeong soon became one of the representative realism playwrights. In other words, Improved *Sinpa* was impressed by realism theatre and intermingled with it. Lee GiSae and Yun BaekNam tried to improve *Sinpa* theatre along with the rise of Western realism theatre. However, their efforts lasted only briefly because Lee GiSae switched his career to media and record, while Yun BaekNam also moved on to film within two years.

On the contrary, the early realistic original plays reflected many characteristics of *Sinpa* Theatre, such as emotional appeals, sensual exaggerations, family ordeals, and the promotion of virtue and the reproof of vice. There appeared many heroes with sick mothers and young sisters who needed to be taken care of, and many early plays ended with catastrophes such as suicide or arson. For example, the hero of *The Death of Kim YoungIl* (*Kim YoungIl ui Sa*) met his death after trying to get money for his trip to his sick mother, and the grandfather in *When the Whistle Blows* (*Gijeok Bulttae*) committed suicide due to harsh reality; they all ended catastrophically unlike realism plays. Kim SoRang, not formally educated in directing like Ihm SeongGu, created *ChwiSeong Group (*聚星座*)* in 1918, which lasted until the end of the 1920s. Kim SoRang did not attempt to improve *Sinpa* theatre much, but his group was loved by the public. His group's repertories were not much different from the early *Sinpa* theatres, but their acting skills improved significantly. Actress Ma HoJung, the wife of Kim SoRang, was known for her acting. The group also got rid of the Japanese scenery and made scenery familiar to Korean.[19] Like Ihm SeongGu's *Renovation Group*, *ChwiSeong Group* presented many charity performances for schools, youth groups, and socially disadvantaged groups. The group had strong affection for the Korean people, and so did the people for the group. The *Sinpa* theatre in the 1920s faced difficulties surviving because of the rising popularity of movies and realism theatres. *ChwiSeong Group* endeavored to keep *Sinpa* interesting by inserting interludes—the most popular songs of those days—between acts. The popularity of interludes was so great that a department of music and songs in *ChwiSeong Group* came about after 1927. Between the interludes of performances, separate music plays were added. Largely owing to the group's efforts, music drama gradually emerged. However, despite all these efforts, *ChwiSeong Group* closed at the end of 1929.

The leaders of *Sinpa* theatre had the will to improve *Sinpa* alongside the appearance of Western realism theatre in the early 1920s. However, the change was not easy. The existing intellectual *Sinpa* theatre leaders soon turned to other emerging industries, such as movies and record companies, while new intellectuals of theatre and media changed their attention to realism theatre. Even though *Sinpa* theatre sought improvements, it inevitably declined as the years went by. The improved *Sinpa* was not enough to attract highly educated audiences, but it was too difficult for the common people, who still sought sentimental stimuli.

2.4 High *Sinpa: The House of Joseon Theatre* (朝鮮演劇舍) and *the Oriental Theatre* (東洋劇場)

In the early 1930s, theatre groups such as *The House of Joseon Theatre (朝鮮演劇舍)*, *The Theatre Market (演劇市場)*, *SamCheon Musical Theatre (三川歌劇團)*, and *New Stage (新撫臺)* emerged. All of them were somewhat related to the *ChwiSeong Group* of the 1920s. Most *Sinpa* theatre companies did not last long; many were created and then disbanded shortly thereafter. *Sinpa* theatre in the 1930s required a new transition due to the spread of realism theatre. To the public who were now familiar with realism theatre, it, as a popular theatre, was demanded more attractive devices in order to attract the audience. It needed grand performances with theatrical elements such as splendid scenery and star actresses.

The House of Joseon Theatre came into being in December of 1929 and planned to be a grand theatre company. Former members of *ChwiSeong Group*, including Ji DuHan, created *the House of Joseon Theatre*. It started as a giant group of 90; it had 30 actors and actresses, 30 band members, and 30 apprentices. It opened with the following repertories: Schnitzler's *The Blind Brother* and a new comedy, *Fifty Thousand Won*, under director Cheon HanSu. Having studied directing once in Japan, he added dance and music to the plays. His directing was well received. This group made four ambitious goals from the beginning: 1) to be a coterie group, 2) to pay salaries as well as dividends—the first attempt to utilize a performance-related pay system, 3) to strip Japanese nuance from their productions and produce original plays, and 4) to build its own theatre auditorium for performance/drama. It was the first theatre company to openly call for submissions of new plays. Thus, many playwrights, like Kim Geon, Park Youngho, and Ihm SeoBang, provided new plays for *The House of Joseon Theatre*. All of them became the leading commercial playwrights of the 1930s. Additionally, Won UJeon, one of the first scenic designers, and Hong HaeSeong, a director from *Chukji* Small Theatre of Japan, joined the group to improve the scenery and directing. Moreover, the company had a talented pool of actors and actresses, such as Lee KyongSeol, Lee KyongHwan, Jeon Ok, and Ji ChoeSun.

The House of Joseon Theatre's productions went beyond the improved *Sinpa* theatre. It employed new plays, some of which even expressed political color, and consisted of realistic sceneries, lighting, and costumes. It also excluded exaggerated acting styles. Ultimately, it became the best and most popular theatre at that time for the public. However, their productions were not exactly like those of Western realism. Yu ChiJin, a leading director of realism at that time, described their productions as "not fully exercised, and somewhat improvised," "a man in a women's role, and no good acting except a couple of Kang HongSik's performances."[20]

The House of Joseon Theatre met a crisis when it produced *The Moon of Silla* in the summer of 1935. *The Moon of Silla* is a love story of a girl hiding her lover, who is a member of the independence movement. Due to its political color, the members of the theatre group got arrested.[21] After this event, *the House of Joseon Theatre* was watched by the Japanese colonial government and faced difficult times. Additionally, when the actress Ji ChoeSun, a daughter of Ji DuHan, got sick, Ji DuHan finally decided to close *The House of Joseon Theatre* with its last performance of *A Maiden in the Island* (*Seom Saeksi*) and *The First Step to Seoul* (上京第一步).[22] Ji DuHan, the source of *the House of Joseon Theatre*'s funding, and his daughter, the best actress of the group, retired from the theatrical world. Ji DuHan's decision could have been out of love for his daughter, but it could have been because of the emergence of *Oriental Theatre*.

Oriental Theatre (Dongyang 東洋劇場) came into being in November of 1935 by the couple, Hong SunEon and Bae GuJa. Bae GuJa, a famous dancer, was the niece of Bae JeongJa, a dancer and a political lobbyist. *Oriental Theatre* was the first theatre exclusive for theatre performance with a rotating stage, a backdrop that ran the length of the stage depicting the horizon, a switchboard-controlled lighting system, and approximately 600 seats.[23] These facilities were a breakthrough for the theatre. *Oriental Theatre* had Choi DokGyeon as its manager and started an exclusive commercial theatre company with directors such as Hong HaeSeong, Park Jin, and Lee UnBang. At first, the directors gathered young generations of actors and actresses and tried to produce a fresh and charming *Sinpa*, though the productions were not fully realistic. The first theatre-exclusive company was called *The Youth Group* (靑春座), and its representative members were actors Park JeHaeng, Hwang Chul, and Shim Young and actresses Cha HongNyeo, Ji GyungSun, and Kim SunYoung. *The Youth Group* implemented an actor salary system.

Bae GuJa's *Oriental Theatre* opened in November with many types of performances, including *The Miracle of the Pipe (Piri ui 奇蹟)*, a music-like theatre called *Akgeuk* (written by Choi DokGyeon), and *The Marriage of the Twins(雙童 ui 結婚)*, a piece of theatre, along with dances, songs, and short skits.[24] *Oriental Theatre*'s repertories foretold its commercial characteristics. Soon, *The Youth Group (靑春座)* followed and performed *A Tragedy of the Temple Room (僧房悲曲)* and *The Border Night (國境ui Bam). Oriental Theatre* also spawned other theatre groups, including *The Comedy Group (喜劇座)* and *The History Group (東劇座)*, but soon these groups combined and became *The Luxury Group (豪華船). Oriental Theatre* with *The Youth Group* and *Luxury Group*, alternated performances in Seoul as well as in other provinces. *The Youth Group* met its golden age during the four years between 1935 and 1939 when the owner Hong SunEon and manager Choi DokGyeon worked together. However, its popularity began to decrease with the sudden death of Hong SunEon in 1938, only three years after its opening. Due to financial difficulties, *Oriental Theatre* went bankrupt in 1939, but it was taken over by a new owner and manager, Kim TaeYun. Although he was not a theatre man, he was very enthusiastic about the art, and created the Theatre Research Institute (演劇硏究所) to train actors. However, along with the change of owner, the primary actors and actresses from *Oriental Theatre* created a new theatre company called Arang. Thus, the heyday of *Oriental Theatre* was on a path of decline.

Oriental Theatre regularly performed six full plays and added skits for the opening and ending of the performances each month. From the beginning of domestic *Sinpa*, it was widely believed that the audience had to cry in order to

Figure 2.1 The Oriental (Dongyang) Theatre Building. Photo from *Encyclopedia of Korean People and Culture* (韓國民族文化大百科事典)

attract other audiences. Thus, playwrights did their best to analyze the tastes of their audience and the characteristics of their actors in order to make the audience cry. Since many of *Oriental Theatre*'s audiences were Korean geishas, their heroines were often women who had fallen into geisha status because of calamitous fates but still kept virtues despite all hardships. In other words, melodramas of family tragedies were very popular at that time. The prominent repertories, which are popular even nowadays, were *Deceived in Love and Crying for Money* (*Sarange Sokgo, Done Ulgo*), *The Power of Mother* (*Eomeoni ui Him*), *Hymn of Death* (*Jugum ui Canga*), *The Revenge of Justice* (*Jeongui ui Boksu*), and so on. *Deceived in Love and Crying for Money* by Ihm SeongGu, for example, was one of the most popular plays, and it was summarized as follows in one newspaper at the time:

> Robbed of love that was more important than life, the heroine finally stabs the enemy with a knife. She is tied up by her own brother, whom she supported his school expenses serving as a geisha. What a nasty fate it is! ... What judgement would the judge make? Could the heroine marry her lover? Tears and sighs will arise as the case end.[25]

The above summary shows outstanding melodramatic features by appealing to emotions and sentimental plotting of reversals. This play is still popular among the Korean people today.

Oriental Theatre became a popular theatre for the masses. It held performances year-round and, thus, easily had dedicated audiences. Through *Oriental Theatre*, many other theatre groups, such as *GoHyeop* and *Arang*, came along. The existence of complete theatre facilities ignited the performance desires of theatre artists. Interestingly, *Oriental Theatre* also had a close relationship with the *Association of Joseon Pansori Singers* (朝鮮聲樂硏究會), a group of master *Pansori* singers. *Oriental Theatre* tried to accommodate *Changgeuk* as well as

Figure 2.2 The Newspapers Advertisement of *Deceived in Love and Crying for Money.*

Sinpa, which were loved by the masses at the time. *Changgeuk* became more theatrical than ever with realism directors, like Park Jin and Kim GiDong. In short, *Oriental Theatre* was the center of popular theatre in the 1930s. The productions, which were sentimental melodramas with a realistic approach, were called high *Sinpa* compared to improved *Sinpa* and early *Sinpa*.

Figure 2.3 A Performance Scene from the *Dengacheu* Company Where Bae GuJa Was a Member in 1932.

Figure 2.4 Bae GuJa in Dancing (1935).

2.5 Technology and Music of *Sinpa* Theatre: *Yeonswaegeuk* (連鎖劇) and *Akgeuk* (樂劇)

There came into being a form called *Yeonswaegeuk* (連鎖劇), a "combined" theatre, in the late 1920s, as *Sinpa* theatre became interested in its stage equipment and scenery improvement. These changes were necessary to attract mass audiences. Motion pictures were used as a scenery in response to the growing popularity of movies. As mentioned previously, Ihm SeongGu, the leader of early *Sinpa,* showed his interest in motion pictures even around the 1920s, and Yun BaekNam, after trying some improvements in *Sinpa*, turned to the film industry in the late 1920s. Since motion pictures were interesting and novel at the time, they became very popular. The directors of *Sinpa*, who had to compete against movies for their popularity, soon took advantage of motion pictures as backgrounds for their *Sinpa* productions. For example, when *Lee Sooil and Sim Soonae* were performed, a clip of the Daedong river scenery was projected onto the backdrop, and then the actors came on stage to meet each other near the riverside. Although most motion pictures were used only for the scenery, occasionally some scenes were replaced with motion pictures instead of live acting. *Sinpa* theatre made the best use of motion pictures at that time. However, when the curiosity of the audience declined, so did the popularity of it. It was not because the combined form itself was less interesting, but because of the poor quality of motion pictures in *Sinpa* theatre compared to the improving quality of movies. Therefore, many theatre critics advised *Sinpa* theatre practitioners to focus on live performances instead. Although the lifespan of *Yeonswaegeuk* was short, it could be regarded as one of the first attempts to utilize cutting-edge technology in plays.

Music and songs were other devices that *Sinpa* theatre practitioners used to attract audiences. Music, similar to that of Westernized musical theatre in the Western musical scale, became a remedy for overcoming the lack of audience. The form was called *Akgeuk* (樂劇), or *Gageuk* (歌劇), and was played during the intermission of *Sinpa* plays. Music theatres of the time were traditional *Pansori* and *Changgeuk*, which were based on the Korean scale, but *Akgeuk* employed Western music. *ChwiSeong Group* developed a Western music department in 1927, and an *Akgeuk* group called *Venus (金星) Opera Group* was initiated in 1929.[26] In the 1930s, *Oriental Theatre* preferred *Akgeuk* since Bae GuJa, the owner of the theatre, had her own group of dancers and singers called the Bae GuJa Akgeukdan. *Akgeuk* flourished in the latter half of the 1940s. *Joseon Akgeukdan* and *Bando Gageukdan* were the most prominent, and both were made by record companies.

The stems of *Akgeuk* were rooted in three ways: the first one was developed in the interlude of *Sinpa* theatre; the second one was the imitation of Japanese *Akgeuk,* such as *Takarazuka*[27]; and the last one was made by record companies for their advertisements. *Akgeuk* groups started from *Sinpa* theatre in the beginning but gradually became affiliated with record companies due to large capital investment. The development of *Akgeuk* in the 1940s was possible partly because of the political situation in which serious realism plays could not be performed and partly because the people were comforted by music as an escape. Furthermore, there were official performances of *Takarazuka* from Japan, which showed the merits of music theatre. Near the end of the Japanese occupation, *Akgeuk* mainly performed pro-Japanese, national plays and served as propaganda of the governor-general. After the Liberation from Japan in 1945, *Akgeuk* remained popular in the turmoil of national establishment and the Korean War. It managed to survive until 1960.

Akgeuk could be considered the first musical in the Western musical scale in Korea, although the first modern musical company *Yegreen Akdan* came into being with the production of *Sneak up to Me* (*Saljjagi Opseoye*) in 1966.[28] *Akgeuk* introduced the taste of musicals to the audience and made the theatre world realize its need. As such, *Akgeuk* that appeared in connection with *Sinpa* theatre was the forerunner of Korean musicals.

In conclusion, *Sinpa* theatre was the first Western-influenced theatre to come to Korea through Japan. Due to the influence of Japanese *Sinpa* theatre, Korean *Sinpa* theatre was once thought of as a genre of sentiment and tears, totally disconnecting Korean theatre from tradition. However, it was neither completely transplanted from Japan nor totally disconnected from tradition. Korean *Sinpa* theatre cleverly took elements from narrative traditions of the *Old Novel* and *Pansori*, though it abandoned traditional acrobatic performance skills. Thus, *Sinpa* theatre contributed to the spread of language-based theatre and played the role of a stepping stone toward Western realism theatre. After the 1920s, when Western realism theatre started, *Sinpa* theatre took its role as popular theatre. For commercial survival and success, it combined other genres such as *Pansori*, *Changgeuk*, motion pictures, music, and dance. Its plots were dramatic, and it appealed to the sentiments of the audience. Thus, it showed many characteristics of Western melodrama. After Korean independence, *Sinpa* theatre did not seem to be officially produced, but many commercial performances adapted the form of *Sinpa* theatre. In this postmodern world, thanks to the revaluation of melodrama, a few *Sinpa* theatres were able to take place after the 1990s. Its elements that appeal to the audience have also been applied to TV dramas and movies. No matter what they may be called, the remnants of *Sinpa* theatre live on through popular art forms in Korea.

Notes

1 Choi, Wonsik. *The Logic of National Literature* (民族文學ui 論理). Seoul, Changbisa, 1982, pp. 37–53.
2 Sohn, JongMuk. *A Study on the Social and Economic Cities of the Enlightenment Period (*韓國開港期都市社會經濟史研究*)*. Seoul, Ilgisa, 1982, p. 379.
3 Ibid., pp. 208–210.
4 Yu MinYeoung, *A History of Modern Korean Theatre* (韓國近代演劇史). Seoul, Danguk University Press, 1995, pp. 216–217.
5 Ibid., 217.

6 *Kyongseong Daily Newspaper*(京城日報), 25 Jul 1907.
7 These were the general opinions of scholars up to 2000.
8 Lee, Meewon. *A Study on the Modern Korean Theatre* (韓國近代劇研究). Seoul, HyundaeMihaksa, 1994, pp. 88–100.
9 Jo, Dongil. *Characteristics of New Novels in the Literary History*(新小說 *ui* 文化史的性格). Seoul, Hanguk Munhwa Yeonguso, 1973, pp. 27–30.
10 Choi, Wonsik. *The Logic of National Literature* (民族文學ui 論理). Seoul, Changbisa, 1982, pp. 68–99.
11 Lee, Jeseon, *A Study on Korean Novels in Enlightenment Period* (韓國開化期小說研究). Seoul, Iljogak, 1972, pp. 57–68.
12 The play is translated as *Sorrows of the Inner Room by* Owen Stampton in *Asian Theatre Journal* in Spring 2022.
13 There are also other minor opinions; Hyun Cheol and Lee GiSe wrote respectively that a military play such as *Hwado Daejwa* or *Soldier's Temperament (Gunin ui Gijil)* was the first performance of the *Renovation (革新團) company.*
14 An, JongHwa. *A Story of the Modern Theatre History* (新劇史 Iyagi). Seoul, Jinmunsa, 1955, p. 27.
Lee, SeoGu. "The Early Unofficial History of Korean Modern Theatre (韓國演劇運動ui 胎兒期野史)." *Sinsajo*(新思潮), Jan 1964.
15 Lee, Duhyun. *Modern History of Korean Drama* (*Hanguk Singeuksa Yeongu*). Seoul, Seoul National University Press, 1966, pp. 38–44.
16 Ibid., pp. 54–58.
17 Ibid., p. 79.
18 *Maeil Daily Newspapers*, 23 Mar 1916.
19 Han, Heo. *The Overview of Joson Theatre History* (朝鮮演劇史概要). Seoul, Gungnipchulpansa, 1956, p. 271.
20 Yu, ChiJin, "After Attending the Performances of Joseonyeongeuksa." *Joseon Daeily Newspapers*, 2 Jan 1933.
21 *Donga Daeily Newspapers*, 11 Jun 1935.
22 *Mail Daily Newspapers*, 16 Jul 1935.
23 Lee, Op.cit., p. 231.
24 Ibid., p. 231.
25 *Mail Daily Newspaper*, 28 Aug 1936.
26 Seo, Hangseok, "Theatre after *Wongaksa*." *The Survey of Korean Arts* (韓國藝術總覽). National Academy of Arts of Republic of Korea (大韓民國藝術院) Ed., Seoul, National Academy of Arts of Republic of Korea (大韓民國藝術院), 1964.
27 It is a Japanese musical theatre company composed only of women. The performances encompass periods from ancient to present and cultures from the East to the West. Their diverse genres include historical drama, fantasy, science fiction, etc.
28 The show employed an exclusive orchestra, choir, and dance company, along with a famous pop singer as the heroine and the best entertainer of the time as the hero. It also had one of the best playwrights, Kim YoungSu, and the best director, Ihm YoungUng. It was said that the total number of the cast was more than one hundred. *Sneak Up to Me* had only seven performances but attracted a total of 16,000 audiences. This large-scale performance was possible because a patron with political power sponsored it. Indeed, *Sneak Up to Me* was the stage event that realized the long-established desire for musicals to become a reality in Korea. In fact, the Korean Musical Association later established October 26 as Musical Day, following the premiere date of the performance.

3 *Singeuk* Theatre

Western Realism Theatre and Social Realism Theatre

After the Samil Independence Revolution in 1919, the Japanese governor-general of Korea switched policy rule from oppression to appeasement. Newspapers and many other journals were allowed to be published. This cultural atmosphere allowed students to give Enlightenment lectures to the public. Along with these lectures, students performed various new plays and music. The renovation of theatre from *Sinpa* to realism appeared with these students' productions. In addition, original modern realism plays and the first academy for actors by Hyeon Cheol also came into being in 1920. All these changes were to shed light on a new kind of theatre, realism theatre.

A few pioneering articles showed the new direction of theatre. The first one was "Theatre and Society" by Yun BaekNam in 1920, which first emphasized the educational function of theatre. "Theatre should grasp the fundamental cultural spirit rooted in a proper mental civilization based on the needs of one's national life."[1] Yun BaekNam believed in theatre's influence on society and its function as social betterment. He rejected the conventional prejudice against theatre and the despising custom of actors. He also pinpointed the possible reasons for the poor performances of the time, such as an insufficient number of plays, no scenery experts, no trained actors and actresses, producers' commercial pursuit over artistic interests, and so on.[2] In short, Yun believed in reformational theatre to nurture and lead national culture. His paper was published during the time of *Sinpa* theatre. His idea of theatre's function accelerated the emergence of realism theatre, which, in turn, brought to light various social ills.

After this article, other articles followed emphasizing the close relationships between theatre and society. The article "The Relation of Theatre to I" by Hyeon Cheol in 1920 preached that theatre should serve society.[3] Then, Ibsen, the father of modern theatre, was introduced to Korean society. *A Doll's House* was finally translated into Korean, and intellectuals anticipated groundbreaking performances in 1922. With the introduction of Ibsen, the term "modern drama" became known to the public. Kim UJin's article "About the So-Called Modern Theatre" was published around this time as well.[4] It summarized the overall meaning of modern theatre, emphasizing its social function. Following Ibsen, representative works of William Shakespeare and

DOI: 10.4324/9781003490708-4

Oscar Wilde were introduced, which eventually opened the door for the translations of the works from the Irish literary revival. Translations of Irish works were intended to highlight nationalism in the works since Ireland was under English colonial rule as Korea was under that of the Japanese. Ultimately, individual awareness and social awakening, centered on Ibsen's dramas, had spread to translation, creation, and theatrical movements.

3.1 The Beginning of Western Realism Theatre with Students' Groups

The Association of Theatre Arts (劇藝術協會), formed by about 20 Korean students in Tokyo in 1920, began as a study group of Western drama. They met every Saturday to study modern and classic drama, such as Shakespeare, Goethe, Gogol, Chekhov, and so on. The group was asked to perform during the summer tour in Korea to raise funds for the hall construction of *DongWuHoe*, an association of self-supporting students. *The Association of Theatre Arts* accepted this offer with the intention of practicing their theatrical ideals on an actual stage as well as helping the students. They wanted to customize the program; therefore, they included musical performances and short Enlightenment lectures in addition to the theatrical performances. Kim UJin, who knew much about modern drama, led the group and directed the plays. He believed in performing original plays rather than translated foreign plays, with the exception of Irish ones, whose national literary movement was developing. The selected plays were *Kim Youngil's Death* (*Kim Youngil ui Sa*), which reflected the lives of the self-supporting students; *The Last Handshake* (*Choehu ui Aksu*), an adaptation of an original Korean novel dealing with a woman's ego and awareness; and a translated Irish play of Lord Dunsany's *The Glittering Gate* (*Chanranhan Mun*). However, because the director Kim UJin was so introverted, the preparation for the tour did not go well. He asked for help from Domoda Geoske (友田恭助), a Japanese modern theatre actor. The performance went on tours in major cities, including Seoul, for about a month from July to August of 1921. The tours were well received. According to a report from *Donga Daily Newspapers*, the audience agreed it was a "true realism theatre."[5] *Kim Youngil's Death* was exceptionally popular, and the lighting of *The Glittering Gate* was said to be new and impressive.

GalDopHoe was another association of self-supporting students in Seoul. It was founded in the summer of 1920 and had its initial performance in December. The association's itinerant theatre was organized into three groups and performed on a large scale from July to early September of 1921. Its tour programs were similar to those of *DongWuHoe*; they included musical performances and short Enlightenment lectures in addition to the performances. *The Fate* (*YunMyong*) and *The Poor* (*Bingonja ui Muri*) were the most popular among their repertories. *The Fate* criticized long-distance marriages through pictures between Hawaiian immigrants and Korean maidens, while *The Poor* described the difficult lives of the self-supporting students. In spite of the lack of funds and time, *GalDopHoe* demonstrated fairly good modern theatres. The audience applauded and wrote reviews with full encouragement along with detailed descriptions.[6] Eventually, a Japan branch of *GalDopHoe* was formed in Tokyo in 1922 and did a summer tour from Busan to Manchuria. *GalDopHoe's* performances were nationalistic and emphasized the enlightenment of the people, although they were an amateur theatre group.

HyeongSulHoe, also a self-supporting students' group in Tokyo, was formed in 1922. Although it planned a summer tour in 1922, the tour was canceled because of a budgetary deficit. Then, *HyeongSulHoe* asked The Association of Theatre Arts to perform during the summer tour in 1923. Many new members, including Jo ChunGwang, Ko HanSeung, and Kim YoungPal, agreed to have the tour in order to let people know about realism theatre. The new members were the second group from The Association of Theatre Arts who did not join the tour of *DongWuHoe* in 1921. *The Association of Theatre Arts* was the most central theatre group that could organize performance tours for other groups. They seemed to have the necessary funds and human resources. The tour group had trial performances in June in Tokyo, which were well received even by the Japanese audience, and started a Korean tour from Busan to the northern cities in July of 1923. The representative repertories were *When the Personality Awakened* (*Gaeseongi Nun Tteun Dwi*) and *The Three Brothers and a Sister* (*Sain Nammae*) by Jo ChunGwang and *A Long Night* (*Jangguhan Bam*) by Ko HanSeung. *When the Personality Awakened* is the tragic story of a coercive marriage without love, and *The Three Brothers and a Sister* is a philosophical debate among three brothers and a sister about humanism, socialism, revolutionism, and romantic love for love's sake, which were the predominant thoughts of the time. *A Long Night* describes the conflict between traditional and modern morals. A hero highlights the modern consciousness that resists conventions. Themes reflected in these plays were the trending thoughts of the 1920s, and the representative playwrights of such plays were Kim Ujin, Jo ChunGwang, and Kim Youngbo. They hoped to write social plays with themes of modern humanity, equal society, and free love. *HyeongSulHoe*'s tour was well received. Its performances were said to be arranged with strong scenery, appropriate costumes, and play scripts. In spite of being an amateur group, their performances excelled those of the extant professional companies and started the new beginning of Korean modern theatre, according to a review from influential newspapers.[7]

ToWolHoe (土月會), also a literary group of students in Tokyo, planned a summer tour in 1923. For their first performances, *Gilsik* by Park SeungHee and one-act modern plays by Shaw and Chekhov were chosen. *Gilsik* is based on modern consciousness, protesting against traditional values, while the others were from Western playwrights. Their performances were highly praised thanks to the stage equipment and the harmonious acting of the characters.[8] *ToWolHoe* did not intend to have more shows after the one above but produced another one in order to pay back the debts from the first show. Among its repertories, Tolstoy's *Resurrection* and *Alt Heidelberg* were great hits.

Thus, *ToWolHoe* was praised so much that it was not modern theatre unless it was a *ToWolHoe* performance.[9] After they compensated for the debts with the second performances, the founding members, except for Park SeungHee, withdrew from *ToWolHoe*. Park SeungHee decided to keep and reorganize *ToWolHoe* and to develop it as a professional theatre company. *ToWolHoe* performed three times in 1924. He signed up with the *GwangMuDae* stage and made it a full-time exclusive theatre of *ToWolHoe* for one year in 1925. However, since Park SeungHee was the only one responsible for most script writings, directing, and fundraising, *ToWolHoe*'s professional performances did not improve much from its early amateur performances.

These students' tours spread the seeds of modern realism theatre based on national consciousness throughout the country, even though they only performed for a short period of time. *The Association of Theatre Arts*, a study group of dramatic works, played a core role in the performance tours. In addition, youth associations, religious groups, and more followed the students' groups and tried to perform modern plays. Eventually, *ToWolHoe* was developed into a professional company and became different from other students' amateur groups. Although the latter performances did not outdo their amateur ones, they greatly contributed to the proliferation of modern theatre—at least symbolically. Since *ToWolHoe* became a professional theatre, many *Sinpa* theatres felt threatened. However, as time went by, *ToWolHoe* had not been successful enough to establish modern realism theatre. It was said that *ToWolHoe* later even regressed to one of the *Sinpa* theatre due to the lack of funds and energy.

3.2 Professional *ToWolHoe* in the 1920s

ToWolHoe is considered the first professional theatre company, which showcased Western realism theatres in Korea. In *Theatre History of Joseon*, Kim JaeCheol wrote that the appearance of *ToWolHoe* in 1922 was the most important event in the history of Korean theatre. *ToWolHoe* was the first company to produce proper realism plays and became the central company of the peninsula.[10] However, its performances were not completely realistic throughout all productions. As examined above, after the success of two amateur performances, which were famous for their realistic sceneries, *ToWolHoe* became a professional company. Its transformation was a great stimulus to *Sinpa* theatres at the time. For the third production, it produced the dance-theatre *Love and Death* (*Sarang gwa Jugmeum*) by Park SeungHee and *The Dream of Grey (Hoesaeg ui Ggum)* in 1924. The orchestra of violins, flutes, and pianos played famous Western music between the acts, which became the origin of the interlude tradition. The fourth production included revivals of *The Resurrection* (*Buhwal*) and *Love and Death*. The fifth was the adaptation of *The Living Corpse* (*San Songjang*) by Tolstoy with added songs, which was a great success. After the sixth and seventh performances, *ToWolHoe* became a popular theatre company like other *Sinpa* theatres. The repertories were those of Japanese *Sinpa* theatre, though *ToWolHoe* insisted its performances to be different from former *Sinpa* theatre's. Since Park SeungHee had to provide almost all the repertories of *ToWolHoe* and also the funds, new plays were always in need and the funds were insufficient.

ToWolHoe finally got an exclusive theatre. It rented *GwangMu* stage for one year in 1925 and performed songs and dances and also adapted the novels of popular artists of the day, like Lee GwangSu. *ToWolHoe* performed his *No Love* (無情) and *Pioneers* (開拓者), which were both well received. However, these performances were not enough to overcome its financial difficulties, so *ToWolHoe* decided to find a breakthrough with *ChunHyangJeon*, a stage adaptation of the traditional *Pansori* piece of the same name. *ChunHyangJeon* was a great hit and relieved the financial difficulties to some degree. Then, *ToWolHoe* went on a tour in the regional areas for more than one and a half months, achieving financial success, but the tour tired the members of *ToWolHoe*. After returning to Seoul, commercial performances continued, but neither the artistry of the work nor financial success were ultimately achieved.

ToWolHoe, having fallen into a slump, sought to make another leap forward by accommodating the famous singer Yun ShimDeok at the time. It again tried to firmly maintain the strong national spirit of culture as well as its theatrical philosophy. It fought against the social prejudices toward theatre; for example, the members of *ToWolHoe* had been despised as if they were a group of depraved people in their conservative families but had been firmly defending theatre.

Their efforts were not different from those of the national activists for the national movement and those of the educators for their students. *ToWolHoe* questioned the differences between the above people and them. *ToWolHoe* strongly believed in the fact that they worked for the betterment of society through theatre. The joining of Yun ShimDeok further strengthened the original intention of *ToWolHoe*.

ToWolHoe made Yun ShimDeok a heroine in adaptations of popular American films such as *The East Road* (東道) and *The Hat Left Over* (Noko Naon 帽子) in 1926. Then, during the New Year by the lunar calendar, the biggest holiday in Korea, *Carmen, The Bear,* and other plays were performed; Yun ShimDeok sang quite a bit in *Carmen* and was very popular. However, actors rebelled against Park SeungHee for running the company arbitrarily, as well as against the manager for treating *ToWolHoe* like an entertainment company without respect for artistic achievements. The main purpose of Park SeungHee and the manager was to pay off the debts of *ToWolHoe*. However, the original members, such as Kim Gijin, Yeon HakYeon, and Yun ShimDeok, left *ToWolHoe* after a week of protests and created another company called Swan Association (白鳥會) in 1926. *ToWolHoe* could not overcome this blow and eventually dissolved after the 56th performance in 1926.

The difficulty of having performances in the 1920s was described in the following article written by Kim EulHan.

> If the level of performance is a little high, the audience may have no idea what this is, or what it means. Then, when the audience goes out one by one, there are half empty seats that were initially full. So, if you lower the level a little, you'll be liked by regular customers, but more sophisticated audiences will criticize whether this is a new theatre movement or a *Sinpa* theatre. This is the biggest headache for the theatre people who are seeking new realism theatre.[11]

The observation above shows the difficulty of *ToWolHoe* in the 1920s. *ToWolHoe* still had recurring performances, such as *This Lord/ Damn Lord* (*Yi Daegam Manghal Daegam*), *The Victory of Death* (*Sa ui Chanmi*) and *The Blood* (*Hyeolyuk*) in 1928. Despite many efforts, *ToWolHoe* was not financially successful. *ToWolHoe* performed a couple of plays sponsored by the owner of Joseon Theatre in 1929. Among them, *The Hill of Arirang* (Arirang Gogae) written by Park SeungHee was the greatest success; it made not only the audience but also the watch-out policemen cry. The play traversed the patriarchal emotions of the Korean people and expressed the deep resentment of the Korean colonial situation. In one performance, a young man threw flyers of the Gwangju Uprising and was held gallantly by the police.[12] As such, the anti-Japanese sentiment of *The Hill of Arirang* was so strong that it was chosen as a place to publicize the student anti-Japanese resistance. Although *ToWolHoe* often produced commercial plays, it always included thoughts of the nation and its people and had pride in contributing to the betterment of society. As *ToWolHoe*'s performances were getting worse due to the lack of budget and talented personnel, it was finally dissolved in 1931, nine years after its foundation. Park SeungHee recalled the reasons for its dissolution: a lack of theatres, good actors, directors, and writers in addition to a lack of audience, owing to the collapse of the middle class. Park tried to reorganize the company with a new name, *The Solar Theatre (太陽劇場)*, with Hyeon Cheol, but it soon turned into *Sinpa* theatre and did not contribute much to realism theatre. The colonial situation inclined toward Japanese war policy played a big role here. Although *ToWolHoe* tried to produce performances in the Western realism style, it was not fully achieved, except for a few productions. However, without the pioneering efforts of *ToWolHoe* toward realism theatre in a poor environment where nothing was prepared for realism, the next generation of theatre could not have achieved realism theatre.

3.3 Original Realism Plays in the 1920s

The development of Korean realism novels started with *Creation* (創造), the first comprehensive literary magazine published from 1919 to around 1925. Original Korean realism plays were developed around the same time. Representatively, *The Resentment in the Wife's Bedroom* (閨恨), *The Fate* (運命), and *The Border* (國境) were written in the 1910s, but many plays appeared in the 1920s. The plays were roughly divided into three groups by the level of achievement of realism.

The first plays were ones in which the protagonists pursued their individual egos but failed to achieve firm egos because they surrendered to traditional conventions or became unclear about what they were trying to seek. In addition, the plot development was not carefully based on causality, and the ending was fierce, unlike most real lives. It also lacked descriptions of a comprehensive external environment. As an example of one of these plays, *The Death of Kim Youngil* (金英一 ui 死) pursued the modern thoughts introduced at the time, namely Tolstoy's humanism, Nietsche's superhumanism, Christian philanthropism, Marx's materialism, and even Dandyism. Ultimately, the play's central claim was not clear because only the protagonist's accented voice was heard.

By 1922, the second group of plays emerged. Compared to the first group, these plays actively challenged conventions and authorities with firm convictions and will. For example, in *A Forsaken* (*Beorim Badeunja*), the protagonist challenges the prejudice of the Church and morals, protests the social prejudice against virginity, and believes in a better tomorrow, even if she fails. In *The End of Old Family* (舊家庭 *ui GgeuNal*), the heroine challenges the authority of a habitual husband and leaves the home like Nora did in *A Doll's House*. The enlightening dialogues and monologues were significantly reduced, and the detailed environmental descriptions of the stages were often noticeable, though not enough, in these plays.

Thanks to the second group, the third group of plays came into existence. They drew attention to the poverty of colonial society rather than to the protests of conventional Confucian morals. *When the Whistle Blows* (汽笛 BulTtae) and *Lee Youngyeo* were representative of this group. The third group's plays had surprisingly natural and objective descriptions of real environments compared to the second group's plays. In addition, these works avoided the Enlightenment speeches or long expressions of direct thoughts and utilized regional dialects as well as everyday language. Even the scenes of death were dispersed to avoid the intense ending in *Lee Youngyeo*. The motto of realism, "there is death but no catastrophe," was achieved. The concept of mass protagonists was also carried out; *When the Whistle Blows* and *Lee Youngyeo* described the lives around the people rather than concentrating only on the protagonist. The plays both addressed societal ills and ultimately dreamed of a better society. In short, Zola's "a slice of life" was achieved in these third group's plays. By the middle of the 1920s, realism plays became the majority and were commonly written thereafter. In other words, playwrights officially came into being in the 1920s.

3.4 The Appearance of Acting Schools

Hyeon Cheol, who studied theatre in Japan, published many articles on modern drama. His insistence on the "people's theatre" powerfully influenced Korean theatre practitioners until the 1930s. Hyeon Cheol, quoting Romain Rolland, who was a French dramatist and novelist with a Nobel Prize for

Literature, said that theatres were not developed in countries where national consciousness was not developed and insisted on a national people's theatre.[13]

Hyeon Cheol thought that it was necessary to have acting schools in order to develop theatre. Thus, he opened *The School for Arts (藝術學院)*, the first acting school, in 1920. The school consisted of departments for theatre and dance and ran for about one year with the plays of Chekhov as exercise scripts. When the actors were dissatisfied with the assigned roles and were anxious to perform on stage, the school closed. Although *The School for Arts* did not have noticeable achievements, its alumni like Lee KyungSon and Kim JeongWon became famous afterward.

Hyun Cheol again opened another acting school called *Joseon Actor's Studio (朝鮮俳優學校)* in December 1924. The motivation of the school, published in *Donga Daily Newspapers*, was to cultivate actors for the stage and movies and to make a lasting monument in the Korean theatre.[14] The school was divided into higher and lower classes, and the monthly tuition was free except for a small amount of enrollment fee. It officially opened in January 1925 with 40 students. In September 1925, *A Doll's House* was performed as an acting exercise. It was said that Bok HyeSuk as Nora was very popular. In February 1926, the school produced its first graduates. Hyeon Cheol formed a theatre company with them and rehearsed a play, but the actors were dissatisfied with the assigned roles once again. Consequently, this acting school was also closed. Although the acting school lasted for a short period of time,

Figure 3.1 Joseon Actor's Studio's *A Doll's House* (1925). Photo from *A Study of Modern Korean Theatre History*, Seoul, Seoul National University Press, 1966. p.viii by Lee Duhyun.

it provided a turning point for training performers. Many actors and actresses were nurtured. This especially contributed to the rise of actresses such as Bok HyeSuk and Kim SuYeon, who later played important roles in theatre and movies.

3.5 The Settlement of Western Realism Theatre: *The Dramatic Art Research Society* (劇藝術研究會)

While a series of students' summer tours and *ToWolHoe*'s performances in the 1920s laid the foundation for the settlement of modern realism, *The Dramatic Art Research Society* in the 1930s solidified it. *The Dramatic Art Research Society* was founded in 1931 and was active until 1939. It served not only as the cornerstone of theatrical history before the Liberation of Korea in 1945, but as an actual achievement of Western realism theatre. Even after the Liberation, the actors, actresses, and directors from the Society led the performances of Korean theatre. Its achievements were highly appraised by Korean theatre historians, as noted below:

> The achievement of *The Dramatic Art Research Society* should be highly appreciated. It was pursued in the 1930s to promote and to establish the modern realism theatre in a truest sense in this land.[15]
>
> In the early 1920s, during the tour performances of *DongWuHoe* led by Kim UJin, the budding of the modern realism theater movement sprouted, and *The Dramatic Art Research Society* took over it, and developed into the full-fledged realism theatre of the West.[16]

The Dramatic Art Research Society had its origin in *The Theatre and Movie Club* (劇映同好會), which prepared the exhibitions of theatre and movies in 1931. With the support of the *Donga Daily Newspapers*, Yun Baeknam, Seo HangSeok, and Hong HaeSeong as the central figures, the *Theatre and Movie Club* exhibited more than 4,000 reference materials for theatre, stage photos, masks, puppets, and movie stills. This exhibition impressed intellectuals, especially theatre practitioners at the time, and people like Jeong InSeop even said that it was "restarting the real new drama movement" and "implying the popularization of a theater laboratory."[17] After this exhibition, it was natural to organize *The Dramatic Art Research Society*; it was thanks to the active support for the new theatre.

The Dramatic Art Research Society started with 12 founding members, including Hong HaeSeong, Seo HangSeok, Yu ChiJin, and Ham DaeHun. Since Yun BaekNam was the eldest senior and often did not attend the meetings, Hong HaeSeong, the next senior, led the group. Most of the members, majoring in foreign literatures at universities, were called "the School of Foreign Literature." The purpose of this group, announced in the newspapers, was to broaden the general understanding of the theatrical arts, relieve the wrongs of the established theatre companies, and establish a true realism theatre. The society planned all projects necessary for the establishment of the new drama, such as the training of actors and audiences and improving the current theatre. It also created a group of 22 students and opened classes for two weeks in August for acting, directing, stage design, lighting, make-up, body training, theatre history of the West and the East, play analysis, and so on. Soon, it organized a company called *The Experimental Stage* in November. First, they recruited 20 research students and then opened up classes. A completion ceremony was held the next year in February 1932, then the second group of its thirteen research students was selected. Classes for female performers also came about, which secured seven actresses, such as Kim GuYeol, Park GeumRye, and Kim YoungOk. After these preparations, *The Experimental Stage* presented an opening performance of *The Inspector General* by Gogol at Joseon theatre. *The Inspector General* was directed by Hong HaeSeong and founding members Seo HangSeok, Yu ChiJin, and Kim JinSeop, and the research student graduates appeared in this show. The performance was well received. It was said that "*The Dramatic Art Research Society* carried out a historical performance," "*The Inspector General* was a great success with its smart selection of the repertory and stylish directing," "wonderous performance that had not been seen lately," and so on.[18] Some theatre critics compared this premiere with that of *ToWolHoe* and advised not to give up the initial purpose of realism theatre.

The Dramatic Art Research Society had a research tendency and, therefore, held many lectures; some of the lectures included hundreds of audience members. This hearty attendance shows an atmosphere of enthusiasm for the new realism theatre at that time. In addition, societal members published criticism on established theatre companies' and students' productions, such as "After seeing the premiere of *SinMuDae*," "*The Power of Darkness* by Yonsei University," "The Theatre Festival by Ewha Women's University," and so on. *The Dramatic Art Research Society* also published journals called *Geukyeosul* (劇藝術), which introduced many articles on modern Western theatre and propagated the ideas of the society. In short, it tried to advertise the ideal realism theatre along with realistic performances.

The performances of *The Dramatic Art Research Society* could be divided into three parts by periods of time. The first period was from May 1932 to December 1934, which was mainly directed by Hong HaeSeong. At this time, many foreign realism plays were introduced and translated, which helped to solidify modern theatre. The second period was from November 1935 to February 1938, led by Yu ChiJin, who emphasized developing original plays by Koreans. The third period, changing its name to *Geukyeonjwa (劇研座)*, was the war period from May 1938 to its disbandment in May 1939. *Geukyeonjwa* tried to survive under the severe oppression of the Japanese governor-general.

The first period when Hong HaeSeong led the group brought many translated Western plays on stage. After the first production of *The Inspector General* (*Geomchalgwan*), *The Generous Lover* (*Gwandaehan Ein*) by Irving and *The Gaol Gate* (*Okmun*) by Lady Gregory followed. These repertories showed *The Dramatic Art Research Society*'s goals, which aimed at realism and nationalism in theatre. Interestingly, the expressionist play *The Sea Battle* (*Haejeon*) by Reinhard Göring was included among the second performances. The performance portrayed a disabled person stuck on the marginal limit of his survival. Unlike other realistic plays, the reviews of *The Sea Battle* were not as positive. A critic said that it was a real pain to pass ten minutes while the actor uttered incomprehensible lines. Some of the crowd easily gave up and left.[19] This meant that audiences of that time were not ready for expressionistic plays.

For its third performance, *The Anniversary* (*Ginyeomje*) by Chekhov, *Gilles und Johanna* (*Ujeong*) by Georg Kaiser, and *A Mud-and-Dung Hut* (*Ttomak*) by Yu ChiJin were performed. Among them, *A Mud-and-Dung Hut* was the most noteworthy. It was an original play performed in a realistic style, probably for the first time. It reflected the poverty under colonial rule and the idea of nationalism. *A Mud-and-Dung Hut* was a story that centered on the families of poor peasants named Choi MyungSeo and Kang GyeongSeon, living in a Korean rural village in the 1920s. Korean peasants actually suffered from poverty due to the exploitation of the Japanese imperial government, and some of them even had to leave their homes because of unbearable debts. In the play, MyungSeo's son, who works in Japan to support his family, returns home dead (in ashes) after being arrested by the Japanese police for being insubordinate and participating in independence movements. The other story of KyungSeon shows that some farmers had to leave their hometown due

Figure 3.2 Chekhov's *The Anniversary* (1933) from *A Study of Modern Korean Theatre History*, Seoul, Seoul National University Press, 1966. p.xiv by Lee Duhyun.

to debts. However, the writer showed some hope with the monologue of MyungSeo's daughter, saying that she should be proud of her brother since he took great actions, which would bring happiness to the poor Joseon people. This play is meaningful not only as the first-performed original play in a realistic style but also as a resistant play under colonial imperialism. It is surprising that this play passed the censorship of the Japanese governor-general at that time. This play also showed the strong influences of the Irish national theatre movement. For example, Sean O'Casey's technique of a tragic-comic character and the disappearance of the main character on the stage were reflected in *A Mud-and-Dung Hut*; there is a farmer character always comical and witty in a tragic circumstance, and the dead son, the spiritual hero of the play, never appears onstage.

Additional performances took place. The fourth performance was *Arms and the Man* (*Mugi wa Ingan*) by Bernard Shaw to commemorate Shaw's journey to Asia. This satirical play showed the British romantic ideas of war and love. The fifth program included *The Imbecile* (*Babo*) by Pirandello, an abridged version of *The Merchant of Venice* (*Venice ui Sangin*) by Shakespeare, and an original play called *A Scenery of the Village with Willow Trees* (*Beodeu Namu Seon Dongri Punggyeong*) by Yu ChiJin. Yu ChiJin established himself as a realist playwright with his play about extreme poverty. It objectively describes a farming village where a son dies as he seeks roots for food in the mountain, and a daughter is sold to be a prostitute at a price lower than that of a calf.

The sixth and seventh programs were two full-length productions performed consecutively in 1934. *A Doll's House* (*Inhyeong ui Jip*) by Ibsen attracted public attention thanks to its huge influence from the West. At the same time, *The Dramatic Art Research Society* devoted a special issue in the journal *Geugyesul* (劇藝術) to Ibsen and introduced materials related to *A Doll's House*.

Additionally, *The Cherry Orchard* (*Beotkkot Dongsan*) was performed to commemorate the third anniversary of *The Dramatic Art Research Society* as well as the 30th anniversary of Chekhov's death. Both multi-act, full-length productions were fairly well received, demonstrating the potential performing ability of the company at the time. Both were directed by Hong HaeSeong, whose experiences in *Japanese Tsukiji* Small Theatre (築地小劇場) were of great help. So far, Hong HaeSeong had directed most of the plays during the first period of *The Dramatic Art Research Society*. Ultimately, the introduction of Western realism plays was well achieved during this first period.

Yu ChiJin led the second period when Hong HaeSeong changed to the paying job at *Oriental Theatre*. Yu ChiJin directed from the eighth to the 17th performances and chose large multipurpose halls like the BuMinGwan except for one performance largely due to financial difficulties. Yu ChiJin further announced that *The Dramatic Art Research Society* would enter its second phase. So far it had introduced new Western theatre with translated foreign plays; now it would feature original plays.[20] As the Little Theatre Movement in the West started from the introduction of foreign realism plays and moved

Figure 3.3 A Doll's House (1934) from *A Study of Modern Korean Theatre History*, Seoul, Seoul National University Press, 1966. p.xiv by Lee Duhyun.

forward to creating original plays, *The Dramatic Art Research Society* followed the same steps. It is also noteworthy that Yu ChiJin proposed the arrangement and revival of Korean theatrical heritages.[21] During the second period, *The Dramatic Art Research Society* performed a total of nine original plays. Unfortunately, some of the plays, such as *The Servants' Quarters* (*Julhaengrang ui Saramdeul*), *Beyond the Dike* (堤坊*ul* Neomunguk), *Toseonang*, and *The Cow*, failed to be produced due to censorship. If these unproduced original plays are counted, the ratio of creative plays written during this time period increases.

For the eighth program, the first performance of the second period, Yu ChiJin planned to perform his own play, *The Cow* (*So*), but the play did not pass the censorship. His earlier play, *A Mud-and-Dung Hut*, celebrated the national spirit by suggesting the independence movement. His next play, *The Cow*, not only failed to pass the censorship, but also the core members of *The Dramatic Art Research Society* were jailed and tortured because of that. After this event, Yu ChiJin declared himself to be a romanticist rather than a realist, but the essence of his style remained realism. However, if Yu ChiJin had not broken the spirit of earlier realism, better works might have been generated. In fact, his early works were the highlights of modern Korean theatre history. *The Dramatic Art Research Society* put tremendous efforts into developing original Korean plays, but most of the plays were one-acts with the exception of a few.

The tenth performance, *A Scholar in a Village* (村先生), was notable since the play had many acts and was the winning work of the *Donga Daily Newspapers'* play contest as part of the V narod movement.[22] After the oppression of the social realism movement by the Japanese governor-general, Korean intellectuals turned to the rural enlightenment movement around farming villages. *A Scholar in a Village* reflects the enthusiasm for the rural movement at that time. This work depicted the conflict between the first and second sons, centering on the protagonist Song, and intended to present a wide range of rural areas' real problems they were facing in the 1930s. In the play, Sir Song returns home after 20 years to protect his hometown. He works with Dalgeun, his second son, to farm and run a night school to enlighten the countryside. One day, the eldest son Dalhoon, a primary school teacher in Seoul, brings his wife to his hometown. The eldest couple, whose lifestyle is suited to urban areas, dreams of a fantastic and romantic rural life. Unable to rid themselves of their improper lifestyle habits from their urban home, the couple encounters the realities of the rural areas, where the farmers are poor, ignorant, indolent, and living in unsanitary conditions. In response to this poverty, the farmers, led by Dalgeun, laugh at the couple's civilized and urban consciousness. While the tensions between Dalhoon and Dalgeun rise, Dalhoon's debts are revealed, and Sir Song makes the eldest son and his wife leave the village. On the other hand, Sir Song insists that his second son remain and become a farmer. This work suggested the view that rural problems could be solved by farmers' own hands. However, this opinion was denounced by some critics as it placed the city and rural areas into a hostile relationship with each other.

Another important creative play of the time was *The Year of Abundance* (*Pungnyeongi*), a work adapted from *The Cow* to pass Japanese censorship. *The Year of Abundance* is a three-act play set in a rural Korean village in the 1930s. A cow is the sole property of the peasant Gukseo's family, and it becomes the symbol of everybody's dream. The eldest son wants to marry a neighborhood girl, who is held back by her family's debt, while the second son, who wants to sell the cow for a share of the profits, secretly plans to go to Manchuria. Also, the supervisor of a tenant farm is interested in taking the cow as overdue farm rent. In order to avoid censorship, the oppressing character is changed from a Japanese landowner to a Korean supervisor of a tenant, thus avoiding the sharp conflict between Japanese and Korean characters. Although the original satirical accusation of the poverty in farming villages changed to comical human-related situations, *The Year of Abundance* was still a strong play, which injected various human desires into the symbol of a cow.

The Story of ChunHyang by Yu ChiJin was another important play in this period. Since this work was a popular repertory of *Pansori*, the intention was to attract audiences and to overcome financial difficulties. However, after the incident with *The Cow*, even *The Story of ChunHyang* was under strict censorship. Fortunately, *ChunHyangjun* was a classic story of *Pansori* from the Joseon dynasty, so it had little need for censorship. In addition, the play received criticism from the theatrical world about whether it was a modern drama or not. Yu ChiJin adapted *Pansori's ChunHyang* into a modern drama of a girl ChunHyang pursuing her own self-realization. This piece is a reminder of Yu ChiJin's proposal to revive Korean theatrical heritage.

As major translated plays of the second period, *Porgy and Bess* by Mr. & Mrs. Heyward and *Blind Geronimo and His Brother* (*Nun Meon Dongsaeng*) by Arthur Schnitzler were notable since they were very contemporary at that time. *Porgy and Bess* paved the way for American musicals in Korea, while *Blind Geronimo and His Brother* introduced psychological realism. *A Tragedy on the Lakeshore* (*Hosang ui Bigeuk*) by modern Chinese playwright Tian Han was the first modern oriental play introduced in Korea. It could be seen that *The Dramatic Art Research Society* in the second period expanded the scope of translated plays and performed them in various ways beyond the boundaries of realism.

In March 1938, the *Dramatic Art Research Society* was disbanded by the Japanese governor-general and reorganized under the new name *Geukyeonjwa (劇研座)*. Despite severe control and sanctions, the organization did discover new playwrights such as Kim JinSu and Ham SeDeok. *The Road* (*Gil*) by Kim JinSu in 1938 and *A Young Buddhist Monk* (*Dongseung*) by Ham SeDeok in 1939 were performed in spite of a national war-like atmosphere. These two playwrights played important roles in the transition of theatre from the colonial era to the new independent Korea. Additionally, notable translated plays were brought from America, such as *Awake and Sing!* (*Kkaeeona Norae Bureuja*) by Clifford Odets and *Winterset* (*Mokgyeokja*) by Maxwell Anderson. The former was a representative realism play from America, and the latter was a famous contemporary play based on a true story. Consequently, *Geukyeonjwa (劇研座)* had to close in 1939. Under Japanese wartime militarism, all theatres had to produce war-supporting theatre, or so-called "National Theatre."

Overall, translated plays took over a large part of *The Dramatic Art Research Society*'s performances. There were 25 translated performances out of the 37 total performances, and most of them were modern plays from the West. At first glance, the works of the Scandinavian peninsula, which were the leaders of Western modern plays, were neglected, while there were many Russian plays, which were situated on the outskirts of Western modern theatre. The reason many Russian plays were introduced was probably the geographical closeness. *The Cherry Orchard* by Chekhov, *The Inspector General* by Gogol, and *The Power of Darkness* and *The Resurrection* by Tolstoy were especially popular and also reproduced many times by other groups. In general, the first period emphasized the translated plays, selecting relatively core modern drama. The second period expanded its interest from the European realism theatre to those of the United States and China. Then, the third period chose contemporary plays according to their popularity.

The Dramatic Art Research Society tried to perform plays directly translated from the original languages—avoiding indirect translations from Japanese. Most societal members majored in foreign languages and literature; therefore, the languages of those original translated plays were at the professional level.

Moreover, these translated plays contributed to improving the standard of plays for theatre practitioners and the audience. Considering the predominance of translated plays at the beginning of modern drama even in the West, many translated plays "were inevitable in Korea as there was no heritage of plays and currently no modern theatrical productions."[23]

In the second period of *The Dramatic Art Research Society*, the members realized the importance of original modern plays. It performed a total of 12 original plays compared with a total of 25 translated plays. Considering the four original plays that failed to perform due to censorship, the ratio of original plays to translated plays was actually higher than mentioned above. In addition to Yu ChiJin, the plays of Lee MuYoung, Lee GwangRae, Lee SeoHyang, Kim JinSu, and Ham SeDeok were performed. Lee MuYoung and Lee SeoHyang were established novelists, while Kim JinSu and Ham SeDeok were found by *The Dramatic Art Research Society*. Lee GwangRae was discovered through the *Donga Daily Newspapers* contest of farmer plays. Lee's *A Scholar in a Village*, which had many acts unlike other plays, dealt with the V narod movement of the early 1930s. However, the play was criticized for demonstrating only vague and emotional rural experiences of intellectuals without a thorough grasp of rural reality. Ham Sedeok's *A Young Buddhist Monk* (*Doyeom*) was the Society's last original play, which lyrically portrayed the human instinct of missing one's mother. The driving force behind the plot was in the mind of a young apprentice monk. Due to its strong lyricism, the play went beyond realism and pioneered psychological realism.[24]

In conclusion, it was *The Dramatic Art Research Society* that achieved a full-scale introduction and establishment of modern realism theatre, and it was in line with the launch of the Little Theatre Movement of the West. Their productions of the first period introduced many modern Western plays with direct translations from the original language. But some selections of the plays were not so different from those of Japanese plays since most translators studied in Japan. The limitation of the Society is that there were more one-act plays than full-length plays and that its productions did not deviate greatly from early realism, i.e., not reaching a modernistic performance level. The works of the second period emphasized original plays. *The Dramatic Art Research Society* was the first theatre group to perform creative plays steadily and tried to find new playwrights. Its plays dealt with criticisms of conventional customs and social satires, which connected society to the spirit of modern realism theatre. Many of the plays were based on rural themes since it was a time of rural movements due to the population of farmers. Despite the oppression of Japanese imperialism and the sentimental commercial *Sinpa* in the 1930s, its merits of establishing realism theatre could not be overemphasized.

3.6 School Theatre Groups

Since there were a fairly large number of higher educational institutions in the 1930s, there were also many school performances. Since there were no schools for theatre, these students' performances were of great help in the development of theatre experts as well as audience engagement. Ewha Women's University first began to hold an annual performance in English in 1930, and performances in Korean followed. The university performed *The Taming of the Shrew* by Shakespeare in 1931, *Justice* by John Galsworthy in 1932, *What Men Live by* by Tolstoy, and *Thursday Evening* by C. Morlay in 1933. Another representative school was Yonsei University, which performed *The Power of Darkness* by Tolstoy in 1931, *The Lady from the Sea* in 1932, *The Tents of the Arabs* by Lord Dunsany and *A Cuckoo* by Max in 1933, and *The Journey's End* by P.C. Sheffery in 1935. In addition, there were many modern plays in the extra-curriculars of other schools, which were not performed by professional companies.

These school performances were heavily influenced by *The Dramatic Art Research Society* in the 1930s. Its members often guided or even directed these school performances. Since school performances were amateur and free from the burden of commercial success, universities could select their plays relatively easily. The school repertories had more diversity than the professional companies at that time, from the classic to the emerging contemporary works. But the students' performances were soon banned in 1936 due to the Japanese military war policies.

Considering the poor conditions of the theatrical world at that time, these students' performances were solid touchstones for the development of diverse repertories without the pressure of money and the perfectionistic demands of realist theatre. The theatre intellectuals wrote criticism of their performances and noted that some of them were better than professional performances. In short, along with *The Dramatic Art Research Society* the school performances helped spread Western realist theatre.

Additional university theatre groups of students were in Tokyo. *The Art Group of Tokyo (東京學生藝術座)* was founded with 15 members, including Kim JinSu and Kim DongWon, one of the best playwrights and actors of the upcoming theatre generation. The group performed *The Cow* (*So*) by Yu ChiJin and *The Dock* (*Naru*) by Ju YeongSeop in 1935; *The Story of ChunHyang*, adapted by Yu ChiJin in 1937; and *Beyond the Horizon* (*Jipyeongseon*) by Eugene O'Neill and *The Plain* (*Beolpan*) by Ju YeongSeop in 1938. It also published a magazine called Act (幕) three times in 1936 1938, and 1939. However, the members were arrested by Japanese police on charges of encouraging left-wing proletarian thought through theatre in 1939. After they were released, the group dissolved in 1940. These student groups in Japan had taken the lead in promoting the latest changes in theatre since the groups had a strong relationship with the Japanese theatrical world.

3.7 Social Realism Theatre

YeomGunSa was the first proletarian arts group that launched as a fanzine in 1922. It had a department of theatre, whose representative members were

Figure 3.4 The Art Group of Tokyo Student's First Performance, *The Cow* (*So*) by Yu ChiJin. Photo from *the Encyclopedia of Korean People and Culture* (韓國民族文化大百科事典).

Kim YoungPal and Song Young.[25] The theatrical department of *YeomGunSa* did not have many noticeable achievements, but it played a fundamental role in the future of proletarian theatre. The beginning of the proletarian theatre movement was led by Kim YoungPal, who was also a member of *the Association of Theatre Arts (劇藝術協會)*, which sprouted modern realism theatre. Kim YoungPal's interest changed from realism theatre to proletarian theatre.

The full-fledged proletariat literary movement began with the organization KAPF (Korea Artista Proleta Federacio in Esperanto), which formed in 1925 with the members of *YeomGunSa* and PASKYULA.[26] While the members of *YeomGunSa* were rookies in the literary arena, those of PASKYULA were established literary men. KAPF, with elderly and young literary men, swept through the literary world once it started. KAPF made three "turns" to stay true to the proletariat. The first change in 1927 was called "The Turn of Purposefulness," which clearly followed the proletarian purpose of the content rather than the unity of format and artistic completeness. It started with the debate between Park YeongHee and Kim GiJin. When Kim criticized Park's work for its lack of formal unity, Park insisted that proletarian content preceded formal unity. Park defined the form as methods for creating playful and decadent beauty of the bourgeois class and insisted that literature should restrain its own formal beauty and be on the frontline of the class struggle. Because of the KAPF members' pressure, Kim apologized to Park. Since then, the proletariat ideal became more important than anything else, and early members who did not have strong beliefs in proletarianism withdrew from the group.

The second turn came after the discussion on art popularization. In 1929, Kim GiJin again brought up the theory of art popularization, to which nobody objected, but his specific proposals, such as the addition of a love story into proletarian literature, were soon criticized. Kim GiJin thought it was impossible to refer to a true proletariat without being conscious of the masses. He focused on the popularity of folklore novels and analyzed which aspects of them captured the interests of the people. Since proletarian literature should express the social, material, and historical causes and motives of incidents objectively and concisely, considering the scope of the ordinary people's opinions and knowledge, the path of folk fiction had to be pioneered. Kim GiJin called folk novels popular novels and made it clear that the masses were workers and peasants. He further defined the popular novels, which should not simply be about temporarily satisfying the popular demands of the masses but also about responding to their fundamental demands, lifting them up, and fulfilling the mission of the current stage of world history.[27] In order to achieve these goals, popular novels should use the methods which include making the writing style and terms plain; making reading comfortable; using concise descriptions and explanations; making most of colorful printings; clarifying psychological descriptions and ups and downs of events; and lowering the price of novels.[28] He insisted on coating proletarian issues with a sweet, a.k.a. love story. Kim GiJin's claims were criticized for being too naive to fight for proletarian achievement by Lim Hwa, An Mak, and Kim NamCheon. Lim Hwa insisted that a more revolutionary struggle was a prerequisite for harming the oppressor and that Kim's claim was fatal, disarming the principle.[29] Eventually, Kim GiJin retreated in 1930, and the debates on art popularization ceased.[30]

The third change was the literary debate on the proletarian status of peasants. The issue of proletarian literature moved from the theory of popularization to the area of peasant literature. The masses included workers and peasants. However, there were only a few workers in Korea at that time; farmers made up the majority of Korean industry. Owing to the debates about peasant literature during the conference of the International Association for Revolutionary Writers in Kharkov in 1930 and the V narod movements of the time, proletarian literature could not ignore peasant literature. In fact, the theory of peasant literature was a strategy that allowed workers armed with class consciousness to hold the proletarian hegemony, consciously recognizing the peasants and using them as allies. In 1931, Ahn HamGwang said that peasant literature should actively instill proletarian thoughts into peasants' minds, but Baek Cheol insisted that peasants should voluntarily respond to the ideology. Both agreed that the poor and the rural reality should be the subject of literature to enlighten the farmers, but there were differences in opinions on methodology. Interestingly, the theory of peasant literature had little effect on the KAPF writers, and in-depth discussions on creative methodologies that fit the purpose-oriented theory did not happen.

In short, the three debates on proletarian literature above were very important not only because of their arguments but also because they laid the foundation for critical Korean literature. This is the first time in the history of Korean literature that such kinds of debates arose, and these debates ultimately led to the development of criticism. In fact, there were more debates than works in proletarian literature. With these discussions, KAPF became more and more like a literary organization faithful to communism. The more KAPF became a communist arts group, the more it was oppressed by the Japanese governor-general of Korea.

After its turn toward proletarian purposefulness in 1927, the theatre department of KAPF opened. KAPF belatedly realized the importance of theatre to spread its ideas and propaganda. The proletarian theatre movements started with three groups: the first one from KAPF; the second one from the regional companies, such as *March Theatre* in Pyeongyang, *Public (大衆) Theatre* in Gaseong, *Gadu Theatre* in Daegu, and so on; and the third one from Korean residents in Japan and Russia. As time went by, most of these groups collaborated with one another and aimed to fight against Japanese imperialism. However, the proletarian theatre performances were not very active in the 1920s for mainly three reasons. The first was that Japanese militarism banned proletarian art; the second was a lack of trained performers to properly perform proletarian drama; and the third was the lack of theatrical infrastructure, e.g., finances, theatre buildings, and human resources.

The first group of proletarian theatre companies included *Yeomgunsa* in 1923 and *Fire Ant (BulGaeMi)* in 1927. However, these companies were not able to perform a single play and disbanded. Then, *the Association of Synthetic Art (綜合藝術協會)* was organized by Yeon HakYeon in 1927, and this group performed an adaptation of a short novel called *He Who Gets Slapped* (*Ppyam Mateun geu Jasik*) by Leonid Andreyev, which had to be closed within three days because of the Japanese police's sanction. The repertory itself was dubious about whether it was a proletarian play or not. The play could belong to the so-called companion artists, who did not join the communist organization but wrote criticisms of bourgeois society.[31]

From the beginning of the 1930s, the proletarian theatrical movement was locally and internationally vigorous. It aimed at enlightening the lives of workers and peasants.[32] *Little Mobil Theatre (移動式小型劇場)* came into being in 1931, and it successfully had performances in early 1932. Due to the realistic constraints that prevented faithful proletarian activities, there was a disturbance inside the troupe, and the extreme left theorist members left the group to perform more clearly defined proletarian plays. The representative repertories were plays such as *The Self-Defense* (*Hosinsul*) by Song Young and *Mr.Park* (*Park Chomji*) by Yu JinOh.[33] The new genre of choric speaking was also attempted. The significance of this troupe was that it was able to perform several times and that it performed representative proletarian plays faithful to realism theatre with dialectic lines.

Megaphone succeeded *Little Mobil Theatre* when *Little Mobil Theatre* was closed due to the censorship. Many members of *Little Mobil Theatre* were in *Megaphone*, which put on performances in June 1932, including *The Hell* (*Jiok*) by Kim HyeongYong, *The Broken JangHanMong*, and *Megaphone*, as well as *The*

Self-Defense and *Mr. Park* from *Little Mobil Theatre*. Although *Megaphone* tried to hide its proletarian color with a famous commercial *Sinpa* play for entertainment such as *JangHanMong*, the company also could not have other performances due to censorship and oppression from the Japanese governor-general.

Following *Megaphone*, *New Construction (新建設)* was founded in August 1932; this group aimed for the construction of a proletarian theatre. Unfortunately, in February 1933, its enthusiastic members were arrested for preaching the propaganda of communism—especially to students—and for having close relationships with the communist theatre groups in Tokyo. Even in this untidy situation, it managed to perform *All Quiet on the Western Front* by Erich Maria Remarque in November 1933. The selection of the repertoire was questioned because it dealt only with the devastation of war that had little relevance to workers and peasants.[34] In addition, the lack of lighting, sound, scenery, and acting skill was also problematic. In spite of the criticism, *New Construction* prepared additional performances as well as a regional tour. It tried to recruit actors and strengthen proletarian ideology.

The Japanese governor-general tried to block the proletarian movement in Korea as well as in Japan. In the summer of 1934, not only the members of *New Construction* but also the core members of KAPF were arrested. The governor-general made the so called "The Event of *New Construction* (新建設事件)" and prosecuted major members. Most of the accused members agreed that they would return to the theatre without insisting on communism. It remains a question of whether they were converted or not, but eventually, KAPF was dissolved. It seems that many of the proletarian artists were ethnic idealists following the trend of the times rather than thorough communists. Only the claims of the proletariat's theatrical movement were tumultuous. It ended only with several performances over the span of ten years. The reasons for the ending were 1) the Japanese military's ruthless oppression, 2) immature proletarian theatre artists, and 3) the fragility of the modern realism tradition. The young proletarian artists had no theatre skills but only ideological ideals. Although the proletarian theatrical artists had only put on a few performances, they were the first to organize a regional and nationwide network of theatre companies.

KAPF was filled with various literary movements and philosophical discussions instead of actual performances. However, two representative proletarian playwrights are worth noting. Kim Youngpal was one of them, a representative of the early proletarian playwrights, a modern realism playwright who turned to proletarian playwright and founding member of *YeomGunSa* and KAPF. He once wrote in his criticism that he created proletarian plays for the culture of the proletariat.[35] Ultimately, he published a number of proletarian plays until he was expelled from KAPF in 1931 because of his job at the Kyungsung Broadcasting Station, a pro-Japanese organization. Kim YoungPal's career as a founding and then excluded member of KAPF showed his characteristics and limitations as a proletarian playwright. His proletarian plays were *The Fight*

(Ssaum), *The Fire* (Buliya), *An Obituary Notice* (訃音), *The Knife of Tripe* (GopChangKal), and *The Family of Three* (三食口).

The Fight (*Ssaum*), written in 1926, is the story of a proletarian husband deserting his bourgeois wife, who refuses to be a bar hostess until she changes her mind. He accuses his wife of being obsessed with the aristocracy and conventional customs. However, this piece is questionable as a proletarian play because selling alcoholic drinks is highly doubtful to be considered sacred labor. Moreover, the man publishes an advertisement with her photo in the newspaper, stating that his wife opens a bar without her consent; the man's actions could be criticized for ignoring the human rights of an individual and a woman, which was against the proletarian manifesto. The man was only true to proletarianism in the sense of his objection to aristocracy and high respect for labor, but he had many problems in the sense that he considered selling alcohol as labor and violated the individual rights of his wife. As such, this play carefully characterized the early proletariat who could not deliver unified proletarian ideas. Because one idea and the preceding idea contradicted each other, the idea of the proletariat stopped with an unfamiliar and abstract slogan.

Another one of Kim YoungPal's plays, *An Obituary Notice* (Bueum) in 1927, is a love story between Jungsuk and KyungSu, who is chased by the Japanese police because of his labor movement. The play begins with the dialogue among JungSuk, her friend, and the landlord. This beginning part, though it has nothing to do with proletarian thoughts, gives a realistic atmosphere to the whole work. They discuss views of women from the old and new generations and criticize the old system of marriage. Even after KyungSu enters, their dialogue remains natural. However, the idea of marriage without dating seems dubious from the perspective of the proletarian belief about marriage. Anyhow, the two characters decide to marry without dating. Then, the younger sister of KyungSu arrives and mentions the death of their mother. JungSuk begs KyungSu to run away, promising a respectful funeral for his mother and taking good care of his young sister. The overall story is a love story in which the proletarian labor movement is inserted.

The Knife of Tripe (*Gopchangkal*) from 1929 also had a similar storyline. However, it devoted much of its story development to acting against the prejudice toward the butcher and fighting against the noble classes. This play strengthened proletarian thoughts without obvious contradictions. This change largely owed to KAPF's turn toward a period of proletarian consciousness. 1929 was also the time when KAPF's proletarian power was most active. Kim YoungPal was expelled from KAPF because he joined the broadcasting station in 1931. Overall, his proletarian plays naturally appeared without the training of proletarian manifestos during the early stage of the proletariat.

Succeeding Kim YoungPal, Song Young was the leading playwright in the development of proletarian plays in the 1930s. Song Young, like Kim YoungPal, was also a founding member of *YeomGunSa* and KAPF. Song Young's first play, *BaekYangHwa* from 1922, was not handed down and is unknown. He published additional plays, such as *Why Mosquitoes Disappear* (*Mogiga Eopseojinen Ggadak*) in 1927, *Justice and Canvas* (*Jeongui wa Canvas*) in 1929, *An Opium Addict* (*Apyeon Jaengi*) in 1930, *Self-Defense* (*Hosinsul*) in 1931, and *New Chairman* (Sinim Isajang) in 1934. His main proletarian plays were performed in the first half of the 1930s. Unlike Kim YoungPal's plays, Song Young's proletarian plays were produced by proletarian theatres, such as the *Little Mobil Theatre* and *Megaphone*. In other words, he was active in the proletarian theatre movement.

Song Young's proletarian plays were not only realistic but also extended to a sort of modernistic, unrealistic satirical style. He wrote social realism plays at the beginning, but he soon realized the awkward decisive endings were meant to provide a positive outlook about the future. For example, in his *An Opium Addict,* the hero, who sells his daughter and buys opium with that money, suddenly decides not to take opium anymore when he becomes impressed by the leader of the labor movement. Song Young knew that the opium addict's sudden change was unrealistic.

Additionally, Song Young tried other formulaic styles to deliver the positive proletarian outlook. In *Self-Defense* (護身術), the protagonist was portrayed like a Braggart Alazon type.[36] He maximized the inverted value of the capitalist in *Self-Defense.* The protagonist, the boss of a company predicting a strike, learns self-defense with his family rather than negotiating with the workers. The play provided a world of inverted values about learning self-defense not to protect against unidentified assailants but to avoid innocent strikers. The irony emerges when his wife gets injured while learning self-defense. This unnecessary protection of the young wife and father goes beyond the affection or filial piety, and points out the bourgeoisie's luxuries. As such, the bragging, unnatural foolishness and inverted world of values, seen through exaggerated characters, spoke for themselves. When the shouts of workers who wanted to discuss their needs were heard, the victory of the workers could be estimated.

In his next play *New Chairman* (新任理事長), Song Young also set an Alazon-type foolish hero who cannot even read the script written for his speech. Also appearing is a protestor, a madman who lost his wife in an accident in the chairman's forest. He pours out accusations at the hero. His aggressive and critical rebellion could elicit censorship from the Japanese government-general if he were not a madman. This accuser reveals the chairman's capitalistic corruption in the forest. It was the most frequently attempted play for performance due to its more aggressive accusations and strong resistance to reality. In general, although Song Young's plays of the satirical group were based on the proletarian idea of the accusation against the capitalist's exploitation and the awakening of the workers, they did not resist reality in full. The satirical play group focused on highlighting the exploitation of the bourgeois capitalists rather than the enlightenment and change of the characters. Therefore, the characters were tangible type-characters from the beginning, and comical situations and satires unfolded because of the tangible nature of the characters. These indirect accusations partly came from the tightening censorship of that time and partly from Song Young's realization of the limitations of realism to carry out the socially positive outlook. As a result, Song Young developed a new unrealistic, formal style to create social proletarian drama. On the other hand, this unique art methodology posed a problem since communism abandoned modernism after the debate of Lukács and Adorno.[37]

Ultimately, the proletarian play was established as one of the main branches of theatre history in the 1930s. The ideology was evaluated as an important theatre of the time. However, compared to the active productions of other theatrical companies, the number of performances of proletarian plays was not as big. This was largely due to Japanese censorship and oppression of the proletariat at the time. Song Young could be considered the best playwright both in his plays and in the proletarian theatre movement in the 1930s. In short, the characteristics of proletarian literary arts and plays: 1) portray materialistic bias with an emphasis on poverty, 2) sharpen the conflict between social classes, 3) advocate excessive rebellion and violence, and 4) emphasize the collective problems of strikes, labor disputes, and tenant disputes based on the trade union movement of farmers and workers.[38]

The proletarian theatre ceased to exist after the event of "*New Construction*" in 1934, and KAPF was disbanded in 1935. Moreover, Japan was entering a period of war. Therefore, any expressions of thoughts other than imperialism were not tolerated. The communist theatre also could not exist anymore. The proletarian theatre practitioners performed pro-Japanese or commercial theatres and then led left-wing theatres when Korea was finally liberated from Japan in 1945.

3.8 The Period of So-Called "National Theatre": Korean Theatre during World War II

Since the war broke out with China and the National Mobilization Act was proclaimed in 1937, the Japanese governor-general of Korea began to put pressure on Korean society to regulate cultural activities. For example, Koreans had to change their names to Japanese in 1940. In addition, Korean magazines and newspapers, such as *Donga* and *Joseon*, were shut down. In fact, the Japanese governor-general did not allow any cultural activities during the first half of the 1940s: the World War II period. *The Association of Korean Theatre (朝鮮演劇協會)* was created with 300 theatre practitioners from nine companies nominated by the Japanese governor-general. The aim was to abandon individualistic thinking and to regulate theatre only to support the country. Therefore, only the so-called "national theatres" that praised and promoted militarism were allowed. As more theatre companies joined, the organization was renamed as *The Association of Korean Theatre and Culture (朝鮮演劇文化協會)*. The Japanese governor-general, along with this association, held three contests for a "national theatre" play in 1942, 19432 1943, and 1945. Other plays representing "national theatre" existed in addition to the plays from the contest. In both cases, the writers, directors, and other participating artists wanted to remain anonymous because they felt guilty after the liberation of Korea. On the other hand, some theatre practitioners desperately refused to write or be involved owing to their patriotism.

The plays in these contests featured topics that supported World War II in order to promote war supply donations or to voluntarily sign up for the war. These plays were generally performed in the realism style. Fortunately, many multi-act plays were developed in a short period of time, but these performances were a disgraceful part of history to the Korean theatre because the plays actively promoted and supported Japanese military policies. For example, *The Jujube Tree* promoted Manchurian migration by propagating Manchuria as a good place to live. Moreover, *The History* highlighted the extreme stubbornness of Confucian tradition in contrast to the Enlightenment, which was linked to Great East Asian Philosophy (大東亞思想). In its admiration for the philosophy, the play further promoted concrete projects of the Japanese authorities, such as volunteering for the war, dedicating resources to campaigns, donating personal property, volunteering for patriotic women's service for the war, and learning Japanese.

The so-called "national theatre" can never be free from its historical meaning, but the secondary meanings could be as follows. First, in the functional aspect of theatre, the national theatres created a bridge between the pre- and post-liberation of Korea from Japan. Since theatre needed the training of actors' bodies and many techniques, it would have been difficult to perform right away if there had been a period of inactivity. Secondly, although empowered by the bureaucracy of Japan, these theatres demonstrated the power of art management with nationwide performances. They made traveling theatre companies visit the audience. Although the left-sided theatre of KAPF planned traveling theatre first, it was the first time that mobile theatre was realized in real surroundings nationwide. Third, many multi-act plays were produced within a short period of time, and the dramaturgies were advanced compared to the 1930s. They were especially good at the development of sudden reversals or complicated plots. Fourth, they were the first and one of the best "purposed" plays. It could be said that they were more effective than the anti-communist plays in the 1950s. Some national theatre plays cunningly propagated their main idea in the middle of the stories without putting it on the surface. They hid the real purpose within the play utilizing popular entertainment and sound cultural consciousness. However, they also gave a lesson that theatre confined to a unified thought is eventually limited in moving the audience's hearts. Even the artists' imaginations and excellent dramaturgies could not lead to deep emotions.

Korean theatre during World War II was performed on behalf of the Japanese military government. It was deprived of its identity, freedom, and individuality, as were the Korean people. With the Japanese surrender, Korea was finally liberated from Japan in 1945. A time of political confusion followed, but mainstream Korean theatre kept the realism trend until the Korean War in the 1950s.

Notes

1 Yun, Baknam. "Theatre and Society." *Donga Daily Newspapers*, 14 May 1920.
2 Ibid.
3 Hyeon, Chul. "The Relation of Theatre and I." *Mail Daily Newspapers*, 30 Jun 1920.
4 Kim, UJin. "About the So-called Modern Theatre." *Hakgigwang*, Oct 1921.
5 *Donga Daily Newspapers*, 18 Jul 1921.
6 Choi, Hyeon. "The Regional Tour Performance of GalDopHoe." *Donga Daily Newspapers*, 1 Aug 1921.
7 "The Performances of Hyeongsulhoe." *Mail Daily Newspapers*, 26 Jul 1923.
8 *Donga Daily Newspapers*, 8 Jul 1923.
9 Park, SeungHee. "Tales of Towolhoe." *Sasanggae*, May 1963.
10 Kim, JaeCheol. *Theatre History of Joseon*. Seoul, Chongjin Seogwan, 1933, pp. 176–177.
11 Kim, EulHan. "Chat about Theatre(演劇雜談)." *Joseon Daily Newspapers*, 8–9 Jun 1926.
12 Park, Jin. *Years and Years*(SeSe YeonYeon), Seoul, Gyonghwa Publishers, 1966, pp. 67–68.
13 Lee, Duhyun. *A Study of Modern Korean Theatre History.* Seoul, Seoul University Press, 1966, p. 97.
14 *Donga Daily Newspapers*, 13 Dec 1924.
15 Lee, Op.cit., p. 218.
16 Yu, MinYoung. *A History of Modern Korean Drama*(韓國現代戲曲史). Seoul, Hongsongsa, 1982, pp. 273–274.
17 Jeong, InSeop. "After Seeing the Exhibition of Theatre and Movie." *DongA Daily Newspapers*, 23 Jun–4 Jul 1931.
18 Lee, Op.cit., p. 175.
19 Park, YongChoel. "After Attending the Second Performances of The Experimental Stage." *Donga Daily Newspapers*, 2 Jul 1932.
20 Yu, ChiJin. "To Promote Our Creative Drama." *Joseon Daily Newspaper*, 3–6 Aug 1935.
21 Yu, ChiJin. "The Road Ahead of the Joseon Theatre-about its Policy and Solutions." *JoGwang*, Jan 1935.
22 Rural movements were developed by young Russian intellectuals in the late 19th century.
23 Kim, GwangSup. "A Proposal to Joson Theatre Companies." *Joson Daily Newspaper*, 1933.
24 The following table lists the repertories performed by The Dramatic Art Research Society. This list shows the advancement of theatrical modernization in Korea at that time.

#	Author(Translator)	Play	Director	Period	Act
1	Nikolai Gogol (Ham Daehoon)	*The Inspector General*	Hong Haeseong	32. 5. 4-6	5
2	Irving(Jang GiJae)	*The Generous Lover*	Hong Haeseong	32. 6. 28-30	1
	Lady Gregory(Choi JongWu)	*The Gaol Gate*			1
	Reinhard Göring (Jo HeeSun)	*The Sea Battle*			1
3	Anton Chekhov (Ham DaeHoon)	*The Anniversary*	Hong Haeseong	33. 2. 9-10	1
	George Kaiser (Suh HangSeok)	Gilles und Johanna	Yu ChiJin		1
	Yoo Chijin	*A Mud-and-Dung Hut*	Hong Haeseong		2

4	Bernard Shaw (Kim kwangSeop, Jang GiJae, Park YongCheol)	Arms and the Man	Jang GiJae	33. 6. 27-28	3
5	Pirandello(Park YongCheol)	*The Imbecile*	Yu ChiJin	33. 11. 28-30	1
	Shakespeare (Jung InSeop)	*The Merchant of Venice*			1
	Yu Chijin	*A Scenery of the Village withe Willow Trees*			1
6	Ibsen (Park YongCheol)	*A Doll's House*	Hong HaeSeong	34, 4, 18-19	3
*	Ferenc Molnar(Jo HeeSun)	*In the Train*	Yu ChiJin	34. 7. 18	1
	JULES RENARD(Lee HeonGu)	*Poil de Carotte*	Hong HaeSeong	34. 9. 6-7	1
7	Chekhov (Ham DaeHun)	*The Cherry Orchard*	Hong HaeSeong	34. 12. 7-8	4
8	Lee MuYoung	*Daydreamer*	Yu ChiJin	35. 11. 19	1
	George Courteline (Lee HeonGu)	*la Paix chez soi*			1
	Yu ChiJin	*The Rite*(祭祀)			1
9	John Galsworthy(Jang GiJae)	*The First and the Last*	Yu ChiJin	36. 2. 28-3.2	1
	Tolstoy (Lee KwangSu)	*The Power of Darkness*			3
	Lee MuYoung	*Free Treatments*			1
10	Lee SuHyang	*Mother*	Yu ChiJin	36. 4. 11-12	1
	Lee KwangRae	*A Scholar in a Village*			3
11	Yu ChiJin	*Sisters*	Yu ChiJin	36. 5. 29-31	3
	田漢 Tian Han (Kim Kwangju)	*A Tragedy on the Lakeshore*			1
12	Adapted by Yu ChiJin	*The Story of Chunhyang*	Yu ChiJin	36. 9. 29-30	4
13	Karl Schönherr (Soe HangSeok)	*Belief and Home*	Yu Chijin	36. 12. 20-22	3
14	Mr & Mrs. Heyward (Jang GiJae)	*Porgy and Bess*	Yu ChiJin	37. 1. 21-23	3
15	Lee Muyoung	*Free Treatments* (reproduction)	Yu ChiJin	37. 2. 25-28	1
	Yu ChiJin	*The Year of Abundance (*the adaptation of *The Cow)*			3
16	Tolstoy (Ham DaeHun)	*Resurrection*	Suh HangSeok	37. 4. 10-11	5
17	Adapted by Yu ChiJin	*The Story of Chunhyong* (reproduction)		37. 5. 15-16	

**	Arthur Schnitzler (Yu ChiJin)	*Blind Geronimo and His Brother*		38. 2. 11-14	1
18	Janet Marks(Lee Suhyang)	*Cuckoo*	Lee BaekSan	38. 5. 28-29	1
	Kim JinSu	*The Road*	Lee SuHyang		4
19	Maxwell Anderson (Jang GiJae)	*Winterset*	Yu ChiJin	38. 7. 8-10	3
20	Clifford Odets (Suh HangSeok)	Awake and Sing!	Lee SeoHyang	38. 9. 14-16	3
21	Yu ChiJin	*The Year of Abundance* (reproduction)	Lee SeoHyang	38. 12. 3-4	2
	Charles Vildrac (Lee HeonGu)	*Le Paquebot Tenacity*			3
22	Tolstoy (Ham DaeHun)	Resurrection (reproduction)		39. 1. 6-8	5
23	Anderson (Jang GiJae)	*Winterset* (reproduction)			3
	Schnitzler (Yu ChiJin)	*Blind Geronimo and his Brother* (reproduction)			3
***	Ham Saedeok	*A Young Buddhist Monk*(Doneom)	Yu ChiJin	39. 3. 3-5	1
24	Yu ChiJin	*The Story of Chunhyang*		39. 4. 8-9	5
	Anderson (Jang GiJae)	*Winterset*		39. 5. 4-7.	3
	Ham Saeduk	*A Young Buddhist Monk*(Doneom)		39. 5. 8-11	1
				39. 5. 8-11	

* Temporary Performances
**first Theatre Competition by Donga Newspaper
***2nd Theatre Competition by Donga Newspapers

25 *A Study of KAPF's Literary Movement.* Yeogsa Munjae Yeonguso, ed. Seoul, History Criticism, 1990, p. 202.
26 The name of an established literary group organized in Seoul around 1923.
27 Kim, GiJin. *The Views on This Literary Age Short Novels (*文藝時代觀 短篇*). Joseon Daily Newpaper*, 9–20 Nov 1928.
28 Ibid.
29 Lim, Hwa. "Towrad the *Muddy Stream*(濁流e Dehayeo)." *JoseonGwang*, Aug 1929.
30 Kim, GiJin. "A Year of Art Movement(藝術運動ui 一年間)." *JoseonGwang,* Jan 1930.
31 Companion artists were the artists who did not join the communist party, but their direction of writings pointed to the anticipation of the collapse of bourgeois society and the arrival of communist society.
32 Sin, GoSong. "The Start of Theatre Movement, —the Present Stage of Proletarian Theatre." *Joson Daily Newspapers,* 29 Jul–2 Aug 1931.
33 Yu JinOh was also a companion artist. Even if he was not affiliated with KAPF, the play went along with KAPF's writing direction.

34 Lee, HeonGu. "After Attending the *New Construction*'s First Performance." *Joseon Daily Newspapers*, 26 Nov 1933.
35 Kim, YoungPal. "Novel No Novel(小說非小說)." *Joseon Daily Newspaper*, 13 Apr 1928.
36 Alazon is one of three stock characters in the comedy of the theatre of ancient Greece. He is an impostor who sees himself as greater than he actually is.
37 György Lukács was one of the founders of Western Marxism, while Theodor W. Adorno was a leading member of the Frankfurt School of Critical Theory and strongly influenced the European New Left. While Adorno advocated modernism, Lukács defended "Realism in the Balance" the traditional realism in the face of rising Modernist movements, such as Expressionism and Surrealism, though he admitted such new movements were a historical necessity. Lukács considered new artistic movements lack what he viewed as revolutionary power. For Lukács, the important issue at stake was not the conflict that results from modernists' evolving oppositions to classical forms, but rather the ability of art to confront an objective reality that exists in the world, an ability he found almost entirely lacking in modernism. Lukács believed that the "social mission of literature" was to clarify the experience of the masses, and in turn show these masses that their experiences were influenced by the objective totality of capitalism. To him, modernism moved toward more immediate, more subjective, more abstracted versions of fictional reality that ignored the objective reality of the capitalist system. Realism was, for Lukács, the only defensible or valuable literary school of the early 20th century.
38 Lee, JaeSoen. *A History of Modern Korean Novels*. Seoul, Hongseungsa, 1979, pp. 302–309.

4 The Liberation of Korea and the Korean War Period

Theatre of Ideology

When Japan unconditionally surrendered to the Allied forces on 15 August 1945 after the atomic attacks on Hiroshima and Nagasaki, Japanese rule over Korea ended.[1] However, it was difficult for Korea to achieve its full independence because it was not emancipated by its own power. Korea was divided into two with the Liberation and was ruled by the United States and the Soviet Union. Korea's intelligentsia were also divided into democrats and communists, who had to contend with each other. Eventually, the liberal democratic Korea led by Rhee Syngman in the South and the communist state led by Kim Il Sung in the North separately built their governments in 1948. However, the political and social conditions continued to be uneasy, and the ceasefire was not stable. Finally, on 25 June 1950, the Korean War began with the invasion of North Korea, and the war lasted until 1953. The Korean War was also a part of the Cold War, and the United Nations against China joined the war. This period from the Liberation from Japan in 1945 to the end of the Korean War in 1953 is commonly called the Liberation and the War Period: the time of turmoil.

The most important thing during the Liberation and the War Period was to build an ideologically correct government that suited each party's beliefs. Theatre groups were also divided into two: the left-wing and the right-wing theatres of the intellect. In addition, there were popular theatres that provided entertainment and comforted the public, who were tired of ideological battles in the turbulent times. Thus, the main intellectual theatres from 1945 to the 1950s in Seoul could be divided into three periods according to the establishment of the Southern government: the first from the Liberation to the establishment of the Southern government in 1948, the second from the established government to the Korean War between 1948 and 1953, and the third from 1953 to 1960. Political changes affected the whole society as well as theatre in the 1950s.[2] Strictly speaking, the Liberation of Korea and the War Period were between 1945 and 1953, but this chapter includes the years between 1953 and 1960 since the scars of the Korean War had strong influences, and new theatrical experiments were not yet distinct. Of course, the left-wing theatres were forbidden and did not exist in the democratic post-war

DOI: 10.4324/9781003490708-5

period in Seoul. This chapter examines the theatres of the turbulent years as they emerged chronologically.

4.1 The Left-Wing Theatre in Seoul

When Korea was liberated from Japan in August 1945, the left-wing theatre immediately became active. The proletarian theatre practitioners created organizations called *The Center of Korean Theatre Construction (朝鮮演劇建設本部)* and *The Alliance of Korean Proletarian Theatre (朝鮮 Proletarian 演劇同盟)*. Then, the two groups united as one and renamed themselves *The Korean Theatre Alliance (朝鮮演劇同盟)* according to the orders of the Korean Communist Party. Since theatres at this time were unable to perform theatrical activities regardless of political sides due to the lack of organized theatre companies, the left-wing theatre formed this organization to carry out its activities as the party's primary group. As the most urgent task, the Korean Theatre Alliance sought the clearing of Japanese and feudal remnants and proposed a theory of *National Theatre* to achieve a national unification of ideas. This progressive *National Theatre* theory emerged based on the need for a new creative methodology to describe ideal realism. It was the independent theatres that dialectically unified the contents for the construction of a progressive democratic state with a progressive outlook and the popular elements of *Sinpa*. In fact, the theory of progressive *National Theatre* was the same as social realism in the 1930s. Its activities were divided into three periods: the first period was from immediately after the Liberation to March 1946 when the central left-wing organization was arranged; the second period was from April 1946 to August 1947 when it actively worked for the popularization of proletarian theatre; and the third period was thereafter until the Southern Korean government was established.

During the first period, the doctrine of the left-wing theatre was established. It intended to clean up Japanese remnants, eradicate feudalism, establish Korean social theatre, and cooperate with international proletarian theatres. The left-wing theatre believed in the full articulation of the people's enlightenment and progressive thought. Its big theatrical event was the performance in the 3.1 Commemorative Theatre Festival in 1946. The 3.1 Movement in 1919 was the biggest independence revolution of the whole Japanese occupation period; therefore, the plays performed were naturally related to the theme of independence. The plays were *An Army for National Independence* (獨立軍), *3.1 Independence Movement and a Manchurian Old Man* (*3.1*運動 *gwa* 滿洲令監), *3.1 Independence Movement* (*3.1*運動), and *Sir* (*Nim*).[3] In addition to these plays were *March 1st in 1919* (己未年*3*月 *1*日) and *Nation and People* (國家 wa 百姓). These plays shared their experiences with the commemoration of the 3.1 Movement, heightened the national spirit, and demonstrated the collective power of the proletariat.

The second period of the Korean Theatre Alliance was most actively engaged in the reformation of social proletariats. It made its voice on various political issues of the time and produced performances that promoted the national spirit of the proletariats. The second 3.1 Commemorative Theatre Festival was a great success, attracting 100,000 audience members in about two weeks. The first part was *The Taebaek Mountains* (太伯山脈), written by Ham SeDeok, who debuted at *The Dramatic Art Research Society* in 1939.[4] Several companies collaborated for the performance of the play. For the second part of the festival, *Great Love* (偉大*han Sarang*), written by Jo YoungCheol, was performed.[5] In addition, a total of 23 independent theatres participated in the Independent Theatre Contest held in July 1947 in order to popularize the proletarian theatre idea. The contents of the plays were limited to anti-feudal, anti-imperialist, and nationalistic themes that could contribute to the construction of a democratic proletarian Korea. In short, it promoted the establishment and popularization of national proletarian theatre.

The last period followed when left-wing performers in Seoul fled to North Korea. In May 1947, as the heads of ministries of the U.S. Military Government were replaced by Koreans and Americans retreated as advisors, the U.S. military government's Korean institution was renamed "The South Korean Transitional Government." As a result of the democratic Transitional Government, left-wing activities were banned, and the Korean Literary Alliance, to which the Korean Theatre Alliance belonged, was also abolished in August 1947. In spite of the oppressions, the Korean Theatre Alliance was reorganized into four theater groups and performed a couple of plays, such as *Moonlit Night* (*Dalbam*) by Kim Isik and *Lonely Lives* by Hauptmann. However, the performances did not go well since the actors were arrested in the middle of them. Although the group planned commemorative performances for the 8.15 Liberation in 1948, they were stopped by the Southern democratic government. Many theatre leaders fled to North Korea: Shin GoSong, Han Hyo, and Song Young fled in 1946, and Ham SeDeok in 1947, followed by actors and actresses such as Hwang Cheol, Sim Young, and Ji GyungSun. These performers played major roles in theatre in North Korea until the Korean War.

The subjects and themes of the left-wing plays during this period mainly consisted of 1) rural enlightenment and emphasis on new proletarian education, such as *Transition* (變換) and *Town of Twilight* (黃昏 *ui MaEul*); 2) willingness to to build a new country, such as *Father who went to Seoul* (*Seoul gattdeon Abeoji*) and *The Cockfight* (*Dalg Ssaum*); 3) historical drama related to independence, such as *An Army for National Independence* (*Dokripgun*) and *3.1 Independence Movement* (*3.1 Deokrip Undong*); 4) the joy of the liberation of nation and classes, such as *The iron chain is broken* (*Cheolswae-eun Kkeuneojyeotda*), *Bottdol's Military Uniform* (*Bottdol-ui Gunbok*), *The Liberation* (*HaeBang*), and *The Pioneers* (*Seonguja*); 5) the justification of the construction of a new communist country, such as *Passenger Train* (*Jeonggaek Yeolcha*) and *General Nokdu* (*Nokdu Janggun*); and 6) the liquidation and satire of Japanese remnants, such as *Twilight* (*Hwanghon*) and *The Old Tree* (*Gomok*).[6] In general, the plays that dealt with the Liberation tried to foretell the bright future of the liberated motherland rather than showing the overwhelming joyous moment of the Liberation—which was commonly done by the right-wing plays. For example, *General Nokdu*, based on the theme of the construction of the motherland, conveyed the lessons of the historical drama by connecting the period of the Donghak Revolution with the period of Liberation. Many of the plays made experimental attempts in short forms in order to be easily performed by the Small Group Theatre. Among the left-wing theatres, *Twilight* (黃昏) by Song Young and *The Old Tree* (古木) by Ham SeDeok were prime representatives. They were outstanding works that showed the proletarian task which ought to be abolished during the Liberation period. They utilized satirical techniques with the characters of the pro-Japanese Mr. Lee and the feudal remnant Mr. Park. They were epitomes of progressive realistic plays during the Liberation Period and were considered to be the highlight of the proletarian dramaturgy written during this period. Indeed, many plays came out in a short period of time compared to the plays of the right-wing theatre. They described the social chaos of the Liberation and instructively explained the obligations of the public during this period. But because they focused on the educational purpose, audiences' dramatic interest was relatively ignored.

Left-wing plays from the Liberation period were created in accordance with the concept of progressive national realism. These works naturally revealed social problems through conflicts among characters with critically minded perceptions of reality. In most cases, their conclusions tended to be consistent with the values of the left-wing party. In other words, the left-wing theatre players during this period developed their theatre performances according to their political nature. In particular, they created progressive realistic plays while dramatizing the abolishment of the remnants of feudalism and Japanese imperialism, which were national objectives during the Liberation period. However, they showed difficulties in coming up with the actual blueprints to construct a new country. Ultimately, the limitation of the left-wing performers at this time was that the artists did not reach the point of presenting new historical perspectives.

The Korean Theatre Alliance arranged an advisory body for the left-wing theatre.[7] It had a council that organized the troupes as well as the actors' groups. It also insisted on independent theatres in order to easily reach people. Independent theatre was the same concept as the Little Theatre during the Japanese Colonial Era, but its aim was to perform for the people, not for the intellectuals. The new creative methodology emphasized the theory of *progressive national theatre*, which was almost the same as social realism in the 1930s. The Korean Theatre Alliance also emphasized the legitimate and critical succession of traditions and made it clear that it inherited KAPF,[8] especially by referring to the spirit of the last proletarian troupe, *New Construction*(新建設) from the Japanese occupation era.[9] It insisted on a concept of national literature that integrated people. National literature consisted of works that reflected the nation's reality based on progressive democracy, i.e., social realism. It tried to make the working class perform in theatrical activities, which was reminiscent of the Mobile Little Theatre Movement (移動式小型劇場) during the colonial period. The most specific practice of the *Theory of Popularizing Theatre* was the effort to revitalize the small theatre circles among workers, farmers, and citizens of intelligence. Therefore, the Mobile Little Theatre Movement was more important for these small groups in order to perform conveniently. The *Theory of Popularizing Theatre* was prepared as the ultimate method to approach the people, but it was not very successful.

After the Liberation, the *Theory of Popularizing Theatre* expanded its characteristics as public art through the exploration of specific theatrical forms, such as the Small Group Theatre (小人劇), an amateur theatre group. It intended to include the audience in the process of revitalizing theatrical circles and to develop the Small Group Theatre, which was accomplished by people with enlightenment purposes. The required performance time was from 30 minutes to an hour, and two to three performances took place at one time with about ten characters and three or four main roles.

The left-wing theatres disappeared after the establishment of the South Korean government in August 1948. The artists who exiled themselves to the North played an important role in the theatrical world of the North until the Korean War broke out. Many of them died during the war or were purged by the North Korean government after the war. Eventually, North Korean theatre began anew with the new North Korean talents.

4.2 The Right-Wing Theatre

The ideological confrontation between the left and right in South Korea during the Liberation period changed in accordance with the policy decisions of the U.S. military government. In other words, the process of the U.S. military government handing over political hegemony to the right-wing forces and the spread of right-wing theatre were in agreement. The right-wing theatre lacked the ability to respond to the left-wing theatre at the beginning, from August 1945 to July 1947. But after the U.S. military government prohibited communist activities in July 1947, the right-wing theatrical organizations began to emerge, such as *the National Association of Theatre Arts (全國演劇藝術協會, October 1947)* and *Korean Stage Arts Center (韓國舞臺藝術院, 1948)*. Since such central theatrical organizations were active, Korean right-wing theatre expanded its influence and grounded itself between 1947 and 1953 without a hitch. However, since the Korean War broke out in 1950 and lasted until 1953, it was a period of tribulation at the same time. The following years that will be discussed, from 1953 to 1960, were not, in fact, called the Liberation and the War period. Still, the scars of war had a strong influence on this period of time, and new theatrical attempts had not clearly emerged yet, so this era can be called the Liberation and the War period in a broad sense. Thus, right-wing theatre could be examined in three periods.

4.2.1 1945–1948: The Period of the Liberation

The first right-wing theatre company was *the National Art Stage (民族藝術舞臺)*, also known as *MinYe (民藝)*, founded in October 1945 and led by Lee GwangRae. This company played a popular repertory of *Resurrection* by Tolstoy in December 1945, which marked the beginning of the right-wing theatre. However, it was nothing new since *Resurrection* was repeatedly performed during the colonial period. In addition to *MinYe*, there were other right-wing theatre companies, such as the *Front Line* (戰線) and *ToWolHoe,* also led by Park SeungHee in the 1920s. The members of *ToWolHoe* performed *Forty Years*, written by Park SeungHee and directed by An JeongHwa, in December 1945 and *The Patriot YunBongGil* (屍倭實記) in 1946. These works recalled the 40 colonial years and paid tribute to the historical patriot Yun BongGil.[10]

The political conflict over the trusteeship of Korea was increasing in 1946.[11] The right-wing theatrical people supported the abolition of trusteeship, while the left-wing people supported the trusteeship. As a result of this political participation, the right-wing theatre artists' voices could reach those outside of the theatre. The former members of *The Dramatic Art Research Society* in the 1930s took the lead and further carried out the V narod movement for the people with the sponsorship of *MinJu* daily newspapers. This V narod movement was a fight against the left-wing theatre. This group also opened up classes for students before performances including, *The Last Moment of Ahn Jung-geun* (*Ahn JungGeun-ui Choehu*), *The National Betrayer* (*Maegukno*), *The Righteous Yoon Bong-gil* (*Yoon Bong-gil UiSa*), and *The Patriot* (*Aegukja*).[12]

At the end of 1946, *The Drama Arts Center (劇藝術院)* was founded, which led to *the Drama Arts Association (劇藝術協會)* in 1947. The group included old members, such as Yu ChiJin from *The Dramatic Art Research Society*, as well as new members, including Lee JinSun, Lee HaeRang, and Kim DongWon, who led the next generation of right-wing theatre. *The Drama Arts Center* performed *The Motherland* (祖國) in February 1947 to commemorate the 3.1. movement, written and directed by Yu ChiJin. The Center was disbanded after the performance. Then, the *Drama Arts Association* was founded with the performance of Yu ChiJin's *A Self-Crying Drum* (自鳴鼓). This company kept going with performances, such as *The Prince in Hemp Clothes* (麻衣太子), *The Price Hodong and the Princess Mokdan* (*Hodong Wangja-wa Mokdan Gongju*), *Milky Way* (*Eunhasu*), *ChunHyangJeon,* and *The Star* (*Byeol*), until it was merged into the Korean *National Theatre* as an exclusive theatre company. Producing more than 20 performances since its foundation, the *Drama Arts Association* played a pivotal role in the right-wing theatre movement.

While the left-wing theatre groups were active around 1947, the activities of the right-wing theatre groups were limited to the occasional events of *National Art Stage*, *The Drama Arts Center*, the *Drama Arts Association*, and the V narod movement. All the performances were one-time only except for those of the *Drama Arts Association*. The right-wing theatres had not yet formed a central theatrical organization that could combine the people's desires into one voice. *The National Theatre Arts Association (全國藝術協會)* finally came into being in October of 1947, led by Yu ChiJin, and it included 12 right-wing companies. Its major members were the former members of *The Dramatic Art Research Society* in the 1930s, but many commercial theatre companies joined this Association. Its most successful production was probably *The Happy Marriage of Sir Maeng's Family* (孟進仕宅 慶事) in 1949, written by Oh Young-Jin in 1943. This play, which sought to find true humanity, is a satirical comedy rooted in folklore. It was a work based on the tradition of showing sound humanism, and it was later ranked as the number one play of the joint production between South Korea and North Korea.This association soon had to split into two: a theatre for theatre's sake and a commercial theatre, since there was strong criticism from the side of theatre for theatre's sake toward the commercial theatre among *National Theatre Arts Association* members. Again, a joint attempt from the right-wing theatre headquarters created the *Korean Stage Arts Center (韓國舞臺藝術院)* in 1948, which included dances, musical theatre, and traditional musical theatre. The public theatrical activities of the right wing were made possible thanks to the *National Theatre Arts Association* and the *Korean Stage Arts Center.* Furthermore, 3.1 commemorative performances and National Theatre competitions were held alongside the national cultural Enlightenment movement. As the activities of the right-wing theatre were not as active as those of left-wing theatre during this period, not many right-wing plays were written. Another challenge was that neither an overseeing theatre organization nor a united policy of right-wing theatre existed at the time.

The most frequent theme of right-wing plays, first of all, was the joy of the Liberation, just as was the truth of left-wing plays. Plays, such as *The Last Days of Imperial Japan* (*Jeguk* 日本 *ui Majimak Nal* in 1945), *The Shaking Axis* (*Heundeulrineun* 地軸 in 1947), and *The Daughter-in-Law* (*MyeoNeuRi* in 1947), brought the theme of joy to life. They made a strong connection between the terrible national realities before the Liberation and the joy of the Liberation. These plays excluded political orientation as much as possible and described situations in a realistic manner. In other words, they described the facts as they were rather than distorting the facts with an assertive outlook for the future. Secondly, there were plays that used history to tell and criticize the current situation, such as *A Self-Crying Drum* (自鳴鼓 in 1947). These works usually made the best of old tales, legends, and historical events and presented the writer's view of the current political situation. *A Self-Crying Drum* expressed opposition to the trusteeship, which was the general opinion of the right wing. Works like *The Story of Ahn JungGeun* (安重根 史記 in 1946) intended to restore national identity by dramatizing the achievements of national heroes during the Japanese colonial period. In short, right-wing plays mostly dealt with the happiness and meaning of the Liberation along with historical plays that metaphorically criticized the political situation of the times. They succeeded in the realism from the 1930s and emphasized dramatic form over content despite their belief in the right-wing political party.

In the midst of ideological debates, the commercial theatre was consistent with the interests of the public; therefore, its activities continued. The representative of commercial theatre was Kim ChunGwang's *Youth Theatre* (青春劇場), which started performing in October 1945 and gained popularity for its historic productions. For example, *The Story of Ahn JungGeun* (*Ahn JungGeun Sagi*) gained much popularity with the visit of a prominent political leader, Kim Gu. However, this historical drama did not differ much from the romantic melodrama because it took a tragic popular character of the era and transformed it to fit the sentimental tastes of the public. These performances put tremendous effort into stage equipments and costumes. The company hired many exclusive actors and actresses since the show included a lot of characters. The exclusive actors were stars with charisma to attract people. Another popular group was *The Golden Seat (黃金座)*, founded in November of 1946. Unlike *Youth Theatre*, it focused on performances that stimulated the tears of female audiences via tragic heroines, characters similar to *Sinpa* theatre. Even in the late Liberation period, *The Golden Seat* was an active commercial group along with the *Youth Theatre*.

Musical-type theatre (*Akgeuk*樂劇 or *Gageuk*歌劇) was another popular theatre form. It aimed for the box office from the beginning, so there were not many criticisms about its performances. Its origin was largely owed to the propaganda concerts of new music in the 1930s, though it originally was not intended as musical theatre. When it was difficult to attract the public's interest by singing alone, dialogues were added to the propaganda concerts, thus becoming a musical-type theatre.[13] *Akgeuk* also looked for national ethnic arts. At the end of the colonial period in Japan, *Akgeuk* avoided pro-government themes by using old Korean tales. While superficially pursuing commercial interests, *Akgeuk* dreamed of reviving the national arts during the Liberation and the War period. The total number of performances in this period came to about 400, showing the popularity of *Akgeuk*. Musical theatre was loved by the masses, who were worn out by heavy ideological debates. This theatre form also influenced the development of *the Korean Gageuk Association (朝鮮歌劇協會)* and ultimately showed its power and influence of the time.

In short, all of these commercial theatres understood the taste of the public, which the left-wing's theory of popularization could not totally grasp. The commercial theatres joined together to organize the right-wing theatre headquarters and, owing to their popularity, even had government-supported performances after the South Korean government was established.

4.2.2 1948–1953: The Period of the Foundation and the Korean War

After the establishment of the South Korean government in August 1948, theatrical artists held a national cultural contest in December 1948 to promote the national spirit. They proclaimed that cultural activities should support the government, while the government should guide cultural activities. In January 1949, the *Korean Stage Arts Center* held a contest of national stage arts, and six proposals for performance improvements were submitted.[14] Among them, the abolishment of the 100% admission tax increase charged by the U.S. military government and the installation of a *National Theatre* were the hot issues of the time. Consequently, the tax was reduced, though not totally, and *the National Theatre* Steering Committee was formed in October 1949. The committee decided to have two exclusive companies, *SinHyeop (新協)* and *GeukHyeop (劇協)*, and the performances were intended to be year-round by two groups bi-monthly.

The National Theatre of Korea finally opened on 30 April 1950 with *Wonsulrang*, written by Yu ChiJin. It was a romantic enlightenment historical drama that indirectly criticized contemporary divided-political reality based on borrowed old history. By dramatizing the historical fact that the Tang Dynasty in the 8th century, who cooperated in the reunification of the Three Kingdoms by Silla, attempted to conquer the Korean peninsula, the play pointed out the analogy of the U.S. and the Soviet Union breaking the Cairo Declaration and Potsdam's Fourth National Assembly after World War II.[15] This work, woven with Wonsulrang's fiery patriotism, saga, and romance with a Guseul maiden, was a personal tragedy of Wonsulrang as well as an expression of Yu ChiJin's grand nationalism. Its performance attracted more than 50,000 audience members within only a week, indicating the possibility of a great theatrical awakening. It was magnificent enough to be called a national epic, and the opening of *the National Theatre* of Korea was a success. The second performance was *The Great Wall* (萬里長城) in the style of *Changguk*, the reformed traditional *Pansori* theatre. The third performance was Opera *ChunHyangJeon* in May. The fourth was *The Thunderstorm* by a Chinese modern playwright in June. The fifth was a dance performance of *The Mermaid* (人魚公主) and was stopped by the outbreak of the Korean War on 25 June 1950. During this period, the establishment of *the National Theatre* and its work were important issues in the theatre industry.

In addition to the establishment of the *National Theatre* and related performances, the first theatre contests for college students in 1949 were influential to many theatre people. The achievements of college theatre were highly praised by theatre leaders and valued even more than those of most professional theatres.[16] The most important thing was that they became the leaders of theatre in the next generation.

First and foremost, the plays in this period showed a strong will to abolish feudal and Japanese cultural remnants. Plays such as *Cosmos* and *Mr. Lee JungSaeng Alive* (*Sala Ittneun Lee JungSaeng Gakha*), both in 1949, belonged to this group. The most important play was *Mr. Lee JungSaeng Alive*, written by Oh YoungJin and performed by *GeukHyeop* in 1949. The author fled from North Korea only with this manuscript, which grasped the problems of the right-wingers during the Liberation period. In the play, the pro-Japanese protagonist Lee JungSaeng is eager to be pro-American after the Liberation. His excessive greediness is symbolized as a big obstacle in the new era. Therefore, even if his fake death leads to his actual suicide, his death becomes a keen

Figure 4.1 *National Theatre* in Myongdong. Photo from *National Theatre* of Korea *70th Anniversary,* Seoul, Gemunsa, vol. History, 2020. p.13.

Figure 4.2 A scene from *Wonsulrang*. Photo from *National Theatre* of Korea *70th Anniversary,* edited and published by The *National Theatre* Company, vol. History, 2020, p.11.

satire of the time. The death of Lee JungSaeng, the old ills' symbol, opened the dawn of a new era. This satire about the pro-Japanese group was regarded as the highlight of the period.

Secondly, certain plays incorporated the ethnic consciousness of national independence, such as *The Star* (*Byeol* in 1948), *The Wall* (障壁 in 1950), *Mother (EoMeoNi* in 1950*)*, and *The Spirit of Motherland (*祖國魂 in 1949). Yu ChiJin's historical plays, such as *The Star* and *The Wall*, were important in dramatizing the contemporary major issues using historical materials, including national independence and the opposition between left and right ideologies. However, by somewhat distorting history on the side of the right wing, the writer's limitation on historical consciousness was shown. *Mother* and *The Spirit of Motherland* have strong right-wing enlightenment characters, so the dramatic plots are arbitrary, and the author's ideology is openly revealed, resulting in melodramatic stories and a lack of consciousness of the dramatic reality.

Thirdly, a group of plays accused of social chaos includes *Blood Veins* (血脈 in 1948), *Tent Village* (天幕村 in 1949), and *The District of the Drifting People* (流民街 in 1949). This group objectively described the poverty of the common people, which had continued from the colonial period, with realistic techniques. In particular, *Blood Veins* was an outstanding work in this period and well portrayed the poverty of people, but it was a passive portrayal of this era by treating social aspects in an episodic manner rather than holistically dealing with the political and social confusion of contemporary society.

During the Korean War, the right-wing theatre people were divided into two groups: one escaped to the south by crossing the Han River, and the other remained in Seoul. Those in Seoul had to cooperate with the Northern military army until the recovery of Seoul for about 90 days. Most performances in these days purposefully supported the war spirit, but there were a few translated Russian plays, such as *The Black Lieutenant Breel*, dealing with racial issues.[17] After the recovery of Seoul, many theatre people, including SinHyeop members, were transferred to newly organized theatre corporations under the Ministry of National Defense and could safely perform, even after the Southern government retreated again to Daegu and Busan. For this reason, Daegu became the cultural center during the war. *SinHyeop*'s *Hamlet* and *Dirty Hands* (*Les Mains Sales*) by Jean-Paul Sartre were the two performances that made a great impact. While *SinHyeop*'s *Hamlet* was said to be the best production of *Hamlet* so far, *Dirty Hands*, the first existential play produced in Korea, received much empathy due to the brutality of the war and the anguish of human existence. After this production, many plays came into being, dealing with the loss of humanity or the damages of the war. All performances tried to highlight the idea of anti-communism since the war had just outbroken. SinHyeop, led by Yu ChiJin, returned to Seoul in 1952 while *the National Theatre*, with Seo HangSeok, was reopened in Daegu in 1953. In Seoul, SinHyeopperformed about 20 plays, such as *The Star*, *The Sisters* (姉妹), and foreign plays, and led the theatre scene in Seoul.

The commercial theatres continued their performances; the *Youth Theatre* (青春劇場) and *The Golden Seat (*黃金座*)* were the two most active companies since the period of Liberation. In the *Youth Theatre*, Kim Chun Gwang was notable since he not only wrote many plays, such as *Wunhyunggung Spring* (雲峴宮 *ui Bom*) and *The Sad Story of Danjong* (端宗哀史), but also directed many works. The *Youth Theatre* tended to produce more domestic tragedies and mystery plays than earlier historical works. Musical-Type theatre (*Akgeuk* or *Gageuk*) also continued to remain popular among the public. However, there were criticisms that these commercially popular theatres did not change much from their performances in the 1930s.

Another popular theatre was women's *Changgeuk (*女性國劇*)*. It originated when *the Women's Club for Korean Traditional Pansori (*女性國樂同好會*)* was founded in 1948. The club launched with the promotion of social gathering for female *Pansori* singers amidst male *Pansori* singers and later became a commercial women's *Pansori* company with the enthusiastic support of the audience. *The Women's Club for Korean Traditional Pansori* performed *The Flower in the Jail* (獄中華), an adaptation of the traditional *ChunHyangJeon*, in 1948, and *The Sun and the Moon* (*Hatnim Dalnim*), an adaptation of *Romeo and Juliet*, in 1949. After the success of *The Sun and the Moon*, the women's *Changgeuk* became the most popular commercial theatre of the 1950s. The origin of its popularity seemed to stem from the gorgeous stage designs, costumes, lighting, and makeup. Additionally, female musicians, who had been alienated from the "male-dominant" music society, played significant roles to show their talent and freedom. As a result, their beauty and freedom became the envy of the audience. Its repertoire mainly consisted of adaptations of old tales and unofficial history along with adaptations of Western classics of love. Since traditional *Pansori* was used for singing, it was easy to come along with old stories; yet its main theme was love stories with splendid spectacles. The outbreak of the Korean War did not interrupt its popularity but the popularity led to the separation of *the Women's Club for Korean Traditional Pansori* and resulted in the creation of nearly 20 new women's *Changgeuk* groups in the late 1950s. The dispersion of the Women's Club deteriorated the overall quality of the performances since almost the same number of performers were divided into many groups. In addition, these companies did not have professional directors and writers, and their styles, neither classic nor modern, were probably tiring for the audience. However, they contributed to the popularization of *Changgeuk* by their splendid spectacles. In the early 1960s, when the *National Theatre* created the *Changgeuk* Group, where famous *Pansori* singers shared their talents, most of the female *Changgeuk* members refused to join, and the female *Changgeuk* theatre faded away.

Indeed, after the establishment of the South Korean government, the division of Korea seemed to be fixed, and so did the division of theatres. The theory of pure Enlightenment theatre was the motto of this period among the right-wingers. In other words, the theatre emphasized national ethnicity in content and accepted the form of realism theatre. *The Grotto* (穴脈) by

Figure 4.3 *The Flower in the Jail* (獄中華) in 1953 by Ihm Chunaeng. Photo from Naver.com and Ihm Chunaeng.

Kim YoungSu and *Cosmos* by Kim JinSu were realistic portrayals of the time, while *The Star* and *The Wall* by Yu ChiJin strongly reflected anti-communistic thoughts. *Mr. Lee JungSaeng Alive* was a keen satire about the pro-Japanese people, which was regarded as the highlight of this period. This realism with democratic national ethnicity became the mainstream of theatre around the 1950s.

4.2.3 1953–1960: After the War Period

Many plays were published after the Korean War. In addition to the established playwrights, new playwrights arose and recorded their experiences of the war. The emergence of the new playwrights in the 1950s was owed to the reinvigoration of the New Year literary contest of each daily newspaper and the newcomer recommendation system of many new magazines when the war was cleared up. Kim SangMin, Ju Pyeong, Ha YuSang, Cha BeomSeock, Ihm HiJae, Lee YongChan, Kim JaRim, Park HyeonSuk, and Oh HakYoung were representative playwrights after the war.

The plays were divided into several topics, such as anti-communism, the damages of the war, moral confusion, economic difficulties and unemployment, and personal desire versus sexuality. Anti-communist plays were based on a black-and-white view and demonstrated the damages of the war. These plays were mainly written by well-established playwrights, such as Yu ChiJin, Kim JinSu, Kim YoungSu, and Oh YoungJin. For example, *The Blue Saint* (*Puren* 聖人) is a love-triangle story during the war. A good hero and an attractive heroine are in love. When the communist army invades their village, Gomi, another village man in unrequited love with the heroine, joins the communist party and tries to kill the hero and rape the heroine. Yet, a grenade intended to hit the hero explodes by mistake, and Gomi gets killed by the explosion. This story is based on the premise that the democratic is good and the communist is bad. So, even before he joins the communist party, Gomi is already notorious in the village. This premise of good and bad, and the frequent dramatic changes of the plot by various chances make the play more a melodrama than a realistic "slice of life." *In the Middle of Fire* (*BulDeoMi SokAeSoe*) by Kim JinSu, the commemorative performance of the Korean War in 1954, is also based on the good and bad equation. The story is about the twists and turns of a professor and his son surviving while avoiding the communist army during the Korean War. Eventually, the daughter of the professor is killed by the communist army after her denial of knowing the whereabouts of her father and brother and her refusal against rape. Seoul is finally retaken and liberated, but the scars of the family remain forever. In short, these established playwrights depicted the war from the democratic perspective of communism being an absolute evil; therefore, they raised the banner of anti-communism in the 1950s.

Ultimately, the new playwrights described the period after the war as the time of moral confusion, economic difficulties, and existential questions. *The Wasteland* (*BulMoGi*) by Cha BeomSeok describes the general post-war society. The family of the elder Choi makes a living by running an old court wedding shop that does not go along with the time. His shabby Korean-traditional old house is surrounded by Western-style houses, and the hero is confronted by his children, who want to sell the house. The eldest son, a war veteran, is unemployed and is arrested by the police for robbery, which was to fund to job hunting. The eldest daughter, who is an aspiring movie star, is deceived, loses her chastity, and commits suicide. Some hope for the future is shown through the second daughter, who works hard as a typesetter. In this way, the society after the war is described realistically, highlighting values in transition, confrontation between traditional Korean and Western cultures, and the conflict between the new and old generations. Additionally, *The Whale* (*Gorae*) by Ihm HiJae portrays the immigrants from North Korea. In spite of their wicked fights, they ultimately show warmth by supporting each other. Beyond the objective and realistic descriptions of everyday life, the play shows the value of common people's humanism. Also, *The Daughters in Free Love* (*Ttaldeur* 自由戀愛*eul* 歐歌*Hada*) by Ha YuSang depicts the generational conflicts between a relatively understanding and moderate couple and their three daughters before marriage. Just as the early plays in the 1910s addressed the problems of old-fashioned marriages, this play depicts the idea of marriage in the transitional period from arranged marriages to free love marriages. Meanwhile, Oh HakYoung was interested in the psychology of human beings rather than realistic portrayals of their circumstances. His maiden play *Flower and Cross* (*Kkotgwa Sipjaga*) traces the psychology of a death-row convict with divided egos. In *The Protest* (*Hangbyeon*), the psychological description of the murder of his sister is excellently drawn. Oh HakYoung was one of the first playwrights to pay attention to human psychology and inner desires.

In addition to the playwrights mentioned above, the appearance of female playwrights, such as Kim JaRim and Park HyeonSuk, should not be ignored. They reflected the society of the time with unique women's perspectives, focussing on the female protagonists and the theme of entangled love in a post-war society. Kim Jalim's debut work *A Whirlwind* (*Dolgaebaram*) is a story of a widowed daughter who dares to find a lover, an internal medicine doctor, and challenges to marry him in spite of the old custom that a widow should never marry again. Park HyeonSuk's *A Female Prisoner* (女囚 *or Sarang ul Chaaseo*) is the story of a woman accused of being a spy when she is actually an ordinary good woman who moves between North and the South Korea following her lover. The tragedy of the division between North and the South Korea is highlighted through this poor woman following love. It is the first time to raise a question of ideology; there is no good man or bad man from the beginning, and it shows the uselessness of ideology before the human instinct of love. For the first time, this play indicated a doubt on the black-and-white view of ideologies. These new female playwrights contributed to anti-established morals arising from the confusion and dissolution of values due to the war and the influx of popular Western culture.

The Korean War and its reflections were the most important topics, even to new playwrights, and their ideologies were not much different from those of the established playwrights. The new playwrights offered diverse themes to the War plays, i.e., war scars, economic difficulties, and psychological problems largely due to the war. In fact, the plays of female writers and of Oh HakYoung which depicted inner desires and psychology began to appear and paved the way to modernism. Even though the traditional order or the absolute power of the patriarchy and the dominant ideology of anti-communism were still enforced, individual desires and sexuality over social ideologies erupted along with women's bold challenging of patriarchal society. With traditions dismantling, distortions inevitably followed but so did the beginning of new values. In other words, the 1950s was a very ambivalent era.

There were only a handful of specialized theatre companies at that time, except for *the National Theatre* and *ShinHyeop,* which was, in fact a part of *the National Theatre*. Additionally, the exclusive theatres were mainly *the National Theatre* and, later, *Wongaksa* in the MyeongDong area. Therefore, the environment was hardly prepared to incubate plays in the second half of the 1950s. The difference between the new playwrights and the established writers was that the new playwrights saw reality through defeated human beings or by revealing the reality of an absurd world. In other words, they tried to express a more anthropocentric perspective and the inner side of human beings. Therefore, although realism was still dominant, modernism also sprang up with its focus on a human's inner world and the invisible reality.

The National Theatre, returned to Seoul in 1957, held a contest for university students. This contest caused a controversy due to the selection of the contest play *Why Fighting?* (*Wae Ssawo?*). Since *Why Fighting?* was a remake of *The Jujube Tree* (*Daechu Namu*), which was a pro-Japanese play and selected as the best play in the so-called *National Theatre* contest during the Japanese colonial period, pro-Japanese controversy arose. Writer Yu ChiJin of SinHyeop thought that he completely reworked the play through its excellent dramaturgy and explained that there was no pro-Japanese element anymore. However, *the National Theatre* Company, led by Seo HangSeok, insisted it was unreasonable to select a pro-Japanese play for a student theatre contest. Thus, this controversy led to the division of the Korean theatrical world into two groups: the groups of *National Theatre* and *SinHyeop*.

This situation stimulated the formation of new companies, including *Production Theatre* (製作劇會), developed from *DaeHak GeukHoe (*大學劇會*)*. *Production Theatre's* birth was owed to *WongakSa (*圓覺社*)*, which was a small theatre of 296 seats, opened in 1958 and free for any experimental performance in the middle of Seoul. It was originally intended for traditional performances, including traditional dances, farmer's band music, *Pansori,* and so on, but also allowed any experimental performances. It only lasted shortly due to the sudden fire in 1960, but it contributed much to theatrical performances due to its free rental and convenient location. The *Production Theatre*, whose members were mostly new students from the university theatre groups, had its first production *The Valiant* (死刑囚), written by Halworthy Hall and Robert Middlemass with the direction of Cha BeomSeok and Jeon GeuYoung, in 1956. It declared the manifesto of modern theatre:

> We believe that our solidarity combined with modern humanism in action and a sense of respect for individuality will guarantee our expressions of the free and creative spirit as well as our ideology to create the modern style theatrical form.[18]

As such, the *Production Theatre's* advocation of the modern theatre style was an attempt to overcome the realism theatre established by the Dramatic Arts Research Society as early as the 1930s and set a monumental new era for contemporary theatre. Like many Little Theatre Movements, the *Production Theatre* also mainly performed at university auditoriums. Its significance was in the discovery of many new theatre artists; it created a turning point in the theatre industry by producing theatre personnel, such as playwrights Cha BeomSeok, Kim JaRim, and Park HyeonSuk; directors Oh SaRyang, Kim GyeongOk, Heo Gyu, and Choi ChangBong; and theatre scholar Lee Duhyun.

Another notable new company was *WonBangGak*, which was organized with the aim of leading contemporary experimental theatre with mostly new playwrights as the main initiative group. The main members were Kim SangMin, Oh HakYoung, Ju Pyeong, and Jang Hangi. The company produced *Rainy Constellation* (*Bi Oneun Seongjwa*) (written by Kim SangMin and directed by Lee GwangRae) and *Life is like a chorus* (*Saengmyeong-eun Hapchangcheoreom*) (written by Oh HakYoung and directed by Lee GwangRae) in 1959. Although it lasted only a short time, its significance should be noted because it produced original plays as inaugural performances and was a much more experimental group than the *Production Theatre*, as their works broke away from realism plays. The productions of *WonBangGak* were also possible due to the free rent of *Wongaksa*.

The educational and international environments of theatre also improved as the years went by in the 1950s. SeoRaBeol Arts School opened in 1953 and became the theatre department of JungAng University in 1959, while the theatre department of DongGuk University opened in 1960. For international theatrical exchanges, the Korean Center of ITI (Inter*National Theatre* Institute) was established in 1958.

The Little Theatre Movement was an attempt by young theatre artists from the post-war period, but it disappeared in the shadow of *the National Theatre* and *ShinHyeop*. This failure was not irrelevant to the reality of the theatre industry; it was difficult to find even a small performance stage before *Wongaksa* opened. However, theatre criticism encouraged the Little Theatre Movement, experimental theatre, and hoped to cultivate new theatre talents in order to revive theatre. The Little Theater Movement in the 1950s eventually showed signs of getting out of the shadow of established realism, and by its earnest activities in the late 1950s, it contributed greatly to building the base of Korean theatre from modern to contemporary.

In conclusion, the theatre of the 1950s was developed as an extension of the modern realism theatre established in the 1930s, but it did not go further from there. This is because the established theatre playwrights and directors who dominated the theatre industry before the Liberation still led the scene in old ways, and newcomers were mostly directly influenced by them. It was a challenging time to devise new theatrical styles due to the social chaos and economic difficulties of the Liberation and the Korean War. Ideology was the main issue of theatre, and the War made this more important. Theatre of this period persistently dealt with the War and its wounds. In terms of ideology, the plays never went beyond the black-and-white view that democracy was the absolute good while communism was the absolute evil. Thus, the theatre remained anti-communist. Of course, some plays dealt with the conflicts between the new and old generations, the decline of traditional values and Westernization, material versatility, psychological love and lust, etc. However, the way of dealing with these subjects did not deviate from a monolithic logic, i.e., an anti-communist view and their portrayals hardly went away from the form of realism. Furthermore, dramatic actions or events often preceded their plot causalities, sometimes giving melodramatic impressions. However, the search for psychology and the absurdity of human existence were slowly noticed after the absurdity of the War started to pass.

On the other hand, commercial theatre was prevalent, which brought comfort to those tired of ideology and the war. In addition to melodramatic and entertaining theatres, Musical-type theatre (*Akgeuk* or *Gageuk*) and *Changgeuk* were popular. In particular, the women's *Changgeuk* gained popularity by stimulating the public's sensibility with the delicateness of women and the beauty of spectacles. Criticisms arose that these commercial theatres did not change much from their performances in the 1930s. However, musical-type theatre paved the way for Korean musicals nowadays, and *Changgeuk* contributed a lot to keeping the tradition of *Pansori* alive, even today.

Indeed, theatres in the 1950s made realism mature while laying the foundation of experimental theatre. As theatre in the 1950s confronted an ideological bias, the division of the country, and the war that followed, it struggled between anti-communism and existentialism, between traditional morals and resistance, and between enlightenment and modernity. Based on these conflicts, Korean theatre found a foothold for an eventual leap to contemporary theatre with diverse perspectives and new techniques in the 1960s.

Notes

1 The exact process of surrender was as follows:
The atomic attacks on Hiroshima and Nagasaki, 10 Aug 1945.
Japan's unconditional surrender to the Allied forces, 14 Aug 1945.
The Japanese King's announcement of surrender to the public, 15 Aug 1945.
The former surrendered by signing the Japanese Instrument of Surrender on 2 Sep 1945.

2 Throughout the years of government establishment and the Korean War, the political situation naturally constrained all activities.

3 Lee, SeokMan. *A Theatre Study of the Liberation Period*(解放期 演劇 硏究). Seoul, TaeHakSa, 1996, pp. 26–27.

4 Ibid., p. 28.

5 Ibid., p. 29.

6 Ibid., pp. 56–109.

7 Shin, Gosong. "Theatre Movement and its Organization." *People(Inmin)*, Dec 1945.

8 KAPF is a proletarian literary group from the 1920s and the 1930s.

9 Han, Hyo. "The Requests of Joaon Theatrical World." *People's Arts (Inmin Yeosul)*, Dec 1945.

10 An independence activist set off a bomb that killed several Japanese dignitaries in Shanghai's Hongkew Park (now Lu Xun Park) in 1932. Immediately after the uprising, he was caught on the spot and sentenced to death at the Japanese Military Court. On November 18 of that year, he was escorted to Japan, imprisoned in Osaka prison on the 20th, and died in Kanazawa on December 19th by firing sentence.

11 The United States and Russia, the Soviet Union at the time, which thought that the preparation process was necessary rather than immediate independence of Korea, divided the Korean peninsula along the 38th parallel and decided to occupy Korea for a certain period of time: the Northern side of the peninsula by Russia and the Southern side by the United States. This is called the trusteeship of Korea, and Koreans' pros and cons were sharply contrasted on the issue of trusteeship.

12 *Joseon Daily Newspaper*, 12 Jun 1946.

13 Park, NoHong. "The Trend of Akguek." *The Movie Era*(Younghwa Sidae), Apr 1964.

14 Yu, MinYoung. *Theatre Movements of Our Time*. Seoul, Danguk University Press, 1990, p.194.

15 The Cairo Declaration and Potsdam's Fourth National Assembly promised the unified independence of Korea, but both the U.S. and the Soviet Union did not give up the Korean peninsula due to the Cold War.
16 Kim, JinSu. "Signal Fire of Realistic Theatre(新劇樹立ue 烽火)." *KyungHayng Newspapers,* 25 Oct 1949.
17 Cha, BumSeok. "Stars are in Every Night (Beoyleun Bammada)." *The Korean Theatre Review*(韓國演劇), Jun 1977, pp. 25–31.
18 Kim, Geongok. "'The Manifesto of Jejak GeukHoe' in The Secret Stories in Jejak GeukHoe (Yeongueukgae Biwha)." *The Korean Theatre Review,* Jun 1985, pp.50–55.

5 The Little Theatre Movement

Just as the theatre of the 1950s could not avoid the scars of the Korean War, the theatre of the 1960s could not be unrelated to a series of political changes, that is, April 19th's Democratic Revolution and May 16th's Military Revolution in the early 1960s. They resulted in total political transformation, followed by fundamental changes in society. After April 19th's Democratic Revolution in 1960, awareness of freedom and individual political consciousness awoke, and civic awareness began to form. There were a few plays regarding April 19th's Revolution, but these plays, unfortunately, failed to initiate a new branch of theatre movements, largely due to May 16th's Military Revolution in the following year. The government after May 16th's Revolution made an anti-communist stance clear and tried to achieve economic development through a centralized political system. *The General Association of Korean Art and Culture (藝總)* was formed to develop integral cultural policies that focused on nationalism. As its subsidiaries, there were various organizations concerning literature, music, art, film, theatre, traditional music, dance, photography, architecture, and entertainment. In the case of theatre, *the Korean Theatre Association (韓國演劇協會)* was founded in 1962. For traditional arts, the government began to nominate the Important Intangible Cultural Property and to hold national folk arts contests regularly. Owing to those contests, revivals of traditional performing arts started, which could be compared to the revivals of the 1930s. As far as theatre was concerned in general, *the National Theatre* mainly presided over the theatre industry until the early 1960s, but two changes took place, which innovated the poor theatrical conditions of the Korean theatrical world. These two changes were the opening of *the Drama Center* and the beginning of the Little Theatre Movement (同人制劇團運動).

The 1960s provided the foundation for developments in contemporary Korean theatre. *The Drama Center* was an exclusive modern theatre ambitiously attempted by the established theatre leader, Yu ChiJin, before the Little Theatre Movement was widespread. In addition, many companies were founded, including the *Experimental Theatre (Silheom Geukjang, 1960)*, *People Theatre (Minjung Geukjang, 1963)*, *Sanha Theatre (Geukdan Sanha, 1963)*, *Bridge Theatre* (*Geukdan Gagyo,*1965), *Free Theatre (Jayu Geukjang, 1966)*, *Women Theatre (Yeoin Geukjang,1966)*, *Ejeotto Theatre* (*Geukdan*

DOI: 10.4324/9781003490708-6

Ejeotto), etc. These theatre companies formed the mainstream of Korean theatre through vigorous activities until the 1970s and 1980s. The *Production Theatre*(*Jejak Geukhoe*), a representative organization of a new coterie theatrical trend in the 1950s, started with a declaration that it would produce a "true modern style of theatre." Through original playwrights, such as Cha BumSeok, Kim GyeongOk, Kim JaRim, and Park HyeonSuk, it proceeded to introduce productions that fit the tastes of contemporaries and also produced translated contemporary plays, such as *The Valiant* (Holworthy Hall and Robert Middlemass), *Youth* (Max Halbe), *Glass Menagerie* (Tennessee Williams), and *Look Back in Anger* (John Osborne).[1] The *Production Theatre* was an example for theatre groups that sought a new theatrical trend at the time, and it served as a catalyst for college intellectuals to take the lead in the theatre movement. This new movement triggered the Little Theatre Movement in the 1960s.

The activities of the Little Theatre Movement were, in a way, a jointly operating system of young theatre intellects. The movement operated with strong solidarity based on similar ideas, such as criticism of established theatre, experiments in contemporary theatre, and a strong will to carry out artistic ideals. Additionally, many of its members were from college extracurricular theatre groups, including companies with coterie awareness in the 1950s. While the new movements of the 1950s revolved around amateur university theatres, the companies of the Little Theatre Movement in the 1960s advocated professional activities, drawing a discriminating mark against the preceding period. The declaration of professionalization by the Little Theatre Movement involved eliminating amateurs in order to start a full-fledged theatre movement with the experiences and accumulated skills of the 1950s.[2] *The Drama Center*, in a way, also participated in the Little Theatre Movement by creating the theatre company *Dongrang Repertory* after Yu DeokHyung, the son of Yu ChiJin, returned from studying in the United States. This chapter will examine the founding of *the Drama Center* and its transition to *Dongrang Repertory* and the important theatre companies of the Little Theatre Movement in order to explore the theatrical movements in the 1960s and thereafter.

5.1 *The Drama Center*

Yu ChiJin, estranged from *the National Theatre*, dreamt of constructing a new theatre with modern equipment in Seoul. He had a chance to have a world theatre tour, which was sponsored by the Rockefeller Foundation, and became familiar with contemporary Western theatres in 1958. With some help from the Rockefeller Foundation in the United States,[3] *the Drama Center*, a theatre with the latest facilities and a thrust stage, had garnered many expectations from its opening.

The opening of *the Drama Center* in 1962 was a dream come true for Korean theatre practitioners. Korean theatre people had not had a theatre solely for theatrical production since the *Oriental Theatre* in the 1930s, which had lasted only briefly. Yu ChiJin chose *Hamlet* for its opening production.

Figure 5.1 *Drama Center*, a Theatre Dedicated to Theatre Founded by Yu ChiJin in 1962. Photo from Seoul Institute of Arts University.

Though it was double cast for the long-term performance, the main members were those from the *SinHyeop* Theatre Company. Lee HaeRang, who had directed *SinHyeop*'s *Hamlet*, co-directed this production with Yu ChiJin. Kim DongWon again played the title role. Thus, *Hamlet* by *the Drama Center* was largely an extension of *Hamlet* by *SinHyeop* in the 1950s, and the acting and directing style were not very different from the former production. It was well received among the intellectuals and critics but without financial success.

The second production was *Long Day's Journey into Night* by Eugene O'Neill with Lee Haerang's directing. The number of audience kept decreasing as the performances went on. After six productions in less than ten months, *the Drama Center* was closed with mounting debts in 1963. Five out of six productions were translated English plays, with the exception of *The Han River Is Flowing* (*Hangang un Heureuda*), Yu ChiJin's original play. Many were disappointed in the decline of the theatre; therefore, many actors and directors left *the Drama Center*. Consequently, Yu ChiJin rented "the theatre to other performing groups and individuals, which invited severe criticism from both public and private sectors."[4] The center was rented for jazz performances, musicals, and even wedding ceremonies.

Figure 5.2 The Drama Center. Photo from Seoul Institute of Arts University.

Yu ChiJin managed to pay off most of the debt in 1963 with the help of a high governmental officer. Ultimately, though, the expectations for a "theatrical renaissance" with *the Drama Center* ended within a year due to its financial difficulties.

As a result, *the Drama Center* contributed to theatre's progress only indirectly, such as by nurturing theatre practitioners and spreading the awareness of theatre rather than by presenting actual theatrical productions. It made an effort to form a foundation for future plays, such as training newcomers through the theatre academy, holding student theatre contests, and presenting the year's winning plays and traditional performances. However, it was also true that the voices of criticism toward Yu ChiJin had grown stronger. His dogmatic activities and problems with the privatization of the theatre were the main reasons for these criticisms. Being conscious of these critiques, Yu ChiJin published the following clarification after declaring that *the Drama Center* would not be privatized:

> I haven't been able to use the latest theatrical facilities during the four years of my business, and it seems that various criticisms have occurred … I will make *the Drama Center* a theatrical stage of everyday performance throughout the year … In order to do this, a budget of 8 or 9 million won per year is required. If this budget is secured for only 3 years, it will be possible to manage the performances without many financial difficulties.[5]

The financial difficulties were always an issue for *the Drama Center* in the 1960s. The sales were always in deficit due to performances that appealed to the Intelli-class but ignored by the public, so despite the initial debt relief, the deficit accumulated. *The Drama Center* could be considered a fraternal theatre, which led the Little Theatre Movement, since its members were peers with Yu ChiJin. Plus, it was a private organization like other fraternal theatres of the time. Yet, unlike these other theatres, the voice of Yu ChiJin was too strong to be equal to any other member's. In short, the 1960s was a period of trial and error for *the Drama Center*.

The characteristics of fraternal theatre became strong when his son, Yu DeokHyeog, began to direct plays upon his return from studying in the United States. After the death of Yu ChiJin in 1974, the name of *the Drama Center* was changed to *DongRang Repertory Theatre* after Yu ChiJin's pen name, DongRang, and the characteristics of the Little Theatre Movement became clear. In 1969, new artist Yu DeokHyeong returned from his studies and began to attract the attention of theatre people by directing and performing full-fledged anti-realistic plays. He made his debut in 1969 in an unusual way: "The 1st Directing Work Presentation." Through this presentation, he was spotlighted for his very poetic, sensuous, and visual directing, and he became the first person to experiment with the introduction of a motion-oriented theatre that Grotowski, Brook, and others attempted after Artaud. These experiments were followed by Oh TaeSeok's *Grass Tomb* (草墳) and Harold Pinter's *Birthday Party*, both directed by Yu DeokHyeong. His efforts became even more full-fledged with the participation of director Ahn MinSu. In the mid-1970s, while establishing the repertory theatre system, which was the will of Yu ChiJin, *DongRang Repertory Theatre* produced movement-focused works that actively utilized audio-visual elements, such as Ahn MinSu's adaptation and directing of *Hamlet*, re-titled *The Prince Hamyeol*, and *The placenta* (胎). These works toured in Europe and the United States and were well received. In the late 1970s, director Kim WuOk (金雨玉) returned from New York to join the group and perform Korea's first Structuralism theatre.[6]

In the mid-1980s, *the DongRang Youth Theatre Company*, dedicated to youth plays under *the DongRang Repertory Theatre*, was launched, expanding the scope of the theatre movement with active performances, such as *Wandering Stars* (*Banghwang Haneun Byeolduel*), *Dreaming Stars* (*Kkeum Kkuneun Byeolduel*), and *Burning Stars* (*Bultaneun Byeolduel*). It was the first time that the theatre received the attention of the youth and was enormously popular. Indeed, the company laid the foundation for the development of youth theatre in Korea.

In 1981, *the DongRang Repertory Theatre* participated in the 5th Korean Theatre Festival[7] with *Self 1122*, written by Kim GiJu and directed by Oh TaeSeok, and in the 7th Korean Theatre Festival with *The Bicycle*, written by Oh TaeSeok and directed by Kim WuOk in 1983. Ahn Minsu directed *King Lear*, in April 1984 at *the Drama Center*. All of these performances, owing to their excellence, are still referred to even today. The *American Lamama Theatre* was invited to the World Theatre Festival held in Seoul and jointly performed *The Trojan Women* in September 1997. The company won the 4th DongA Theatre Award[8] for *Human, Truly Human* in 1967, the 8th DongA Theatre Award for Murray Schisgal's *Luv* in 1971, the 10th Baeksang Arts Award[9] for *Grass Tomb* (草墳) in 1973, and the 16th Baeksang Arts Award in 1979 for *When Spring Comes, in the Mountains.* These awards suggest that *the Drama Center*—and later *the DongRang Repertory Theatre*—stood at the center of Korean theatre. This company brought about a huge change in the Korean theatre industry through the anti-realistic and experimental theatre movements in the 1970s.

5.2 The Beginning of the Little Theatre Movement

The Little Theatre Movement also meant that Korean society had transformed from a traditional Confucian to a democratic, modern one. In other words, it was a process of moving from a unified culture under a centralized administration, such as *the National Theatre*, to individualized theatres. Western culture was widespread in Korea after the Korean War, and the civic consciousness and free will that awakened after the April 19th Revolution accelerated this movement. Of course, the first step of this movement was the *Production Theatre* (製作劇會), founded in 1956, which actively struggled for the creation of a new play for a new era. It was said to be a catalyst in establishing many small fraternal theatre companies.

As the 1960s was a period of political and social turbulence, a drastic change occurred in the theatre world. The fraternal theatre companies, which began to grow in the late 1950s, began to lead Korean theatre in the 1960s. In the late 1950s, as the artists associated with *ShinHyeop*, a representative theatre company, went to the film industry, the established companies gradually languished. Meanwhile, young theatre artists, who had been doing theatrical activities at the universities, boldly established fraternal theatre companies where they experimented with new trends in theatre. Many fraternal theatre companies followed, such as *the Experimental Theatre (實驗劇場)*, *the People Theatre (民衆劇場)*, *Sanha Theatre (山河)*, *the Bridge Theatre (假橋)*, *the Free Theatre (自由劇場)*, *the Women Theatre (女人劇場)*, *the DongRang Repertory Theatre (the successor of the Drama Center)*, and so on. In fact, these fraternal theatres blossomed in the 1970s when the General Association of Korean Art and Culture, a government-supported organization, subsidized nine selected companies from 1974 as a five-year project for theatrical revival. Its intentions were "to promote new [original] plays, to help the moribund Korean theatre to keep running, and to provide theatrical culture for citizens in the provinces."[10] Although there were not many plays of lasting quality, many new original plays were produced with experimentation, and the audience could enjoy a variety of performances. In fact, these fraternal theatres led the Korean theatre industry until the 1980s, and some stayed active until the 1990s. The following are the representative fraternal theatres to be explored when studying contemporary Korean theatre.

5.2.1 The Experimental Theatre (實驗劇場)

The Experimental Theatre (實驗劇場), founded on 3 October 1960, was regarded as the first and the most active theatre company among the small fraternal theatres. While the *ShinHyeop* led the theatre industry in the 1950s, *the Experimental Theatre* led the Korean theatre industry in the 1960s. This is supported by the fact that the number of performances in the 1960s reached 31. Despite such a large number of performances, the time when they began to attract the attention of a large audience was probably in the 1970s. This company performed popular works, such as *The Marriage of Figaro* and *The Happy Marriage of Sir. Maeng's Family* (孟進仕宅 慶事); set up small theatres, such as in Unni-dong; discovered young directors, such as Yun HoJin, Jeong JinSu, and Kim YoungRyul; and began to produce box-office hits, such as *Equus* in the 1970s. In particular, *Equus* was evaluated as the cause of a perceptual change in Korean theatre history since it accentuated the merits of *the Experimental Theatre* with its record-breaking box-office hit.

The activities of *the Experimental Theatre* could be roughly divided into three periods: the first period from the establishment in 1960 to the establishment of a small theatre in Unni-dong in 1975, the second period of the small theatre in Unni-dong from 1975 to 1993, and the third period from 1993 to the present. If the first period was called the era of a purely fraternal theatre, the second period was a period of professional theatre with the characteristics of fraternal theatre. The third period was a lull due to the frequent moves of its small theatre, the death of the long-run leader Kim DongHun, and the departure of core members, like Yun HoJin. It was only until the mid-1990s that *the Experimental Theatre* could be counted as one of the leading companies of Korean theatre.

One of the founding members disclosed the motive for the foundation of *the Experimental Theatre* as follows:

> The start of *the Experimental Theatre* started with the question, "What is the problem with Korean theatre?" We were just breathless with the desire and aspiration for a "good performance," and we had the youthful honesty and humility that qualify ourselves as "Korean theater force[s]" … The plays of the 1950s may have been good for technical reasons, but there was clear lack of poetic passion. Most of them were already old. Moreover, there was no place to train young people … we think what we need most is not technical success but the power of theatre that shakes us, "the Inner Revolution of Humans" or "the Awakening of Humans and Society" that Ibsen and Bernard Shaw have shouted.[11]

For this reason, young theatre artists who had the power and desire to shake the human spirit united under the same ideology, and the first fruit of that was the birth of *the Experimental Theatre*. The founding declaration showed the characteristics of *the Experimental Theatre* more clearly. This inaugural declaration was introduced in detail because many fraternal companies were founded with a similar purpose.

1. We formed *the Experimental Theatre* with a pledge to become an experimental tool for capable and enthusiastic theatre artists
2. We organize ourselves as navigators who will even sacrifice ourselves for the theatre
3. Our purpose is to establish an experimental stage and to establish a theatre of ideology on this land
4. We grow *the Experimental Theatre* with our own dues
5. Our basic operation method is as follows:
   a. Aiming for a general theory in all areas of the theatre, we pursue experimental and concrete experiences centering on the stage
   b. We plan the composition goals of the stage and the directing techniques.
   c. Through the experimental stage, we can each discover and nurture our own talents.
   d. For a staged work, priority is given to the work of fraternal colleagues. In the case of a foreign work, a new playwriting method or stage theory is selected.
   e. In addition to the experimental showcases, complete performances with the audience are regularly conducted.

Since *the Experimental Theatre* started with such idealistic and academic attitudes, it became a leader of Korean theatre at that time.

The founding performance of *the Experimental Theatre* was Ionesco's *The Lesson* (directed by Heo Gyu in a small theatre at Dongguk University). Considering the fact that the repertories of the established theatre at the time was persistent with realism theatre, it can be guessed what the reaction was like. Yeo SeokGi, the main critic of the time, praised the fact that the selection of the repertory fitted well with the purpose of *the Experimental Theatre*, but he doubted how much the director understood the work because the commentaries on the playwright or his play were insufficient.[12] Considering these reactions at the time, it is presumed that the founding performance of *the Experimental Theatre*, *The Lesson*, attracted much attention in its attempt but did not achieve much as an experimental performance or receive any financial success.

As performances went on, it was not easy for poor young people to open their wallets every time and to keep ideological clarity. It was around this time that some members of the group argued the need for transformation into a professional theatre. Eventually, with the performance of the fourth production *Holy Occupation* (GeoRukHan 職業, written by Lee GeunSam), a dual system of organization came into being: a professional theatre company and an academic company. Plus, when *the Drama Center* opened in 1962, many of its members moved there, and *the Experimental Theatre* faced a crisis of dissolution. Fortunately, the members, such as Choi DeokSu, Heo Gyu, Yu Dalhun, and Kim UiGyeong, who had strong affections for *the Experimental Theatre*; Lee SunJae, who came back from military service; Lee NakHun, who returned from studying in the United States; and newly joined Kim HyunYoung and Shin MyungSun, were able to take charge of *the Experimental Theatre* with a stronger team.

The Experimental Theatre changed its trajectory to a full-fledged professional theatre company at their ninth performance of *10 Indian Dolls*. This performance, written by Agatha Christie, a popular British mystery writer at the time, aimed to attract a large audience and make up for the company's financial losses. In 1964, *the Experimental Theatre* participated in the performance festival commemorating the 400th anniversary of Shakespeare's birth with *King Lear* (directed by Heo Gyu). This performance mobilized a large audience for the first time since the founding of *the Experimental Theatre* and also for the first time in theatre history. This performance won the first DongA Theatre Awards: Best Actor (Lee NakHoon) and Best Supporting Actor (Ham HyunJin).

After the thirteenth performance, *the Experimental Theatre* realized it was straying far from the founding ideology, so the company resurrected the pure ideological attitude of its founding. As a result, "Saturday Salong" (土曜 Salong) was formed. These were organized and regularly occurring performances for the purpose of theatrical experimentation. [13]

In 1967, *the Experimental Theatre* began to follow a commercial trend. It selected for its repertoire the French melodrama *Fanny* by Marcel Pagnol. The financial success of this performance, which intended to make up the deficit resulting from the previous low box office sales, made the troupe a considerable surplus. Thus, it openly made the transition to a professional theatre company in 1969. Not surprisingly, *The Marriage of Figaro* (by Beaumarchais) and *The Happy Marriage of Mr. Maeng's Family* (by Oh Young Jin) also attracted large audiences.

In 1970, in celebration of the tenth anniversary of the founding of *the Experimental Theatre*, Oh YoungJin's *Mr. Heo* (許生傳) was performed, and attendance again broke the record. However, after the play's success, it became difficult for actors to devote themselves only to theatre due to the rising TV industry. An overall review of the ten-year *Experimental Theatre* suggests that it performed a lot but had only a few performances that brought the "experimental theatre" name to light.[14]

It was in 1975 that *the Experimental Theatre* built a new home in Unnidong. Having a 150-seat theatre next to DeokSeong Women's University provided an opportunity to transform itself into a theatre-centered company and a full-fledged professional theatre company 15 years after its foundation. At this time, the management methods were also drastically revised to pay regular salaries to personnel in each department. New young directors, such as Yun HoJin, Jeong JinSu, and Kim YoungRyeol, joined the group and brought vitality to the company. In short, the company was reorganized as a professional theatre with its own theatrical space and the payment of wages to its members. Notable performances during this period include *Equus*, *Ireland*, *Green Julia*, *Tumbling Doll Riding a Roller Skate*, and *God's Agnes*. *Equus*, which was performed to commemorate the opening of the theatre space, achieved the mobilization of more than 20,000 audiences for the first time in the history of modern Korean theatre and set a record for consecutive performances for three months. With this performance, *the Experimental Theatre* reached its prime. The performance of *Equus* had three major contributions to the theatre of that period: the establishment of a long-term performance system, the opening of the small theatre era, and the expansion of the audience.[15] In 1992, when the city plan for the restoration of the old palace was established, the Experimental Little Theatre space in Unni-dong had to be closed. Even though the company occasionally performs nowadays, its influence on the contemporary theatrical world is limited.

What is the significance of *the Experimental Theatre* in theatre history? First of all, the era of full-fledged fraternal theatre opened. After the founding of *the Experimental Theatre*, new companies, such as *People, Sanha, Free, Squares, Bridges, Women*, and so on, appeared one after another, giving a fresh stimulus to the theatre world. In addition, by introducing a wide range of works of European writers, such as Jean Anouilh, Max Frisch, Marcel Pagnol, Beaumarchais, Kafka, and Peter Shaffer, the range of translated plays broadened, and new Korean playwrights, such as Lee GeunSam, Kim UiGyeong, Lee JaeHyun, Shin MyungSun, etc., were discovered.

5.2.2 The People Theatre *(民衆劇場)*

The People Theatre was founded in January 1963 with the representative Lee GeunSam, a professor and playwright. Most of the founding members were

Figure 5.3 *Equus* in 1975. Photo from *Yesul Jisikbaegwa* (藝術知識百科) https://www.culture.go.kr/

Figure 5.4 Reproduction of *Equus* by *the Experimental Theatre* in 2022. Photo by *the Experimental Theatre.*

actors from *the Drama Center* and *the National Theatre.*[16] In addition, the central members were characterized by the fact that they studied abroad like Lee GeunSam (University of North Carolina, USA), Kim JeongOk (Sorbonne University, France), and Yang GwangNam (Brigham Young University, USA).[17] *The People Theatre* had adopted a collective leadership system among the three people above. The founding ideologies of *the People Theatre* were as follows:

1. We find a play in which we can breathe with the people
2. We inherit the legacy of great theatre and pursue a new future in theatre
3. We reject the old-fashioned attitude of the established theatre and defend the assertion of a true stage artist[18]

The People Theatre aimed for a thoughtful theatre company with harmonious repertoires; the method was by "creating a playful and elegant play." As indicated in the declaration of *the People Theatre*, the confidence in its human resources enabled the company to challenge itself to rectify the wrongs of the established theatres and the general public. In other words, the composition of its artists, which included middle-aged, new artists, and three major professor-theorists who studied in Europe and America and could speak English and French,[19] solidified the human resources of *the People Theatre.*

The activities of *the People Theatre* could be divided into three periods. The first period was from its foundation to 1973 and was considered the period characterized by many translated French comedies. This period was the time of discovery to find direction. The second period was from 1974 to 1983 when many American comedies were introduced and the company's stylistic re-establishment took place. Through the resurgence, a "new expression" was achieved, which was different from that of the first period. The third period was from 1983 to the new millennium when *the People Theatre* started to move toward popular and musical dramas. *People Theatre*'s *Guys and Dolls* was the starting performance of the third period, which announced the characteristics of *People Theatre* in the 1980s and the arrival of the musical era.

The founding performance was Felicien Marceau's *The Egg* in 1963. This work premiered in Paris in 1957 and was accepted as a representative work in France at that time. The outstanding feature of the work was the use of first-person narration. The protagonist, Majis leads the play by switching her role from a commentator to an actor in the play. Kim JeongOk, who was in charge of its directing, used the technique of overlapping short scenes, recreating the performance he saw in France. A stylized stage set, rare for the time, was also presented. The performance was well received by critics, who remarked that "the delicacy of this play lies in the philosophy of the egg and the cheerful comedy."[20] The inaugural performance was overcrowded and, ultimately, became a huge success.

For the second performance, a salon drama was tried out for the first time at the Bando Hotel—now called Lotte Hotel—in November 1963. Since there were no small theatres in Korea, the company rented the hotel's banquet hall and decorated it with a small theatre atmosphere. Sacha Guitry's *The Villa For*

Figure 5.5 The Egg from *People Theatre*. Photo from *Encyclopedia of Korean People and Culture*.

Sale, directed by Heo Gyu, and Ionesko's *The Bald Soprano*, directed by Kim JeongOk, were successfully produced. The audience could easily enjoy the humor of *The Villa For Sale* since it was a popular comedy. On the other hand, *The Bald Soprano* was an unfamiliar and esoteric absurd play, so the company was keen on the reaction of the audience. Kim JeongOk, an international student in France who had a deep understanding of European culture, had ambitious directing goals. He said, "It is inevitable to experiment with absurd drama in order to find an escape from the dead end where only commercial drama hit."[21] The audience was confused but curious about a completely new form of play, and critics well accepted *The Bald Soprano* as anti-theatre. For example, Yu MinYoung said, "He [Kim JeongOk] was good at interpreting the absurd play like a poet. *The Bald Soprano* contributed to the settlement of absurd drama in Korea along with *the Experimental Theatre*."[22]

The year 1964 was the 400th anniversary of Shakespeare's birth, a memorable year for the theatre world. The festival was the biggest event in the history of modern theatre and lasted about a month from 22 April to 23 May with the cooperation of theatre, academia, cultural groups, and mass media. Six groups—*National Theatre Company*, *ShinHyeop*, *People Theatre*, *Experimental Theatre*, *Fraternal (同人) Theatre*, and *Sanha Theatre*—held performances together, including a contest on the same stage in one place, i.e., various theatre people united and mobilized 40,000 spectators.[23] *The People Theatre* participated in this event with *As you like it*—translated by Kim JaeNam, directed by Yang GwangNam—and gathered 5,278 audiences in ten performances.[24] This event was a great success, but some critics bemoaned that the performances at that time had no aesthetic considerations in the Korean localization of the Western classics.[25]

Noteworthy original plays were also produced by *the People Theatre* during this period. The first one was Park JoYeol's *Rabbit and Catcher* (*Tokki wha* 砲手), directed by Kim JeongOk and performed on *the National Theatre* stage in September 1965. It won the 2nd DongA Theatre Awards for "Best Play" and "Best Actor" and received 300,000 won as the prize.[26] This work was a mixture of the comedy of manners and Molière's comedy of character and was said to be a sophisticated comedy that made the audience laugh while educating them with a keen criticism of society at the same time.[27] Another important play is Lee GeunSam's *There Is Something Extra* (*GukMul IssSaOpNiDa*), directed by Yang GwangNam. This play came into being as a part of the DongA Theatre Awards. In order to discover original plays, the DongA Theatre Awards provided the winning troupe with enough money to perform a new play in commemoration of the Award. Thus, *the People Theatre*, which won the 2nd DongA Theater Award, produced *There Is Something Extra* in the following year. Through the secular success of a young man, this work revealed the current social changes after the war and its structural contradictions in a humorous and satirical way. It ironically suggested the trend of status-seeking and money-worship. It was a sharp criticism of the shameful materialistic values created by the industrial society in the late 1960s.[28] It also received attention for presenting the characteristics of epic theatre in Korea for the first time.

A critic compared the theatre of the 1960s to a period of blueprint when any play was welcomed to be performed to diagnose future directions of theatre.[29] During this period, *the People Theatre* attempted many social satire comedies, whether they were translated or original. There were more translated performances, totaling 12 performances from its inception until the end of the first period in 1973. In other words, the first period of *the People Theatre* was strongly influenced by Kim JongOk, who had mainly pursued French absurd comedies. "Because of the influence of absurdity, which was the dominant literary trend in the West in the 1960s, absurd works were also mainly performed in the Korean theatrical world."[30] Because of Kim JongOk, French plays appeared as a distinctive feature of *the People Theatre*; their performances were valuable owing to the trend of modernity at that time. In short, the first period of *the People Theatre* significantly provided direction on how to proceed in the future.

The People Theatre, which brought forth a fresh perspective in the Korean theatre world, experienced a period of suspension for three years. This was because the founding members, around the age of 30, left the theatre one by one in search of making living as they grew older. As a result, relatively young directors took the lead. Lee HyoYoung and Jung JinSu produced one of America's anti-war plays, *We Bombed in New Haven* by Joseph Heller, in 1974.[31] This production rebuilt *the People Theatre* and, thus, the second period began. The reconstruction of *the People Theater* pursued two novelties: one was a performance system centered on small theatres, and the other was the nurturing of new talent.

The People Theatre made its popular purpose clear: many performances sought amusement. Therefore, the company largely focused on commercially proved performances of translated dramas, such as *A Taste of Honey* by Shelagh Delaney; *Cactus Flower, a Farce* by Abe Burrows; and *You Can't Take It with You* by Moss Hart and George S. Kaufman. The box office results were generally favorable.[32] In addition, the company produced the children's play *Cinderella*, extending their scope of performances to include various age groups. For original plays, Lee HyunHwa's *Kadenza* (1978) and Lee GeunSam's *Gesani* (1983) premiered in Korea. Since the establishment of the studio in 1978, the company produced winning plays of the New Year's Drama Contest with the aim of discovering talented new playwrights, actors, and directors. Plus, the Excellent Creative Short Play Competition, in partnership with the workshop led by Yeo SeokGi, took place.

If the first period of *the People Theatre* pursued authentic French comedies, which suited the taste of Kim JongOk, the second period could be considered a period of full-fledged professional theatre with an extensive search for more diverse plays. A total of 44 performances were held in the second period. Although not included in the number of performances in the second period, steady workshop activities took prominence. The workshop activities played a part in developing the competencies of the members. Excluding the "re-performances," there were more translated plays than original plays; 27 translated plays were performed compared to 17 original plays. Among translated plays, an overwhelming number of 17 were American plays, in addition to some from Germany, Switzerland, and Poland. It is interesting to note that the representative repertoires of *the People Theatre*, such as *A Taste of Honey*, *Cactus Flower*, and *You Can't Take It with You*, premiered during this period. In short, this period marked a leap forward to becoming a popular professional theatre company. In addition, the direction of the repertoires gradually shifted from the French to the Anglo-American style in this period.

The third period of *the People Theatre* began with the full-fledged, Broadway-style musical *Guys and Dolls*, which marked the arrival of the musical era in Korean theatre. The musical *Guys and Dolls*, premiered in December 1983 in Korea to commemorate the 20th anniversary of *the People Theatre* and directed by Jeong JinSu, earned stable returns for a long time. Moreover, owing to the end of the Cold War in the late 1980s, *the People Theatre* also introduced Brecht in Korea. When the prohibition of Communist works was lifted with the inauguration of the new government in 1988, *the People Theatre* produced *The Threepenny Opera* by Brecht under the direction of Jeong JinSu in December 1988. In fact, as democratic fever surged in Korean society starting in the mid-1980s, plays of social accusation and social satire became very popular. The plays of the Soviet Union and Eastern Communist countries, as well as those from South America, which had long been ruled by military regimes, were introduced and became popular in Korea. *Ah, Chernobyl*, directed by Jeong JinSu, which deals with the nuclear accident that caused an environmental disaster, was also introduced in Korea in 1989.

In addition to those plays above, many new and contemporary translated plays were produced, such as Sam Shepard's *True West*, David Mamet's *American Buffalo*, and Simon Gray's *Otherwise Engaged* under the project of "A Series for Contemporary Intellectuals." Also, important original productions, such as *Gesani* (Goose, 83), *Anarchist from the Colony* (*Sikminji eso on Anarchist*, 84), *Pioneer* (*SeonGuJa*, 87), and *The Village of Seven Mountains* (*Chilsanri*, 七山里) (89), drew the attention of theatre people.

The musical *Little Shop of Horrors*, performed at Jeongdong Theatre in 1995, was the first trial of inviting the original members from Broadway. This performance was choreographed by Edie Cowon, who choreographed the musical on Broadway in 1982. Cowon's visit to Korea was supported by an American cultural expert program created by the U.S. Public Information Service to promote cultural exchanges between Korea and the United States. Along with his choreography, the scary reversals of *Little Shop of Horrors* attracted many audience members.

Excluding the "re-performances" during this period, the number of translated dramas was overwhelming, with a total number of 42. Most of the translated plays were mainly English and American contemporary popular dramas. Plays by popular comedy writers, most notably Neil Simon and

Murray Schisgal, were performed side by side. Also, during this period, musicals, the most prominent theatre genre in the United States, began to grasp the attention of Korean theatre people. American plays introduced during this period were continuous sources of popular entertainment in Korean theatre.

In conclusion, the contributions of *the People Theatre* were largely summarized into five categories. First of all, it aimed at the popularization of theatre. The concept of popularization of theatre was viewed as "let's widely spread the plays that can be understood, sympathized, and enjoyed by those who have completed high school education and above."[33] As a way to popularize theatre, it showed interest in musicals and refined comedies as well as children's and adolescent plays.[34] If the success or failure of the popularization could be considered with the number of audiences, *the People Theatre* succeeded in popularizing theatre. Secondly, *the People Theatre* introduced well-known Broadway musicals in Korea, especially *Guys and Dolls*, which was produced very true to the Broadway production. This production showed the authentic style of the Western musical to the Korean audience. Thirdly, *the People Theatre* introduced a variety of translated contemporary plays, especially in the later period, focusing on translated English and American plays, which were generally intertwined with timeliness and popularity. *The People Theatre* premiered *Guys and Dolls*, *Cactus Flower*, *A Taste of Honey*, *You Can't Take It with You*, *M. Butterfly*, *True West*, and *American Buffalo* (from English); *The Egg*, *The Bald Soprano*, and *Who's Who* (from French); *The Threepenny Opera* and *The Visit* (from German), and other works such as *Ah, Chernobyl.* Fourth, from the second period, *the People Theatre* tried to discover new talented people because it had its own small theatre at that time. Many new playwrights, who participated in the Korean Drama Workshop led by Yeo SeokGi, were able to accommodate high-quality productions of their one-act plays. The playwrights included Lee ByongWon, Kim ByeongJong, Choi InSeok, Kim HanYoung, Kang ChuJa, and Jeon JeonJu, and most of the writers who won the New Year's literary drama competition at that time. Although it was a workshop performance with no admission fee, the high-level directors, including Kim DoHoon, Kim HyoGyung, Yun HoJin, Kim GiJu, and Jeong JinSu, produced them. *The People Theatre* consistently held workshops, earning income through general public performances and spending that money in order to find new talented theatre artists. Fifth, *the People Theatre* had various small theatres in various locations, according to its financial situation, and made the most of them. Although each small theatre did not last long due to financial difficulties, it was noteworthy that *the People Theatre* tried to overcome the shortage of performance halls and realized the spirit and effective operations of a small theatre. In short, as such, the historical significance of *the People Theatre*, which took the lead in establishing the popularization of theatre, should not be overlooked.

5.2.3 Sanha (山河) Theatre[35]

At the turn of the 1960s, most theatres stood between the two goals of "re-establishing *the national theatre*" or "the popularization of theatre." *Sanha Theatre* chose and endeavored to achieve the goal of "popularizing theatre." This goal was closely related to the difficult financial situation of most theatre companies at the time. In the case of *the National Theatre*, it operated without much financial difficulty as it was funded by the tax put in place, yet there was a clear limit to the selection of its repertoires under the regulations of national policy. In contrast, *the Drama Center*, the only private theatre of the time, suffered from financial difficulties and internal conflicts. *The Experimental Theatre*, which was founded in 1960, had not settled down as an established company yet. Cha BumSeok, the core member of the *Production Theatre* in the 1950s, saw the need to found the new company *Sanha* when the members of *the Experimental Theatre* doubted their company's identity. Theatre critic Yu MinYoung also explained the situation at the time when the *Sanha Theatre* was founded:

> It seems that 1963 was in an inevitable situation where a theatre company was forced to emerge. It is because *the Experimental Theatre*, *the People Theatre*, *the New Stage Experimental Theatre*, etc., which were wandering under ideology, had not yet found their paces, and the dream of *the Drama Center*, where the energy of the entire theatre world was concentrated on revitalizing the theatre, had been destroyed. As a result, there was no solid vocational theatre company to lead Korean theatre. Of course, the *SinHyeop*, which had a long tradition, was separated and rebuilt from *the Drama Center*, but the *SinHyeop*was not a theatre company that could realize ideals, at least for young and ambitious theatre players.[36]

Cha BeomSeok and Kim YuSeong, with their artistic comrades, founded *the Sanha Theatre* on 28 September 1963. At this time, many members of *the Experimental Theatre*, *the People Theatre*, and *New Stage Experimental Theatre* formed a united front. Voice actors, who were popular on the radio at the time, also joined, and a total of 28 people participated. Their motto could be summarized as "the theatre must be with and for the public" and "the popularization of the theatre." It aimed to produce plays that could present high artistry and breathe with the public at the same time.[37] Cha BeomSeok recalled the foundation of Sanha as follows:

> We didn't even have a declaration that was as grand as the other theatres when we started ... The only thing we wanted was bringing the audience back. Theatre wasn't about pickpocketing fraternal members or selling the tickets to the members so that they could enjoy for themselves, but the idea was to gain a larger audience and spread the joy and value of

> theatre to the audience more widely. We used to describe it as "the popularization of theatre".[38]

The slogan of the "popular theatre" was very realistic. Cha BeomSeok, based on his desperate experience gained through the *Production Theatre*'s activities in the 1950s, introduced the system of a theatre management committee to organize the *Sanha Theatre*'s status as a professional theatre company. For those who thought of the *Sanha Theatre* as a successor to the *Production Theatre*, they learned that the characteristics of the *Production Theatre*, a fraternal theatre, and *Sanha Theatre*, a professional theatre, were quite different.

As a founding performance of the *Sanha Theatre*, Son ChangSeop's novel *The Surplus Man* (剩餘人間) was adapted by Ihm HiJae and performed on *the National Theatre* stage for four days from 14–17 March 1963. *The Surplus Man* is a work mainly depicting the mental and material trauma caused by the Liberation and the Korean War. Cha BeomSeok said, "I wanted to take *The Surplus Man* as an opportunity to settle and heal the mental debt of the past." The audience's reaction to *The Surplus Man* and the box office sales were decent, but the responses of critics and scholars were cold.

In March 1964, *the Sanha Theatre*, which planned to present four performances a year, performed *The Blue Tiled-Roof House* (靑Giwa Jip by Cha BeomSeok) on *the National Theatre* stage, directed by Lee WonGyeong. The box office result was a devastating defeat. The income was affected by the economic recession that swept the theatre industry despite its insistence on the popularization of the theatre. Subsequently, *the Sanha Theatre* performed *The Taming of the Shrew* as part of the celebration of the 400th anniversary of Shakespeare's birth, directed by Cha BumSeok. At this time, the production recorded a surplus, largely owing to the success of the Shakespeare festival itself. As the fourth performance in 1965, the Sanha Theatre produced

Figure 5.6 *The Surplus Man*, the Founding Performance of *Sanha Theatre* in 1963. Photo from *Encyclopedia of Korean People and Culture.*

Thomas Wolfe's *Look Homeward, Angel* (天使*yeo,*故鄕*eul Bora*) with newcoming director, Pyo JaeSun. This performance won two awards for the troupe, i.e., the 2nd Korean Theatre Awards; Rookie Director of the Year Award, and the Leading Actor (Lee SunJae), and the 2nd DongA Drama Awards; Best Leading Actor (Kim SeongOk) and Best Stage Art (Jeong WuTaek). It was the best year for the company to establish its position despite the operating committee members suffering from financial difficulties at that time. In 1966, stimulated by the awards of the previous year, Cha BeomSeok wrote *Tropical Fish* (熱帶魚) and produced it in April, *Beckett* by Jean Anouilh in September, and Cha BeomSeok's revival of *Burning Mountain* (山*Beul*)[39] in November. *Tropical Fish* tackles intergenerational problems and the issue of racial discrimination that began to spread in Korean society at that time. The play specifically addresses the superiority complex of a Christian character. 1966 was also a significant year because *Sanha Theatre* developed *the Cooperative Theatre Council.* It joined hands with other theatre companies: *the Experiment, People, Free, Fraternal,* and *Square Theatres* to lead the way for the theatre industry. The details of this council were shown in a newspaper at that time:

> The six theatre companies pledged to solve mutual financial difficulties and do research on various issues related to the activities of the theatre through "the Cooperative Theatre Council." It plans to install "Theatrical Finance" in order to support a better-equipped stage and better theatre performances. "Theatrical Finance" means that 300,000 won is invested by six theatre companies as part of a performance fund. In addition, in cooperation during the performances, the member theatres will purchase tickets and distribute them among the members, while also aiming to expand the paid audience. In addition, the performance PR people will also collaborate to provide mutual assistance, such as giving a preview of a member theatre's performance in their program booklet.[40]

From this article, it could be assumed that *Sanha Theatre* would reach the level of a major theatre company within the first three years.

According to the performance records of *Sanha Theatre*, Cha BeomSeok wrote an overwhelming number of works from 1963 to 1969. Even if the scope of writers was extended to the 1970s, young artists, such as Yun DaeSeong, Oh HakYoung, and Park YangWon, were the only outside artists who performed at the *Sanha Theatre.* Ihm HiJae and Ha YuSang were excluded from the plays despite their participation in the company from the beginning. In addition, the plays of Yu ChiJin were also excluded, even though Cha BeomSeok made his debut with Yu ChiJin's recommendation. Other performances of translated plays showed signs of being very conscious of the public. Since *Sanha Theatre* was so concerned about catching the public fancy, it, ironically, became isolated from the public; it could neither satisfy the tastes of the sophisticated audience nor expand to a new audience.

Figure 5.7 The 6th Performance of *Beckett* by Jean Anouilh in September 1966. Photo from *Sanha Theatre Company*.

Another characteristic of the works of *Sanha Theatre* was its strong social awareness. It was faithful to Cha BeomSeok's philosophy of theatre, which declared that the works should be related to current society. Most of all, the theatre consistently insisted on the modern idea of amusement to attract the audience. In any case, the company adjusted the ratio between original and translated plays in spite of its efforts for amusement[41]—and endeavored to maintain this approach until it disbanded in 1983. Representative playwright Cha BeomSeok consistently maintained the belief that the repertory system should be selected to attract the audience; thus, original plays as well as translated plays should fit or adapt to the sentiments of contemporary Koreans. Most performances of *Sanha Theatre* did not deviate from this belief.

Cha BeomSeok's insistence on popular theatre brought about the "Popularization Debate" in 1964. Theatre critic and playwright Lee GeunSam published an article in the Seoul newspapers under the title "Theatre and the Public," as if it were talking about Cha BeomSeok. He worried about the plain taste of theatre under the label of popularization.

> Among playwrights who try popular theatre, there is a person who greatly misunderstands. That is, first, the public hates translated plays, and, second, the public only likes plain original plays .... In the reality of

> Korean theatre, the masses refer to the "total audience" with heterogeneous social backgrounds and heterogeneous psychologies.[42]

Kim UiGyeong, who expressed concern over the commercialist trend, and Yeo SeokGi, who had the view that "theatre is a sort of minority art", sympathized with Lee GeunSam. About a year later in 1965, Cha BeomSeok also published a kind of refutation in the same newspaper, "Theatre to the public," which used almost the same words, but the content was completely different. He questioned the people of so-called intellectual theatres who believed that theatre could continuously exist without the support of the general public. He believed that theatre could and should not exist only for a chosen audience, i.e., the intellectual class. Director Lee HaeRang agreed with Cha BeomSeok that the popularization of theatre was to increase audiences as much as possible with easily understandable plays. The debate on popularization at the time, which ignited due to the *Sanha Theatre*, raised the question of for whom theatre was created: how to secure the existing audience and how to attract new members to the theatre. These worries have not changed, even today, and the debate about popularization was the starting point for modern professional Korean theatre. The Popularization Debate in the 1960s was a confrontation over the sensitive issue between the commercial theatre, represented by the *Sinpa* theatre, and the high research theatre arising out of the experimental theatre movement. Those who accused the *Sanha Theatre*'s catchphrase of popularization wanted to preserve the purity of theatre as an art, while those who tried to expand the audience base of theatre wanted to overcome the chronic financial difficulties of the theatre industry. Ultimately, the *Sanha Theatre* was meaningful in that it provoked this debate with professionalism and commercialism.

In short, the *Sanha Theatre* introduced many new original plays and translated plays for a total of 52 performances—including several returning performances—until it was disbanded on 31 March 1983. Since the number of original plays they produced was about 40% of the entire performances, even if this is not over half, it could be said that it succeeded in contributing to the promotion of original work, which was its objective at inception. In the case of translated plays, American works were the most numerous, followed by those from the United Kingdom, France, Norway, and France. Although there were a few classic pieces of Shakespeare and Greek tragedies, most of them were modern realism plays and were in harmony with the realistic interests of the *Sanha Theatre.*

The basic direction of the *Sanha Theatre* was closely related to the concept of popularization. Both original and translated plays were socially relevant at the time. The efforts of the *Sanha Theatre* were aimed at real-time communication with the audience through authentic realism. Its attempt was closely related to its intention of popularization. This trend went along with its belief in realism. *Sanha Theatre*'s efforts continued through local performances in regional areas, which were rare at that time. It discovered outstanding actors and actresses, such as Lee SunJae, Kang HyoSil, and Cheon SeonNyeo, in the days when there were few professional performers. Above all, the company pursued the goal of "popularizing theatre" all the time, which provoked the Popularization Debate.

The Sanha Theatre was the only company that was disbanded in 1983 after 20 years of operation when most theatre companies moved on to the second generation. In this process of moving to the second generation, each theatre company changed its original beliefs and ways of direction significantly. *The Sanha Theatre*'s disbandment implies that the influence of the leader Cha BeomSeok was great, but it also suggests a willingness to realize the foundational goals of realism theatre and popular theatre. In an age when the importance of these goals diminished, the troupe dismantled unlike other fraternal companies. Indeed, *Sanha Theatre* was one of the leading companies of the Little Theatre Movement and provided a driving force to modern Korean theatre. It carved its name in Korean theatre history with only the performance of Cha BeomSeok's *Burning Mountain*, which is considered the peak of Korean realism drama by many critics. Above all, *Sanha Theatre* is a role model for many other theatre companies that wander without direction, as it boldly put forth the aim of popular and realism theatre and consistently followed those ideas.

5.2.4 The **Bridge (架橋) Theatre**

The *Bridge Theatre* was launched on 20 March 1965 with two main intentions: one was that the young theatre majored graduates from colleges wanted to be professional theatre practitioners, and the other was that they agreed to communicate with one another as well as with the audience as the word *Gagyo* (bridge) implied. According to the inaugural statement, its purpose was "to provide a common plaza in the society where dialogue is not blocked" and "to create performances of pleasure for the public." It declared to maintain "a thorough academic attitude" and also planned "seminars and lectures for the Enlightenment in theatre." The statement also commented that performances "will faithfully portray the trends and techniques of the past through internal and external classics and will not neglect to experiment with new possibilities but will not forget the old in order to find new ones."[43] The timeline of *Bridge Theatre* performances could be divided into three periods. The first period in the 1960s focused on national tours with Bible dramas, and the second period from 1970 to 1993 turned to a variety of experiments, like a tent theatre, and introducing the combination of many original and translated plays. After 1993, it focused on *Akgeuk*, a musical-style theatre, starting with the performance of *The Tavern without Address* (番地 *YeopNeun* 酒幕).

As the founding performance, Lee GeunSam's *The Trial of Demostes* (*Demostes ui* 裁判) was presented at the Newspaper Hall, directed by Lee SeungIl. This performance was evaluated as "lacking in sophistication," but "sincere and fresh like young theatre students."[44] As the second performance, Lee GeunSam's *Holy Job* (*GeoRukHan* 職業) and Edward Albee's *The Zoo Story* were shown, reaffirming their original purpose of "a new experiment" and "discovering an original play." The media gradually began to show interest in its performances, reporting that the group was part of an "Active Salon Drama Movement." "Salon drama" seemed to be the solution to the difficulty of securing a performing hall at that time, but it did not continue for long.

In March 1966, the first national-scale tour took place with *The Miracle of the Compost Tower* (堆肥塔 *ui* 奇蹟), written by Lee GeunSam and directed by Lee SeungGyu, which was considered Lee GeunSam's first musical. Taking this first tour as an opportunity, the *Bridge Theatre* planned to tour more often. Prisons, churches, military units, and rural towns were mainly targeted as performance venues. From this time on, the company joined hands with Christian groups and devoted itself to performing Bible plays for a while. With the support of the Bible Theatre Committee of the Audiovisual Education Bureau of the Korean Christian Federation, the *Bridge Theatre* developed Bible theatre and went on tours in prisons, churches, women's shelters, Christian secondary schools, and universities around the country. But, after the company secured its financial status from doing Bible theatres, it then moved on to performing regular plays. In 1969, with the sponsorship of the Catholic Church's Hansen Disease Project Council, the company produced *The Stupid Mr. Fate* (*Miryeonhan PaljaDaegam*), written by Lee GeunSam and directed by Kim SangYeol, and went on a national tour for 96 days. The company performed in a mobile hospital car in any place where many people could gather, such as a school playground, where they obtained the record-breaking audience of 250,000.[45] The significance of this performance is as follows:

> 1) Recognizing the correct interpretation of modern medicine that leprosy was not an incurable disease, 2) Providing a full-fledged play with places around the countries that were culturally alienated, 3) Experimenting with the possibility of Korean musicals according to Korean sentiment, 4) By liberating performances from proscenium theatres in confined conditions promoting the popularization of theatre by performing outdoors, like mask-dance theatres had in the past.[46]

What is important here are the "experimenting with the possibility of Korean musicals" and "popularizing theatre by performing it outdoors." These are the exact expressions of the *Bridge Theatre's* performances until 1970.

The *Bridge Theatre* opened up its new phase in the 1970s with Ionesco's *The Bald Soprano* (*Daemeori Yeogasu*) directed by Kim JinTae. This work was a little different from the nature of its former repertories. From 1970 to 1977, the theatre actively engaged with performances that could possibly get out of the label as a "Bible theatre specialist." In fact, 18 non-Bible performances were staged in 1971 alone, and three or four new works were steadily released after 1973, excluding re-performances. A representative of these was

1971's *The Comedy of Errors*, which was presented at *the National Theatre*, directed by Lee SeungGyu. This performance was highly praised for "marking a turning point in the 60-year history of modern Korean drama because of its first Korean-ization of the Western classics."[47] The play, which Lee GeunSam translated, was transformed by Kim SangYeol into the three old kingdoms of Korea, i.e., Goguryeo, Baekje, and Silla. The media at the time described the secret to the success of this work in five points as follows:

> Some of the reasons why Shakespeare's early romantic comedy was such a great hit is because of the Korean-ization of the Shakespearean play, including ① setting the place and time in the Three Kingdoms period of Korea, ②employing the indigenous nature of language and costume, ③ the involvement of mask dances, folk songs, and the attempt of *Pansori* (唱), ④ the devices and movements that are like fairy tales or cartoons, and ⑤ drawing the rhythm of lines to *Pansori*.[48]

In short, this was one of the first attempts to incorporate theatrical Korean heritage into the Western canon, and these experiments continued to go on for many years to come.

In addition, the *Bridge Theatre* was the first to try "tent theatre." The first performance took place in July 1973 with Tom Jones's *The Fantasticks* (directed by Lee SeungGyu), which first opened at Daecheon Beach resort, followed by 15 performances. It was a mobile theatre that could accommodate 200 people. Later, major fraternal theatre companies participated in tent theatres. Under the title of "79 Summer Tent Theatre Festival," six theatre companies from Seoul held the theatrical festival for one month, including the *Bridge Theatre*, *Theatre 76*, *Theatre Hometown, People Theatre, Modern Theatre,* and *Free Theatre*. The achievement of this Tent Theatre Festival was not significant, but it was a chance to realize the need for a new style. The audiences and actors could become intimate with each other within tent theatre performances since a freer style than a dialogue-based realistic performance could fit on the stage. The participating companies pledged to have a more sufficient plan for repertoires for the next festivals. The *Bridge Theatre* participated in this festival with *Lee SooIl and Shim SunAe* (adapted by Ha YuSang, directed by Kim SangYeol) and received relatively positive responses. For one reason, whenever the scene changed, the so-called "interlude actor" came out and sang popular songs with the audience, and the characters also sang a song of the time when the mood of the play heightened. This fit well with the characteristics of tent theatre. Also, the fact that a real prototype of *Sinpa* theatre was seriously reproduced suited the tastes of the audience. The script was rewritten based on the testimony of an older actor, Go Seolbong—at the time, 67 years old—who worked for the *Oriental Theatre*, a representative high *Sinpa* theatre company in the 1930s. Aside from the fervent response at the festival, the *Bridge Theatre's Lee SooIl and Shim SoonAe* held another significance in their attempt to restore the original form of *Sinpa*.

Figure 5.8 The Fantasticks in 1973. Photo from The *Bridge Theatre*.

Around this time, the activities of the *Bridge Theatre* were falling into a lull. In addition, when Lee SeungGyu, who had been the representative of the company, left for the United States in 1979 to study abroad with the help of the Literary Arts Promotion Agency (文藝振興院), Park InHwan took over the company. Park InHwan commissioned playwright Lee GeunSam, journalist Go MyungSik, lawyer Han SeungHeon, and critic Seo YeonHo to advise on the company's repertories and theatre activities.[49] They prepared a stage for their first production with *The Great Wall of China* (written by Max Frisch, directed by Lim JunBin), a performance commemorating the 15th anniversary of the *Bridge Theatre*. As a result, the company received the DongA Theatre Award. However, after this performance, the theatre's activities slowed down.

The *Bridge Theatre* came back with a new style of performance called *Akgeuk*; *A Tavean without Address* in 1993: the beginning of the *Akgeuk* period. Since 1993 the company had performed more than 100 performances, and except for three works by Peter Weiss, Tom Jones, and Lee GeunSam, the rest of the works were all *Akgeuk*, Korean musical-style theatre. However, *Akgeuk* did not get much attention from the audience as well as theatre people, and the influence of the *Bridge Theatre* on Korean theatre almost disappeared in the 1990s.

In conclusion, the significance of the *Bridge Theatre* on Korean theatre history was, first of all, that it had steadily performed purpose-driven theatres. This included Bible theatre, theatre based on the theme of medicine, and so on. Secondly, it tried to increase the number of audiences. These actions were closely related to its efforts to become a professional theatre. Thirdly, reflecting the general interest in Korean traditions in the 1970s, it tried to utilize those traditions and Korean emotions, sounds, and movements. Various performances were produced in this attempt, such as *The Miracle of the Compost Tower*, *The Sound of Mask*, *The Comedy of Errors*, *Lee SooIl and Shim SoonAe*, and so on. Fourth, it attempted musicals, as seen in *Endless Aria*, *Fantastics*, and *Porgy and Bess*. The musical was a very popular genre at the time, and it was a genre that many other companies were interested in. The musical helped the *Bridge Theatre* to secure its popularity. Fifth, it produced many anti-realistic original plays, especially written by Lee GeunSam and Lee GangBaek, and proved its capability of producing them. Therefore, the *Bridge Theatre* played an important role in the production of anti-realistic plays. Lastly, there were efforts to "popularize" theatre through many tour performances, tent theatre, and reproducing *Sinpa*. Eventually, the *Bridge Theatre* had much influence on the theatre world at the time, and it even created trends of the time, such as touring performances. In short, like the company's name, the *Bridge Theatre*, it was a bridge between the old and the new, the stage and the audience, and the theatre and the public.

5.2.5 The Free Theatre (自由劇場)

Founded in June 1966 with Kim JeongOk and Lee ByungBok as the main pillars, the *Free Theatre* received attention with its distinctive works among the Little Theatre Movement in the 1960s. Its unique theatrical flair attracted not only critics but also the public. In addition, the *Free Theatre* led active overseas performances in the 1980s and 1990s, attracting considerable attention abroad. Its splendid award-winning shows exemplify its appeal: it won the grand prize at the 3rd DongA Theatre Awards in 1966 for *Poverty and Nobility* (*TTaragi ui* 饗宴), the golden prize at the 7th DongA Theatre Awards in 1970 for *Where Shall We Meet in What Shape?* (*Eodisoe Mueosi Doeeo Mannarya*); the grand prize and the best work prize at the 8th Baeksang Arts Awards in 1971 for *The Ballad of the Sad Café* (*Seulpeun Cafe ui Norae*), written by Carson McCullers and adapted by Edward Albee in 1963; the grand prize at the 9th DongA Theater Awards in 1972 for *The Barber of Seville* (*Seville* 理髮師); the grand prize and the best work prize at the 15th Baeksang Arts Awards in 1978 for *What Will It Be?*(*Muoesi Doelgo Hani?*); the stage art prize at the 28th DongA Theatre Awards in 1991 for *Poverty and Nobility* (*TTaragi ui* 饗宴); and the grand prize and the stage art prize for *Hamlet* at the 30th DongA

Theatre Awards in 1993.[50] All of these awards indicate the leading position of the *Free Theatre* had in the Little Theatre Movement.

Even before the foundation of the *Free Theatre*, Kim JeongOk played an active role in other companies of the Little Theatre Movement, such as *the Experimental Theatre* and *the People Theatre*, which were already established. He directed major works of *the People Theatre*, including *The Egg* (*Dalgyal*), *The Bald Soprano* (*Daemeori Yeogasu*), *Thieves' Carnival* (*Dodukdeul ui Mudohoe: Les Bal des voleurs*), and *The Rabbit and the Catcher* (*Tokki wa* 砲手). The *Free Theatre* covered a wide range of works, including absurdist plays, French Boulevard plays, and original plays, but what penetrated these works was the lightness, as revealed earlier in *The Egg*. The "light touch," "speedy tempo," and "upbeat comic tone" captivated the audience before the ideology of the esoteric absurdist drama. Kim JeongOk's work sought the balance between "experimentation" and "popularity," which became even more full-fledged after the foundation of the *Free Theatre*.

The *Free Theatre* expressed its ambition to "create today's true contemporary Korean theatre by inheriting and succeeding Western theatre that originated from Greek drama."[51] By clarifying the "succession of Western theatre," the *Free Theatre*'s performances foreshadowed the sophisticated Western theatre that Kim JeongOk presented during the days of *the People Theatre* company. It was important to provide enjoyment to the audience while mainly performing Italian and French comedies. Accordingly, in June 1966, the inaugural performance of *Poverty and Nobility* (*TTaragi ui* 饗宴*, Miseria e nobiltà*) by Italian Eduardo Scarpetta was performed and directed by Kim JeongOk at the stage of *the National Theatre* of Korea. Yet, the company did not neglect original plays, starting with Oh YoungJin's *A Woman Diver on Land* (海女 *Mute Oreuda*) in 1967. Original plays were occasionally put on stage, especially from Choi InHun (崔仁勳), Lee HyunHwa (李鉉和), and Kim YongRak (金容洛). The company's major works included Eugene Ionesco's *The Bald Soprano* in 1969, Choi InHun's *Where Shall We Meet in What Shape?* (*Eodiseo Mueotsi Doeeo Mannarya?*) in 1970, Goethe's *Faust* and Lee GangBaek's (李康白) *The Marriage* (結婚) in 1975, *Endgame* by Samuel Beckett in 1977, *What Will It Be?* (*Mueosi Doelggo Hani?*) by Park WuChun in 1978, *Flowers Are Blossoming in Windy Days* (*Baram Bunen Naledo kkocheun Pine*) in 1984, *Blood Wedding* by Federico Garcia Lorca in 1985, *Hamlet* in 1993, *Phaedra* by Jean Racine in 1999, *19 and 80* by Colin Higgins in 2003, and many other works.

The Free Theatre had more re-performed works than any other theatre company. For example, *Poverty and Nobility*, which was the first performance, was repeatedly performed until the 1990s, and the same was true for *Where Shall We Meet in What Shape?*, which was an early work for the company. *The Bald Soprano*, which Kim JeungOk premiered during his time at *the People Theatre*, was also a representative repertoire since it was performed as an opening commemorative performance for the *Café* Theatre in 1969. The company performed many re-produced plays while also producing two to six new plays or domestic premieres annually in the 1970s and 1980s. According to its performance yearbook, the production of new works reduced significantly after the mid-1980s. Although it did not totally neglect new productions, the *Free Theatre* continuously reproduced its representative repertories. In order to examine the characteristics of the *Free Theatre*, it is better to examine its complete works together rather than divide them into periods.

One of the characteristics that contributed to the uniqueness of the *Free Theatre* was its preference for European theatre, primarily France. Since the Little Theatre Movement in the 1960s advocated contemporary theatre experiments, it showed great interest in Western contemporary theatre. Unlike Western plays in the colonial period, which were accepted via Japan, Western contemporary plays were directly accepted almost around the same time they were produced. Despite the general trend of emphasizing original plays in this period, the repertoires of the Free Theatre were more concentrated on translated plays. As far as French repertories were concerned, Kim JeongOk directed 20 French plays while the Free Theatre performed 28 French plays from 1961 to 1979.[52] Kim JeongOk's farcical cheerfulness and Lee ByungBok's splendid costumes made the plays' sensational lightness shine. The meeting between director Kim JeongOk and scene designer Lee ByungBok from the inaugural performance revealed the unique tastes and sophisticated sensibility of the *Free Theatre*. Of course, the translated plays of the *Free Theatre* were not limited to comedies; many experimental plays of Eugene Ionesco and Fernando Arrabal were also performed. Ultimately, though, comedic works such as *Poverty and Nobility*, *That Woman* (*Cette femme-là: Geu 女子 Saram Japne*), *Thieves' Carnival* (*Les Bal des voleurs: 盜賊 deul ui 舞蹈會*), *The Marriage of Figaro*, *The Barber of Seville*, and *Tartuffe* (*Sarang gwa 僞善 ui Heujeong*) found great appeal among the public and were re-performed until the 1990s, forming a clear trend of the *Free Theatre*.

Another characteristic of the *Free Theatre* was the opening of *Café* Theatre and the pioneering of salon drama. The performances of the *Free Theatre* in this space included *The Bald Soprano*, *The Zoo Story* (*Dongmulwon Iyagi*), *Prayer* (*Gido: Oraison* by Fernando Arrabal), and other experimental plays from the contemporary Western world. They had styles and views different from realism. The theatre's French sense and style were extended to original plays such as Lee GangBaek's *Marriage*, which ran for a long time. Many premiered plays at *Café* Theatre continued to be performed as the repertoire of the *Free Theatre* even after the *Café* Theatre was closed. In fact, *Café* Theatre was not a theatre exclusively for the *Free Theatre*, nor was it a theatre dedicated solely to plays. The best box office hit at *Café* Theatre, *Tumbling Doll Riding a Roller Skate* (*Roller Sakte reul Taneun Ottugi*), was a monodrama by Kim DongWon of *the Experimental Theatre*. In addition, not only theatrical performances but also traditional performances, such as *Pansori*, took place there, and famous celebrities of the day, like *Pansori* singer Kim SoHee, had starred. By experiencing traditional performances at *Café* Theatre, the *Free Theatre* could expedite the exploration of traditional Korean theatre in the 1970s.

These experiments with Korean traditions became the features of the *Free Theatre* and, therefore, allowed the *Free Theatre* to become global. In November 1970, the *Free Theatre* performed *Where Shall We Meet in What Shape?* by Choi InHoon, who had already gained his fame as a novelist. Choi InHun published the play titled *Princess PyeongGang*, but Kim JeongOk encouraged the production of the play with the new title *Where Shall We Meet in What Shape?* in spite of many colleagues' opposition. He was particularly attached to this work from the beginning because of the work's freely re-interpreted historical folktale. Kim JeongOk referred to this play as an "anti-historical drama" in his writings, inclining toward an abstract style away from realism. Kim JeongOk read the play from the view of absurdist drama while actively adopting elements of Korean heritage in his directing.

Overall, the 1970s was the time when interest in traditions was growing throughout the Korean theatre world. In the 1970s, the *Free Theatre*, which had mostly pursued Western sensibilities before, showed interest in traditional performances. As a result, a full-scale exploration of Korean theatrical heritage began with a series of works in the 1970s. *Dongrijajeon* (東理子傳), written by Kim YongRak and directed by Kim JeongOk in 1974, started an

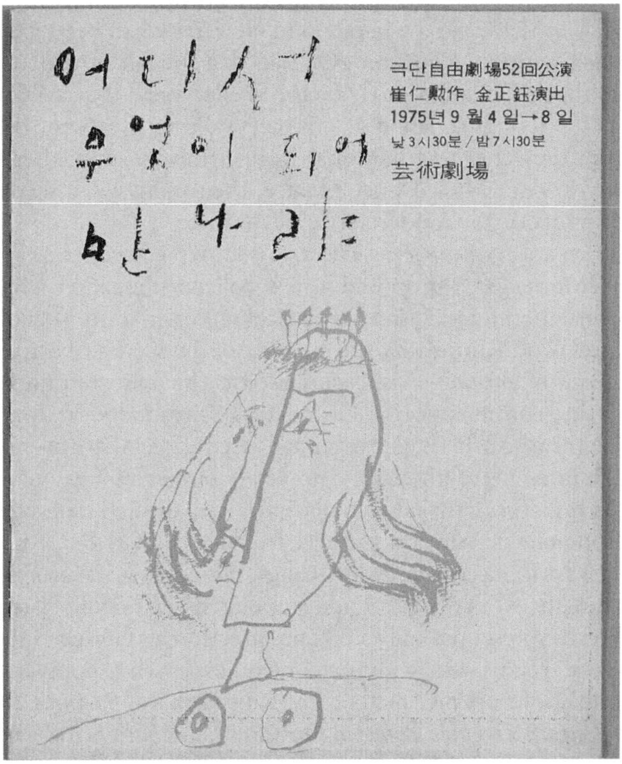

Figure 5.9 The Poster of *Where Shall We Meet in What Shape?* (1970). Photo from Seoul Museum of History.

inquiry into Korean cultural identity. Based on the classic novel *Tiger's Reproof* (虎叱), Kim JeongOk completely transformed the proscenium stage of the Myeongdong Arts Theatre into a playground. The second-floor auditorium and the stage were connected and a real tiger-like presence appeared in the auditorium. It was a work based on the classics of the Joseon dynasty. In the play, when a corrupt local governor is dispatched, the governor appears in a handcart, which was the director's attempt to add modernity.

The Free Theatre started the new experiment of so called "Collective Creation" along with a search for traditional theatrical heritage. In 1978, the *Free Theatre* made a significant transformation with the production of *What Will It Be?* It conducted lectures on traditional theatre, modern dance, *Pansori*, *Samulnori* (percussive traditional beats), and martial arts in their rehearsals. Although the company started with Park WuChun's play, actors contributed to writing new scripts during the process of the group's creative workshops. *The Free Theatre* attempted the Collective Creation because of its mission to find the identity of Korean theatre. Since the tradition of Korean theatre was actor/theatre-centered rather than play-centered and, at the same time, had the characteristics of a total theatre, it naturally resulted in the idea of group creation. Additionally, Kim JeongOk's observation of Peter Brooke's *The Birds Meeting* (1973) in a workshop in New York had been greatly stimulating. Strangely enough, Kim JeongOk said that the performance was similar to traditional theatre, like Korean *Yangju Sandaenori*, a Mask-Dance theatre near Seoul. Kim JeongOk felt that advanced Western experimental theatre was somehow connected to traditional Korean theatre, and, therefore, if he properly knew Korean Mask-Dance theatre, then there was a way to create a Korean yet internationally modern style of theatre.

The group creation of the *Free Theatre* used two core concepts: Collective Creation and Montage. It proposed a new collective creation while denying the conventional method of faithful theatrical representation. It endeavored to create theatrical productions that sprouted from the scenes of actors and their practices. The term "montage" is usually used as cinematic terminology, but it is inherent in the representation of Eastern and Korean arts. In Korean poetry, painting, and theatrical heritage, montage is considered to be more than a simple form; it provides rhythm and complexity by assembling and connecting elements. *The Free Theatre* tried to replace the idea of such montages with the logical development of Western theatre. In *What Will It Be?*, Kim JeongOk intentionally tried to insert traditional songs, dances, martial arts, shamanistic rituals, and designs so that poetry and popular singers could naturally intervene. The director presented only a certain direction and induced the actors to choose poetry or trendy arts. Traditional melodies as well as popular songs were adopted from famous poems, such as Lee SangHwa's *Is Spring Coming to the Lost Lands* (*Ppatgin Deuledo Bomeun Oneunga*) and Kim SoWol's *Invocation of the Spirits of the Dead* (*Chohon*). The reaction of the audience to this work was varied. *What Will It Be?* caused conflicting reactions in the theatre world, but it contained important issues of contemporary Korean theatre, such as the modernization of tradition and controversy over the deconstructive methodology. Overall, the audience's reaction was favorable, but some theatre experts had negative criticisms. Because of this work, the *Free Theatre* continued the methodology of group creation and produced many works, such as *Flowers Bloom Even on Windy Days* (*Baram Buneun Naledo kkoteun Pinda*), *Nameless Flowers Fall in the Wind* (*Barame Ireumeopneun Kkoteun Gigo*), *If a Rooster Does Not Cry, Even a Hen* (*Suttagi An Ulmeyon Amttakirado*), *And They Died* (*Geurigo Geudeuleun Jugeo Gatta*), and *Birds Flying in the Sunset* (*Noeuleul Nalaganeun Saedeul*).

The Free Theatre's methodology extended not only to original plays but also to reconstructing translated plays, such as Lorca's *Blood Wedding* and Shakespeare's *Hamlet*. In particular, *Blood Wedding*, which was produced as the opening performance of the General Assembly of the International Theatre Institute in 1995, was reconstructed with the collective creation of the *Free Theatre*; its new interpretation of the play and the employment of Korean theatrical traditions received worldwide attention. Kim JeongOk emphasized death as the passion in the original work, thereby opening a new dimension of meaning to the original work. The fate, captured by passion, resulted in contemplation and death in the Korean production. Additionally, in the reconstructed stories, the Korean folklore and clowning related to marriage had little to do with the original plot. However, the performance showcased all the folklores of Korean marriage and presented an overall Korean atmosphere. The work also connected the past and present, as well as the regional distance between Spain and Korea, through clowning and criticisms on realities. The unique interpretation of the *Free Theatre* was noteworthy.

The Free Theatre would probably be the company that most frequently performed abroad among Korean theatre companies in the 20th century. Its overseas performances began in November 1979 with *Tango in a Pocket* (*Jumeoni Sokeseo Tangoreul*) and *What Will It Be?*. Together with Mr. Fukuda, the representative of Japan's *Subaru Theatre Company* and the chairman of the Japanese Contemporary Theatre Association, the Korean-Japanese theatre exchange was established. First, in October 1979, Mr. Fukuda performed *The Deep Blue Sea* (*Gipgp Pureul Bada*) at a small theatre in Seoul. A month later, the *Free Theatre* performance was held in Japan with *What Will It Be?* and toured Nagoya and Osaka after the performance at the 300 Theatre of Tokyo. After that, Kim JeongOk participated in the "Third World Theatre Festival" held in Seoul in March 1981 with *What Will It Be?* receiving great reviews from domestic and foreign theatre officials. Taking advantage of the favorable reviews, the *Free Theatre* was the first Korean theatre company to participate in the International Theatre Festival held overseas and to engage in active overseas performances during the 1980s. *What Will It Be?* was invited to perform at the Caesar Theatre Festival in Spain in October 1981, and, subsequently, in November for the Rennes Music Festival in France, and the Royal Tropical Museum in Amsterdam. The second collective created work, *Flowers are Blossoming in Windy Days*, was first premiered at Jinjin, a

Japanese theatre in March 1984, followed by a performance in Korea with *Blood Wedding* in June. It continued performing in the Nansy World Theatre Festival and Epinal Festival in France, then House of World Cultures in Paris, and Hammamet World Theatre Festival in Tunisia. Subsequently, in June 1985, *Flower Is Blooming Even on a Windy Day* performed in Tokyo, Osaka, Hiroshima, Kyoto, Sapporo, and so on for a month, and *Blood Wedding* was performed at various theatre festivals in Spain and France in July. The Free Theatre was invited to various theatre festivals around the world afterward. Its performances, created by the collective group processes based on Korean theatrical heritages, became the major repertoires after 1982. Notably, overseas performances occupied a large proportion of its activities.

In short, the *Free Theatre* largely attributed its success to the creativity of director Kim JeongOk. In his early days, his performances contributed to the creation of sophisticated and absurdist plays in the Western style, and, in his later days, it advanced into the world through collective creation based on Korean heritage. Consequently, the *Free Theatre* gained worldwide recognition along with Kim JeongOk, who became the first Asian president of the International Theatre Institute.

5.2.6 The Women's Theatre (女人劇場)

The Women's Theatre was founded in October 1966 under the leadership of Kang YuJeong. Considering that women's theatres all over the world began in earnest in the late 1960s, the birth of the *Women's Theatre* in Korea coincided with the global trend. The time when the *Women's Theatre* was founded was not a favorable time for female theatre artists. However, the theatre industry enjoyed its boom with improved qualitative performances and stable audiences, adding vitality to the establishment of the *Women's Theatre.* At that

Figure 5.10 Blood Wedding (1984). Photo from *Free Theatre.*

time, the creation of a theatre company exclusively for women was accepted by theatre artists as "an exotic event."

In fact, the *Women's Theatre* was not the first in Korea to create a theatre company only for women. In 1947, just after the Liberation, the *Women's Little Theatre* was born under the leadership of Park NoGyeong, a professor and theatre artist at Ewha Women's University, who graduated from Waseda University in Japan. A total of seven performances, such as *Homeland* (by Hermann Sudermann), *A Doll's House* (by Ibsen), *Wgatch on the Rhine* (by Lillian Hellman), *Tomorrow, the World!* (by James Gow and Arnaud d'Usseau), and *Othello* (by Shakespeare), took place, and the company was disbanded by the Korean War in 1950. About 20 years later, in the mid-1960s, the group called the Women's Theater formed to continue their efforts.[53]

When the company was founded, Korean society was still under feudal rule and patriarchy; therefore, women's activities were very restricted. In fact, theatre artists at that time paid attention to the *Women's Theatre* simply out of curiosity. Yet, the *Women's Theatre* was founded to serve as a stepping stone in expanding the activities of female theatre artists, expressing femininity through the perspective of women, and contributing to society with performances and voluntary services. These were clearly evident in the purpose of the founding of the *Women's Theatre*, as seen below:

> *The Women's Theatre*, as its name suggests, is a theatre where only women gather their will. [...] We would like to proudly present all the wisdom of housekeepers based on the delicacy and persistence of women only. Just as women do good home, wouldn't the theatre movement also require the wisdom of a housekeeper? ... It is a firm belief that the driving force of the Women's Theatre that spurs the revitalization of theatre will greatly contribute to the benefits of theatre. [54]

In short, the purpose of the *Women's Theatre* could be summarized as follows: first, seeking the popularization of theatre; second, contributing to society through theatre; and third, expressing femininity. Looking at the founding purpose of the *Women's Theatre*, its aim of feminism was not achieved, but it recognized the necessity of developing femininity and women's culture.

In order to effectively examine the repertoire of the *Women's Theatre*, the period of its activities could be divided into three. The first period, from 1966 to 1969, was the initial period of practicing the founding mission. The second period, from 1970 to 1989, was the time to develop original plays and introduce diverse translated plays. The third period, from 1990, saw a decline in activity because of leader Kang YuJeong's old age .[55]

As the founding performance of the *Women's Theatre*, Anton Chekhov's *Seagull* was staged at *the National Theatre* stage in November 1966, directed by JinSun Lee. With the selection of Chekhov's *Seagull*, the *Women's Theatre* has implied the intention of advocating realism theatres. For its fourth performance, Kang YuJeong directed Garcia Lorca's *The House of Bernard Alba*

(*Bernard Alba ui Jip*) in July 1968. Since this work, the plays of the *Women's Theatre* kept being directed by Kang YuJeong, and she began to show interest in women's plays. *The House of Bernard Alba* showcased only women and was a highly poetic, satirical play from Spain. In December, the company performed *People Who Made Miracles* (*Gijeokuel Mandeuneun Saramdeul*), modeled after Helen Keller, with direction from Kang YuJeong. This work was centered around female characters like *The House of Bernard Alba*. This performance was sympathetic, and at the climax, it strongly conveyed its emotion. It was highly praised by critics, and the audience expresses good responses, too. The show performed again in January of the following year. With this performance, Kim MiYoung, who played Helen Keller, won the DongA Theatre Award. In February 1969, Kang YuJeong directed *The Women of Shakespeare* as a charity performance to help lepers. In November of the same year, the *Women's Theatre* at last performed a Tennessee Williams' play. *The Streetcar Named Desire* was directed by Kang YuJeong, and Shin Gu won the DongA Theatre Award for Best Male Actor. Tennessee Williams as well as Garcia Lorca became important playwrights that the *Women's Theatre* performed in the future. The theatre even published an anthology of Tennessee Williams' plays for the first time in Korea.

The first period of the *Women's Theatre* took advantage of a motherly image, which was the acceptable image of women of the time. Through this image, the Women's Theatre tried to break the prejudices against female theatre companies. It also tried to contribute to society with charity performances. This was the beginning period of the company trying to find its suitable repertories and, finally Tennessee Williams and Garcia Lorca were chosen. In addition, *Women of Shakespeare* and *People Who Make Miracles* were also discovered in the company's early days.

The Women's Theatre's full-fledged activities took place in the second period. At this time, it premiered many translated plays in Korea and paid attention to the development of original plays. Many Tennessee Williams' plays premiered: *The Night of the Iguana* (*Iguana ui Bam*) in 1970, *Suddenly Last Summer* (*Jinan Yeoreum Gapjjagi*) in 1971, and *Out Cry* (*Gohae*) in 1972. The other premieres were Jean Genet's *The Maids* (*Hayeodeul* written 1947) in 1973, Terrence McNally's *Next* (*Geu Daum*, written 1968) in 1975, and Hugh Leonard's *Da* (written 1973) in 1980. These premieres were the plays with delicate femininity or which only women appear or were the most contemporary controversial works. In addition, many notable translated plays were produced: Wolfgang Hildesheimer's *The Trojan War*, August Strindberg's *Miss Julie*, Noel Coward's *Blithe Spirit* (*JangnanGgureogi* 幽靈), Peter Shaffer's *The Public Eye* (他人*ui Nun*), Arthur Kopit's *Oh Dad, Poor Dad, Mamma's Hung You in the Closet and I'm Feelin' So Sad* (O Appa, Gayeopseun Uri Appa). Somerset Maugham's *The Constant Wife* (*Anaeraneun* 職業*ui* 女人), and Tom Stoppard's *Dirty Linen and New-Found-Land* (*Deoreoun Sogos*).

Figure 5.11 The Poster of *The Street Car Named Desire* (1988) by *The Women's Theatre*. Photo from DA-Arts (Digital Archive of National Theatre Museum of Performing Arts) archive.atck.or.kr.

Many original plays were developed, and many of them premiered. Starting with Lee JaeHyun's *The Sleepwalking Patient* (夢遊病 患者) in 1970, six creative plays followed in 1974 and 1975. The next performance was Moon JeongHee's poetic play called *The Birth of a Butterfly* (*Nabi ui* 誕生), which was derived from the tale of the three kingdoms, or the three countries of the old Korea. Both the writer Moon JeongHee and director Kim JeSun were rookies in this performance. Next, Jeon JinHo's *The Hiccups of the Moon* (*Dalnara ui Ttalgugjil*) performed in Seoul and was followed by a tour in the Chungbuk region. In January 1975, the *Women's Theatre* celebrated "the World Women's Year" set by the United Nations and had a commemorative performance in April, where Kang SeongHee's *Backlight* (逆光) depicted the creative pains of a woman. Roh KyungSik's *Daljip*,[56] Oh YoungJin's *The Dancer* (舞姬), Lee JaeHyun's *The Red-fruit Spicebush* (*Bimok*), and Hwang SeokYoung's *Mountain Chrysanthemum* (山菊) followed. The *Women's Theatre* participated in the Second Korean Theatre Festival (大韓民國演劇祭) with Hwang SeokYoung's *Mountain Chrysanthemum* directed by Kang YuJeong in 1978, which won the company the Best Works Award, the writer Hwang SeokYoung the Drama Award, and actor Lee JuSil the Women's Acting Award. This play was known as the people's national tragedy during the Enlightenment period and the colonial era, and was staged for Korean Americans, touring in Hawaii, New York, Washington, Chicago, and Los Angeles throughout February of 1979. In this period, the *Women's Theatre* also opened a small theatre called "Edinburgh Little Theatre" in April 1972. It was an exclusive theatre of the *Women's Theatre*, which hastened to open. However, it had to close three months later due to the financial difficulties.

In the first half of the 1980s, the *Women's Theatre* again won the Korean Theatre Festival Drama Award in 1981 with Cha BumSeok's *O Crane, My Love* (*Hakiyeo, Sarangilraera*). Regarding the play, Cha BeomSeok and Kang YuJeong said,

> The folktale from the distant past that three women transformed into three islands in the morning may be the symbol of "truth, goodness, and beauty" or "knowledge, affection, and will" that humans want to pursue. This is how we took the motives of this work.[57]

This play was staged for the tour in the U.S. in commemoration of the 100th anniversary of diplomatic relations between Korea and the United States in 1982. Roh GyeongSik's *The Tower* (塔) performed in May 1984. *The Tower* is a story about Queen SeonDeok of Silla and a man Jigwidongja who admires her. With Yun JoByeong's *Bonfire Morning Dew* (*Modakbeul Achim Iseul*), which was staged in September 1984, the *Women's Theatre* again participated in the Eighth Korean Theatre Festival. Yun JoByeong received the Best Play Award and the actor Shim YangHong received the Best Male Acting Award. This performance depicted true human nature in a life or death situation, when five miners are trapped due to a gas explosion in a coal mine. This performance also won the Best Prize of Production, Drama, Lighting, and Music Composition by the Korean Theatre and Film Arts Awards (currently Baeksang Arts Awards, established by the Hankook Daily Newspapers) as well as the Theatre Critics' Awards. It was a performance that showed Kang YuJeong's belief in realism theatre. Critic Han SangCheol said, "Kang Yujeong's directing had reached its peak in this performance."[58] *The Organ Sound* (風琴 *Sori*), which participated in the Ninth Korean Theatre Festival in 1985, illuminates the lives of two women in their mid-60s who lived at the end of Japanese colonial rule. This performance showed the maturity of Korean realism drama. This play of Yun JoByeong's also received the Best Drama Award. A critic said the following:

> In particular, Yun JoByeong's realism deepened the realism initiated by Yu ChiJin in the 1930s as much as possible … As Lukács pointed out, true realism is the dialectic of reality. Considering that the effort to overcome the pain and find a brighter life is the world of realism, Yun JoByeong's work is outstanding. In particular, it is excellent to bring the lost folk songs and dialects to life in the work. The realism Korean drama has reached its peak of maturity.[59]

When the *Women's Theatre* celebrated its 20th anniversary in 1986, *Across the River to NeoBuSil* was performed along with the reproduction of *Oh Dad, Poor Dad, Mamma's Hung You in the Closet and I'm Feelin' So Sad* and *Respectable Whore* (*Jongyeung Halmanhan Changyeo*). Many theatre people celebrated the *Women's Theatre* with comments on its activities and contributions, including the following:

> The power of *the Women's Theatre (女人劇場)* comes from the spirit of Kang YuJeong (姜由楨). While she possesses the sensibilities of the femininity, she also has a remarkable driving force and strong will... Another contribution of the *Women's Theatre* may be the productions of Tennessee Williams. The characters of Williams, such as Blanche, have consistently been loved by Korean women. Kang YuJeong's works of Williams have succeeded in mobilizing many audiences. There is no more convincing evidence of success.[60]

Another comment follows:

> As a woman, Kang YuJeong began to cultivate the land with a hoe- her passion for plays in a barren theatre where even men could hardly cultivate anything. With tireless energy and fighting spirit, she has overcome many hardships and trials. To this day, she has performed total of 77 performances and, in particular, several overseas—all over the United States—performances. Through such activities, the *Women's Theatre* has made various contributions to the Korean theatre world. Appealing to the hearts of Koreans with original realism plays, the *Women's Theatre* has also intensively performed several works by Tennessee Williams to reflect on the pain of female existence. For the tenth anniversary of its founding in 1976, the *Women's Theatre* first published an anthology of Tennessee Williams's plays. Now is the time to find a more certain identity as an mature theatre company. I can't stop looking forward to the development of a unique theatre company by establishing its own personality.[61]

Commentors, including the above two, highly regarded Kang YuJeong's leadership in the *Women's Theatre*, agreed that the *Women's Theatre* did a solid job with the works of Tennessee Williams, and also performed many original realism plays.

In addition, the *Women's Theatre* sought original plays for women's liberation from a woman's perspective. Yun JeongSeon's *Free Spirit* (自由魂) was performed in September of 1987 as a participant in the Korean Theatre Festival. *Free Spirit* was "fresh in drawing the love and life of Hwang Jini, a female poet and geisha of Joseon dynasty, from the feminine liberation perspective."[62] The director Kang YuJeong said, "Hwang Jini, who was born in such an era, wanted to be a woman and a human being and resisted with her times ... fighting for freedom."[63] Although it was limited to personal resistance, Hwang Jini's critical mind was significant and she could be considered the first feminist in Korea.

When looking at the second stage of the *Women's Theatre*, the most obvious feature was the effort to match the ratio between the translated and the original plays. During this period, 47 translated plays were held—while 36 plays were original, some of the others were reproductions of them. It tried to accommodate a greatly more original plays compared to the early days. There were 22 translated plays and 19 created plays, though not all of them were premiered.[64] As a result, it could be said that the *Women's Theatre* seriously recognized the lack of original dramas, which was a chronic problem in Korean theatre overall, and contributed to its development. Also, performances during this period did not fully practice the ideas of feminism, but at least dealt with women's lives. Many works, such as *The Maids*, *Daljip*, *Across the River to NeoBuSil*, *Free Spirit*, and *Mother* illuminated the stories of women's lives. Through these works, a variety of women's roles, including sisters, wives, neighbors, mothers, and daughters, were brought up on the stage. Although their feminist representations were not strong enough for liberal feminists, the *Women's Theatre* evoked the roles of women in the patriarchal society and provided opportunities to female theatre artists.

The third period started with the staging of two different prominent works. Jo WonSeok's *Return* (歸路) in 1990 dealt with the controversy over sexual violence. About the tragedy of the court's actual ruling that protected chastity as worthy of protection, the director Kang YuJeong said, "I made this work, thinking that one day when we are liberated from the bonds of women's chastity stipulated by history, we will be able to declare that we are the same human in true sense."[65] In September of the same year, Bae BongGi's *Season of Infertility* (不姙*ui* 季節), a participant in the Seoul Theatre Festival, was staged. This work, which dealt with the problem of secondary education, was criticized for the failure of effective stage-language in spite of its clear theme.

In February 1991, William Shakespeare's *Macbeth* was performed in commemoration of the 25th anniversary of the *Women's Theatre* as well as its 100th performance. It was a big event, but it did not get remarkable results worthy of its scale. In 1992, Anton Chekhov's *Three Sisters* performed and was well received. This was the second time the *Women's Theatre* performed Chekhov's plays; *Seagull* was its first and founding performance. Chekhov's women were the characters whom the *Women's Theater* could fully embrace. This performance was "a sensational performance with music and visual effects and brought out the essence of Chekhov's drama well expressing dreams and ephemerality of life."[66] In 1996, the 30th anniversary of the Women's Theatre included the productions of Lee HyunHwa's *Kirie*, which dealt with pro-Japanese issues to commemorate the 50th anniversary of the Liberation; Edward Albee's *The Tall Three Women*, which won the Drama Desk Award of the United States for Outstanding Play in 1994; and Park JeHong's *Useless Man* (*Sseulmo Yeopneun* 人間).

Though the third phase of the *Women's theatre* is still in progress, the active period of the *Women's Theatre* seemed to end with Kang YuJeong's death in 2005. The *Women's Theatre* is very meaningful for a reason that it has maintained a female theatre company in the male-centered theatre industry since its foundation. Overall, the company has contributed to Korean theatre with excellent translated and original productions, and many of them were premiered; it nurtured numerous talents, including female theatre artists and kept pioneering spirits regarding the women's movement. It criticized Korean male-centered theatre world and laid the foundation for the more active feminist theatres, though it did not portray the depth and diversity of feminism. Indeed, the *Women's Theatre* is truly a living witness of the history of feminism in Korea by constantly exploring and demonstrating women's skills and power.

5.2.7 The Ejeotto Theatre

The *Ejeotto Theatre*, which was launched in 1967, was probably the most important experimental company with tenacity and individuality at the beginning. The *Ejeotto Theatre* agreed with other fraternal theatre companies of the Little Theatre Movement to establish the artistry of theatre, to challenge the established theatres, especially commercial theatres, and to pursue the spirit of experimentation for the creation of theatre in a new era. Bang TaeSu, the representative of the *Ejeotto Theatre*, recalled its start and beliefs as follows:

> The name "*Ejeotto*" came from interjections, such as "E...Jeo...Tto...," and its start was like those interjections without definite meaning. The *Ejeotto Theatre* thought that theatre should reclaim the nature of human being, and believed that theatre should start again from human nature. We were to prove with the proposition that theatre was human confirmation and theatrical expression was human expansion. To that end, we held a debate and deepened ourselves in the Eastern philosophy. Above all, the *Ejeotto Theatre* tried to share a common consciousness through commune together and desperately intending to make their assembly a creed. The *Ejeotto Theatre* professed itself as the "avant-garde system" of Korea.[67]

Even among the fraternal theatre companies, the *Ejeotto Theatre* was neglected by and somewhat isolated from the others. The *Ejeotto Theatre* attempted extraordinarily experimental performances from its beginning. These performances were attempts to change audiences' perceptions through experimenting with the structure or form of plays. Bang TaeSu divided the period of *Ejeotto's* activities into two: the period from 1966 to 1976 of experimental theatre and that of conventional theatre afterward. Thus, the earlier part of its activities is considered historically more important than the later part in the development of Korean theatre. As Bang TaeSu said, the experimental

Ejeotto Theatre might resemble the Little Theatre Movement of the Western theatre and was the most avant-garde among the experimental companies of the Korean Little Theatre Movement from the 1960s.[68]

The name "*Ejeotto*" was acquired with the opening of its small theatre, and the members were from Deonguk University's theatre department and *the Drama Center*. The *Ejeotto Theatre* was the first fraternal theatre that owned a small theatre space at that time, and pantomime was performed as the opening performance. Although it was claimed to be the first experimental mime performance in Korea, the performance itself was a presentation of mime-like gestures. Even so, it got good responses from the audience who were looking for experimental performances, and every performance was sold out. The admission was free; a donation box was installed at the entrance instead. The audiences of the *Ejeotto Theatre* were either those who demanded new experiments or who had family-like, unconditional solidarity with *Ejeotto*. Bang TaeSu recalled this pantomime performances as saying,

> having a pantomime performance presupposed understanding of the audience and dissemination of pantomime, but above all, it was an experimental theatre as a part of the Little Theater movement. Pantomime was introduced as a type of avant-garde theatre. Performances involved portraying a fragmentary story with gestures.[69]

The *Ejeotto Theatre* continued to experiment. On 20 December 1969, graffiti from public restrooms was collected, and a joint composition without a specific author was performed. The company also created works through interviews with 150 pairs of young lovers on the back-wall road of DeokSuGung Palace. On 1 July 1970, in front of the Myeongdong Arts Theatre, a street performance was tried with a crowd, but the actors were arrested by the police. Another street play was prepared; on 15 August 1970, a long street work from Sajik Park to the Han River was performed, but the production team was handed over to a summary trial.[70] All of these experimental performances at that time seemed to be regarded as merely strange behaviors that destroyed social order. However, it was true that the more it was persecuted, the more it became famous. On the significance of street theatre, Bang TaeSu said,

> [e]ven if it is not pushy, the theatre must experiment from various angles toward the bright future. Even if an experiment was not fruitful, it should be continued as a challenge toward the authoritatively established theatres and as a proof of the free spirits of artists.[71]

Additionally, the characteristics and status of the *Ejeotto Theatre* at that time were summarized by Cha BeomSeok, as follows:

> In the theatre world, the name Bang TaeSu was still unfamiliar and unknown. However, he expressed his faith to maximize his experiments with his voices and gestures. His theatrical ideology and approaches to show the energy of youth while rejecting all existing theatre: the company belonged to a kind of heresy. And his emphasis to place importance on gestures, that is, movements instead of language, could be seen as his unique work attitude.[72]

Another critic considered the *Ejeotto Theatre's* attempts to break down the old wall of fixed ideas had fairly well reached the audience. He explained its work for the future of Korean theatre.

> Rejecting language and trying to deliver stories through gestures, desiring to build a full-fledged theatre space without separating the audience and the stage, expanding the means of expression to break away from the premise of traditional theatre, and exploring....We know that everything was *Ejeotto's* contribution to the future of experimental theatre.[73]

The assessment above, which showed the perspective of the theatre world well, clearly told the characteristics and reputation of the *Ejeotto Theatre.*

The interest in mime, which was shown in the opening performance of the *Ejeotto Theatre*, continued in the 1970s. In March 1972, *Folk Mime* was presented by Kim SeJung at the *Ejeotto Theatre.* With this opportunity, the Korea Mime Research Institute was founded in the fall of 1972 with the intention of creating a new theatre by actively introducing mime to theatre. *The Unfair Thief* (*Eokulhan Doduk*) (by Kim YongRak, directed by Bang TaeSu) was then performed in commemoration of the founding of the Korea Mime Research Institute. Through this play, the first generation of pantomimists in the early 1970s, including Yu JinGyu, Kim SeongGu, and Kim DongSu, came into being.[74] The *Ejeotto Theatre* also held the following symposium titled "Reform of Acting" on 2 March 1974. Kim SeJung emphasized the importance of reviving traditional movements, as follows: "The reform of acting will be achieved when it utilizes Korean traditions, such as dance-movements and *Pansori* vocalization."[75] It was a meaningful event in that it attempted to introduce Korean folk theatrical traditions into Western mime gestures.

The *Ejeotto Theatre* hosted the First Young Theatre Festival in May and June 1973. The festival attracted more than 2,000 audiences, with more than 100 young artists participating from the total ten fraternal theatre companies, including the *Bridge Theatre, Dongin Theatre, Contemporary Theatre, Ejeotto Theatre, Folk Arts Theatre, Experimental Theatre, Ark Theatre,* etc. Although the Young Theatre Festival was not financially successful, the hundred amateur theatrical artists pursued their own theatrical expressions. It showed enough motivation to break away from the stereotypes of conventional theatres with themes, gestures, and directing techniques. Such young theatres were significant in that they were aimed at post-Broadway and experimental theatre. The *Ejeotto Theatre* submitted the production of *Scent* (*Hyanggi*) for this festival and received positive responses from the audience.[76]

Soon after the Young Theatre Festival, The *Ejeotto Theatre* tried psycho-drama along with the *Bridge Theatre* in the neurology ward of Ewha Woman's University Medical School in September 1973. Psycho-drama is one of the treatment techniques founded by Jacob Moreno as a method of group therapy. Basically, it originated from improvisational theatre in which the therapist, its assistant and the lead patient were interwoven. At that time, *Pattern* (*MuNuii* directed by Bang TaeSu) and *My You* (*Na ui Dangsin*; directed by Lee SeungGyu) were performed.[77] These were Korea's first psycho-drama performances written with the purpose of treating mental health patients.

The *Ejeotto Theatre's* small warehouse theatre (倉庫劇場) opened on 15 May 1975, as its third small theatre space. Among small theatres that *Ejeotto* owned, this small warehouse theatre was the most suitable for the *Ejeotto Theatre's* experimental performance. Its arena stage was a variable stage with 100 seats; it was a mixture of a protruding stage and a circular stage. There were entrance doors and underground passages on both sides of the stage, which were effective in creating changes and three-dimensional effects. Therefore, this narrow space completely eliminated the sense of separation and distance between the stage and the auditorium, so the audiences were able to enjoy completely different theatrical atmosphere from that of the conventional proscenium theaters. The opening commemorative performance was *Setani* (poetry by Park JeongOk, play adaption by Lee EonHo, directed by Park JeCheon). The celebratory performances by six theatre companies were followed by the performance of *Snake* on 25 July.[78] *Snake,* with sharp social consciousness and criticism, aroused sympathy and mobilized 3,500 audiences, which could be a success in a small theatre with the size of 100 seats. In the experimental performance of *Snake*, the 27-year-old young director Bang TaeSu used all the sounds that could be produced by human bodies, solemnly visualizing primary human instincts, and creating the harmony between individual and group acting. Despite the successful staging of this new attempt, the controversy on whether this show was a theatrical performance or not was seriously debated, not only among the audiences but also among the theatre artists. Regarding the new attempts shown by the young theatre company, some advocated the work as showing the possibility of a new type of theatre to the audience who tired of realistic plays, while others believed the work aroused confusion, ambiguity, displeasure, and anger within the audience. Also, there were accusations of exposing the ugliness of life. With enough attention to arouse fierce debates, the performance was successful in mobilizing the audience, but the content of the work was severely transformed due to the censorship. For example, the Performance Ethics Committee ordered that the scenes of the assassination of John F. Kennedy and Martin Luther King, Jr. had to be changed because they were too violent, but allowed the scenes in the Garden of Eden. As a result, the artist's intention to contrast how human

Figure 5.12 The Reproduction Poster of *Snake* (1978). By *Ejeotto*. Photo from DA-Arts.

corruption shown in the Bible and in the modern history could not be seen in the performance. Such a case was just one example in which the censorship of the authorities distorted the content of the work.

As examined, the first part of the *Ejeotto Theatre* was engaged in enthusiastic experimental activities with passion. Its active experiments began with the opening of *Ejeotto's* second small theatre in 1972. The experiments explored mime theatre, street theatre, and experimental theatre based on sounds and body movements.[79] During this period, mimes performed eight times, original plays 15 times, and translated plays six times out of a total of 29 performances, i.e., they had more creative plays than translated plays. In the case of original plays, *Illustration at the Crossing* (*GeonNeolMok ui Saphwa*), *Voice* (*MokSoRi*), *Confusion and Arrangement in the Museum of Art* (美術館*eseoui* 混沌 *gwa* 整理), and other non-realistic works were performed. In terms of playwrights, four pieces were from Yun JoByeong; three from Kim YongRak; and three from Yun DaeSeong were presented among a total of 15 original drama performances. In particular, during this period, the *Ejeotto Theatre* got involved with playwright Yun JoByeong, whose plays changed from the non-realistic to the realistic, which influenced *Ejeotto's* performances turning toward realism. In the case of translated plays, the works of Megan Terry and Jean-Claude Van Itallie, who were the writers of the American avant-garde theatre, appeared on the stage. Two of Beckett's absurdist plays and two of Jean-Claude Van Itallie plays were performed out of a total of six translated plays. Ultimately, the translated plays were mainly experimental in the early period of the *Ejeotto Theatre*.

The *Ejeotto Theatre* began to change when it participated in the First Korean Theatre Festival, hosted by the Ministry of Culture in 1977. The festival became the first opportunity for writers and directors to further evaluate the potentials of the theatre company.[80] As a result, nine theatre companies participated in the First Korean Theatre Festival, which showcased a total of 105 performances and mobilized 3,800 audience members. The *Ejeotto Theatre* was honored with the Minister of Education's Award for *Sparrows and Locomotives* (*ChamSae wa* 機關車), written by Yun JoByeong. The *Ejeotto Theatre*, with direction from Bang TaeSu, successfully participated in the Korean Theatre Festival with Yun JoByung's three plays on farming areas. In 1981, *Farmland* (農土), a participant in the Fifth Korean Theatre Festival, won the Best Theatre Award and the Best Male Acting Award (Kim JongGu). It was also awarded the Best Theatre and Drama Awards at the 18th Korean Theatre and Film Arts Award Ceremony (now known as the BaekSang Award), hosted by the *Hankook Daily Newspaper*. *Farmland* was highly praised by many critics at that time as a performance that showed the development and achievement of realism in Korea. What made this work stand out was that the writer sharply captured the problem of the rural community being alienated in the process of modernization. In 1982, *The Woman-Farmer* (農女) participated in the Sixth

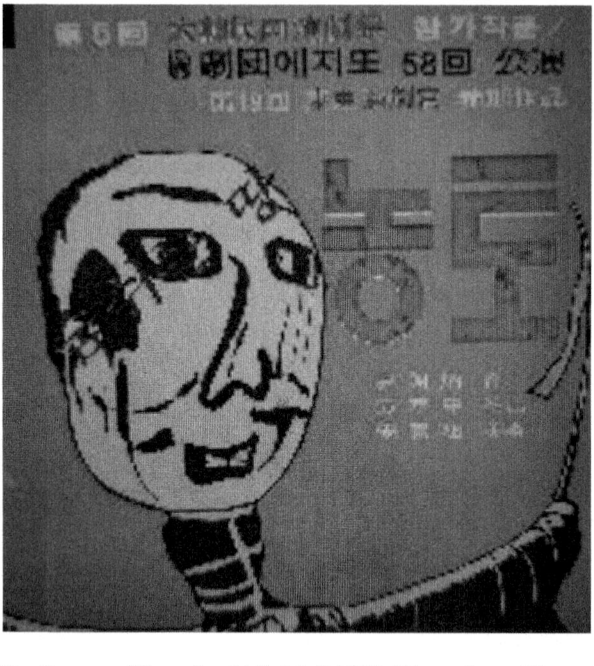

Figure 5.13 The Poster of *Farmland* (農土) (1981). Photo from *Ejeotto Theatre*.

Korean Theatre Festival. It is a work depicting the life of a woman who was born as the daughter of a servant and persistently defended the farming countryside, along with the social changes of the time. The play reminded audiences of the downfall of the countryside realistically in her lonely fights and deepening isolations. In addition to *Farmland*, it was very noteworthy in that it opened up another possibility of realism that showed restraint in expressing emotions and event-centered plots. In 1983, *The Farmer (農民)*, the last work among the farming triology by Yun JoByeong, raised the farmers' past slavery issue, but it failed to show the contemporary problems.

It was financially sound for the *Ejeotto Theatre* to attend the Korean Theatre Festival and receive awards, but the company lost its original experimental impetus and characteristics. Thus, its performances in the second period were not considered critically as important as those of the first period. Its contributions in Korean avant-garde theatre history were mostly achieved during the first period. Regrettably, the *Ejeotto Theatre* moved its headquarter from Seoul to Busan after 1997, and it was isolated from the mainstream theatrical world.

Overall, the *Ejeotto Theatre* 1) was ahead of the times with many avant-garde performances, 2) was a center for young people new to the theater industry, 3) presented performances centered on original plays, i.e., more creative than translated plays, and 4) owned small theatres as many as seven theatres. Indeed, the *Ejeotto Theatre* was a pioneer in that it had already shown its avant-garde characteristics before the experimental theatre circumstance in the 1970s was established. Since this led to the participation of the audience, the *Ejeotto Theatre* contained some of the seeds of postmodernism, the main discourse of the theatrical world today. *Ejeotto's* activities were, in a few words, "a history of rebellion," as Robert Burstein expressed it.[81] Just as Western theatres have a history of backlash against traditional theatres up to this day, *Ejeotto* tried similar actions. Its activities were carried out as the reaction against the existing conventional theatres. Although the *Ejeotto Theatre* was not deeply rooted in the history of Korean theatre—even theatre practitioners thought of the company as a cult, its issues were noteworthy because they presented the further direction for avant-garde theatre. Ultimately, the historical significance of the *Ejeotto Theatre* was that it deviated from the existing conventional theatre and prepared a new alternative method for contemporary Korean theatre.

Conclusion

The Little Theatre Movement, which began in the 1960s, was a joint operating system of young theatre artists with strong solidarity based on ideological homogeneity. Many other fraternal theatre companies joined the Little Theatre Movement in addition to the theatre companies discussed above. The examined companies were the representatives of this movement indeed, not in name. They renovated Korean theatre with active contemporary theatrical experiments, criticism of established theatre, such as *SinHyeop* and *the National Theatre*, and new artistic visions.

These fraternal companies actively worked until the 1980s, and they demonstrated the rapid generational changes in the Korean theatre world, providing the foundation for diversity and modernity. They consequently broadened the scope of Korean theatre; they had urged the establishment of new ideologies or approaches to theatrical performances. Their aesthetics were to exercise experimental theatres. In short, the Little Theatre Movement aimed at experimental theatre as a way to break away from realism at that time.

The other objective of the Little Theatre Movement was the expansion of the audience group. The declaration of "professionalization" led the awareness of the audience as the basis of theatrical activities and to find new audience members. As seen from the progress of the "Theatrical Popularization Debate," which took place sporadically from 1964 to 1967, the popularization of theatre meant showing high-quality theatres to a larger number of the audience more often. The progress of this debate revealed that theatre companies were still lingering in elitism, even though they had declared their awareness of the public. However, compared to the earlier periods, the audience started to grow little by little over time, centering on college students. It was an opportunity for theatre players to identify a new audience of college students.

The true contributions of the Little Theatre Movement to Korean theatre lay in the theatre companies' contemporary introductions of wide-range Western theatrical styles, such as absurdism, boulevard theatre,[82] musicals, and so on, and in their efforts to discover original plays with their theatrical experiments. Also, their experiments in utilizing Korean theatrical traditions took place and made Korean theatre known to the Western world. It was the Little Theatre Movement that demonstrated the possibility of theatre with tools other than language, thus setting the beginning of contemporary theatre and the seed of the so-called postmodern theatre today. The movement tried to find new ways of expression against realism theatre. The innovations consequently brought about the turning point that placed Korean theatre into the paradigm of contemporary world theatre.

Notes

1 Jeong, Hosoon. *Little Theater Movement in Korea*. Seoul, Drama and Humans, 2002, p. 42.
2 Ibid., p. 72.
3 The initial funding was $100,000.
4 Cho, Oh-kon. *Korean Theatre: From Rituals to the Avant-garde*. Fremont, Jain Pub Co, 2015, p. 251.
5 Yu, ChiJin. "The Drama Center is Not Privatized." *Korean Daily Newspaper*, 1 Sep 1966.
6 It was advocated by Kirby, who was influenced by Structuralism, and analyzed the play structurally and expressed it in a minimalist manner.

7 The Korea Theater Festival is the theater festival organized in 1977 by the Korea Culture and Arts Promotion Agency, a subsidiary of the Korea Arts Council. The purpose was to promote the development of Korean theater through the cultivation and performance of original plays. Starting with the 11th Theater Festival in 1987, the hosting organization was transferred to the Korea Theater Association, and the name was renamed and reorganized to the Seoul Theater Festival. Other theater festival that developed from this Korean Theater Festival is Seoul Performing Arts Festival, which has been inviting many foreign excellent performances and attracted many audiences.

8 The DongA Theater Award is a prestigious annual theater award hosted by the Dong-A Newspaper, established in Nov. 1964.

9 This is an awards ceremony established in 1965 to develop Korean pop culture and arts and to boost the morale of artists. It is a comprehensive arts award given to the production crew and performers of TV, movies, and plays that were broadcast or screened during the year. The name was the Korea Theater and Film Arts Awards from the 1st in 1965 to the 19th in 1983, the Korean Theater, Film and Television Arts Awards in the 20th and 1985 and the 21st in 1985, and the Korea Baeksang Arts Awards in the 22nd in 1986. It was changed to the Baeksang Arts Awards from the 23rd in 1987 and has been used to this day.

10 Cho, Op. cit., p. 241.

11 Kim, UiGyung. "Start and Re-start of *the Experimental Theatre*." *10 Years of the Experimental Theater*, 1970, p. 35.

12 Yeo, SeokGi. "Korean Theatre in the 1960s and *the Experimental Theatre*." *The Record of 40 Years of the Experimental Theatre (實驗劇場40年史)*, 2001, p. 38.

13 The following works were performed: 5 June 1965 <*5 Days*> (by Zeiger)/ 12th <*The New Republic*> (by Shin MyungSun)/ 19th <*Women*> (by Oh HyeRyeong)/ 26th <*Sold Antiques*> (by Ha GyeongJa)/ July 3rd <*A Bright Morning*> (by Kintero Brothers) performed at KBS Hall for 6 weeks.

14 Lee, GeuSam. "Young Company." *The 10 Years of the Experimental Theatre.*, 1970, p. 50.

15 Yu, MinYoung. "The Meaning of the 40th Anniversary of *the Experimental Theatre* in Theatre History." *The 40 Years of the Experimental Theatre*, 2001, pp. 34–35.

16 Yu, MinYoung. *The History of Drama Movement in Our Time*. Seoul, Dankook University Press, 1990,. p. 315.

17 Seo, YeonHo, and Lee SangWu. *100 Years of Our Theatre*. Seoul, Hyunamsa, 2000, p. 202.

18 "The 'Popular Theater' Is also Born." *Seoul Daily Newspaper*, 30 Jan 1963.

19 Yu, MinYoung. "The Popular Theater's 20 Years." *The Korean Theatre Review*, Jan 1984, p. 20.

20 Yeo, SeokGi. "Review of *the Egg*." *HanGukDaily Newspaper*, 30 May 1963.

21 Shin, HyunSuk. "French Drama." *Western Drama in Korea*. Seoul, Sohwa, 1999, p. 284.

22 Yu, MinYoung. *The History of Drama Movement in Our Time*. Seoul, Dankook University Press, 1990, p. 315.

23 Lee, JinSoon. "The History of Korean Theater." *The Korean Theatre Review*, vol. six, Jun 1978, p. 46.

24 Ibid.

25 Yeo, Seokki. *The Reality of Korean Theatre*. Seoul, Donghwa Publishing Co., 1974, p. 168.

26 At that time, 300,000 won in currency was equal to the total budget cost of producing one production.

27 Shin, HyunSuk. "A Study on the Acceptance of French Theater in Korea." *The Articles of Duksung Women's University*, vol.25 1996, p. 9.

28 Seo, YeonHo. "Korean Theater and Realism: Recognition and Development." *The Korean Theatre Review*, Apr 1987, p. 41.
29 Jeong, ByungHee. "Performances of tran slated plays in Korea." *The Korean Theatre Journal* (演劇評論) *V.5*, Apr 1971, p. 33.
30 Shin, Op. cit., p. 111.
31 Yu, MinYoung. "20 Years of the People Theater." *The Korean Theatre Review*, Jan 1984, p. 20.
32 Lee, Meewon, and Kim Bangok. "The History of Korean Theater in 50 Years of Liberation." Korean Research Foundation Ed., *50th Anniversary of Liberation, Articles 7*. Seoul, Korea Research Foundation, 1995, p. 295.
33 Jeong. JinSu. "The Trend of Translation in 1991." *Culture and Art*, 25 Nov 1991, p. 25.
34 Jeong, JinSu. "On the Popularization of Theater." *Korean Theater Society Symposium*, 2000.
35 Sanha literally points out the mountain and the river, which inclusively means "Nature."
36 Yu, Minyoung. "The history of *Sanha Theatre Company*". *The Korean Theatre Review*, Aug 1976, p. 44.
37 *Sanha Theatre Company ed., 10 Years' History of the Sanha Theater Company*, 1973.
38 Cha, BumSeok. "The Dream of 10 Years Ago." *10 Years' History of the Sanha Theater Company*, 1973.
39 *Buring Mountain* is the representative play of Cha BeomSeok in 1962 before when the Sanha was not founded yet. The play was total of five acts and performed from 25–29 December 1962, by the National Theater Company performed on the National Theater under the direction of Lee Jin-soon (李眞淳). The intention of this work was to portray the originality and dignity of human beings during the War based on ideological divisions, the misery, and destruction and killing. The background of the play was also during the Korean War and the mountain village where partisans are haunted. At that time, a Partisan, a former teacher named Gyubok, visits the house of Jeomrye's house, a young widow, and asks for her to the hide. They soon fell in love, but Sawol, the neighboring's widow, notices their relationships and offers to take care of Gyubok together. However, the far-fetched relationship among these three is bound to end as soon as the Southern Government's subjugation is unfolded. In other words, the ROK Army put fired at on the large bamboo-forest where Gyubok is hiding. Gyubok is burned to death, Sawol pregnant with GyuBok's child commits suicide, and Jeomrye loses her mind. This play is considered as not only the representative Cha BeomSeok's play but also the representative of Korean realism War plays. Thus, the reproduction of *Buring Mountain* was very meaningful to Sanha Theatre.
40 "Mutual Aids Behind the Stage." *Korean Daily Newspaper*, 25 Oct 1966.
41 Out of a total of 52 performances, there are 18 creative plays. The company tried to produce popular plays to easily reach the public, but it tried to match roughly the ratio between original plays and translated plays to 1:2. It was easy to determine the public's preference for translated plays that had already been performed even in foreign countries.
42 *Seoul Daily Newspaper*, 29 Apr 1964.
43 "The Foundational Declaration of the Bridge Theatre." 20 Mar 1965. Phamplet of the Bridge Theatre in 1965.
44 Yu Min,Young. *The History of Korean Theatre Movemnent* (韓國演劇運動史). Seoul, TaehakSa, 2001, p. 409.
45 SeungGyu, Lee. "Theatrical Company Bridge, 10 Years of Touring." *The Korean Theatre Review*, Jan 1976, p. 64.
46 Report request for *The Stupid Mr. Fate*, Mar 1969.
47 *Dong-A Daily Newspapaer*, 13 May 1971.
48 Ibid.

49 "The Bridge Theatre with a New Operating System, Appointment of Four Advisors Including Mr. Lee GeunSam." *Il-gan Sports Newspapers*, 19 Jan 1980.
50 The chronology of Free Theatre. https://encykorea.aks.ac.kr/Contents/SearchNavi?keyword=자유극장&index=0&tot=2
51 Yu, Op. cit., p. 413.
52 Shin HyunSuk, "French Drama." *Western Theater in Korea 1900–1995*. Shin JeongOk, Shin HyunSuk etal. Ed., Seoul, Seowha, 1999, p. 282.
"The difference in the frequency of the second place Lim YoungWung (9 plays) and the Warehouse Theater(倉庫劇場) (11 plays) shows that Kim JeongOk and the Free Theater occupy an unrivaled position in the introduction of French theater."
53 Yu, MinYoung. "Opening a New Field ⑧—The History of the Women Theater." *The Korean Theater Review*, Oct 1982, p. 27.
54 Ibid.
55 Kang YuJeong was born in 1932 and died in 2005.
56 *Daljip* is an event in the evening of the full moon of the lunar New Year. A pile of fresh pine trees tied together to lighten it up to burn away the old and the evil.
57 Cha, BumSeok, and Kang YuJeong. "Three Cranes Met on the Road to Liberation." *The Korean Theatre Review*, Oct 1984, p. 45.
58 Han, SangCheol. "The Women Theater that Survived for 20 Years." The program of the 78th regular performance of the Women Theater, *Across the River, NeoBuSilo*, Mar 1986.
59 Yu, MinYoung. *Theatrical Culture of the Later 20th Century*. Seoul, Korean Academy of Education, 2000, pp. 522–524.
60 Kim, EuiGyeong. "The 20 Hard Years of the Women Theatre." The program of *Across the river to NeoBuSil* Mar 1986.
61 Han, Op. cit.
62 Kim, SeongHee. "Free Spirit." *Art World*, Nov 1987.
63 Kang, YuJeong. "Life of the Pioneer Hwang Jin-I." Phamplet of *Free Spirit*, Sep 1987.
64 The 2nd period of original plays were: *The Sleepwalker* (Lee Jaehyun), *Flower Wind* (Cha Bumseok), *The Birth of a Butterfly,* (Moon Junghee), *The Hiccups of the Moon* (Jeon Jinho), *Backlight*(Kang Seonghee), *Daljip* (Roh GyeongSik), *Dancer* (Oh Youngjin), *Red-fruit spicebush* (Lee JaeHyun), *Mountain chrysanthemum* (Hwang SeokYoung), *O Crane, My Love* (Cha Beomseok), *Sir Lee, Damn Lee* (Park SeungHee), *Tower* (Roh Gyeong-sik), *Bonfire Morning Dew* (Yun Jo-Byeong), *The Organ Sound* (Yun Jo-Byeong), *Across the river to NeoBuSil* (Roh Gyeong-sik), *Free Spirit* (Yoon Jeong-seon), Mothe (Park JeHong), *Buring Mountain* (Cha BeomSeok), *Return* (Jo WonSeok) (in order of performance).
65 Kang, YuJeong. "Director's Note," Phamplet of *Return*, Feb 1990.
66 Kim, SeongHee. "A Painful Life and a Vision of Overcoming It." *Young Lady*, Aug 1992.
67 Bang, TaeSu. "Ejeotto's Gathering of 8 Years." *The Korean Theatre Review*, Jan 1978, p. 69.
68 Han, SangCheol. "Reflection of Korean Theatre Studies: Directing of Contemporary Korean." *The Korean Theatre Journal*, vol. six, 1994, p. 31.
69 Bang, Op. cit., p. 68.
70 Ibid., p. 69.
71 Han, Op. cit., p. 45.
72 Cha, BumSeok. "Cafe Theatre and Ejeotto Small Theater." *Art World*, Aug 1991, p. 75.
73 Yeo, Seokki. "That Personality, That Conviction." The Egeotto Theatre's 41st performance *My Name is Hobby*.

74 The protagonist of *The Unfair Thief* were Yu JinGyu, Kim SeongGu, and Kim DongSu, and were the first generation of pantomime who had been developed in the form of experimental theatre by introducing mimes to Korea. From the mid-80s, various types of mimes such as clowns, objets, and sound-mimes were introduced. Wu HongYoung, Lim DoWan, Park SangSuk, and Shim CheolJong were the second generation of modern mimes representing this era. The 3rd generation of the current mime world were French studied schools such as Nam GeungHo, Yu JinWoo, and Park MiSeon, and they were expanding their breadth to post-mime forms such as combining with other genres or including sound and music. "Korean Modern Mime Departure in the 1960s." *Daehan Daily Newspaper*, 1 Oct 2002.

75 Lee, TaeJu. "Contemporary Korean Theater and Criticism." *The Korean Theatre Review*, Mar 2000, p. 58.

76 Kim, MunHwan. "The 1st Young Theater Festival." *Seoul Daily Newspaper*, 15 Jun 1973.

77 Seo, YeonHo, and Lee SangWu. *100 Years of Our Theater.* Seoul, Hyeonamsa, 2000, p. 258.

78 Lee, Op. cit., p. 56.

79 Bang, TaeSu. "The Wanderer Dreaming of Built-In." *The Korean Theatre Review*, Aug 1986, p. 31.

80 Yu, MinYoung. "Lessons of the 1st Theater Festival and Prospects for the New Year's Theater." *Theatrical Culture of the Late 20th Century.* Seoul, Korean Academy of Education, 2000, p. 358.

81 Brustein, Robert. *The Theater of Revolt.* Methuen, T&A Constable ltd, 1962, p. 4.

82 Boulevard theatre consists mostly of comedies but also had dramas. Starting from the second half of the 18th century, popular and bourgeois theatre alike took up residence on the Boulevard du Temple, then was nicknamed "Boulevard du Crime" due to the many melodramas and murder stories shown there. In addition to the many attractions on display there—fireworks, pantomime, acrobats, etc.—a so-called "boulevard" repertoire emerged separate from upper-class theatre. In general, the characters are simply drawn, ordinary, or easily understandable. There is a strong tendency to avoid touchy subjects, such as politics and religion. The style is not designed to challenge preconceived ideas or offend. Brunet, Brigitte. "Le Théâtre de Boulevard," *French Studies*, vol. 59, July 2005, pp. 417–418.

6 The Beginning of Experiments and Innovations for Modernizing Theatrical Traditions

A prominent characteristic of 1970s' theatre is the experiment to incorporate Korean traditions into modern drama. The Little Theatre Movement from the 1960s was firmly established in the 1970s and sought another new experiment. Although there had been a few theatre people seeking Korea's theatrical roots early on, such as Oh YoungJin, it was not until the 1970s that Korea began to embrace its traditions in an overwhelmingly Western-oriented Korean modern theatre. As a preliminary step to this movement, a movement started to preserve Korean cultural traditions, including Mask-Dance theatre from the late 1960s, and, thus, these traditions became designated as National Intangible Cultural Property.

The new theatrical experiments were deeply related to the social atmosphere of excavating the roots of Korean culture and national identity at that time. Historians explored the origin of autochthonic Korea, and, in turn, modern literature also tried to connect its history to this autochthonic origin. In other words, the subject of national cultural identity became important to Koreans, and people tried to be reconnected through finding cultural traditions. It is also interesting to note that cultural pluralism, such as interculturalism, began to arise, and post-colonial scholars began to criticize the Westernization prominent around the world at this time. The seeking of cultural identity and recreating theatrical traditions today seems to be common in non-European cultures, especially in Asian countries that have embraced Western traditions as their contemporary theatre. Ultimately, the issues of finding the roots of Korean theatre, the modern acceptance, and recreation of the traditions were the major concerns and objectives of the Korean theatrical world in the 1970s.

Owing to the atmosphere explained above, attempts to apply traditional theatre practices, such as masks and dances, to Western-style modern Korean theatres emerged in the 1970s. Yu DeokHyeong and An Minsoo of *the Drama Center*, Heo Kyu of the *Folk Art (民藝) Theatre*, and Kim JeongOk of the *Free Theatre (自由)* were the representatives of these experiments. Each director had his own approach to incorporating traditions. The theatre companies of these traditional experiments were also the representative companies of the 1970s. In other words, the applications of traditional theatrical practices were the most popular issue of the time. This chapter will attempt to position these

DOI: 10.4324/9781003490708-7

valuable efforts of the 1970s into the context of modern Korean theatre and examine their achievements and limitations.

6.1 *The Drama Center*: Integration with Contemporary Experimental Theatre

The Drama Center, which opened with *Hamlet* in April 1962 with the support of the Rockefeller Foundation of the United States, experienced new momentum with "A Homecoming Directing Presentation" by Yu DeokHyung in 1969. *The Drama Center* of the 1970s presented the concept of Total Theatre while experimenting with new anti-realistic theatre. Yu DeokHyung, Ahn MinSu, and Oh TaeSeok were the main pillars, and the Korean and Eastern Asian traditions they showed were actually the byproducts of these experiments. Their acceptance of tradition was in line with the experiments of post-realism Total Theatre that took place in the West in the 1960s.

The application and re-creation of Korean traditions became a noteworthy issue. For example, some critics argued that Ahn MinSu's *Prince of Hamyeol* (*Hamyeol Taeja*) showed some traditions of Chinese Peking Opera, Japanese Noh, and Kabuki in addition to Korean traditions.[1] Despite these criticisms, the experimental plays of *the Drama Center* clearly achieved the two objectives that any other experiments did not achieve before. One was that Korean traditions had been revived and were presented as modern theatre, and the other was that they made the Westerners aware of Korean traditions, i.e., the globalized Korean traditions. In other words, by using Korean traditions to accommodate the experimental direction of global Western contemporary theatre, Korean theatre's modernity and internationality were established.

The above characteristics can be analyzed and examined in *Grass Tomb* (草墳) (1973) and *The Placenta* (胎) (1974), the representative works of *the Drama Center* during this period. When *Grass Tomb* is discussed from the perspective of applying tradition within modern theatre, it is a challenge to connect the two. While Western theatre is usually composed of *tension and confrontation* toward the climax, Eastern theatre can be characterized as *anti-tension and reconciliation*, which is episodic. The mood that was consistently felt in *Grass Tomb* was strong confrontation and tension. The so-called order of the island and the order of the land clashed with each other tightly, and intense conflicts and tensions persisted. The English title of this work is *Order*, which clearly explains the structure. Although the plot was not based on Aristotle's *Poetics*, i.e., development, crisis, climax, and finale, the highlights of this composition were strongly conveyed. Even lines that were repetitive and concise evoked images rather than directly conveyed their meaning. These features were Western avant-garde rather than traditional Korean.

The traditional aspects appeared in the subject matter rather than in the plot. By using a unique aerial sepulture[2] known as *Grass Tomb* (Chobun) as the subject, the work had an inseparable relationship with special Korean locality and customs. And even though the *Grass Tomb* was not a well-known tradition, it was connected with the reproduction of intergenerational traditions up to the present day. Furthermore, the taboo and tradition of the village were inseparably related to the subject matter. The so-called rational order of land and the illogical customary order of the island were traditions that could be easily encountered in Korea. Therefore, it gave legitimacy to the conflict in the work and became a clue to understanding of the order on the island, which could only be "illogical and absolute."

In addition, traditions could be found in the choice of words. When the role of the auditory image was more important than the transfer of meanings in dialogue, the choice of language was directly related to the atmosphere of the work. The work featured forgotten traditional words and indigenous words. Strong repetitive words, such as *JeongSuRi* (Crown-Head), *Mut* (Dry Land), and *JaMaegJil* (Diving), were used. Also, inserted *sounds* expressed in the passages became *magic rhymes.* As such, *Grass Tomb* was an appropriate application of traditional Korean elements to the most Western and modern avant-garde composition. Just as logical meaning in the avant-garde is meaningless, the meaning of aerial sepulture, which only reminds us of a distant exoticism with a unique burial custom, was meaningless in itself in *Grass Tomb.* Only the order presented and the experience of the village-commune were consequently emphasized in the performance.

At the time, director Yu DeokHyeong wanted to strengthen the basic direction of this play. He regarded this work as "the power of dual compliance and rebellion." This becomes more evident in the director's words, as shown below:

Figure 6.1 A Performance Scene from *Grass Tomb* (1973). Photo from *the Encyclopedia of Korean People and Culture.*

Figure 6.2 The Poster of *Grass Tomb* (1973). Photo from DA-Arts.

> I have been looking for a formula in the maximization of the dual power of all works. I believe that there would be one point in which the two forces of yin and yang finally meet in another unified state. It is looking for a way to express the unified state of yin and yang in a thorough theory of motion.
>
> [...] In order to find the method of expression, "In the Eastern side, we discussed Yin-Yang, the Five Elements theory, the Zen, Eastern Asian plays in Thailand, Japan, India, the beliefs of shamanism and totemism, and so on. And on the Western side, we discussed grotesque situations, Absurdism, Dionysus and Apollo, the ancient old Myth, and the new theatrical trends...".[...] Not only that, "the creativity of the movements of primitive consciousness—I believe that there will be a gesture of our consciousness. What we lean on for the natural movement that can be neither East nor West, but also be East and West at the same time, and as I gradually discovered what it was, the training started to gain strength and speed."[3]

Essentially, the director's note made it clear that the performance of *Grass Tomb was* intended to be more about the avant-garde than about the revivals of Korean traditions.

Criticism at that time also paid attention to the theatrical songs, not just the language, but also the body movements in the performance of *Grass Tomb*. This recognition of theatrical songs and body movements set a new turning point in contemporary Korean theatre, which meant a focus on theatricality itself rather than the message. Ultimately, the specific acting methods did not matter and theatrical decisions were of Korean heritage. The following question of a panel discussion at that time clearly expressed the limits of "Koreanization" in *Grass Tomb*. "That does not mean that the movement is Korean. Can't we feel that it would have failed if the director put Korean tradition rashly?"[4] In other words, the "Koreanization" of *Grass Tomb* did not meet the expectations of Korean audiences. There were complaints, for example, that the Korean lines were not delivered well enough to be "rhythmic, resonating, or a cry" and that many Korean audiences felt neglected.

Overall, *Grass Tomb* was a preliminary work that applied Korean traditions to Western avant-garde theatre and provided an opportunity to escape from language-oriented theatre. It also revived the subject matter of aerial sepulture that was mostly forgotten even by Koreans, and the strong ritualistic atmosphere consequently contributed to the global acceptance of Korean traditions. This was certainly not a retro-representation but absurdist avant-garde. It also had great significance for showing a new direction of applying Korean traditions. Though its application was limited to the subject and the atmosphere in *Grass Tomb*, it clearly showed a method of applying Korean traditions in a modern and global way.

The Placenta also adapted traditions but was less avant-garde than *Grass Tomb*. First of all, the author Oh TaeSeok used much more logical language than in *Grass Tomb*. A tragedy in Korean history, the tragedy of King Danjong and his loyal six retainers, was conveyed. Later, when the shock of the premiere had disappeared, a critic noticed that the political reinterpretation of the event was stronger than that of its cruel expressions.[5] However, not only in the direction from Ahn MinSu but also in the writer's own performance, the original "animal obsession with bloody life" was more prominent than the historical and political message. *The Placenta* belonged to the experiment of applying traditions to avant-garde theatre like *Grass Tomb*. The story of protecting bloodlines led to the human instinct to preserve the race. In other words, the story of two accomplices, in switching their own children between Park JungRim's granddaughter-in-law and a female servant, was interwoven with the royal conspiracy surrounding King Danjong. A female servant who gave her child as a scapegoat to be killed cried out her son's name in madness. Thus, the play was historical as well as personal, while the story was from the past but its instinct for blood was contemporary. Ultimately, the story "explores the relationship between the ruler and the ruled by honoring the tenacious tendency of the life that Koreans have continued in spite of many deaths."[6] In addition, the brutal sensations strongly expressed the meaning of life and death, and our existence. Therefore, *The Placenta*, which was both a historical and anti-historical personal drama, was clearly linked to modern absurdist drama.

In short, the application of tradition was limited to the subject matter, as shown in *Grass Tomb*. Due to its clear historical epoch, it was retro unlike *Grass Tomb*, but it was difficult to have a special historical meaning since the brutal sensations were clear. Rather, anti-historical elements—e.g., umbilical cord made of red cloth, which were unusual in historical stories, gave significance to the work. These very breakthroughs made well-known historical facts free from their time and connected to modern interpretations. Ahn MinSu's directing was praised by many critics, as shown in the example below:

> Ahn MinSu's stage was so intense and shocking that it completely blocked the possibility that there could be another director of this work. For example, the scene of executing six loyal subjects was cruel, forming bizarre moldings with spouting blood. In addition, there were grim sounds and desperate movements of prayer in the scene. All made the performance uniquely gruesome and terrible.[7]

Indeed, the performance of *The Placenta,* like *Grass Tomb,* was in the same context as the experimental theatre of the West in the 1960s and the 1970s.

As seen in the two works above, the experimental theatre of *the Drama Center* never intended to preserve or restore traditions. The shock they brought to Korean theatre was their theatricality. Yu DeokHyeong and Ahn Minsu of *the Drama Center* approached traditions as sources for their

Figure 6.3 The Premiere Program Book's Front Page of *The Placenta* (1974). Image from DA-Arts.

avant-garde experiments. The *Center* added Korean traditions to contemporary Western experiments. The applications of the traditions in performances largely came from their locality, rituality, and anti-Aristotelian theatrical traditions that contemporary Western experiments sought. Plus, the applications were not authentic, but only vaguely Korean; they included oriental traditions from many other countries, such as India and Japan, and even included the Dionysian rituals of ancient Greece. Though the two directors did not seek to preserve or revive Korean cultural elements, they ironically suggested a wonderful way to modernize and globalize them. For this reason, some critics at that time denigrated their productions as lacking originality and having a tendency to imitate. However, there are no objections today that these experiments were ultimately linked to the modernization and internationalization of Korean traditions.

6.2 Heo Gyu's *Folk Art (民藝) Theatre*: Discovery of Indigenous Roots

Heo Gyu, who led the *Folk Art Theatre*, focused on the successful reproductions of Korean traditions. In 1973, he held the opening performance of the *Folk Art Theatre* with *The Man of Korea, TteogSoe* (高麗人 *TteogSoe*), and made it clear from his declaration that "we study and create original theatrical semiotic systems in order to make unique theatre arts for our nation."[8] This led to the discovery and reproduction of tradition and the spirit of its playfulness that would develop into the idea of festive culture in the future.

Heo Gyu also attempted to accommodate *Changgeuk* into Korean modern theatre. He confessed the change of his directorial perspective, as follows:

> From the beginning of my study in directing, I was deeply immersed in Western theatre theory for a long time and followed it like a belief in all my theatrical works. But I changed my direction in the 1970s and took on the task of creative applications of Korean theatrical traditions.[9]

Hoe Gyu's creative directing in the *Folk Art Theatre* with his own original plays is worth noting. Heo Gyu and the *Folk Art Theatre* researched the country's folk traditions, such as legends, ritual-plays, and shamanistic funeral rituals, and adapted them for the stage. *Muldori Village* (Muldori-dong) (1977) and *DaShiRaGi* (DaShiRaGi) (1979) are the representative works of these adaptations. Therefore, this section will analyze Heo Gyu's original plays, e.g., *MulDori Village* and *DaShiRaGi*, as representatives. Their characteristics do not encompass all of Heo Gyu's efforts to embrace tradition—especially his efforts to modernize *Changgeuk* and his theory of Festive Culture cannot be overlooked—but they clearly suggest one direction of integrating traditions into modern Western-based theatre of the 1970s. In addition, these works well represented the experiments with traditions that Heo Gyu steadily tried from the 1970s.

MulDori Village, the first Presidential Award-winning work of the Korean Theatre Festival that was proposed to promote original plays, was the first to incorporate old legends into plays. The story of "A Lad Heo," a legendary Hahoe mask maker, is intertwined with the story of SeoNang Goddess of the same Hahoe Village. In other words, when Lad Heo receives a manifestation from a shaman god, he places a forbidden rope on the pavement and makes a mask with all his might. He dies from vomiting too much blood without completing the jaw of the last Imae mask, while his worried lover peeps at him. Along with this legend, another legend of a woman who becomes a widow as a virgin after marrying the dead was also intertwined in *MulDori Village*.

When it comes to integrating legends, the play first reconstructed the times and characters. Thus, the story is retro and traditional. Though there is no specific clarification on the era of the play, it feels natural that this is the time of Lad Heo's mask production. The names of the characters were also the characters of the Hahoe special ritual-play *Pyolsin Kut*, including DoRyeong, GakSi, ChoRaengI, IMae, SeonBi, and Yangban. Partial shaman rituals or partial Mask-Dances were inserted into the performance of *MulDori Village*. Here again, the director's efforts for the excavation and collection of traditions were conveyed. The director explained his intention of the production as follows:

> In addition to the nine Hahoe masks that have been preserved, the three masks (ByolChae, TToegDari, DoRyeong) that have been restored by taking into account of their roles, characters, sculptural methods, and the oral data of the masks in the special ritual-play, *Hahoe ByeolSin-GutNori*. It should be also clarified that it was recreated based on the cultural heritages of the Korean, such as *Pansori*, folk songs, lyrics, Shaman songs, Mask dances, etc., that the members have learned and practiced since the foundation of the *Folk Art Theatre*.[10]

It was clearly stated that the direction of this traditional experiment was, most importantly, about the application of authentic Korean traditions.

However, the problem was that this application did not show the abundant and essential beauty of the traditions, which were shrouded by partial integrations. This acceptance not only let tradition remain remote, but it also promoted the distance from current living traditions. Additionally, most original Korean narratives were interpreted by Western logic. It clearly shows that Lad Heo's death was logically explained, that is, Lad Heo was killed as a scapegoat by the village leader, not as a curse due to the peeping of his lover. This was the artist's personal reinterpretation of his death, and it represented the characteristics of modern narratives. But, rather than making the story feel modern, the story seemed to fall flat. The mysterious story was only interpreted with a logical understanding, and that made the play look partially traditional when put into a Western composition.

In addition, miscellaneous insertions, such as shaman songs and Mask-Dances, resulted in the failure to achieve a unified effect. Therefore, the solemn

Figure 6.4 A Scene from *Muldori Village*. Photo from *the Encyclopedia of Korean People and Culture.*

atmosphere of a village ritual, which was the background, did not create a unified atmosphere or aesthetic effect appropriate to the entire work. This lack of unified aesthetic was insufficient for the audience to experience live traditional effects beyond satisfying their simple curiosities. This could be seen as a defect in the traditional aims of the *Folk Art Theatre*. The representation of tradition without consideration of the overall aesthetic effect limited the audience's impressions and empathy. Despite the discovery and reproduction of pioneering traditions shown by the *Folk Art Theatre*, its integration seemed apathetic, and overall gave off a monotonous feeling. Indeed, based on this experience, the next step forward would be a task left to future generations.

There is no significant difference between *MulDori Village* and *DaShiRaGi* in the directions of integrating traditions. However, since they basically reproduced the humorous folk theatres, *DaShiRaGi*, which had been handed down during the funeral in Jindo Island, had more aesthetic unity overall. While recreating *DaShiRaGi*, the *Folk Art Theatre* was successful in pursuing "the modern meaning of life through the contrast between the fear of death and the joy of new life's birth, which is the deep-rooted emotion of human beings" to some extent.[11]

The work was within the atmosphere of the original Jindo *DaShiRaGi*, a funeral folk theatre. In particular, the appearance of the Grim Reaper, which was not found in Jindo *DaShiRaGi*, is striking, and, through it, the absolute boundary between life and death is broken by depicting the underworld as an extension of this world. In the Jindo *DaShiRaGi*, the Monk is in a love triangle with the Blind and the Shaman wife, whereas in this work, instead of the Monk, the Grim Reaper replaces his place. Originally, *DaShiRaGi* was performed at a funeral to mourn the dead; therefore, the play's expansion of the art world across life and death was truly appropriate. The will of a good life not only confronts and fights against the Grim Reaper but also captures and confines him and goes to rescue the wife that the Grim Reaper captures. Also, humorously, the birth of a baby is portrayed for a prolonged period. The blind suddenly dies when a baby is born. This naturally expresses a cyclicality and reincarnation of life and death. Indeed, the philosophy of life and death, expressed through the simple humor of the traditional Jindo *Dashiragi*, is deepened and accepted.

In short, the significance and limitation of this experiment of integrating traditions in *MulDori Village* and *DaShiRaGi* are in line with the significance and limitations of Heo Gyu's *Folk Art Theatre*. Heo Gyu utilized theatrical traditions from Mask-Dance theatre, folk puppet theatre, and *Pansori*, the singing monodrama. In order to utilize these works, he had to retrain actors and actresses to be able to practice these skills. He began to teach vocal techniques necessary for singing traditional songs and to train dance movements, as well as fine art techniques for making masks and puppets. The *Folk Art Theatre* led by Heo sincerely tried to restore authentic theatrical traditions in modern Korean theatre. At the same time, the company's works were sometimes criticized for trying to restore the tradition too precisely and not attempting to retest or revitalize it today. Overall, these experiments were at the beginning stage and contributed much to reviving theatrical traditions. Thus, the experiments of the *Folk Art Theatre* have laid the foundation for traditional theatrical experiments in contemporary Korean theatre history.

6.3 *The Free Theatre*: Montage Technique and Group Creation

The *Free Theatre* presented refreshing performances of translated Western plays, such as absurdist plays and French boulevard plays, characterized by comedy and lightness, which were lacking in Korean theatre. However, in 1970 with Choi InHun's play *Where Shall We Meet in What Shape?*(*Eodiseo Mueotsi Dwaeeo Nannarya?*), a change took place. This change was directly connected to the application of Korean traditions to contemporary theatre. Through these experiments, the globalization of *Free Theatre* became possible.

The success of *Where Shall We Meet in What Shape?*, which premiered in the fall of 1970, was highly praised and provided an opportunity for the *Free Theatre* to turn their attention to Korean traditions. Its performance of Choi InHun's *Ondal* in 1969 was based on a well-known folk tale of *Ondal*, who became the son-in-law of a king and a general from a poor bachelor from a countryside mountain of the old kingdom, Goguyeo. The play reinterprets the *Ondal* folk tale and makes it cyclical with a traditional Buddhist atmosphere.

> I saw the most dramatic encounter in the *Ondal* story. The absurdity of meeting, the mystery of meeting even though one didn't choose it, and

> the meeting of Ondal and Princess I would like to see as a prototype for the fundamental human experience.[12]

As the director intended, a mystical and causal Buddhist relationship appeared as if on an axis. The princess happened to encounter Ondal. To convey this illogicality, mysterious encounters and separations were exemplified by dreams, and the gratitude tale of "Magpies and a Snake" was grafted into the *Ondal* folk tale. In the end, the logical composition of the modern narrative was attributed to this mysterious network of encounters and ties among people. The performance of the *Free Theatre* focused on highlighting these mysterious encounters. Anyway, this play was the beginning of a tradition-based original contemporary drama.

Where Shall We Meet in What Shape? of the *Free Theatre* was not necessarily intended to integrate the traditions but rather focused on the reproduction of the atmosphere of the play. The stage space, such as all scenic elements and costumes, seemed abstract in comparison to that of the historic forms. Ondal's house on stage consisted of several abstract stones and wires instead of a realistic thatch, and the costumes were obviously traditional but unknown to the times. As much as possible, the clear division between dream and reality was avoided.

Figure 6.5 A Scene from *Where Shall We Meet in What Shape?* (1970). Photo from Seoul Museum of History.

Once the performance successfully ended with "an unexpectedly large audience," this work became a repeating repertoire of the *Free Theatre* and provided important momentum. As a result, it was a performance that showed the use of traditions earlier than any other performance and also aroused the necessity to do so. It also showed the direction of future experiments with Korean traditions. In fact, the abstract representation of *Where Shall We Meet in What Shape?*, chosen for the necessity of the work, was in line with the abstraction of traditional integration that appeared in "Montage" or "Total Theatre" of the *Free Theatre* in the future. As described above, *Where Shall We Meet in What Shape?* opened the eyes of the *Free Theatre* as well as the Korean theatre industry to the importance of utilizing Korean traditions and the possibility of commercial success.

What Will It Be? (*Mueotsi Doelggo Hani?*) (1978) was the first collaborative work to establish the practice of integrating the traditions that *Where Shall We Meet in What Shape?* began in the *Free Theatre* style. Although the writer Park WuChun was still specified, this was the beginning of Collective Creation and Total Theatre that the *Free Theatre* advocated afterward. Group Creation was "to move the axis that depended on the creativity of the director to the actor." It attempted to create a collective production; every member of the production created their own work out of their idea, and the director only gradually made them harmonious. Meanwhile, Total Theatre was "to expand the expression style of the theatre by bringing all kinds of artistic activities and cultural patterns in our society to the stage." In other words, through Collective Creation and Total Theatre, the new theatre was advocated as follows:

> With the ideal of Group Creation and Total Theatre, while highlighting the cycle of life and death, the new theatre takes place in the encounter or conflict between Western theatre and Korean theatrical heritage. We declare the Third Theatre as the theatre of today.[13]

What Will It Be?, the beginning of a theatre experiment that fit this ideal, first dismantled the basic grammar of Western theatre. In other words, the play ignored the dramatic composition of logical causality, took the actors' quick transformations to other characters according to the various situations, including improvisations and encouraged harmonious joint acting without star actors or actresses. In addition, it tried to recapture the traditional circular view of life and death and to utilize traditional images in modern plays. The clash between the legacy of traditional performance and the latest Western theories—the idea that combined traditional visual and auditory images of montages with the politics and sociality of people's lives—attracted attention. The question was how much of aesthetic unity and philosophical depth of the successive images could be achieved in such miscellaneous montages.

It is thought that *What Will It Be?* still lacked enough depth in the overall integrated meaning created by the combination of the aforementioned elements. Despite these limitations, its stylistic experimental spirit of integrating traditions deserves attention. Unlike the incidental traditional atmosphere, which was attained in the midst of avant-garde experiments at *the Drama Center* and the rather plain reproduction of tradition at the *Folk Art Theatre*, the *Free Theatre* boldly reconstructed or dismantled traditions and employed visual and auditory images as new method of theatre composition. At least in terms of style, it borrowed theatrical traditions to provide audiovisual images with modern applications and further clarified its own aesthetic position. However, some critics criticized these experiments for not achieving aesthetic unity and philosophical depth.

These deficiencies were closely related to the fact that the company did not pay much attention to the spiritual aspect of Korean heritage. In other words, the superficial borrowings of traditions were successful to some extent, but they were not rooted in the traditions' intangible meanings. This is the remaining homework of the *Free Theatre* as well as contemporary Korean theatre, which keeps experimenting with the integration of traditions today.

Although *What Will It Be?* was sometimes criticized for lacking aesthetic and philosophical unity, the meaning of this experiment cannot be reduced to the so-called "'Export performance' aimed only for foreign markets." Even though it was a formal and stylistic integration of traditions, it presented its own unique method of integrating traditions and became a milestone toward the achievement of a complete re-creation of traditions in contemporary Korean theatre. In this sense, the *Free Theatre* played an important role in the 1970s. Its techniques of Collective Creation and Montages played a key role in the company internationalize later.

In conclusion, the achievements and significance of the first period of integrating tradition were enormous. The 1970s was the time when the movement to find cultural roots began in modern Korean history. Additionally, discussions on the starting point of autochthonous modern or modern literature began, and discussions on the preservation of Korean heritage also began in earnest. Most of the Mask-Dance theatres had been designated as intangible cultural properties, and modern theatre was able to recognize the need to apply traditions.

As examined above, *the Drama Center's* experiments showed outstanding unity and aesthetics in Korea's directing history, but the integration of traditions was rather limited to the subject matter and the atmosphere of ritual, as its achievements were byproducts of following the Western avant-garde movement. On the other hand, Heo Gyu's *Folk Art Theatre* tried to faithfully discover and reproduce the traditions, including *Pansori*, shaman songs, dance, and so on. The level of traditional training was an achievement that no other theatre company had accomplished. However, the representation of tradition was not well-connected with modernity, so it appeared rather one-dimensional. Meanwhile, the *Free Theatre* began to pay attention to tradition from Choi InHun's performance of a folk tale play and experimented with actor-centered theatre through Collective Creation and Montages. Despite the accusations of lacking overall aesthetic unification or the construction of connected meanings, the experiments the company conducted revitalized the traditions by using excellent visual and auditory images.

Considering that today's experiments with traditions still have similar problems, the results of the experiments in the first period should not be lightly evaluated. Although the experiments of the first period only followed modern Western experiments, reproduced old traditions, or did not succeed in forming a consensus of aesthetic meaning by visualizing the spiritual elements, they are significant in that these were the first series of attempts and paved the way for future experiments. Especially nowadays in this internationalized and diversified world, contemporary theatre based on its own traditions is easily connected with worldwide postmodern theatre. These experiments are clearly milestones toward the establishment of a "contemporary Korean theatre," and they laid the foundation for the applications of traditions in Korean theatre. Considering that these companies were the representative companies of that time, the main issue of the 1970s was a post-colonial national theatre looking for its cultural identity.

Notes

1 Yeo, Seokki, Lee Sangil, and Han Sangcheol. "Panel Discussion: The Controversial Works of This Issue." *The Korean Theatre Journal*, V.15, Winter 1976, p. 61.
In particular, in this performance, styles such as Chinese Opera (京劇) or Japanese Noh and Kabuki (歌舞伎) are revealed, so in terms of expression, it is Japanese rather than Korean. For generations who don't know Japanese culture, there is a great deal of risk of causing the illusion that such a technique is a new attempt at Korean expression.
2 Aerial sepulture is a double funeral method where the body is placed on an airy tree branch, and only the bones are buried after the body is completely rotten.
3 Yu, DeokHyung. "Notes for Directing *Grass Tomb*." *The Korean Theatre Journal*, V.8, Summer 1973, pp. 52–56.
4 Yeo, SoekGi et al. "Panel Discussion: The Controversial Works of This Issue." *The Korean Theatre Journal*, Summer 1973, p. 122.
5 Kim, MunHwan. "Oh Taeseok: A Sense of Reality in Unrealistic Play." Oh Taeseok, *Collection of Oh Taeseok's Play 2: Why Had Shimcheong Thrown Twice into the Indang Sea?*. Seoul, PyeongMinSa, 1994, p. 348.
6 Han, SangCheol. *Issues and Reflections in Korean Theater*. Seoul, Hyundae Mihaksa, 1992, p. 218.
7 Gu, HeeSeo. "The String of Life—Clearly Emphasizes the Meaning of *The Placenta*." Oh TaeSeok, *Oh TaeSeok's Playbook 1: On the Moonlit Night of the Baekma River*. Seoul, PyeogMinSa, 1994, p. 266.
8 Heo, Gyu. "The Man of Korea, TteogSoe." *National Drama and Traditional Art* (民族劇 *gwa* 傳統藝術). Seoul, Munhak SegyeSa, 1991, p. 277.
9 Ibid.
10 Heo, Op. cit., p. 226.
11 "DaShiRaGi." *The Anthology of the 3rd Korean Theatre Festival*,. Korean Culture and Arts Foudation, Ed., Seoul, Hanguk Munhwa YeSul Jinhungwon, 1980, p. 358.
12 Choi, InHoon. *Literature and Ideology*. Seoul, Munhak gwa Jisungsa, 1979. pp. 251.
13 A program book of *Now Only a Quarter Century*.

7 *Madanggeuk*

The Contemporary Sociopolitical Theatre with Traditions from Korean Heritage

Madanggeuk is often identified as a representative form of socio-political theatre due to its themes of resistance to social injustices. Furthermore, the style of *Madanggeuk* has been established so distinctively that it is seen as a genre of its own in modern Korean theatre. Since the 1970s, modern Korean theatre has continuously strived and, to a certain extent, succeeded in incorporating elements of traditional performances, yet *Madanggeuk* is the only form recognized as a unique genre. Simultaneously, it is also the only theatre genre that has adapted and stylized Korean traditional performances into a form of modern theatre. Thus, the study of *Madanggeuk* should be examined as socio-political theatre and as the reapplication of Korean traditions. This chapter examines *Madanggeuk* according to these two aspects.

7.1 *Madanggeuk* as Sociopolitical Theatre

Madanggeuk's origin is rooted in the citizen-artists who came into being in the late 1960s and were most active during the 1980s. In fact, these artists were not just any citizens but mostly groups of university students who protested against the political situation at the time. They created a theatre of protests, now called *Madanggeuk*, and campaigned for their concerns. *Madanggeuk* is basically a social theatre that exposed the unspoken views of pressing socio-political issues. Since the students were highly educated, many of them were talented and became professional theatre personnels later on; however, they were initially amateurs.

Madanggeuk began in the late 1960s when Park's regime became oppressive.[1] A student group protested the political issues of the time, such as the establishment of Korean and Japanese amity since World War II and the amendment of the Constitution, which increased the length of the president's term. Many demonstrations followed to protest against these political decisions. Short theatrical performances were added to these demonstrations in order to broadcast aspects not covered by the mass media due to the censorship and to enhance the spirit of protests. *Rituals for Invoking the Spirit of Patriots* (鄕土儀式招魂*Gut*) in 1969 is one of the earlier versions of these performances known even today. The ceremony consisted of three parts: invoking

DOI: 10.4324/9781003490708-8

of the spirits, a satiric performance criticizing the servitude to a stronger nation, and a folk festival. The performance is noticeable not only in its spirit of protest but also in its theatrical form. It made the best use of traditional Korean Mask-Dance theatres and Shaman ceremonies. Indeed, it is one of the first attempts to revive traditional performances in modern Korean theatre. Though the text and various aspects of this performance were not recorded, they were handed down among students by word of mouth.

Madanggeuk became more active and popular among students in the 1970s, and it began to gain recognition as a form of theatre. Some of its texts were written down, and the performances were not necessarily connected to the protest demonstrations, but they were often combined. Even though it had characteristics of demonstrations and events, *Madanggeuk* was, in essence, a performance. Many leaders of *Madanggeuk* in the 1960s and 1970s became well-known theatre directors in the 1990s.

The topics of *Madanggeuk* broadened over time, but they still criticized the Korean upper class and government for their irresponsibility. The topics generally fall into the following categories: 1) current social and political problems, 2) the problems of farming villages, 3) the problems of urban poor workers, 4) the reinterpretation of history, especially in relation to the United States and Japan, 5) Korean ethnicity and the matter of self-existence and self-respect, and 6) the advent of the savior Messiah.[2] These topics all pay attention to the problems of Korean society. Of course, plays on social subjects existed, but since there was no theatre that consistently dealt with social issues like those mentioned above, *Madanggeuk* was established as a social and political theatre in Korea.

Madanggeuk returned to its activist origins in the 1980s owing to the political situation. In 1979, the assassination of President Park, a military dictator who was in power since 1961, increased the hope for democracy. In the spring of 1980, many students who were imprisoned during Park's regime returned to the campuses. There were many demonstrations supporting the new labor movements and political parties, and *Madanggeuk* was an active part of those demonstrations. However, the 1980 massacre at Gwangju by the new military government of President Jeon silenced many demonstrators and shadowed the political and cultural atmosphere of the 1980s. *Madanggeuk* became a part of the underground labor movements and democratic parties, and developed itself into an underground theatre. *Madanggeuk* reached its prime in June 1987 when the civil resistance movements finally changed the oppressive policies of the military government.

Through these resistance movements, Korean society finally became a free and democratic society and entered its path to globalization and postmodernization. In 1988, the festival of *Madangguk* took place, which was the first appearance of *Madanggeuk* on a professional stage. However, when *Madanggeuk* became a part of the established theatre circle, its decline began. Though it became an established branch of theatre, its passion and ardor seemed to have faded. Its social satire and criticism became dull with the newly democratic society. Ultimately, *Madanggeuk* began to die out when the ban against it was finally lifted. The amateur theatre based on the protest demonstrations was likely to fade away when those protests were no longer necessary.

Madanggeuk aims to achieve the following four principles in its performances: 1) displaying factual and circumstantial truth beyond the press-media reports, 2) creating collective festivity, 3) introducing a typical ideal folk model for the future of ordinary citizens, and 4) allowing variations depending on performance situations. In other words, *Madanggeuk* attempts to tell the audience hidden facts and different views of an event beyond what the political and economic ruling class wants the masses to believe. It also tries to suggest a heroic model of ordinary people and create an atmosphere of merry festivity. Additionally, it aims to be a performance that can adjust to different performance conditions, especially demonstrational situations. The theatrical frame can accommodate any situation, which allows it to be part of the demonstrations.

Madanggeuk has similarities to the epic theatre of Brecht. They both ultimately aim at social reformation. Though the employed techniques are varied, Aristotle's linear plot is broken with various dances, songs, and signs in both forms. *Madanggeuk* even sometimes employs discussions on social issues among actors and audiences; the audiences are invited to participate in the discussions during the performance. In order to protest and enlighten, *Madanggeuk* as well as epic theatre try to avoid empathy. However, unlike epic theatre, *Madanggeuk* aims for a concrete struggle in the form of a wide-open structure. In other words, the composition of theatre can be flexible depending on the performance situation. For instance, it juxtaposes scenes of hypothetical play and actual reality and ignites the energy suitable for protesting in real life. Of course, it also includes traditionally handed-down festivities that tie the performers with the audiences.

Unlike traditional theatres, *Madanggeuk*'s playfulness and openness presuppose a clear consciousness of life. *Madanggeuk* argues that theatre should go beyond simple materialism and have the so-called ideal folk model to show a vision for the future. Lukács, a Marxist philosopher and literary historian, argued, "The perspective is the most important in works of art."[3] Similarly, the perspective of pointing out social injustices and offering a vision for the future is the most important part of *Madanggeuk*. In short, in *Madanggeuk*, the intention to secure the realities of people's lives as the subject matter is universally pursued; current social issues and reinterpretations of historical facts are carried out.

On the other hand, the clarity of perspective in *Madanggeuk* can pose a problem. The strong orientation toward the typical folk ideal model and future vision raises concerns about turning art into a method of ideology. In other words, problems such as schematic object recognition or mechanical solution by ideology have been pointed out as weaknesses of *Madanggeuk*. Schematization itself is not necessarily harmful to the form of theatre—theatrical activity itself may be a schematized convention—but there is a great concern that the clichéd and uniform ending could turn the entire theatre into a simple slogan. This problem has already appeared in the failures of social realism, such as the theory of non-conflict. In fact, even when looking at some productions of *Madanggeuk*, their portraitions seem awkward except for their interested parties. The question of how to make ideological art artful is an immediate task of *Madanggeuk*. Overall, the ideal concept of *Madanggeuk* is as a theatrical form with a national spirit based on traditional theatre's playfulness and openness while accusing today's society for its lack of welfare for the people and the absence of a positive outlook for humanity's future. Indeed, the emergence of *Madanggeuk* was an important part of Korean theatre in the transitional period of self-awareness.

The state of separation in the 1980s between the established theatre and *Madanggeuk* was largely due to *Madanggeuk*'s extreme theatrical experimentations with a touch of political protest and its amateurism. The established theatre was not open enough to accept *Madanggeuk*. Meanwhile, the task of overcoming the amateurism of *Madanggeuk* also appeared. A movement developed to differentiate between "Du-Le-Pae" and "Tteun-Pae" in *Madanggeuk* and to make "Tteun-Pae" a specialized theatre company. *Madanggeuk* required more proficient and professional theatre training in the 1980s.

It is difficult to accurately grasp the actual status and data of *Madanggeuk* performances up to the 1980s. Because of the political repression of the time, no records were made, and performances were quietly shared among *Madanggeuk's* activists. Plus, the texts of *Madanggeuk* are semi-fixed; they are neither written texts like most Western drama nor dictated oral texts like traditional folk theatre. Furthermore, most texts of *Madanggeuk* are usually co-created by main actors, and there is much room for improvisation. Depending on the performance situations, lines and songs can be easily added or pulled out. Among the four aesthetic principles of *Madanggeuk*[4], the situational variations are largely due to the semi-fixed texts. Even though some texts of *Madanggeuk* are written by a specific author, the flexibility of texts is still retained.

Fortunately, some texts have been published to show the outlined situations in the late 1980s. *People's Theatre in Korea* (edited by Chae HuiWan and Im JinTaek, 1985), *Madanggeuk* (*Minjeokgeuk*) *Scripts 1 and 2* (edited by People's Drama Research Society, 1988), and *Madanggut Script Collection of Jeonlado* (edited by Shin Myung Players, 1989) are representative examples.[5] The main subject areas of the existing *Madanggeuk* are classified, and the works that are frequently discussed in each field are to be examined one by one. In a strict sense, this methodology has a problem of randomness in the selection of works and in the difficulty of grasping the recent trends of *Madanggeuk*, as well as the exclusion of performances. However, it is now almost impossible to trace the former performances due to the lack of records, and what is left are only a handful number of *Madanggeuk* texts that have been handed down. Selected fields and works are as follows.

1) Subject of Ethnic Issues: *Insensitivity* (*Bulgamjeung*)
2) Subject of Rural Issues: *Hampyeong Sweet Potato* (*Hampyeong Goguma*)
3) Workers, Urban Poor Location: *The Story of Deoksangol* (*Deoksangol Yiyagi*)
4) Material of Social Current Affairs: *True Donga Gut* (*Jin Donga Gut*)
5) Material for Reinterpretation of History: *The Revenge of the Army Raised in the Cause of Justice* (*Uibyeong ui Boksu*)
6) Material where the Messiah appears: *Hongdongji* (*Hongdongji*)

First of all, *Insensitivity* is highly dependent on a realistic composition, which is a little peculiar to *Madanggeuk*. Under the eight subtitled episodes, almost every scene develops a new situation, but every episode points toward a unified subject of its own. In particular, the consolation letter read with the voice of a young girl at the end brings up the issue of the ironic inter-Korean confrontation, further indicating the unnatural division of Korea. In addition, the construction leading to the climax through allusion-expectation-achievement—waiting and fulfillment—is the traditional realistic compositional method since Ibsen.

Since it is far from orthodox realism, *Insensitivity* shows all perspectives simultaneously. These include Private Kang, who was drafted into the military by forcible conscription; Private Han from a rural village with a father who was in prison because his brother got away to the North; Sergeant Peng, a veteran soldier who lost his father to the Communist Party; and so on. The play shows multiple perspectives without a fixed viewpoint of a single speaker. This multiplicity and simultaneity are thought to be linked to the episodic composition of traditional theatre.

While pinpointing the nation's biggest problem—the insensitivity toward the division of Korea—the play also conveys, in realistic ways, the tragic realities caused by the division of the nation, internal problems in the military, and the issue of the presence of U.S. military troops. Ultimately, the play evokes the urgent problems of the reality of the division today, which Korean people tend to turn away from and forget.

Hampyeong Sweet Potatoes addresses "The Hampyeong Sweet Potato Case" in 1978, when farmers who suffered enormous damage from the agricultural purchase policy of the Agricultural Cooperatives conducted "a collective damage compensation campaign to urge the government to buy the promised purchases."[6] First of all, the composition takes the form of a play that is close to a traditional performance, unlike *Insensitivity*, and there is no tension or excitement from the development of the plot. Interestingly, the main compositional form of question-and-answer and repetition, as is the case with folk games and folk dances, leads to a well-established satirical story. The farmer's music is essential to this performance, and the success or failure of the dance determines the success or failure of this performance. Though it is still a work of amateur playwriting, the basic composition of *Hampyeong Sweet Potato* is a cyclical plot in the form of a traditional play, and it consists of a sub-theme, questions, and repetitions as constituent units. When a sub-topic is selected, a question about it follows and is repeated, and then one sub-composition is finished. The repetitions of the sub-compositions make a play. Most importantly, *Hampyeong Sweet Potato* shows the victory over the government at the end of the struggle; its main aim was to protest the government for its inconsistent farming policy and to show that the farmers can achieve their goals by uniting. Thus, it is linked to the ideology of *Madanggeuk* in that it proclaims and suggests a solution to the current rural problems.

The Story of Deoksangol in 1977 is a case-investigation play dealing with the murder of a member of the demolition group at Mt. Mudeung in Gwangju, known as the Tarzan Incident of Mt. Mudeung.[7] It pleads for the life of Park Heungsuk, a poor urban worker who was sentenced to death, by telling the audience the untold story behind his accidental killing of an officer during a house evacuation. It starts with *Gut* and the story unfolds in *Madang* and *Geori*, which could respectively be considered acts and scenes in Western drama. However, *Madang* and *Geori* are not gradual and connected to plot development but rather reveal the full picture of the event through a fragmentary sequence of scenes. In this sense, the composition of this play differs from realistic dramatic techniques even though it is influenced by them. Moreover, unlike the diverse perspectives of characters in *Insensitivity*, the hero Park Heungsuk's personal viewpoint is fixed, and he stands out as a clear protagonist. While defending Park Heungsuk's murder case, the play criticizes the mass media's bias that manipulates public opinion and the old, vested generation including bureaucrats, clergymen, judges, and so on. However, it does not deviate much from established ethics in order to gain sympathy from the common people for Park Heungsuk's life. Since it was performed as part of an actual plea for Park's life, it was a work with a high level of practicality.

When President Park's regime oppressed the freedom of speech in the 1970s, advertisements were banned in the *DongA Newspaper*, which published news against the president. Thus, some elites and students advertised their personal notes or encouragements in the *DongA Newspapers*. At the same time, some reporters of the *DongA Newspapers* who proclaimed the Declaration of Free Press Practice in 1974 were fired. *True DongA Gut* in 1975 told the reporters' testimonies of the *DongA Newspapers*.[8] The performance at that time was performed in *Guchidade* style[9] without a script while including the report of the case. Performers wore nib-shaped reporters' masks made of newspapers to demonstrate the immediate image of newspapers and to hide their faces from surrounding policemen. "The songs sung by the audience according to the instructions of the performers reproduced the contents of *DongA Newspaper*'s real situation, not broadcasted in media. A considerable amount of donations was collected on the spot for encouraging advertisements."[10] It was reported that "a spontaneous protest of 1,500 student-spectators followed after the performance was over."[11]

True DongA Gut was an improvised play aimed at finding out the truth of the incident and was recorded later. At the time, it took an inflammatory position on a current story. Therefore, the ethics of *circumstantial truthfulness* and *situational variations at sites* were important. Participation of the audience was crucial. Reproducing the content of *DongA Newspaper*'s real situation with the audience's songs and spontaneous protests showed examples of on-site movement. If the play were to be performed today, the impact would be insignificant. Therefore, once the significance of the current event passed, it was necessary for *Madanggeuk* to impose universality on the work.

The Revenge of the Army Raised in the Cause of Justice is a work that exposes the fabrication of the so-called noblemen's army and the power of the people under Japanese rule. The work is composed of a *Gut,* a shaman ritual, at the beginning. Most of the piece borrows the structure and characters from traditional Mask-Dance theatre and ends with group dances. In addition, scenes used quick role changes since the three members of *Pansoe*, *Madangsoe*, and *Deokjindaek* continuously changed their roles. The pretense of the Nobleman's sickness contrasted sharply with the loyal soul of the people's army, which was described to show the patriotic spirit. Particularly, the play showed the camp of the people and the Japanese military simultaneously with the scene of the innocent child rhyme-songs and group dances. However, the question remains of whether it is an interpretation of history without distortion. Since the people and the nobleman are treated in terms of good and evil, the writer's perspective seems to be solidified and also to be based on a black-and-white view. Overall, the play tries to reinterpret the forgotten history and succeeds in showing the people's patriotism.

Hong Dongji is anthropomorphic, comparing the foreign powers of the United States and Japan to a tiger and a cat, respectively. In addition to using personification, *Hong Dongji* is the central symbol of the work, known as "the vision for the future." Structurally, it is also divided into *Madang* and *Geori* with the beginning road play and *Gosa*, the ritual for the performance, so the style is based on the structure of the traditional Mask-dance theatre and *Gut*, the Shaman ritual. However, because the structure is simple, the fun comes from comical moments or satire rather than tension from the dramatic events. *Hong Dongji,* which rejected foreign powers and expressed national independence, represented the savior of people. Unlike other *Madanggeuk*, the image of a powerful Messiah is highlighted, so the play is included in a new division involving the emergence of the Messiah.

As the six examined works generally show, the contents are limited to the criticism of reality and the reinterpretation of history. Since most of *Madanggeuk*'s viewpoints are aimed at accusing and correcting established ethics and values, *Madanggeuk* works are often progressive. But some of the works are suggestive enough to be called "one-off." Plus, the subjectivity is often so clear that its obvious intention can be felt. Acquisition of universality in one-time current events and overcoming the black-and-white logic of typicality are required in *Madanggeuk.* Despite these shortcomings, *Madanggeuk* emphasizes social criticism on the side of the socially weak, shows a post-colonial view toward foreign countries, and holds strong beliefs in social justice and equality. Indeed, *Madanggeuk* opened a new chapter in sociopolitical theatre in the history of Korean theatre.

7.2 *Madanggeuk* as a New Theatrical Form with Influences from Korean Heritage

As *Madanggeuk* was interested in national subjectivity, its form naturally turned toward familiar traditions. As mentioned above, traditional theatrical arts played an important part in the formal structure of *Madangguk*. Episodic or circular plot was often employed instead of the linear plot of Aristotle. Characters were usually type characters, like those in Korean Mask-Dance theatre, often representing social classes. In a sense, they were even more exaggerated in *Madangguk*; they were caricatures or icons of various classes. They had only a few characteristics of real people in order to show the contrast among characters, to deliver the messages, and to preserve the traditional merry spirit of performances. Many traditional vocalizations and songs were employed, as well as dances and stylized movements. There was hardly any scenery except for a few props to indicate a location. The writing of *Madanggeuk* was often the collective work of a leading group that shared the experience of a specific event. The collaboration was valuable because *Madanggeuk* tried to criticize the ruling class and protect the everyday lives of commoners. Additionally, the stage of *Madanggeuk* was a bare empty space surrounded by audiences or a part of demonstration, but it could also be a proscenium stage. No scenery was necessary, and only a few props were employed. Music was fairly important to the performance of *Madanggeuk* as it was in traditional Mask-dance theatre; the traditional music orchestra of *Changgu* (an hourglass-shaped drum beaten with a long stick), *Buk* (a drum beaten with a hand or a thick stick), *Kkaengguri* (a brass drum), *Ajaeng* (a stringed instrument), and sometimes *Piri* (a wind instrument) was a part of the performances. These traditions of *Madanggeuk* are examined in two parts, i.e., its intangible traditions and its stylistic elements.

7.2.1 Adoption of Intangible Traditions: The Aesthetics and Consciousness of **Madanggeuk**

The spiritual orientation of *Madanggeuk* heavily relies on intangible elements of traditional theatre. Among these, *Madanggeuk* is most influenced by the concepts of *people's consciousness*, *playfulness*, and *openness*. These concepts and their relation to *Madanggeuk* are examined one by one.

7.2.1.1 People's (Minjung) *Consciousness*

It is common knowledge that traditional Mask-Dance theatre has depicted society from the perspective of common people, *minjung*, who enjoyed this genre as a type of folk art. While the word *minjung* has been defined in various ways, the term essentially refers to the common people and the public as seen in the traditional Mask-Dance theatre. Out of all episodes in the traditional Mask-Dance theatre, the three most prominently dramatic are the episodes of the noblemen, the apostate priest, and the old couple. In the noblemen episode, the protagonists are not the noblemen but their servant, while the main character is a good-for-nothing of the village in the priest episode. Furthermore, in the old man and old woman episode, which depicts the reality of the common people's lives, the story progresses from the old woman's point of view—a person who would have normally been a social underdog in patriarchal society.

Madanggeuk inherits the *minjung* consciousness of common people. *Sori-gut Agu*, for example, is critical of Japanese sex tourists who come to Korea yet defends the sex workers saying, "Nevertheless, we can't put all the blame on those poor girls." Such an inclination is in line with the traditional Mask-Dance theatre that mocks the deceptive bad behavior of the apostate priest but keeps a neutral attitude toward the female concubine shaman. The style can be very forgiving toward commoners who struggle to survive. In *Jinogui-gut*, the whole community becomes one with the people playing a central role in fighting against goblins who harass the common people in various forms, such as tenant goblins, foreign crop goblins, and natural disaster goblins. These goblins represent the complex and structural problems of society, so the play can establish a critical rapport with society from the people's perspective. *Pig Dream*, another example, realistically depicts the difficult lives of common people, capturing their optimistic attitudes and warm relationships. The people in this play warmly embrace a maid who has become pregnant out of wedlock. Moreover, in *The Hawk of Jangsan Cape*, a foreign intruder hunts and kills a hawk, which is believed to be the guardian of the people, and the people come together to drive the intruder out despite their severe suffering. The last scene, in particular, features an army of farmers holding up a flag of a dragon. This scene deeply touched the audience, as it suggested the victory of the common people. As the examined *Madanggeuk* cases show, all *Madanggeuk* works criticize society from the perspective of common people, *minjung*.

Yet, the *minjung* portrayed in *Madanggeuk* are more autonomous and enlightened than the *minjung* depicted in Mask-dance theatre. While Mask-Dance theatre is composed of stories that have been improvised by the people over long stretches of time, the narratives in *Madanggeuk* were created anew by university students through a collaborative creative process. Despite having been considered the intellectual elite, university students during the epoch of *Madanggeuk* strongly strived and sharply criticized contemporary society from the people's point of view. This perspective can characterize *Madanggeuk* as a form of political theatre and makes it a modern style of theatre that inherits the intangible traditional spirit of the people's consciousness. No existing style of modern theatre can rival *Madanggeuk* in having been intentionally created for the people and having adopted the *minjung* consciousness. It is this *minjung* consciousness that is the very essence of *Madanggeuk*, which gathers various forms of *Madanggeuk* together under a single genre.

7.2.1.2 Playfulness (Nori)

While it is difficult to succinctly define *playfulness* in traditional performances, its similar expression collective festivity, or *SinMyeong*,[12] can be represented by the concept of *heung* (merriment) or perhaps by the concept of transcendent festivity in Western culture, where the self and the world become one and the self is completely lost in the process. Just like Mask-Dance theatre cannot be discussed without referring to the concept of *playfulness*, *Madanggeuk* is more often characterized by its playfulness than by the fluidity of its narrative.

Mask-Dance theatre was traditionally performed after a street procession or a shamanistic ritual dedicated to the prosperity of the villagers or during a religious village feast. The fact that the Mask-Dance theatre was performed after community rituals shows that it was fundamentally a community activity for fun and pleasure—a relaxing event after solemn rituals. Mask-Dance theatre, beginning with a ritual dance, would soon transform into a scene of *Sinmyeong*, which denotes collective excitement and fun.

Madanggeuk tried to revive this playfulness of traditional theatre in the modern context. For example, *Sori-gut Agu*'s dialogues, songs, and dances were entertaining despite their underlying sharp criticism of sex tourism. Musical numbers like "If you tell me to take off my clothes, I will," "Money Song," "Please, Don't," and "Wishing Happiness," despite their satirical aspects, play a comical role while mercilessly disclosing the problems of society to the audience. *Jinogui-gut* goes even further. Every subject of criticism is depicted in the form of goblins that are rebuked severely and delightfully. Even though it is a serious drama, which reports and seeks solutions for the desperate reality of farmers, the play ends with exuberant percussive music and an extravagant group dance, which creates quite a commotion. This kind of ending generates merriment and joyfulness, concluding the whole event as a festivity. In addition, *Hampyeong Sweet Potato*, depicting the farmers' victory over their struggles against the government's purchase of sweet potatoes, is inevitably a story to enjoy. It ends with the scene in which farmers shout with joy, "Farmers are the masters of their own lives!" *Pig Dream*, while portraying the difficulties of common people's lives, ends with a group dance and joyous music celebrating the marriage of Wangcho and Misun. The stage direction states, "The dance celebrates the marriage of Misun and Wangcho. Their vows symbolize their willpower to stand firm in the face of painful adversity." It further describes that "the dance gains more and more energy and the entire theatre becomes the site of a festival until all of the audience stands up to dance and play together."[13] *The Hawk of Jangsan Cape* dramatizes the folktale about a hawk from Jangsan Cape village. It is an exciting depiction of the people's rebellious spirit. It begins with the village's shamanistic ritual for a plentiful fishing season, which is an exemplary representation of the playfulness of the villagers. Furthermore, the last scene in which the people rise to fight rhythmically escalates until "the atmosphere reaches its peak, the light goes out, and the play ends."

Playfulness, shared with the audience in the above exemplary *Madanggeuk* works, cannot be easily found in contemporary modern theatre. *Madanggeuk* breaks free from the formula of modern Western theatre. It tries to provide the audience with a truly playful experience while satirizing the here and now in society. Ultimately, it believes that theatre is a festivity.

7.2.1.3 Openness: Madangness

The *madangness* of *Madanggeuk* derives from the performance venue where *Madanggeuk* was performed.[14] The concept of *madang* expands to *madangness*, which refers to an *open structure* of the performance, allowing ever-changing variations according to the audience, location, or performers of each performance. The concept of openness encompasses important characteristics of *Madanggeuk*, such as its variability, open structure, collectivity, and on-site presence.

Ihm JinTaek, who was the first to analyze the spatial characteristics of *Madanggeuk*, asserts that the term *madang*, which refers to "a flat area inside or outside a house," implies common, rather than individual, ownership. From this, he further interprets a strong sense of "collectivity" or "sociality" from *Madanggeuk*.[15] Lee YeongMi, adding to Ihm JinTaek's view, explains that the spatial "openness" is the most prominent feature of *Madanggeuk*. Here, openness signifies that "the space between the stage and the audience is left open" and simultaneously that "the pervasive sense of a familiar environmental reality surrounding the stage prevents the audience from being immersed in theatrical illusion."[16] Furthermore,

> *madang* is both a temporal and spatial situational concept. It constitutes the grounds for life as well as the grounds for generating a culture which can help to perceive and express these lives. It is, above all, a place for the community to gather.[17]

In other words, "it is a space, which does not create a theatrical illusion but which is open: all of its elements, including the stage, auditorium, and the external everyday spaces are all open toward each other"[18] While *madang* may seem similar to an arena stage, it fundamentally differs, as it does not require stage sets, installed props, or dramatic illusion. Hence, *Madanggeuk* maintains "a relative, multiple, and omniscient attitude" toward everything within the stage.[19] Kim JiHa expands the concept of *madang* in which the sacred and the vulgar become one, in which countering forces such as the transcendental and the gravitational rules of life—e.g., giving birth, living, eating, excreting, and vulgar rules—come together in harmony, creating the musical world of *Yulryeo* (律呂), heavenly harmony, as a scientific art. His theory can be associated with modern spatial theories that recognize the ideological significance of spaces that go beyond their practical purposes.[20]

Openness is derived from a philosophical reflection of *madang*. It is directly connected to a state where anything is possible, as a force of "active nothingness," or "due to its relativity and multiple points of views." Thus, *Madanggeuk*, with the structure of traditional Mask-Dance theatre, such as *Sori-gut Agu*, *Jinogui-gut*, *Hampyeong Sweet Potato*, and with stories in a realistic style, including *Pig Dream* or *Jindonga-gut*, allows for the spontaneous insertion of seemingly unrelated stories. For example, in *Pig Dream*, the female factory worker episode can be omitted without ruining the overall structure, or another episode about a construction worker can be added. In *Jindonga-gut*, any news report can be inserted or eliminated. Also, according to its progression, a performance can run for longer or shorter than planned. The duration of the performance can vary according to the degree of playfulness the show might attract or the rate of interaction with the audience.

Madang, means a scene, or "a site where things are happening now." Thus, *madang* in traditional theatre often refers to the "here and now." *Madanggeuk* embraces this element and develops it into "a situational reality" or "on-site political participation." *Madang* is not only a "site for entertainment and fun" but also a "site of struggle against all external conditions which oppress life." Also, the spirit of *madang* can be seen as open magnanimity, encouraging competition to enhance the productivity of life, to strengthen the internal solidarity of a community, and to ultimately enable reconciliation and even friendship between the opponents.[21]

In this way, *Madanggeuk* interprets and extends the concept of traditional *madang* in the modern context. As a result, in *Sori-gut Agu*, the main character returns to play with the women despite having been beaten up and chased away by Jjokbari. In *Jinogui-gut*, people use all their means to persuade Mangmakdaegol, a wealthy farmer, to become reinvolved in the reformation. In *Pig Dream*, Wangcho warmly welcomes and marries Misun, who has returned pregnant with another man's baby. These scenes go beyond existing morals, revealing a sense of open magnanimity. As seen in these examples, openness with magnanimity is one of the core characteristics of *Madanggeuk*.

Furthermore, *madang* can take place anywhere, because it does not require a specific setting. In other words, it has unlimited variability. Any site that has a surrounding audience can become a *madang*. The stage of a *Madanggeuk* can take place in any *madang*, which includes any indoor space or theatre building. This limitless adaptability of space exemplifies how *Madanggeuk* has seamlessly embraced the traits of traditional Mask-Dance theatre.

Madang can also be perceived in terms of its group collectivity in the sense that it is a place that many share. A *madang* inside a house is a shared space, as is a *madang* in a marketplace. As a *madang* stage is only formed once an audience gathers around it, it can be identified for its collectivity in the sense of "us" rather than "I." Therefore, *Madanggeuk*, even when it recounts a personal story, symbolizes something beyond the story of this individual; it projects a story about *us*; therefore, a representative story of individuals that narrates a collective struggle.

As examined, *Madanggeuk* inherited the spirit of traditional performance: *minjung* consciousness, playfulness, and openness—the very spirit of an open and alive community. It is significant that these traditional and intangible cultural assets have continued to exist in modern theatre. Furthermore, this spirit of tradition can be extended to existing theories of *Madanggeuk*, where the intangible spirit of tradition remains at the center.

7.2.2 Traditional Stylistic Heritages of Madanggeuk

7.2.2.1 Episodic Structure

Generally, *Madanggeuk* features an episodic structure. For this reason, it fundamentally differs from Aristotelian theatre, in which the plot serves as the most important element of drama. Among the six elements of drama—plot, character, thought, language, music, and spectacle—thought is the most important element in *Madanggeuk*. In this sense, the genre is classified as that of ideological drama like Brechtian theatre. The dramatic structure of *Madanggeuk* can be altered to best express an idea or a theme. It is taken for granted among theatre scholars that "when one judges the expressive methods of *Madanggeuk*, the criteria should not be based on Western theatre aesthetics."[22] The dramatic structure of *Madanggeuk* is influenced by the role of *Geori* (scenes) or *Gwajang* (episodes) in traditional Korean theatre. In traditional Mask-Dance or shamanistic rituals, scenes and episodes are not necessarily interrelated. What is important is that the episodes as a whole express a contemporary sentiment that reflects the perspective of *minjung*, the people.

Episodic or multiple-story structure is a prominent feature of *Madanggeuk*, not only in those based on Mask-dance theatre compositions, such as *Sori-gut Agu*, *Jinogui-gut*, *Hampyeong Sweet Potato*, but also in those based on the realistic structure, such as *Pig Dream* or *Jindonga-gut*. In *Pig Dream*, which has the most similar structure to a Western plot, it is more like a collection of episodes from the people's lives than a linear plot. In fact, all *Madanggeuk* mentioned in this chapter have episodic or multiple story structures. Except for the opening and closing scenes, one or two episodes can easily be inserted or deleted without affecting the essential message of the drama. In addition, frequent songs, dances, as well as the repetition of certain words or phrases and of certain behaviors, are a strong testament in favor of *Madanggeuk*'s connection to tradition.

7.2.2.2 Repetition and Circular Structure

Repetition is often found in traditional performances, especially in folk theatre. For example, the Miyal and the Old Man are reunified after each character repeatedly gestures the other person's action in the same manner. Another example is the simple act of recognizing a monkey, which results from the repetition of asking similar questions to the monkey. The noble class becomes the subject of satire through the continuous repetition of phrases that share a similar structure. These repetitions are adopted in *Madanggeuk*, especially in those works that utilize creative narratives with the Mask-Dance format. For example, *Sori-gut Agu* or *Jinogui-gut* uses many Mask-Dance-style repetitions. The following are a few examples of these repetitions:

Agu: Give me some money.
Musician: What did you do with the money you earned?
Agu: I was swindled into giving all of it to the street girls.
Musician: I don't have any either.
Agu: Give!
Musician: I can't!
Agu: Give!
Musician: I can't![23]

Ttaette: We'll buy a collective cow.
Malttuk: We'll buy a collective cultivator.
Ttaette: We'll buy a collective thresher.
Malttuk: We'll buy a collective dryer.
Gaedochi: We'll have a collective sales shop and raise pigs.
Ttaette: We'll raise chickens.
Malttuk: We'll raise silkworms.
Gaedochi: We'll raise fish.
Ttaette: We'll raise rabbits.
Malttuk: We'll grow great water rush and mushrooms.
Gaedochi: We'll grow mulberry and poison ivy.
Ttaette: Ha ha ha ha. We'll raise poisonous snakes, big and small, and sell them to the city folks in Seoul who lack in stamina, hee hee hee.[24]

As seen in the examples above, the repetition of similar words enhances the themes and rhythms of the dialogues. This method of repetition, originally employed by Mask-Dance theatre, later influenced *Madanggeuk*.

The repetition method is found not only in dialogue but also in the dramatic structure. For example, the nobleman scene has a circular structure. This circular structure is especially prominent in the *Bongsan* Mask-Dance theatre, presumed to be the latest of the traditional Mask-Dance theatre. The nobleman scene in the *Bongsan* Mask-Dance theatre, as has already been studied by Jo Dong-il, repeats the structure, comprised of 1) the dignity of the nobleman, 2) Malttuk's rebellion, 3) the angry rebuke of the nobleman, 4) Malttuk's denial, and 5) the relief of the nobleman.[25] Seemingly disparate merry dance sequences are inserted in between these dialogues. Furthermore, no apparent cause and effect can be applied to these moments in between blocks of dialogue. The sample dialogues clearly show the repeated structure of the nobleman episode:

1. Malttuk: The nobleman enters!
2. Malttuk: His title simply means he is a son of a dog and as low as a table.
3. Nobleman: What did you just say?
4. Malttuk: I just said the three brothers of the noble Lee family are entering.
5. Nobleman: Oh, the noble Lee family.

After this dialogue, the nobleman and Malttuk merrily dance, and then another bit of dialogue continues, as follows:

1. Nobleman: When accompanying noblemen, you must arrange somewhere for us to sit instead of simply wandering around!
2. Malttuk: I did arrange a nice place with a door opening out to the sky.
3. Nobleman: What did you just say?
4. Malttuk: I did set the place in the center of five directions, chose a house with eight balustrades and five pavilions, and dipped your cigarette in pig shit.
5. Nobleman: What did you just say?
6. Malttuk: That I dipped it in honey water.
7. Nobleman: He dipped it in honey water.[26]

In spite of the variations of lines, it is still a repetition of the same structure. Here, the repetition is in the form of a circular structure. In other words, the noblemen scenes have a complete circular structure, and the dance sequence functions as a buffering device. As seen in the examples above, each part is a satire in itself. Neither linear plot nor cause and effect relationships exist between each satirical part.

Furthermore, in this circular structure, repetitive parallel insertions were added. For example, when asked where he has wandered without properly accompanying the noblemen, Malttuk gives an unnecessarily long answer:

> Yes, yes, I went to look for the nobleman. So I ate cold rice and soup for a meal, and then I went to the barn, and drew out a donkey, and brushed its back nicely, and I rode on it, and stepped on and around the West and the East, as if I stepped on ripe fermented soybeans, and then, eastern Yeoul, western Guwol, southern trees and northern mountains, I searched every corner of the nation, every village and town, even between rocks and stones, and deep in the dirt, and in every crack of the fir trees, I looked everywhere but I could not find any fellow who remotely looks after my nobleman. Then, I remembered the old saying how about I go back home and see if you could find the person. Finally, I went to the nobleman's family mansion in Seoul; even there I could

> not see the nobleman or the young nobleman. The lady was all alone, so with my hat on, and with my whip on the side, and with my hair well wrapped in cloth, on my knees, I did it and did it; I did it twice.[27]

The point of this inserted dialogue is for Malttuk to reveal that he has slept with the lady twice. It is a parallel insertion in the middle of the plot.

In addition, many oral formulaic phrases are found. For example, the expressions

> eastern Yeoul, western Guwol, southern trees and northern mountains, I searched every corner of the nation, every village and town, even between rocks and stones, and deep in the dirt, and in every crack of the fir trees, I looked everywhere

are commonly used in classical texts to express the efforts of searching for someone or something. As Parry and Lord emphasize, such expressions are commonly shared throughout a society as official phrases that have been orally passed down.[28] Therefore, Malttuk's answer verifies that the verses of Mask-Dance theatre have been orally passed down by multiple authors. Simultaneously, it shows how a commonly known oral text has been inserted into the performance. In short, the nobleman scene is based on a circular structure with each episode narrated with repetitions or parallel insertions. The repetition, led by Malttuk's long speeches, enables a satirical depiction of the nobleman. Thus, this scene is an exemplary model of a scene based on a circular structure.

This circular structure is one of the most revealing elements of *Madanggeuk*. For example, *Jinogui-gut* is clearly based on this circular structure: the peasant goblin, the foreign grain goblin, and the flood damage goblin harass the farmers in turn. In this way, the repetition progresses to become characteristically circular. It is upon this circular structure that the linear structure of the farmers' autonomous actions is applied. The basic composition of *Hampyeong Sweet Potato* is also based on such a circular structure in the form of traditional Mask-Dance theatre. It is comprised of a sub-theme, an associated question, and repetition. See below for examples.

> ***A sub-theme***
> Sweet Potato: This is what those jerky officials bullshitted to us! "Well, we've decided to purchase all of your sweet potatoes, produced with your sweat and blood..."
>
> ***A question***
> Farmer 1: I think I've heard something like that before. So?
>
> ***A confirmation of the sub-theme***
> Sweet Potato: Well, so ... those jerks promised to buy all the sweet potatoes declaring their promise on the newspaper, the radio, the TV, and even

through the loudspeakers owned by the head of the village, and then...
Farmers: (simultaneously) and then... (pause)

Answer to the question
Sweet potato: (suddenly in a loud voice) The promise was kicked to the curb!
Repetition -Just like Cha Beomgeun kicks a soccer ball.
-Just like a Japanese person kicks a Joseon man.
-Just like an American kicks a Korean.
-Just like a gangster kicks a girl.
Farmer 1: (to the rhythm) Just like a business owner kicks a laborer.
Farmer 2: Just like a police officer kicks a college student protesting.
Farmer 3: Just like a cow kicks a dog.
-And so on-

Repetitions and circular structure in *Madanggeuk* are actually based on the structure of the traditional Mask-Dance theatre. This signals the departure from the Western Aristotelian drama by realizing a new modern theatrical style. Such innovative attempts found in *Madanggeuk* can certainly be seen as a pioneer of up-and-coming styles and changes in the theatre.

7.2.2.3 Music and Accompaniment

In traditional Korean Mask-Dance theatre, musical accompaniment leads the movement of the drama, and songs are inserted whenever possible. Without music, the performance would not take place. *Madanggeuk* also uses music in this way. Hence, it is quite common to see traditional musicians seated on the outskirts of a *Madanggeuk* performance. In *Madanggeuk*, musical accompaniment leads the progression of the drama, determining changes in the tempo and speed.

Furthermore, many *Madanggeuk* performances feature songs that have been inserted into the scenes. For example, *Sori-gut Agu* inserts many songs to raise the rhythmic feeling and merrymaking. *Jinogui-gut* features not only songs at various intervals but also employs minor-key *Pansori* to express a sense of despair. The use of songs and dances seems quite natural in *Hampyeong Sweet Potato*, which celebrates the victory of the farmers. Even *Pig Dream*, a *Madanggeuk* piece in the style of realism, concludes the performance with dancing and singing to celebrate the wedding of Misun and Wangcho. Music or musical accompaniment is integral to traditional Mask-Dance theatre in the same way that it is essential to *Madanggeuk*. Thus, *Madanggeuk* is a pioneer in introducing music and musical accompaniment in modern theatre.

7.2.2.4 Colloquial Language and Dialogues Like Folksongs

The traditional Mask-Dance theatre is scripted with extreme forms of colloquial language and folk-song-like dialogues. Mask-Dance theatre was collectively made rather than of a single author to serve the public enjoyment. *Madanggeuk* adopts its predisposition for the public; hence, the language used is also similar to that of Mask-Dance theatre. Despite having been initiated by the elite, the verses of *Madanggeuk* utilize the spoken language of the common people. For example, in this context, the narrative is often revealed to the audience through the use of simple questions or the linking of homonyms. Below is an example:

Musician: You are quite attractive (*sam-sam*).
Agu: Ah well, total strangers *(nam-nam*).
Musician: Strangers *(nam-nam*)?
Agu: Yes, why not strangers *(nam-nam*)?
Musician: Buster, I am a stranger (*nam*) to you and you are a stranger(*nam*) to me, so we are strangers (*nam-nam*), buster.
Musician: "Strangers (*nam-nam*)" are over there.
Agu: Where?
Musician: There. (He points to the business owner and a few women.)
Agu: Buster, they are not strangers (*nam-nam*) but a man (*nam)* and a woman (*yeo*). Man-Women (*nam-yeo*), man and woman (*nam-and-yeo*).
Musician: If they were just man and woman (*nam-yeo*), that would be good.
Agu: You mean, they are not even man and woman (*nam-and-yeo*)?
Musician: The pig trotters (*Jokbal*)
Agu: Ah, you mean pig trotters that make such a good side dish for the rice wine?
Musician: A Jap. (*Jjokbari*)
Agu: Ah, do you mean you have to suck on them hard (*Jok jok para)* for your health? Well, I can't stomach that.
Musician: You buster, can't you see that a Jap (*Jjokbari*) business owner crossed the seas to flirt with not one but two Korean girls?[29]

As shown in the example above, colloquial language is used to ask questions or repeat different variations of homonyms. As a result, the simple language acquires a rhythmic musicality. Such use of language is light and easy for the audience to understand, making it suitable for expressing *minjung* consciousness in a satirical way.

7.2.2.5 An Open Relationship with the Audience

In *Madanggeuk,* it is possible for the audience to cheer, shout interjections, or even join the play in the middle of the performance. For example, in my personal attendance to see *Jindonga-gut* during my college years, the reading of the proclamation of free journalism was met with enthusiastic applause and cheers from the audience. This kind of open relationship with the audience is even possible in the most Westernized and tightly structured type of *Madanggeuk*. For example, in *Pig Dream*, drinking scenes naturally involve drinks circulated among the audience to amplify the sense of merriment. *Madanggeuk*, in comparison to Western theatre, allows the audience to easily participate. The actors may even insert improvised lines in response to the audience's reactions.

Such an open relationship with the audience is part of the heritage that has been passed down through traditional Mask-Dance theatre. Its open structure allows performances to last for many more—or even fewer—hours according to the audience's response. While it has become rare today, at one time the elder dancing together with performers of Mask-Dance theatre at a corner of the playground could often be seen. The dances of audience members were also seen as part of the performance by other audience members. *Madanggeuk* has adopted this open structure by leaving ample room in the script. The audience can participate and create the work together. The open structure in *Madanggeuk* is all the more significant nowadays because the word "text," which is in the process of a completion of meanings, has become more commonplace than the word "play," a completed form. Ultimately, *Madanggeuk* has played an assertive role in introducing the concept of an audience participatory text in modern Korean theatre.

7.2.2.6 Use of Stock Characters

In traditional Mask-Dance theatre, it is widely accepted that performers play stock characters. For example, even if the character Malttuk appears in various Mask-Dances, each Malttuk is called by the same name, wears a similar costume, and acts in accordance with his persona. Such characteristics of particular characters in traditional Mask-Dance theatre are the products of a long process of repetition during which the actors and the audience have gained a common understanding of the characters' scope of actions. Hence, it is possible to predict how a character might react to certain situations. For example, the double-sided nature of Malttuk's persona guarantees that he will instantly, if superficially, obey the nobleman when given an authoritative order. It is also this double-sidedness that pushes Malttuk to revise his response. He reiterates that he had dipped the nobleman's cigarettes in honey water, rather than in pig's shit. Malttuk's response signals to the audience to wait even more eagerly for him to satirically recount the sex scene with the lady in which he says it was "not just once but twice." Stock characters can be found in Mask-Dance theatre, including Apostate Monk, Buddhist Monk, Young Shaman, the Prodigal, Nobleman, Servant Malttuk, Old Woman, Old Man, and so on.

The genre of *Madanggeuk* emulates Mask-Dance theatre's use of stock characters. In *Sori-gut Agu*, Agu resembles the Prodigal of Mask-Dance theatre, while *Jinogui-gut's* Gaedochi is similar to Malttuk, the servant. These stock characters may not be identified as clearly as in the sociopolitical forms of *Madanggeuk*, which feature stock characters due to the dichotomous nature of the plot. For example, in *Jindonga-Gut*, the contrast between good and evil is quite distinct between the journalists and the entrepreneurs. Even in realistic

Madanggeuk, such as in *Pig Dream*, each of the characters exhibits their individual traits, yet they are still associated with stock characters because they represent the people of today and depict their thoughts. Thus, *Madanggeuk* draws on stock characters of traditional Mask-Dance theatre, adapting them for a modern context.

7.2.2.7 As a Collaborative Teamwork

Traditional Mask-Dance theatre was not created by an individual but was a product of accumulation, transmitted by word of mouth through the ages as a collaborative project and even as an embracement of the audience. In old rural Mask-Dance theatre, the performances could not take place without the occurrence of common village rituals. More recent urban Mask-Dance theatre was often associated with festivals, such as *Dano*.

On the contrary, most *Madanggeuk* was created by the creative elite. Yet, the performance emphasized collaboration. This can be seen through the longevity of *Madanggeuk* troupes. Hence, such reverence for collaboration in *Madanggeuk* originates from its roots in traditional Mask-Dance theatre.

Conclusion

Madanggeuk produced in the 1970s and 1980s is a form of contemporary theatre that was clearly established as a political and social drama with inherited traits of traditional theatre. The achievements of *Madanggeuk* in modern Korean theatre history can be summarized as follows: 1) it was the first underground theatre, which protested against current political and social issues, 2) it made the best use of Korean traditions and succeeded in reviving traditional theatrical forms and their intangible spirits, and 3) it consequently awakened cultural nationalism among the audiences.

In fact, *Madanggeuk* is the only form of contemporary theatre that has been settled as a consistent genre, which was founded in traditional theatre. It has not only inherited the intangible nature of tradition, that is, people's (*minjung*) consciousness, playfulness, and openness, but it also has realized visible stylistic characteristics, such as episodic composition, repetitive structure and dialogue, the use of music and colloquial language, and an open relationship with the audience. Indeed, among the numerous experiments that have taken place regarding tradition, only *Madanggeuk* has managed to stand firm as an established genre of theatre.

Furthermore, *Madanggeuk*'s method of adopting tradition ties the genre to the age of postmodernism. It has embraced the concept of people's (*minjung*) consciousness within the perspective of today's studies on postcolonialism, and without being limited to the archetypes of tradition, has succeeded in considering tradition as a means of multiple expressions. In fact, owing to such contemporary modifications, *Madanggeuk* could become the genre that exists today. In a sense, *Madanggeuk*, its emergence coinciding with the rise of postmodernism, could be the precursor to Korean postmodernism. There is, however, an unbridgeable gap between *Madanggeuk* and postmodernism. Since *Madanggeuk* accepts tradition as part of national consciousness, it is far from the diversity of postmodernism that emphasizes globality and individualism. Plus, the fact that *Madanggeuk* began to lose its power as soon as postmodernism began to be accepted in earnest also distances it from postmodernism.

It seems that the *Madanggeuk* of today has lost its sense of purpose and, therefore, its popularity has diminished. This may be either because people's (*minjung*) consciousness has become too serious theme in today's individualized and diverse society or because those who had once fought for democracy shifted their attentions to the politics themselves. Perhaps this is why the *Madanggeuk* of today deals mostly with environmental issues rather than political issues. Regardless, in order to revitalize *Madanggeuk* again, it should be reborn with today's social and theatrical needs.

Notes

1 President Park became the president after the 5.16 military coup in 1960. He showed a strong desire for political power from the end of the 1960s, which appeared in the three-term constitutional amendment in 1968. Afterward, a confrontation with the people who wanted democracy arose, and he suppressed them. His achievements in economic development and his persecution of democracy are always opposed to each other.

2 *People's Theatre in Korea (韓國ui 民衆劇)*. Chae HuiWan and Im JinTaek, eds. Seoul, Changjak gwa Bipyongsa, 1985, pp. 6–7.

3 Lukács, George. *The Realism of Our Time*, Munhal Yeosul Yeongguhoe, Trans. Seoul, Ingansa, 1986, p. 33.

4 As mentioned above, Madangguk ideally aims to achieve the following four principles: 1) showing factual truthfulness, 2) creating collective festivity, 3) suggesting typical folk ideal model, and 4) adjusting to situational variations.

5 Chae, Op. cit.; *Madanggeuk (Minjeokgeuk) Scripts.* People's Drama Research Society Ed., vol. 1 and 2. Seoul, Pulbit, 1988.; *Madanggut Script Collection of Jeonlado*, Shin Myung Players, ed. Gwangju, DeulPul, 1989.

6 Chae, Op. cit., p. 131.

7 Ibid., p. 239.

8 Ibid., p. 273.

9 It is a style of acting with spontaneous dialogue by actors without a script, using only the outline of the plot, and was often used in early Sinpa Theatre.

10 Due to the military government pressure, DongA Newspapers' advertisers canceled advertisements, so advertisements could not be displayed. In order to help its financial crisis, individuals donated money to support DongA Newspapers' the Declaration of Free Press Practice.

11 Chae, Op. cit., p. 273.

12 *SinMyeong* is the state in which the playful spirit reaches its peak.

13 Chae, Op. cit., p. 237.

14 *Madang* means an open outdoor space that is flat and large enough for people to gather.

15 Im, JinTaek. "For New Theatre: A Few Ideas about Madanggeuk." Ulrim ed., *Essays on the Establishment of People's Theatre*, vol. 2. Seoul, Uri Madang, 1987, p. 52.

16 Lee, YeongMi. *The Principles and Characteristics of Madangguk.* Seoul, Korean National Research Center for the Arts, 1996, pp. 172–173.

17 Chae, Op. cit., p. 224.
18 Ibid., p. 176.
19 Ibid., p. 177.
20 Kim, JiHa. *The National Aesthetics of the Mask-Dance Theatre*. Seoul, Silcheon Munhak, 2004, pp. 88–136.
21 Chae, Op. cit., p. 224.
22 "From Madangguk to Madang-gut." *The Present Status of Korean Literature*, Chae HuiWan and Im JinTaek, eds. Seoul, Changjak gwa Bipyongsa, 1982, p. 217.
23 Ibid., p. 56.
24 Ibid., p. 104.
25 Jo, DongIl. "The Compositional Principle of the Nobleman Scene in Bongsan Mask-Dance Theatre." *The Ideology of Mask-Dance Theatre*, Chae Hui-wan, ed. Seoul, Hyunamsa, 1984, p. 44.
26 Jo, DongIl. *History and Principles of Korean Mask-Dance Theatre*. Seoul, Hongseongsa, 1979, pp. 200–202.
27 Lee, Duhyyn. *The Collection of Korean Mask-Dance Theatre*. Seoul, Geyomunsa, 1997, p. 189.
28 Parry, Milman. "Studies in the Epic Technique of Oral Verse-Making 1: Homer and Homeric Style." *Harvard Studies in Classical Philology*, vol. 41, 1930, pp. 73–147.
29 Sori-gut Agu. *People's Theatre in Korea*, Seoul, Changjak gwa Bipyong, 1985, pp. 54–55.

8 Toward the Postmodern Theatre

Korean society reached a turning point with the achievement of democratization in the late 1980s and the hosting of the Seoul Olympics in 1988. As the subject of the Seoul Olympics symposium was "postmodernism," a new tide of changes occurred in Korean society as well as in Korean theatre. Due to political changes in the late 1980s, *Madanggeuk*, which had come from the underground to the established theatre industry with the changes in society, gradually lost its influence. Perhaps because *Madanggeuk* was ultimately an underground sociopolitical drama, when the democratic political issues disappeared, its influence also dissipated.

The period of the 1990s was more complex and internationalized than ever, so individualism and interculturalism were widely accepted. International exchanges of theatre were also active. It seemed that a new era would surely come, moving out of the influence of cultural imperialism. As the 1990s went on, the words "postmodern" and "post-industrial society" were no longer unfamiliar. The so-called central values were dismantled, and none of the values in the name of diversity were dominant. In this decentered and uncertain era, "populism" alone was rising, which was closely related to the industry of popular entertainment. Like the flow of this culture, theatre had come to a place where popular values became important, turning away from elitism. Because of these changes and areas of diversity, it is very difficult to discuss this period at a glance. In this chapter, firstly, the new changes in the theatre industry during this period are summarized, and then the predominant theatre companies that led the transition to this period and the major theatre companies and directors of the 1990s are discussed.

8.1 The New Theatrical Trends of the 1990s

The characteristics of 1990s' theatre, first of all, emphasized the entertainment elements of theatre. The problem of theatre existed not in the entertainment itself but in the lightness of the commercial culture, which was based on the mass. The sense of vocation associated with modern theatre disappeared, and the belief in social edification was also greatly diminished. Commercialized independent performances were identified as excellent performances and

DOI: 10.4324/9781003490708-9

showcased the professionalism of theatre companies. There has never been a period when the commerciality of theatre was ignored, but it was rare when it was openly established as a part of the main performance value. The problem was that the dissolution of the central value went beyond the respect for diversity and eventually led to an absence of value, leaving only playfulness. This was almost no exception in the theatre of the 1990s. The performances in the back alleys of DaehakRo[1] were mostly dominated by pornographies and light comedies.

Owing to this light-hearted trend, caricatures and parodies dominated writings of original dramas. Indirect communication through reversal and irony emerged. So the artist lowered his or her voice as much as possible rather than giving omniscient instructions. The meanings were fluid and fragmented, but none of them were clearly explained, and, through the participation of the audience, performances even induced audience writing.[2] Such composition was certainly not a typical playwriting of reaching a climax and gaining catharsis through heightened conflicts and tensions. The emphasis was on how the parody and the multiplicity of fragmentations were connected to the emotions or moods of the entire work. Meta-drama, superimposed images, and physical movements rather than language were explored, so this new form of theatre was led by dramaturgy techniques more than ever. In other words, the emphasis on sensibility took precedence over the literary and philosophical depth of theatre. Thus, scene by scene had to provide a viewer with something to see that stimulated the senses. These changes brought a new perspective to realistic Korean theatre, but despite the smooth progress of techniques, the freshness eventually decreased due to the limits and repetition of the techniques.

The rise of the term *cultural industry* was also another characteristic of this period. This started in the movie and video industry, in which large corporations had expressed strong interest, and their interest also spread to theatre. The Samsung Movie Business Team produced the musical *42nd Street* in 1996 in collaboration with the American Theatre Company in the United States to convey the essence of Broadway musicals. In conjunction with this concept of a cultural industry, musicals emerged as a powerful genre contributing to the popular trend of pursuing pleasure and sensibility.

This trend also led to the spread of translated light comedies. A small portion of these comedies were overall good performances with ensemble acting and scenery, adding to the comical fun. However, having both commercial and artistic qualities was rare. Most of the comedies stimulated only peripheral senses. Plus, since companies wanted to obtain maximum effect while minimizing investment costs, performance budgets, stage art, and actors were generally insufficient.

To make matters worse, taking advantage of the commerciality of the theatre industry, a so-called "stripping theatre," or adult theatre, appeared in the early 1990s. They were addicted to solicitations with loud compromising slogans, and the performances were crude while most exposed scenes took place in blackout. Most of the audience who came to the show out of curiosity left the theatre feeling defrauded rather than enjoying it. It was difficult to find satisfaction in these plays of eroticism, and it was also misleading to say that they were pornography or adult theatre. Indeed, it was just another failed commercial theatre that disappeared near the end of the decade.

The emergence of the concept of *cultural industry* was certainly a welcomed addition because it showed the beginning of competing with the world's commercial theatre and getting out of small-scale theatre. However, when investments sought only short-term profits, investment profits were not guaranteed; short-term profits only made the audience leave theatres due to the low quality of performances, which, consequently, devastated the theatre industry.

Remarkably, the genre that emerged in the 1990s was musical theatre. In addition to Broadway-style musicals, experiments in Korean-style musical theatre steadily continued. Because the popularity and sensibility of theatre were emphasized, the expectations for the commercial viability of music theatre were greatly increased. This change reflects the trend of the European and American theatre industry, where musicals are the predominant forms of commercial theatre. Individual musical companies also came into being owing to this musical atmosphere. Sinsi Musical Company—founded in 1988—and ACOM—founded in 1994—were representative companies. Sinsi Musical Company was famous for its *Akgeuk*, Korean-style musical, and later Western-licensed musicals, and ACOM for its original musicals, such as *The Last Empress* (*Myongseong Hwanghu*), which was also performed on Broadway.

Western-style musicals have grown rapidly in quantity and quality since the early 1990s. *Nonsense*, *Don Quixote*, *Cats*, *Chorus Line*, *Guys and Dolls*, *Les Misérables*, *42nd Street*, and *Subway Line 1* were performed frequently in the 1990s, becoming familiar repertoires. In addition, original musicals were also steadily staged. Various performances continued, such as the familiar repertoire of *DongSungDong Sonata*, *Lee SooIl and Shim SoonAe*, *Winter Traveler* (*Gyoul Yeonga*), *Love in the Rain*, *Blue Saigon*, and *The Last Empress*, which is the only one that gained attention through overseas performances. Also in rotation were outstanding Korean adaptations with musical formats in small theatres, such as *Subway Line 1* (*Jihacheol 1 Hoseon*), *Sworn Brothers* (*Uihyongje*), and *Mosquito*, led by Kim MinGi, which also attracted much public attention. In short, in the first half of the 1990s, vocal performances were somewhat poor, but remarkable growth in dance, other acting ensembles, and spectacles took place. By the middle of the 1990s, musical productions increased, so there was not a day when musicals were not performed throughout the year, and thus, performances began to grow in size. In other words, musicals established themselves as a concept of the "cultural industry." During this time, musical and theatre audiences began to differentiate; musicals were for popular and wealthy audiences, while theatre was for more intellectual audiences.

The commercial success of musicals emphasized the importance of Korean music performances as well, and experiments to revive traditional music plays continued. First of all, interest in *Pansori*-related *Changgeuk* and Women's *Changgeuk* increased. Discussions on the modern acceptance of *Changgeuk* were also diversified, and the Women's *Changgeuk*, which had been rarely performed since the early 1960s, was also revived. In particular, in 1998, *Changgeuk*, *BaekBeom Kim Gu*, and Women's *Changgeuk, Love of Jin Jin*, were directed by a new generation director. The fact that these performances showed signs of a generational change was of great significance because the generational changes show the possibility of the continuation of genres. In addition, music-style theatre *Akgeuk* centered on popular songs and were performed intermittently, particularly by *Bridge Theatre* and *Sinsi Musical Theatre*, and they gained popularity among the middle class and elderly people. Although it was a large-scale performance, the stage or acting fell into mannerism of the old sentimental story of *Sinpa* style, and that was not enough to gain the attention of the new generation and critics. Ultimately, *Changgeuk*, Women's *Changgeuk*, and *Akgeuk* were experimented with Korean-style music theatre thanks to the advancement of Western-style musicals.

Accepting tradition and re-creating experiments were major issues in the 1990s. In accepting the so-called post-industrial society, the re-creation of tradition went beyond the confirmation of national identity and became valuable sources of infinite creations. Through the re-creations of tradition, a new objective was given to the globalization of Korean theatre: how to modernize the tradition and make it a living culture. Oh TaeSeok and Lee YunTaek were representative directors of these experiments.

Another characteristic of this time was the expansion of long-term programed performances. These kinds of performances, which are only possible with solid economic foundations and artistic visions, gradually increased in the 1990s. Although the visible effect was still insignificant, some projects were definitely settling down and leading the path for quality performances. For example, the *Seoul Arts Center* played an excellent role as a public theatre, enhancing the quality of performances with the series "Today's Playwrights" and "Theatre of Our Time." Meanwhile, *Hyehwa-dong First Theatre Lab (Hyehwa-dong Silhyomsil 1 Beonji)*, organized by young directors, became a mecca for producing young directors. In addition, international exchanges increased exponentially. In particular, the Seoul International Theatre Festival, the biggest theatre festival in Korea, was established in 1998 after the ITI General Assembly and its World Theatre Festival in 1997. With this opportunity, regular overseas performances and international performances in Korea were programed. Many public theatres progrmaed similar events likewise.

Minority theatre, such as feminist, youth, and children's theatres, also made a leap forward in the 1990s. Feminist theatre especially made rapid progress. Since Simone de Beauvoir's *A Disgraceful Affair* (*Wigi ui Yeoja*) was performed in the late 1980s by *Sanwoolim*, a fraternal theatre founded in 1969 and subsequently settled in a small theatre in 1985, feminist theatre attracted many female audiences. This company continued to perform foreign feminist works, such as Virginia Woolf's *A Room of One's Own* (*Jagiman ui Bang*), Caryl Churchill's *Cloud 9* and *Top Girls,* Barbara Walker's *Amazon* as well as original adaptations of Korean works, such as Park WanSeo's *Are You Still*

Dreaming? (*Geudae Ajicdo Kkeum Kkugo Itteunga?*) and Ju ChanOk's *What Does a Woman Live By* (*Yeoja eun Muoet euro Saneunga*), introducing a wide range of women's issues from sexual violence to the delicacy of women. The original plays of Jeong BokGeun and Um InHee followed. Indeed, the performances of *Sanwoolim* made a big impact on society at the time and attracted housewives to the theatre, forming a new audience group—loyal, middle-aged female audiences like the audiences of Women's *Changgeuk* in the 1950s. The long-forgotten women's theatre strongly took hold in the 1990s but rather subsided in the 2000s. However, due to the worldwide "Me Too" movement, feminist theatre has been rejuvenated starting in the late 2010s.

The trends of the 1990s were new in the history of Korean theatre. Theatre based on an intellectual audience lost its value and gradually blurred its border with commercial theatre. The values of modernity, which led up to the 1990s, were mostly replaced by new postmodern values. Before such full-fledged postmodern movements took place, the two theatre companies that were active in the 1980s should be examined. They are *Yeon Wu* and *Theatre 76*, which were formed in the late 1970s. While they had the characteristics of fraternal theatre companies from the 1960s, they also caused changes in the theatre industry in the 1980s, making it easier for people to accept postmodern theatre of the 1990s.

8.2 Transitional Companies toward Postmodernism: *Yeon Wu and Theatre 76*

While most companies founded in the 1960s came to a lull in the 1990s, new theatre companies that formed in the late 1970s became active. Among them, the companies of *Yeon Wu* and *Theatre 76* were notable. They were ultimately fraternal companies founded in the late 1970s and were on missions to bring about changes in the stagnant theatre world. These two theatre companies, composed of new artists in the established theatre world, tackled society with social criticism and new artistry. Since the Gwangju Democratization Movement and Massacre happened in 1980, the entire art world was under military control and suppressed, so the resistance of these companies was of great significance, like the underground *Madanggeuk* in the 1980s.

Yeon Wu Theatre was a fraternal company that gathered graduate members of the drama club of Seoul National University. It started as a study group centered on Jeong HanRyong in 1977 and was finally approved as a theatre member of the Theatre Association in 1978. From the beginning, the company insisted on original plays. Since it was difficult to find original plays, it adapted many novels and poetry into plays. *Yeon Wu* Theatre tried to create plays centered on its members, so instead of looking for actors that fit characters, it rewrote the plays for *Yeon Wu* members. In addition, it made it clear that *Yeon Wu* created works based on social consciousness. As the inaugural performance, *In the Morning, I Was Always Alone* (*Achimeeun Neul Honjayeyo*, written by Kim KwangRim, directed by Jeong HanRyong) took place in

1978. The company continued to perform original plays and planned a series called the "Rediscovery of Modern and Contemporary Korean Canonical Plays (Hanguk Hyundae Yeongeuk ui Jaebalgeon)." Although the chairperson changed from Jeong HanRyong to Park InBae, then to Kim SeokMan, and then to Jeong HanRyong again, the initial principles of the company remained in place. The representative works were *JangSan Cape* (*JangSan got Maru*) in 1980, *The Chronicles of Mr. Han* (*Hanssi Yeondaegi*) in 1985, *Birds Are Also Rising* (*Saedeuldo Sesangeul Tteuneunguna*) in 1988, *In Search of Love* (*Sarangeul Chajaseo*) in 1993, *Come and See Me* (*Nalboreo Wayo*) in 1996, *Mr. Kim Chiguk Goes Crazy* (*Gimchiguksi hwanjanghada*) in 1998, *Thee* (*Yi*) in 2000, and the series performances of "Rediscovery of Modern and Contemporary Korean Canonical Plays."[3] The plays in the 1980s emphasized social resistance, while the plays in the 1990s focused on postmodern experiments with traditional influences.

In the early years, *YeonWu* strongly expressed its intention to participate in social issues and attack problematic reality through theatrical activities. In the 1980s, *YeonWu* was close to being an avant-garde theatre group responsible for converting *Madanggeuk* into an indoor theatre as well as lleading satirical criticisms of society. As indoor staged works of *Madangguek*-type theatre, there were *Did the Bier That Stopped Not Have a Chief Mourner?* (*Meomchwo seon Jeo Sangyeoneun Sangjudo Eopdadeonya?*) in 1982 and *My Hometown Where I Lived* (*Naui Saldeun Gohyangeun*) in 1984. *The Chronicles of Mr. Han* further explored the possibilities of Korean epic theatre in 1985. However, at the turn of the 1990s, *YeonWu* embraced the postmodern era

Figure 8.1 A scene from *Mr. Kim Chiguk Goes Crazy*. Photo by *YeonWu* Theatre Company.

Figure 8.2 A Scene from *Thee*. Photo by *YeonWu* Theatre Company.

Figure 8.3 The Poster of *Thee*. Photo by *YeonWu* Theatre Company.

and showed active experiments in dismantling text along with micro-discursive thoughts and perspectives. A generational change also took place and produced new playwrights such as Yun YoungSeon, Jang WuJae, Kim TaeWung, and Ko SeonWung, and directors such as Min BogGi, Kim HakSeon, and An KyeongMo. In particular, Yun YoungSeon's *Squint's Question Answer* (*Sapaltteugi Seonmundap*) in 1994 and *My Braggart Father Has Cancer* (*Tteoli Uri Abeoji Ame Geolriseottne*) in 1996 were deconstructive plays that were close to *Yeonwu*'s satirical expression of reality and marked the full-fledged start of postmodernism since the 1990s. Even the divided Korea was caricatured in *Mr. Gim Chiguk Went Crazy* in 1998. The play symbolizes the confrontation between North and South Korea with twin brothers, whose mothers appear to remind them that they are one with each other at the end. Despite each other's hatred, they are portrayed as indistinguishable even by the wife. It borrows the motif of the classic folk tale of *Onggojip* and heightens the connection between tradition and the postmodern technique.

Starting as a small fraternal group, *YeonWu*, based on humanistic literacy, aimed to criticize reality and contribute to society through theatre. It also explored various theatrical methods to express social realities. Above all, no theatre company had tried to promote original drama as much as *YeonWu*. Thus, the company made a significant contribution to revitalizing original play productions in Korean theatre history.

Theatre 76, was a theatre company that launched an experimental theatre movement centered on so-called absurd plays in 1976.[4] It was led by young theatre artists, including Kim TaeWon, who was also interested in movies and dance, and young actor Gi JuBong, and was planned in close solidarity with films and paintings. With the goal of launching the Little Theatre Movement, this theatre company, which was founded with the performance of Sartre's *Vomitage* (*Gutto*), suffered financial difficulties. It began to revitalize when director Gi GukSeo took over the company. In particular, in 1978, when Peter Handke's *Desecration of Audience* (*Gwangaek Modok*) was put on stage, *Theatre 76* began to attract attention as a young and ambitious experimental theatre. *Desecration of Audience* was popular with approximately 430 performances as part of the company's fixed repertoire for 10 years.

Theatre 76, received extra attention with the production of the *Hamlet* series. The massacre of Gwangju citizens by government military forces in 1980 cast a political shadow over most of the 1980s. Under these circumstances, the political *Hamlet* came into being. Gi Gukseo, the director, adapted *Hamlet* and made it into a series of political confrontations. *Hamlet 1* in 1981 was set in modern times and was performed by 70 young people in jeans. The director said that *Hamlet 1* paid attention to the numb outsiders of history rather than to intrigue the surroundings of the murder of Hamlet's father in Denmark.[5] Owing to the fame of Shakespeare, the changes to the original work went unnoticed by the government in the beginning. Gi Gukseo made a series of five *Hamlets* between 1981 and 1990. It is said that the theatre was surrounded by 500 policemen during

Figure 8.4 The Poster of *Desecration of Audience* (2022) by *Theatre 76*. Photo by *Theatre 76*.

performances of *Hamlet 3*. Indeed, *Hamlet 1, 2,* and *3* were the new and timely Korean interpretations of *Hamlet* as a political caricature. The director Gi Gukseo broke down the motifs of *Hamlet* and arranged them to show the modern issues of society. Though he did not break any binaries, such as the right and wrong of *Hamlet*, he first introduced the idea of deconstruction of an original play and rearranging it according to his intentions. In other words, the director's rearrangement can be seen as the forerunner of deconstructionism in Korea.

Yeon Wu and *Theatre 76*, founded in the late 1970s and actively performing in the 1980s, were fraternal groups that belonged to the Little Theatre Movement. They represented the experimental indoor theatres in the 1980s, while *Madanggeuk* actively initiated underground performances. Though these two companies also performed in the 1990s, they did not attract the same attention as they did in the 1980s.

Figure 8.5 A Scene from *Hamlet 6—Next to the Chrysanthemum in Samyang-dong* (2012). The *Hamlet* Series, Which Began in 1981, Continues until *Hamlet 6* in 2012. Photo by *Yonhap News* and Gi Gukseo.

8.3 Major Theatre Companies and Directors in the 1990s

Important theatre companies of the 1990s, such as *MokHwa*, *YeonHidan Players*, and *MiChu*, were different from the fraternal theater groups. These were groups centered on powerful directors, and they received attention for their new experiments suitable for the postmodern era. The major directors were often major playwrights of the 1990s. They deconstructed the causal development of plots and emphasized elements other than language, such as visual or audio images, along with physical movements. They particularly experimented with making Korean heritage come alive and made themselves internationally known with the Korean-ization of Western classics.

The modernization and globalization of traditions in the 1970s focused on tradition itself or combined the traditions with Western avant-garde experimental theatre. The modernization and globalization of traditions in the 1980s were intercultural and melded into contemporary Korean theatre. In the 1990s, as Korean society entered the postmodern era, the globalization of tradition accelerated. *Samulnori,* the traditional performance of percussion instruments, became popular in numerous overseas performances, enough to become a common noun. Additionally, Mask-Dance theatre took place in various regions beyond its origins. *Bongsan* Mask-Dance theatre and *Yangju Byeolsandae* Mask-Dance theatre performances increased in earnest overseas. Not only that, an international Mask-Dance theatrical festival was organized in Korea; the "*Andong International Mask Dance Theatrical Festival*," which was promoted in 1997, is a prime example. *Madanggeuk* also participated in the "Asian Council for People's Culture," which focused on the modern integration of traditions, such as masks, and collaborated with various Asian theatre players to make *Cry for Asia* in 1990, 1995, and 1998.

Traditions were widely applied in contemporary theatres and were viewed as a resource for diverse experiments of the postmodern era. Though the experiments in modernizing theatrical traditions began progressing in the 1970s, the reconstructions of traditions in order to keep them alive began in the 1990s. The theatre companies that pioneered in the 1990s were those that led experiments with traditions, which propelled postmodern theatre.

8.3.1 Oh TaeSeok with The MokHwa Theatre Company

The *MokHwa Theatre Company* was one of the leading companies in the 1990s, founded in 1984 by director and playwright Oh TaeSeok.[6] He had been a member of *the Drama Center*, founded by Yu ChiJin, but created his own company. With the founding of *MokHwa Theatre Company*, he was free to pursue his theatrical dreams. The two themes of his theatre company were "Korean tradition" and the "Korean War." These themes originated from his experience of his father dying after the Communist army took him away during the Korean War.[7] Oh TaeSeok then spent his childhood with his grandmother in the countryside, where Korean traditions remained untouched, unlike in the cities. Nature and Korean tradition, which healed the scars of the war, left a strong impression on his mind. His dramas utilized traditional Korean motifs with bold imagination. He opened *MokHwa Theatre* with his original play, *Africa*, in 1984. His directing included many sporadic and contingent elements. The structure of the story was far from Aristotelian causality, as it was synchronic rather than chronological, which often left the audience flummoxed. In short, the text was full of unexpected sensuousness and fancifulness. Therefore, due to his multiplicity, ambiguity, and anti-causal plot, TaeSeok's work is studied from various perspectives, such as surrealism, semiotics, and postmodernism.[8] There are few Korean playwrights with as many multidisciplinary influences as Oh TaeSeok.

The varieties of his texts could ultimately be encompassed in the modernization of the Korean tradition. No matter what kind of cultural and literary trends were applied, most of Oh's plays, such as *Cloudy Tower (UnsangGak,* 1990), *Why Did Simcheong Throw Herself Twice into the Indang Sea* (*Wae Simchongieun Dubeon Indangsu ui momeul Deonjotneunga*,1990), *White Gull, Don't Hopping Fly* (白鷗ya, Kkeongchung Najimara, 1991), *Baekma River Under the Moonlight* (白馬江 Dalbame, 1993), and *Bellflower* (Doraji, 1994), were rooted in Korean tradition. Two plays, *Why Did Simcheong Throw Herself Twice into the Indang Sea?* and *Baekma River Under the Moonlight*, are analyzed in reference to Oh TaeSeok's reconstruction of Korean tradition and the acceptance of postmodernity.

In *Why Did Simcheong Throw Herself Twice into the Indang Sea?*, the famous Korean folk classic is utilized. The writer presents the fin-de-siecle circumstances by applying ShimCheong's well-known tale to his play. In this play,

ShimCheong, who sacrificed herself in the Indang Sea to open the eyes of her blind father and all blind people in the country, meets the Dragon King at the underwater palace and goes sightseeing in modern times before marrying the king of her country. Watching the life of a young man named Yun Semyeong, a human being whom the Dragon King chose to test, ShimCheong despairs at his harsh reality. Finally, she is appalled by the trafficking of girls and society's indifference toward them and throws herself as a scapegoat once again into the sea in order to draw attention from society.[9]

Except for the fact that the activist is ShimCheong and that she jumps into the sea as a scapegoat, the tale of ShimCheong and this play have no other similarities. Nevertheless, by presenting ShimCheong as a witness to contemporary problems of Korean society, the work is at once connected with the classics and gains a tremendous depth by comparing yesterday to today. Moreover, in the composition of minimizing ShimCheong's individual character, the archetype of ShimCheong in the old tale is inherited as the heroine of the play. Therefore, ShimCheong, as a critic of the modern world, is a virtuous character from the beginning, and this justifies her jumping into the sea as a sacrifice to protest against the trafficking of girls. In addition, the world of ancient ShimCheong and the world of today are contrasted and highlighted. In ancient times, the goodness of ShimCheong is represented by filial piety, opening the eyes of the blind all over the country, but in modern times, her goodness pushes the male protagonist into an even more miserable situation due to her lack of understanding of his situation. She throws herself into the sea again, but no one can be saved.

At a glance, the stage of *Why Did Simcheong Throw Herself Twice into the Indang Sea?* was distracting, diverse, and chaotic. The stage was full of the waste of contemporary byproducts: discarded packing and boxes, human targets in entertainment venues, prostitutes used in human trafficking, and so on. The work appealed to the audience with maximum sensational stimulations (even toward the grotesque),[10] multiple progressions, a sense of speed, diversification of perspectives, and elements of shock. All of these could be symptoms of postmodernism. In addition, the work applied a new technique of reviving the traditional spirit. It was difficult to find fragmented traditional images or dances in the performance. However, only with the fragmentary borrowing of the heroine's name from the well-known folk tale, this play became inextricably linked with tradition. By choosing the name of the activist for the modern world as ShimCheong, the play acquires a classic character and a scapegoat motif. Ultimately, its meaning becomes amplified, and, at the same time, it is connected to the world of the past. It may be called a kind of parody without the intention of mocking the old story. There was little contrast between the two works. However, the breathtaking connection between the two works is in Oh TaeSeok's novelty in crossing the worlds of the old tale and modern reality. Indeed, *Why Did Simcheong Throw Herself Twice into the Indang Sea?* was of great significance in a new contemporary method of integrating traditional tales. Thus, Oh TaeSeok was successful in showing the signs of postmodernism and suggesting a new way of reviving tradition.

Unlike *Why Did Simcheong Throw Herself Twice into the Indang Sea?*, *Baekma River Under the Moonlight* places tradition at the center of the work. Thus, traditional elements can be found easily. The play shows the roots of tradition through *Daedongje* (village ritual) held in a town of the old kingdom of Baekje. Through the godly shamans in *Daedongje*, the unofficial history of the destruction of the Baekje Kingdom is caricatured from a contemporary perspective. *Daedongje* is like a playground of historical ghosts and a meeting point of the past and the present. The caricature of its history adds playfulness to *Daedongje*, which ultimately aims at the unification of the whole village and the demonstration of traditional roots. Oh TaeSeok's spirit of play, which is rooted in Korean tradition, is fully shown in this work. The visual effects of the characters are also excellent: the loyal subject SeongChung is crippled, King Uija's limbs are bound, and General Gaebaek appears as a spider because he murders his family.[11] In other words, Oh TaeSeok used the village ritual and the history behind it to show his own meta-logical storytelling; he made the work diverse and gave multi-meanings with his postmodern reinterpretation, caricature, and images.

In conclusion, the major characteristics of Oh TaeSeok's way of integrating traditions into the above works are anti-causal novelty and playfulness. Furthermore, his storytelling is deconstructive since he rejects Aristotelian

Figure 8.6 A Scene from *Why Did Simcheong Throw Herself Twice into the Indang Sea?* In Abandoned Boxes, Women Wait for Customers. Photo by The *MokHwa Theatre Company*.

causality in the development of the plot. The unfolding of a discontinuous story goes back and forth between the past and the present, and between this world and the other life. This storytelling strategy also showcases the infinite imagination and playful wit that only Oh TaeSeok could provide. Additionally, the unique parallel communication method among characters is noticeable. Unlike a Western-style debate, it involves sitting in a row and talking without looking at each other.[12] Therefore, his performances can be discussed as postmodernism or deconstructionism. However, even in the midst of modernity and novelty, he ultimately aligns the artist's perspective with Korean traditions. Consequently, his performances do not advocate or insist on integrating traditions, but Korean traditions appear as the roots of his performances. The era in which the most traditional Korean-style stories connect with the latest Western theories is termed postmodernism, and Oh TaeSeok's artistic sensibilities played a prominent part in it.

8.3.2 Lee YunTaek with YeonHidan Players

YeonHidan Players, founded by Lee YunTaek in 1986, emerged as the most active company in the 1990s along with *Mokhwa Theatre Company*. The two main pillars of Lee YunTaek's performances were sociality and playfulness.[13] He had a belief in the sociological role of theatre and strongly opposed the idea of theatre as simply entertainment. Though he deeply realized that today was a post-industrial society more than ever, he still emphasized the powerful message that theatre should play the role of a social critic. Theatre for social change is not only strongly expressed in his political and historical works dealing with accusations against absolute power but also expressed in the works that focus on playfulness, including caricatures and parodies.

Playfulness appears throughout Lee YunTaek's works. He uses calculated playfulness appropriately in any performance, and the basis for it is rooted in Korean traditional performance. He insisted that the origin of Korean plays is in *Gut*, a shaman ritual, and it should not be stuck as a "fixed and unchanging text" but treated as a "living *Gut*, which lies at the intersection between ethnicity and contemporariness."[14] In other words, by insisting on "the living *Gut*, he sincerely tried to revive tradition. This "living tradition" raised debates about *Gut*, suggesting a new direction for the integration of tradition. None of his works are irrelevant to tradition, but to examine Lee YunTaek's integration of it, the representative works *Ogu* and *The Problematic Human, Yeonsan* will be examined.

Ogu is a work that caused a series of so-called "*Gut* (shaman ritual) debates" about the acceptance of tradition and raised the issue of "living tradition."[15] As the title suggests, *Ogu*, a shaman ritual for the dead, is a play for the dead. However, since death, the most dramatic incident, comes as a part of the entire process of life, it is difficult to find conflict in the work. Even the psychopomps[16] that guide the dead mom have the same desires as human beings;

therefore, what *Ogu* shows is a mess and feast of life. It is pointless to find a logical plot or direct message in the work.

While taking a nap, the old mother meets King Yeomla, who rules the underground world. When she wakes up, she asks her son for an *Ogu* ritual as her last wish to prepare for death. In the middle of the ritual, when the shaman's frenzy is taking place, the old mother suddenly dies after leaving the words, "I'm returning." The psychopomps appear to take the old mother with them. The underworld psychopomps bargain for the journey's guide money,[17] have an affair with the widow, engage with humans to play card games, and even judge the issue of human inheritance. The fear or sorrow of death is diluted and caricatured in the process of thorough reification of death, normalization, and objectification. In the mourner's house, people, including relatives, constantly complain of hunger, sleepiness, and inheritance, and play card games to earn money. Through these everyday routines, the essential drives of life—material and sexual desires—are highlighted. Recalling that this reification has been the subject of many comedies, it is rather natural that the ritual of death, *Ogu*, becomes a comedy.

Ogu focuses on reviving tradition rather than presenting its aesthetics. It was controversial that *Ogu Gut* was interpreted to fit contemporary life and became a play itself. The artist regarded the *Gut* ritual as an intangible prototype of a Korean play. In addition, he asserted that "old ancestors did *Gut* in the old way, and we must do *Gut* in our way"[18] and insisted on integrating "the tradition alive today." In other words, the methodology of integrating traditions shown by *Ogu* includes its emphasis on intangibility and present-ness. Of course, traditional dances and melodies are well-utilized, but these are only the surface elements of *Ogu*'s traditional experiment. The circle of life and death and playful chaos are indeed the essence of the Korean comic spirit that has been forgotten in the turbulence of modern history. Beyond the reproduction of the original ritual or the aesthetic reconstruction of the traditional image, the conscious effort to incorporate the spirit into contemporary times opened a new era for the adaptation of Korean traditions.

On the other hand, *The Problematic Human, Yeonsan* interprets tragic human contemplation from a contemporary perspective. The perspective of the playwright, who grasped the nature of the *Yeonsan* tragedy as the confrontation between Confucianism (foreign powers) and Shamanism (indigenous powers), was new and convincing.[19] The intellectuals of Confucianism in old times took advantage of their interests due to the so-called Confucian philosophy and Chinese power. The writer criticized the opportunism of intellectuals as well as the bureaucrats in political strife at that time. In other words, the work was inextricably linked to the integration of living traditions and provoked criticism of the opportunism by modern intellectuals through the interpretation of King *Yeonsan's* tragedy. In short, the interpretation of history and political power led audiences to think about the social power balance. The writer aroused public interest with the rewriting of King *Yeonsan*'s

Figure 8.7 The Happy Mother during the *Ogu* Gut. Photo by *YeonHidan Players.*

Figure 8.8 The Curtain Call. Photo by *YeonHidan Players.*

history. This reinterpretation strongly reflects the influence of postmodernism. However, it is a regret that the writer has a bit of an arbitrary interpretation of the history, and the individual character of *Yeonsan* is somewhat unclear.

The entertainment aspects were also well realized in this play. Theatrical attractions were varied, such as a realistically yet symbolically slanted stage and a pool of gazebos in the center of the stage. In addition, the contemporaneity is felt in the traditional costumes, stage arts, and short displays of traditional dance and acting.[20]

Ultimately, the popularity of and praise for this work originate from the postmodern pluralism of the performance. The tragedy of King *Yeonsan* and the dark political struggles of power in history are revived for contemporary audiences, and traditional elements are seen everywhere in popular entertainment. Since a historical fact is used as the subject, the play is connected to the intangible meaning of history as well as tradition, and so it is essential to have a tangible representation of traditional scenes, costumes, and sounds. When representing traditions, the performance does not insist on its originality; traditions become internalized tangibly and intangibly in *The Problematic Human, Yeonsan*. In other words, through modern interpretation and modern sensibilities, *Yeonsan* emerges as a person of the past as well as of today. The slogan of the tradition that began in *Ogu* is achieved in *The Problematic Human, Yeonsan* with a relatively large consensus. Indeed, the playwright presents a so-called social play in the post-industrial society and uses Korean tradition as a part of postmodern diversity. In this way, Lee YunTaek's integration of tradition advocates for the revitalization of the intangible spirit. The root of his plays is traditional enough to insist that the original form of Korean theatre is *Gut*, a shaman ritual. In addition, his company's skill in traditional artistry surpasses that of any other theatre company's. Since the proficiency of traditional artistry is demonstrated, the company's traditional experiments are even more exciting. Lee YunTaek's method of traditional integration has also has been applied to the productions of Western classics, such as *Hamlet*, *King Lear*, and *Mother Courage*, and attracts worldwide attention. This reinterpretation of tradition is mainly connected with one of the postmodern methods.

8.3.3 Son JinChak with **MiChu Theatre Company**

Another notable company in the 1990s is the *MiChu Theatre Company*. It was founded in August 1986, centering around Son JinChak, who was the representative of the *Folk Art Theatre*, *MinYe*, along with about 30 other members. *MiChu* was launched in 1987 with the founding performance *Guardian* (*GiKimi*) on the stage of the Arts Center Grand Theatre and was active in the 1990s. *MiChu* presented works that harmonized with society through a wide range of topics and was evaluated as a theatre company with national sentiment in various forms, crossing a wide range of fields from traditional to modern musicals. In 1996, the company moved to *Yangju*, a suburb of Seoul, and established *The Mountain Place of MiChu* (*Michusanbang*) with facilities such as a 200-seat indoor theatre and an outdoor theatre. In March 1998, *MiChu* Theatre School, a one-year actor educational program, was established.[21]

Since Son JinChak was originally from the *Folk Art Theatre MinYe*, which had practiced traditional Korean arts since the 1960s, he has been deeply interested in the revitalization of tradition. In particular, its core members helped to solidify the genre called *MaDangNoRi*, which had been formally established in the theatrical world since 1981, years before the company was founded. It was an effort to turn *Madanggeuk*, which was an underground genre in the 1980s, into an indoor performance. He pursued a more complete theatrical aesthetic by showing brilliant stagecraft and skilled traditional acting in cooperation with a TV company. *MaDangNoRi*, which employed traditional dances, songs, and movements, remade old tales, and *Pansori*, along with new stories. This genre became popular thanks to the company's outstanding traditional artistic techniques and the massive promotion by large capital support. The form of *MaDangNoRi* was exclusive to the *MiChu Theatre*, which created a modern genre with influence from the traditions. As *MiChu Theatre* declared in its inaugural manifesto, *MiChu Theatre* had a strong belief in *Madang*, the traditional open playground, as its stage. Thus, the name *MaDangNoRi* came from a Korean word *MaDang* meaning "playground" and *NoRi* meaning "play." Though *MaDangNoRi* is performed on indoor stages, the stage is not a proscenium and can freely move around. *MaDangNoRi* is the first successful example of reproducing tradition with large commercial investments, media advertisements, and public popularity. The form is a successful case of integrating traditional theatrical heritage with post-capital investment, which is one of the characteristics of postmodernism.

MiChu's other major works were also related to Korean traditions. They retold the stories related to Korean history, old tales, and traditional artists' lives in plays such as *The Sky of Namsadang* (*Namsadangui Haneul*), *The Silver World* (*Eunsegye*), *In the Mountains and Fields, When Spring Comes* (*Bomi Omyon Sane Deule*), and others. For example, *The Sky of Namsadang* shows the philosophy and sorrows of old artists through the female chief of *Namsadang*, a group of nomadic entertainers. The legendary story is expanded to include *Namsadang*'s philosophy that originated from the belief that an artist has sinned in heaven and has been driven into the human world; thus, one must entertain people to compensate for their sins despite the difficulties of reality.[22] The heroine's excellent skills and beauty make her unfortunate life even more appealing, while it clearly conveys the belief in *Namsadang*'s art. However, it is difficult to find her individual characterization, which is shaped by the causality or events of the play. The personal history of the heroine has been reduced only to the story of *Namsadang*. Since the play detaches the heroine from an individual, the play has a distance from personal involvement, i.e., a sense of Brechtian alienation. In other words, since the stage was arranged in a series of *Namsadang*'s talents and skills, the success or failure of this performance depended on how many actors could reproduce the skills of old *Namsadang*.

Reviving the skills of *Namsadang* is key to enjoying the performance since all characters, including the heroine, are detached from their stories but all act the well-known tale of *Namsadang*. In a sense, they are marionettes of *Namsadang* players, and their skills are emphasized as the form of the play. Thus, the performance is connected to the present, which claims the form rather than the content. As members of Michu Theatre had been interested in Korean traditions for a long time, the six traditional theatricalities of *Namsadang*[23] were successfully revived in this performance along with songs and dances. Yet, it failed to achieve the original range and excitement of the old *Namsadang*, whose performers devoted their whole lives to developing their roles and skills. Thus, the integration of tradition in *The Sky of Namsadang* is only partially achieved.

Figure 8.9 A Scene of *The Sky of Namsadang*. Photo by *Michu Theatre Company*.

MiChu Theatre also participated in social criticism. *The Toenail of General Oh* by Park JoYeol attacks the nonsense of the political and military system, and *Death and the Maiden (Jukmeun gwa Soyeo)* by Ariel Dorfman criticize the unjust deaths under the military regime. The relationship between Ariel Dorfman and *MiChu Theatre* led directly to Dorfman's work, *The Other Side* (*Gyeongeseon Neomeo*), also directed by Son JinChak in South Korea in 2005. *The Fairy in the Wall* (*Byeok Sokui YoJeong*) raises the question of ideology in the age of the Cold War in Spain. In short, *MiChu* tried to alert audiences to political issues, such as war, ideology, and dictatorship, and to defend life and nature.

In these accusatory plays, *MiChu Theatre* always tried to add elements of Korean traditions whenever possible, reproducing them most harmoniously and effectively as a whole and considering modern reinterpretations from today's perspective. The company considered traditional Korean heritage as a new theatrical source of the postmodern period rather than needing to be authentically reproduced. For this reason, the company was able to create a new genre, *MaDangNoRi*, based on the tradition with the contemporary entertainment industry.

8.3.4 Other Notable Directors

In addition to the above directors, who mostly turned to traditions for post-modern theatrical sources, some other directors focused more on postmodern techniques. Choi YongHun, who led *Little Miracle Company (Jakeun Sinwha)*, was one such representative. Through co-creation, the company presented the individualistic and fragmented phenomena of modern society with ultra-modern technology and ensembles. *War? Music! (JeonJaeng? Eumak!)* started with many techniques similar to the postmodern ones. It was influenced by many experimental exercises, such as improvisation, transformation, and co-creation. However, these applications were not simply duplications or imitations.[24] This performance was fully ensembled with rapid scene changes, transformations, and improvisations. For another example, *Mr. McKinto Ssi!*, a modernized Korean adaptation of Dario Fo's work, also contains scenes of improvisation, a mechanical ensemble of physical acting, rapid changes of multiple roles, computer video and sound effects, and so on. In addition, "the idea of virtualization of a cutting-edge mechanized future society first drew attention, and its limitations were well-drawn from the perspective of humanism."[25] It "convincingly presented the problems of the future society, such as modern people's sense of alienation and dwarfishness, environmental problems, abortion problems, and the hypertrophy of the mass media." The title of the play also made a pun, i.e., *Mr. McKinto, Ssi,* could mean McKintosi, the clogged city.[26] Above all, the entire performance was speedy but kept a rhythmic flow. Indeed, *Mr. McKinto Ssi!* presented a virtual reality of a cutting-edge civilization that destroyed humanity by utilizing these techniques to the maximum.

In short, *Little Miracle Company* focused on the overall ensemble rather than one main character, emphasizing the stereotype of fragmentary characters and mixed realities, such as the inclusion of a nightmare, as well as techniques of improvisation, transformation, co-creation, and rapid scene changes. The company often reflected the consciousness of young people in new ways. All these characteristics are the recollections of postmodernism.

Chae YunIl and Lee ByungHun are also notable directors of postmodern techniques. Chae YunIl, along with playwright Lee HyeonHwa, presented many plays, such as *0.917*, *Cadenza*, and *Bulga Bulga*. He was probably one of the first directors to pursue brutal sensory theatre and to diffuse or blur meanings in Korea. His directing of *The Mask of Fire—The Form of Power* is the Korean version of *Caligula*, which blurs the boundaries between meaning and meaninglessness with a persistent confrontation between power and knowledge and madness and reason. His *BulgaBulga* was probably one of the first deconstructive theatre pieces, which broke the binary of truth and falseness and righteousness and wrongness. *Bul* means "no," while *Ga* means "yes." Thus, *BulgaBulga* means both "yes" and "no" depending on how someone reads it; it is "inevitably possible" (*Bulgabul Ga*) and "absolutely impossible" (*Bulga Bulga*) according to the vocal breath-pronunciation. Ultimately, the binary of truth and falseness became vague.[27] It blurs what is true and what is false from the title, saying the exact opposite fact that the title may or may not be permissible at the same time. Lee ByungHun was unique in his innovative visualizations. His *Hunchback Kingdom* directly delivered violence and

Figure 8.10 A Scene from *War? Music!* Photo by *Little Miracle Company.*

madness, demonstrating that brutality can also be beautiful.[28] In other words, he broke the binary that brutality tends to be ugly and bad.

In short, these directors were all related to postmodern techniques, and they ultimately broadened the diversity of Korean theatre by visualizing total theatre using audiovisual images, ensembled physical movements, deconstruction of dichotomies, and appealing to cruelty and violence. They broke the long-held belief of Aristotelian causal storytelling and opened a new era. They paved the way for postmodernism.

8.3.5 Non-verbal Performance

Non-verbal performances were also were on the rise in the 1990s, like *Nanta*.[29] From its premiere in October 1997 to the present day, *Nanta* was the first recorded non-verbal and mixed genre performance in Korean theatre history. The story of *Nanta* is simple. Three cooks happily prepare the dishes, but the manager appears out of the blue and suddenly asks them to prepare various dishes for a wedding. The basic storyline is a hustle and bustle for this preparation.

The performance innovated many theatrical strategies, which showed the characteristics of postmodernism. First, it is theatrical because it eliminates all conversations from the performance but does not destroy the meaning of the plot. Since the music and percussive rhythm lead the performance, it could be considered a concert. This performance uses kitchen furniture, not ready-made real instruments. At the same time, the rhythm of traditional Korean

Samulnori is harmonized with the rhythm of modern Western popular music, such as jazz. In addition, the movements of the actors, as in traditional Korean Mask-dance theatre, are always in accordance with the rhythm. As a result, they could be considered some sort of modern dance. As such, *Nanta* was the emergence of a full-fledged postmodern performance that clearly declared the fusion of the performing arts.[30]

Various considerations for communion with the audience also emerged. Before the start of the performance, the performers tried to induce the audience's sense of rhythm by practicing applause or stomping on the floor with the audience. In addition, since the performance does not employ any conversations, it used other theatrical devices for dramatic changes. For example, water was boldly poured into the audience seats, and in order to bring the audience closer to the performance, some audience seats were placed in the orchestra, naturally incorporated with the stage scenery.[31] In addition, as traditional wedding ceremonies increased over the years, they were turned into theatrical events. Essentially, men and women are selected from the audience to experience a traditional Korean wedding ceremony and to participate in the performance. Also, several attempts to break down the walls between the stage and the auditorium are incorporated, such as throwing many colored balls from the stage to the audience, throwing sweets to the audience to taste, and utilizing the cooking odors, which stimulated the sense of smell. These methods, along with the music, enhanced communications with the audience. Percussion sound underscores throughout the performance; it controls the pace of the performance and monitors the excitement according to the speed of the beat.

Nanta has been commercially successful in Korea as well as abroad. Before Covid-19, there were three dedicated halls for this show in MyeongDong, Hongdae Station, and Jeju-Island, i.e., theatres based on mass popularity.[32] It is the first non-verbal performance to make use of traditional heritage and ceremonies in Korea, but also makes the performance very contemporary and enjoyable for the masses. The director of *Nanta*, Song SeungHwan, also directed the opening ceremony of the 2018 PyeongChang Winter Olympics, which was well received.

Jump is considered another representative performance that was successful along with *Nanta*. If *Nanta* was born and succeeded within the theatre industry, *Jump* appeared like a comet outside the theatrical world. In fact, all of the actors were martial arts practitioners and masters of Taekwondo, Taegyeon, Karate, and Hapkido. *Jump*, premiering in 2002, was able to build an exclusive theatre quickly, like *Nanta* and succeeded as a non-verbal performance.

Jump seems to have succeeded *Nanta* because it combined comedy with acrobatic movements and high-level martial arts. However, the dramatic composition is rather unnaturally structured, so it seems like a forced comedy. From a theatrical point of view, *Jump* may be insufficient in many ways, but the factor of its popularity was ultimately due to the traditional martial arts.

Ultimately, this performance must be understood as a complex genre. There is no doubt that martial arts are the strongest contributors to the performance.

Figure 8.11 A Cooking Scene from *Nanta*. Photo by *PMC Production*.

However, it would not have attracted the interest of the audience as much as it did if it only presented martial arts without any storytelling. The plot is about a day when a special guest, a martial arts master, comes to a family who is busy preparing to welcome the guests. It is a rather strange story in that the guest falls in love with the daughter of the house, and then a clumsy thief enters, upsetting the family. But the thief is soon caught by the guest, the martial arts master. The performance is successful in combining comedy and a high level of martial arts and acrobatic movements. The incorporation of martial arts attracted interest from the modern audience, who was enthusiastic about action performances. In addition, there were no language barriers, as it was a non-verbal performance.

It was also a performance that showed that popularity was not only achieved through artistic achievement, but it could also be easily gained through physical movements and spectacle. It was awarded the Foreign Press Promotion Award in the Culture Category by the Foreign Correspondents Club in 2004, ranked first at the Edinburgh Fringe box office in the UK in 2005, sold out at the Peacock Theatre in the West End in 2006, and then on Broadway. It also has theatres in Seoul and Busan exclusive for itself. "It established itself as a representative cultural product of Korea enjoyed by all people around the world."[33] The popularity of *Jump* could be understood in the same context as the popularity of Hong Kong martial arts movies. It was a performance that succeeded in commercializing and popularizing the martial arts traditions, such as Taekwondo, Taegyeon, Karate, and Hapkido in performance form. Although it was somewhat unfamiliar because it was not based on an orthodox theatre tradition, *Jump* was a successful work in terms of accommodating various traditions. The traditional martial arts that had been forgotten were brought to life and were presented for modern audiences. With martial arts, a genre outside of theatre art, the show pursued multi-faceted and spontaneous fun through multiple and episodic compositions. Martial arts and erratic actions were more enjoyable than providing unified meanings. Also, like *Nanta*, it was easy for audiences to approach. As such, it was a performance that connected to the popularity of postmodernism, giving priority to public enthusiasm over the aesthetic perfection of a play. *Jump*'s impact on the theatre world was not negligible. It is necessary for theatre to expand the scope of performances by considering the fact that traditional martial art is receiving worldwide attention.

Traditions have been passed down in various ways according to the tastes of the public. There have also been attempts to dismantle and synthesize theatre and other genres. For example, in the 1990s, through performances such as *Breath 4323* and *You Wear a Crown There*, the company of *Breath 4323* used language only when absolutely necessary and combined play and dance with bodily movements.

These postmodern trends have found their way into many other performances, forming a new theatrical trend. Even if a writer or director did not to advocate theatricism, many theatrical techniques, such as meta-drama and transformations of the proscenium arch, were easily applied. Regardless, what stands out most in the experiments of the 1990s was the reconstruction of traditions and the dissolution of modern theatre. While the first group of postmodern experimental directors from the West, such as Peter Brooke and Eugenio Barba, actively utilized elements of traditional theatre in the third

Figure 8.12 A Martial Arts Scene from *Jump*. Photo from the *Jump* Official Website

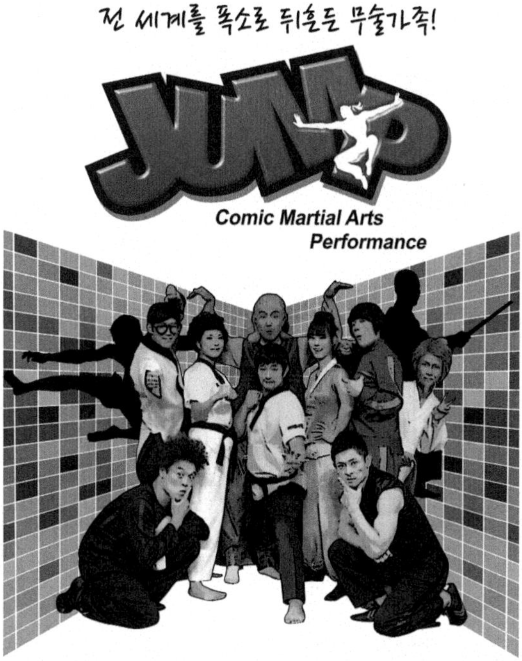

Figure 8.13 The Poster of *Jump*. Photo from the *Jump* Official Website

world after they rejected fully follow Aristotle's principles, the performances of "alive tradition" in Korea follow this global context. The attempt to create traditional theatre by dismantling and reconstructing it, not restoring it, is closely connected with the spirit of postmodernism and the globalization of Korean theatre. What stands out with the dissolution of the tradition is the break from the concept of modern drama. Here, as meta and narrative techniques and anti-logical attempts (fragmentation of lines, disregard of time and space, etc.) continue, sensation and shock appear as important effects.

8.4 Toward the New Millennium

Many theatre artists made new theatre companies, such as *HakJeon* in 1994, *ChaIMu* in 1995, *BaekSu GwangBu* in 1996, and *YeoHaengJa* in 1998. *HakJeon* took the lead in small theatre musicals with the representative Kim MinGi and was particularly famous for *Subway Line 1*, a German musical that he adapted into a Korean situation, which was praised by the original German director.

ChaIMu, inducted by Lee SangWu, produced many comedies, unlike most other companies, and created many social satires. The representatives of the above two companies, Kim MinGi and Lee SangWu, were former members of *YeonWu* Theatre and, thus, reached the apex of their time. In the meantime,

Figure 8.14 Many Foreign Audiences Waiting When *Subway Line 1* Was Reproduced in 2021. Photo by *HakJeon Theatre Company*.

two other leaders, Lee SeongYeol of *BaekSu GwangBu* and Yang JeongWung of *YeoHaengJa*, were emerging artists who led the next generation. Yang JeongWung actively applied Korean traditions to the Western canon, and Lee SeongYeol created works with neatly harmonized images. They led the experimental theatre movement in the new millennium.

In addition, many new directors started to draw attention in the late 1990s. Each of them presented their own plays with their own styles of directing. As in the past, newcomers were trained not only from the United States, England, Germany, and France but also from various countries, such as Russia and Japan presenting fresh influences on Korean theatres. For example, the performances of Kang RyangWon from Russia were based on physical movements, while Song SeonHo from Japan introduced contemporary Japanese plays, which showed the delicate deconstruction of everyday lives in isolation.

The notable playwrights in the late 1990s were Park GeunHyeong, Ko SeonWung, Lee HaeJe, Oh TaeYoung, and Bae SamSik, who debuted at the end of 1990 and led the playwriting scene of the 21st century. Some of them, such as Park GeunHyeong and Ko SeonWung, also served as directors. Their characteristics were as follows: Park GeunHyeong hyper-realistically described realities, which often turned to absurdity; Ko SeonWung conducted

Figure 8.15 A Scene from *Inspector* Directed by Kang RyangWon. Photo by *Theatre Dong*.

various theatrical experiments by exploring the loss of dreams, sexual corruption, alienation, paranoia, and repressed violence with a heroic protagonist; Lee HaeJe showed insight in humanity and social consciousness through his excellent use of indigenous poetic language, multi-sensory space, and fantasy crossing reality and illusion; and Oh TaeYoung kept silent after arguments of *Prostitution* in 1988, but in the late 1990s, he suddenly released a series of unification plays and drew attention. He pursued unification through subversive imagination and the forms of satire and allegory. Bae SamSik wrote plays like oriental paintings that contained blank space and thought, and, based on humanistic insights, he captured the poetic mood, ample humor, and the ephemeral nature of life. All of these playwrights were somewhat related to postmodernism in that they looked at life from a corner rather than from the center, often presenting ancillary characters as main characters in original plays, adding audience-conscious public entertainment and experimenting with various formats and styles. They led 21st-century Korean theatre, accelerating its diversity and forming their own audiences through various audiovisual images, formatted experiments, and fantasies.

The theatrical trends of the 1990s can be summarized again as follows: 1) 1990s theatrical experiments seem to be obsessed with form. The modern drama's sense of devotion to society had already disappeared; the charms of plays were no longer the depth of intellectual or philosophical content and shifted to the novelty of forms. 2) The art of theatre was more emphasized than ever. How to act became more important than why or what to act. For

Figure 8.16 A scene from *Get the Sun on the Haunted House* Written by Lee HaeJe. Photo by *Inhyeok Theatre Company.*

a performance that connected the tradition and the present, the East and the West, it was necessary to acquire both skills, so actors who learned traditional performing arts, such as *Pansori* and Mask-drama, learned Stanislavski's method as well. Stage artists and technicians were also more important in performances than ever before. 3) Inter-culturalism and post-colonialism became more prominent and widespread, especially in the 1990s. Now, it was clear that Korean theatre tried to recognize the legitimate values of Korean culture by breaking away from the cultural imperialism of the colonial era. 4) The concept of *cultural industry* emerged, and many planned theatre festivals and performances took place. 5) With the rise of music theatre, the musical firmly established itself as a genre, and Korean-style music theatre, such as *Changgeuk*, Women's *Changgeuk*, and *Akgeuk*, became active styles. 6) The experiments of Korean traditions continued, and artists actively applied Korean traditions to the Western canon. 7) In the absence of central value due to the individualism, the spirit of playfulness and entertainment emerged as the two greatest values. This is not irrelevant to the play's obsession with form, but it is linked to the emphasis on the ritual and common experience of theatre. In other words, the ritual function of ancient theatre seems to demand a common experience and a role as public entertainment in today's marginalized postmodern society. 8) International exchanges of theatre were expanded with the 1988 Olympics, and the Seoul Theatre Festival expanded to the Seoul

International Theatre Festival in 1998, greatly contributing to international exchange. 9) The rise of caricatures and parodies was clear, and emotional sensibility started to become important while social interest and responsibility diminished. 10) Minority theatre, such as feminism theatre, youth theatre, and children's theatre, grew. 11) The underground *Madanggeuk* was incorporated into an established theatre but then again declined. 12) Theatre was pushed out of DaeHakRo due to the high rent of theatres.

Korean theatre embraced postmodernism in the 1990s. As the countries of the world drew closer together, Korean theatre moved in line with the major trends of world theatre. The application of technology was also a factor that Korean theatre in this period strived to follow in order to remain in line with world theatre trends.

8.5 Theatre after the New Millennium

New changes after the new millennium began to appear around 2010 when the generational shift gradually became visible in the theatre world. Before that, Korean theatre had not been changed much, and the leading playwrights and directors of the 1990s were in power. The postmodern trend was further deepened, and various methodologies, such as de-constructionism, performativity, postcolonialism, and the concept of post-drama, were specifically applied to Korean theatres around the new millennium. Many new theatre artists came into being around 2010. This is closely related to "production theatres," which have been active since around 2010.[34] Doosan Art Center, Namsan Art Center, the Creative Platform of the Seoul Theatre Company, and the Next-Generation Artist Project of the Arts Council supported young talents.[35] These emerging new theatre artists received education that more cared about unique personalities and therefore had deeper interest in social and gender issues.

The Korean theatrical world also began to more actively apply Korean traditions to the Western canon, and some, such as Yang JeongWung and Oh TaeSeok, acquired global recognition. Korean traditions infused in the Western canon provided with different meanings to the original works, increasing the diversity of meanings and, at the same time, spreading the beauty of Korean traditions to the world. These experiments emerged as visible international results in the new millennium. For example, Yang JeongWung's directing of *A Midsummer Night's Dream*, his representative work, was introduced at the Edinburgh Fringe Festival in 2005, at the Gdansk International Shakespeare Festival in Poland, and, for the first time in Korean theatre history, at the Barbican Center in London, UK in 2006. His work attracted international attention, and he was invited to the Globe Theatre Festival held in commemoration of the 2012 London Olympics. Oh TaeSeok's adaptations are another example of international success; his *Romeo and Juliet* was performed at the Barbican Center in London in 2006, and his *Tempest* was performed at the Edinburgh International Festival, which received enough attention to win him the Award of Herald Angels in 2011.[36] The modernization and application of Korean theatrical heritage probably met its heyday during this period.

Due to the Sewol ferry disaster in 2014, Korean society was left in deep shock. Consequently, many writers and directors have treated this accident as their subject matter for plays. The ferry Sewol, which was on its way from Incheon to Jeju Island, sank in the sea near Jindo-gun, Jeollanam-do, in 16 April 2014. Among the 476 passengers on board, including high school students who were on a school trip, 304 people died, and a few of them were not recovered. The Joint Investigation Headquarters of the Prosecutors and Police Department announced that the Sewol ferry sank due to the illegal overloading of cargo, poor securing, excessive hull extension, and poor driving skills of the helmsman. The government was sweating over the controversy over "gwanfia ((官僚) bureaucrats + mafia)," which was pointed out as the cause of collusion and corruption in the shipping industry. In the process of probation, the government was confused, and Korean society suffered for a long time over the controversy surrounding the Sewol Special Act. The case soon became an important subject of plays, and for the first time, a kind of documentary drama started.

In addition, there were two major socio-political events related to these changes. One is the protest of artists against the "Black Lists"[37] in 2016 and the other is the "Me Too Movement" in 2018. The main cause of the Black

Figure 8.17 A Scene from Yang JeongWung's *A Midsummer Night's Dream*. Photo by *YeoHaengJa* Theatre Company.

Figure 8.18 *Hamlet*, Directed by Yang JeongWung in the City of London Festival (COLF), London. Photo by *YeoHaengJa* Theatre Company.

Figure 8.19 A Fire Scene from Oh TaeSeok's *Tempest*. Photo by *MokHwa Theatre Company*.

Figure 8.20 A Scene from Oh TaeSeok's *Tempest*. Photo by *MokHwa Theatre Company*.

Lists case was the exclusion of so-called leftist artists from the selections for public supporting funds during the former right-wing presidents' regime. After the protests, the Black List fact-finding committee was launched, and the committee reported its investigation results in a report in 2019.[38] It is doubtful that all of its reports are true, but it was an opportunity for artists to reconsider the issue of appeasement, censorship, and exclusion nowadays.

Another case, the "Me Too Movement" was also accelerated these changes in society in general. "Me Too Movement" in theatre broke out in 2018 after successive Me Too confessions in the literary circle beginning in 2016 and public prosecutors in early 2018. When actresses' Me Too confessions came out one after another, many established male directors and actors were accused. Female audiences formed a kind of fandom called "With You," supporting young female directors and actresses.

These two incidents, along with the Sewol ferry disaster, brought about profound changes in the theatre world. The Sewol ferry disaster made artists realize the corruptions of society as well as their own social negligence of themselves. They tried to recreate the entirety of the Sewol ferry accident in performances by visiting the accident site, interviewing the parents of the victims, etc. In other words, their efforts became the beginning of documentary theatre. There were performances ranging from plays showing the lamentations and sorrows of the mothers of dead students to plays condemning an irresponsible government. The Black Lists case induced artists to become

Figure 8.21 Another Scene from Oh TaeSeok's *Tempest*. Photo by *MokHwa Theatre Company*.

more sensitive and active about social issues. In a way, artists who had taken for granted the mild censorship—different from the strict and dictatorial censorship of the 1970s and 1980s—began to protest against it. In particular, there was a lot of criticism against the *national theatre* or national and public organizations that received government subsidies. As a result of the Me Too movement, questions arose about the existing hierarchical relationship among theatre-related artists, and the artists sought a symbiosis based on equality and cooperation. After these incidents, the theatre world's attention turned to social issues such as labor, gender, and disability. Such deep concerns for women also led to other interests in sexual minorities like queers, and their theatres also started to appear in the established theatre. Many of these new performances are collective company's creations, not individual works, and the directors are also relatively less established than before. The subject matters are mainly confined to reports of labor movement, gender discrimination, and the problems of disabilities. Their biased interest in the socially underprivileged and the minority, in a way, narrows the spectrum of theatre and tends to lower the overall aesthetic quality of performances.

In conclusion, a generational shift is in progress in the theatre world. Many new budding young artists have sprung up. It is encouraging that they are working hard, but there are only a few remarkable performances yet. Among new artists, directors Lee GyungSeong and Jeong JinSe have just settled in and are getting noticed. Indeed, Korean theatre is in the middle of new changes. 'The new artists' enthusiasm for a rightful society foretells upcoming social theatre which utilizes postmodern techniques after postmodernism, though nothing is settled yet. Whatever theatre it may be, the future of Korean theatre will hopefully keep pace with world theatre and seek its own unique color to contribute to the world as well.

Notes

1 It is a district of Seoul, Korea, where many theatres are located similar to Broadway and off-Broadway.
2 For example, the narrator of a play asks the audience what kind of ending they want, and depending on the answer, the ending is changed for each performance.
3 *The Thirty Years of YeonWu*, YeonWu, ed. Seoul, HanWul Publisher, 2008.
All following lists of performances are quoted from this book.
4 The name of the company 76 comes from the year it was founded.
5 "Shakespeare's Hamlet, An Experimental Production with 70 Young People in Jean." *Josun Daily Newspapers*, 15 Apr 1981.
6 The name of the theatre company "MokHwa" means cotton, which was the symbol of their mindset of creating theatre with a spinning wheel.
7 Lee, Sangran. *A Study on Oh TaeSeok's Theatre* (*Oh TaeSeok Yeonjeuk Yeongu*). Seoul, Seogang University Press, 2011, p. 21.
8 For further consult,
Myong, InSeo, and Choi JunHo. *Oh TaeSeok' Theatrical World* (*Oh TaeSeok ui Yeonjeuk Segye*). Seoul, Hyundae Mihaksa, 1995.
Oh, TaeSeok, and Seo YeonHo. *Oh TaeSeok's Theatre: 40 Years of Experimentations and Challenges* (*Silheom gwa Dojeon ui 40 yeon*). Seoul, Yeonguek gwa Ingan, 2002.
Hanguk GeukYesul Hakhoe. *Oh TaeSeok*. Seoul, Yeongeuk gwa Ingan, 2010.
Lee, Sangran. *A Study on Oh TaeSeok's Theatre* (*Oh TaeSeok Yeonjeuk Yeongu*). Seoul, Seogang University Press, 2011.
9 Oh, TaeSeok. *Throw Herself Twice in Indang Sea* (*Wae Simchongieun Dubeon Indangsu ui momeul Deonjotneunga*). Seoul, Pyongminsa, 1994.
10 Yu, InGyong. *"The Grotesque of Oh TaeSeok's Theatre." Oh TaeSeok*. Hanguk Geukyesul Hakhoe ed., Seoul, Yeongeuk gwa Ingan, 2010, pp. 247–274.
11 General Gaebaek originally killed his family before going to the final fight with Silla because he was thinking of dying in the fight. So, it was an unofficial tale to praise the loyalty of Gaebaek. However, Oh TaeSeok interpreted the tale oppositely; Gaebaek sinned and transformed into a spider.
12 Oh TaeSeok named this method the dialogue of "ridge between rice paddies."
13 Lee, Meewon. *Contemporary Korean Playwrights*. Seoul, Yeongguek gwa Ingan, 2003. pp.233.
14 Lee, YunTaek. "To Change the Perception of *Gut* and Theatre." *The Korean Theatre Review*, Aug 1990.
15 The debates of *Gut* are a series of debates between Lee YunTaek and Lee SangIl. Lee SangIl criticizes Lee YunTaek's hasty application of *Gut* into theatre, saying *Gut* is *Gut*, while *theatre* is *theatre*. Lee YunTaek replies that *Gut* is the origin of traditional Korean theatre and that he now tries to restore its living tradition in theatre.
16 Psychopomps, literally meaning the "guide of souls," are creatures, spirits, angels, or deities in many religions whose responsibility is to escort newly deceased souls from Earth to the afterlife.

17 It is believed that there is a long journey from this life to the next, and the journey's guide money refers to the travel expenses required to go on this journey.
18 Lee, YunTaek Op. cit.
19 Lee, YoungMi. *Hangyeore Daily Newspapers*, 15 Jul 1995.
20 Choi, JunHo. "Semiotics in Korean Contemporary Theatre: The Problematic Human." *The Korean Theatre Reviews,* Sept. 1995.
21 http://www.michoo.co.kr
22 Kim, BangOk. *DongA Daeily Newspaper,* May 1993.
23 They are Korean traditional percussion, acrobatic feats, dish-spinning tricks, tight-rope walking, Mask-Dance theatre, and puppet theatre.
24 Choi, YongHun. "Director's Words." *The Program of War? Music!, 1991.*
25 Lee, Meewon. *Korean Theatre in Postmodern Period.* Seoul, Hyundae Mihaksa, 1996, pp. 191–192.
26 Ibid.
27 Lee, Meewon. "Lee HyunHwa and Postmodernism." *Contemporary Korean Playwrights.* Seoul, Yeongeuk gwa Ingan, 2003, pp. 214–215.
28 Lee, Meewon, *Korean Theatre in the Postmodern Period.* Seoul, Hyundae Mihaksa, 1996, p. 53.
29 "*Nanta*" means beating or hitting in Korean.
30 Lee, Meewon. "A New Experimental Performance: *Nanta.*" *Age of Globalization/ Theatre in Deconstruction* (Segewha Sidae/Haechewha Yeongeuk). Seoul, Yeongeuk gwa Ingan, 2001, p. 241.
31 Ibid.
32 from *Nanta* homepage, https://www.nanta.co.kr/
33 http://www.yeegam.com/jump/ENG/introduction/01_about.asp
34 "Production theatre" is a theatre production system specifically by the theatre company to produce its own productions. Mostly, this system was identified as employing young artists. The name was derived after the young artists in the 1950s called their new company "production theatre." Since then, this term has been broadly used.
35 Kim, BangOk. "Korean Theatre and the Power of Feminism in 2010s." *The Korean Theatre Journal,* vol. 96, Spring 2020, p. 167.
36 Lee, Meewon. *Korean Traditions and Performances in Postmodern Era.* Seoul, Seoul National University Press, 2016, pp. 233–246
37 Blacklists are prepared for the purpose of vigilance, surveillance, or disadvantage against the target, and most of the blacklists created for the purpose of discrimination are illegal and can cause social controversy. A typical example is a company creating a blacklist of workers who have joined a labor union to hinder their employment, and according to the Labor Standards Act of Korea, blacklisting for the purpose of hindering workers from getting a job is prohibited.
38 *The Report of Blacklist in the World of Arts and Culture: Committee of Fact Investigations and System Improvements.*Blacklist Fact-Finding Committee ed., Seoul, Munhwa Cheyuk Gwangwanbu, Feb. 2019.

Selected Bibliography

An, JongHwa. *A Story of the Modern Theatre History (新劇史 Iyagi)*. Seoul, Jinmunsa, 1955.

Bang, TaeSu. "Ejeotto's Gathering of Eight Years." *The Korean Theatre Review (韓國演劇)*, Jan 1976.

———. "The Wanderer Dreaming of Built-In." *The Korean Theatre Review*, Aug 1986.

Best, Steven, and Douglas Kellner. *Postmodern Theory*. New York, The Guilford Press, 1991.

Brunet, Brigitte. "Le Théâtre de Boulevard." *French Studies*, vol. 59, July 2005.

Brustein, Robert. *The Theater of Revolt*. Methuen, T&A Constable ltd, 1962.

Carlson, Marvin. *Performance*. London and New York, Routledge, 1996.

Cha, BumSeok. "Cafe Theatre and Ejeotto Small Theater." *Art World (藝術世界)*, Aug 1991.

———. "The Dream of 10 Years Ago." *10 Years' History of the Sanha Theater Company (劇團山河十年史: 1963-1973)*. Seoul, The Sanha Theater, 1974.

———. "Stars are in Every Night (Beoyleun Bammada)." *The Korean Theatre Review*, Jun 1977.

Cha, BumSeok, and Kang YuJeong. "Three Cranes Met on the Road to Liberation." *The Korean Theatre Review*, Oct 1984.

Chae, HuiWan, and Im JinTaek. "From Madangguk to Madang-gut." *The Present Status of Korean Literature (韓國文學 ui 現段階)*. Kim YunSu et al. ed. Seoul, Changjak gwa Bipyongsa, 1982.

Cho, Oh-Kon. *Korean Theatre: From Rituals to the Avant-Garde*. Fremont, Jain Publishing Company, 2015.

Choi, Hyeon. "The Regional Tour Performance of GalDopHoe." *Donga Daily Newspapers*, 1 Aug 1921.

Choi, InHoon. *Literature and Ideology (文學 gwa Ideology)*. Seoul, Munhak gwa Jisungsa, 1979.

Choi, JunHo. "Semiotics in Korean Contemporary Theatre: The Problematic Human." *The Korean Theatre Reviews*, Sept 1995.

Choi, Wonsik. *The Logic of National Literature (民族文學ui 論理 1)*. Seoul, Changbi, 1982.

Choi, YunYoung. "The Acting Style of Sinpageuk Actors in 1910s (1910 年代 韓國 新派劇 俳優ui 演技 樣式)." *Theatre Education Journal (演劇教育研究)*, 2011.

Danguk University's Dongyanghak Yeonguso. *Anthology of Dongyanghak38:* 日常生活 *gwa* 近代 結婚制度, 新聞編. Seoul, Minsokwon, 2010.

"DaShiRaGi." *The Anthology of the 3rd Korean Theatre Festival (第3回 大韓民國演劇祭戲曲集)*. Korean Culture and Arts Foundation, ed., Seoul, Hanguk Munhwa YeSul Jinhungwon, 1980.

Formation Process of Modern Literature (近代文學eu 形成過程). Korean Association of Traditional Literature, ed. Seoul, Munhak gwa Jiseongsa, 1983.

Fortier, Mark. *Theory/Theatre*. London and New York, Routledge, 1997.

"The Foundational Declaration of the Bridge Theatre." 20 Mar 1965, Pamphlet of the Bridge Theatre in 1965.

Gu, HeeSeo. "The String of Life--Clearly Emphasizes the Meaning of *The Placenta*." Oh TaeSeok, *Oh TaeSeok 's Playbook 1: On the Moonlit Night of the Baekma River (Oh TaeSeok 戲曲集 1: Baekmagang dal Bam-e)*. Seoul, PyeogMinSa, 1994.

Han, Heo. *The Overview of Joson Theatre History (朝鮮演劇史概要)*. Seoul, Gungnipchulpansa, 1956.

———. "The Requests of Joaon Theatrical World." *People's Arts(人民 藝術)*, Dec 1945.

Han, SangCheol. *Issues and Reflections in Korean Theater(韓國演劇ui 爭點gwa 反省)*. Seoul, Hyundae Mihaksa, 1992.

———. "The Women Theater that Survived for 20 Years." The Program of the 78th Regular Performance of the Women Theater, *Across the River, NeoBuSilo*, Mar 1986.

Heo, Gyu. "The Man of Korea, TteogSoe." *National Drama and Traditional Art(民族劇 gwa 傳統藝術)*. Seoul, Munhak SegyeSa, 1991.

Hyeon, Chul. "The Relation of Theatre and I (演劇 gwa 吾人 ui 關係)." *Mail Daily Newspapers(*每日申報), 30 June 1920.

Im, JinTaek. "For New Theatre: A Few Ideas about Madanggeuk." *Essays on the Establishment of People's Theatre (民族劇 Jeongrip-eul Wihan 資料集)*, vol. 2. Ulrim, ed., Seoul, Uri Madang, 1987.

Interculturalism and Performance. Bonnie Marranca and Gautam Dasgupta, ed. New York, PAJ Publications, 1991.

The Intercultural Performance Reader. Patrice Pavis, ed. London and New York: Routledge, 1996.

Jang, Hangi. *Korean Theatre History(韓國演劇史)*. Seoul, Dongguk University Press, 1986.

Jeon, GyongOk. *History and Principles of Korean Mask-dance Theatre (韓國假面劇ui 歷史wa 原理)*. Seoul, Yeolhawadang, 1998.

Jeong, ByungHee. "Performances of Translated Plays in Korea." *The Korean Theatre Journal (演劇評論)*, Apr 1971.

Jeong, Hosoon. *Little Theater Movement in Korea (韓國 ui 小劇場 gwa 演劇運動)*. Seoul, Drama and Humans, 2002.

Jeong, InSeop. "After Seeing the Exhibition of Theatre and Movie." *DongA Daily Newspapers*, 23 Jun–4 Jul 1931.

Jeong. JinSu. "On the Popularization of Theater." 2000, Korean Theater Society Symposium.

———. "The Trend of Translation in 1991." *Culture and Art (文化 wa 藝術)*, 25 Nov 1991.

Jin, Bonggyu. *Pansori: Theory and Practice (Pansori: 理論 gwa 實際)*. Seoul, Suseowon, 1989.

Jo, DongIl. "The Compositional Principle of the Nobleman Scene in Bongsan Mask-Dance Theatre." *The Ideology of Mask -Dance Theatre (Talchum ui 思想)*, Chae Hui-wan, ed. Seoul, Hyunamsa, 1984.

———. *The Esthetics of Korean Mask-Dance Theatre (韓國 假面劇 ui 美學)*. Seoul, Hanguk Daily Newspaper, 1975.

———. *History and Principles of Korean Mask-dance Theatre (Talchum-ui 歷史wa 原理)*. Seoul, Hongseongsa, 1979.

Kang, Hanyoung. *Pansori*. Seoul, Sejong Daewang Giyeomsayeophoe, 2000.

Kang, YuJeong. "Director's Note: Recognition of an Independent Personality as a Wife." The Program Book of *The Constant Wife (Anaeraneun 職業ui 女人)*, April 1990.

———. "Life of the Pioneer Hwang JinIi." The Program Book of *Free Spirit* (自由魂), Sep 1987.

———. The Program Book of *Return*, Feb 1990.

Kim, BangOk. "Korean Theatre and the Power of Feminism in 2010s." *The Korean Theatre Journal (演劇評論)*, vol. 96, Spring 2020.

———. "A Study of Madangguk." *Journal of Korean Theatre Studies Association (韓國演劇學)*, vol. 7, no. 1, 1995.

Kim, Dongwon. *Curtain Call at the Age of 88*. Seoul, Taehaksa, 2003.

Kim, EulHan. "Chat about Theatre (演劇雜談)." *Joseon Daily Newspapers*, 8–9 Jun 1926.

Kim, GeongOk. "The Manifesto of Jejak GeukHoe." *The Secret Stories in Jejak GeukHoe (制作劇會 祕話). The Korean Theatre Review*, June 1985.

Kim, GiJin. "The Views on this Literary Age Short Novels (文藝時代觀 短篇)." *Joseon Daily Newpaper*, 9–20 Nov 1928.

———. "A Year of Art Movement (藝術運動ui 一年間)." *JoseonGwang*, Jan 1930.

Kim, GwangSup. "A Proposal to Joson Theatre Companies." *Joson Daily Newspaper*, 1933.

Kim, Hakdong. *A Study on Korean Poetry of the Enlightenment Period (開化期 詩歌 硏究)*. Seoul, Simunhaksa, 1981.

Kim, HakJu. *Plays of Popular Entertainments of China (中國ui 戲曲 gwa 民間 演戲)*. Seoul, MyongMunDang. 2002.

Kim, Heunggyu. *Pansori*. Seoul, Jeonbuk Aeyang Bonbu, 1988.

Kim, IgDu. "Poetics and Politics: The Formal Characteristic and Political & Social Meaning of Sinpaguek (新派劇 ui 詩學gwa 政治學)." *Korean Performance Journal (韓國公演文化硏究) vol 11*, 2005.

Kim, Jaecheol. *Theatre History of Joseon (朝鮮演劇史)*. Seoul, Chongjin Seogwan, 1933.

Kim, JiHa. *The National Aesthetics of the Mask-Dance Theatre (Talchum ui 民族美學)*. Seoul, Silcheon Munhak, 2004.

Kim, JinSu. "Signal Fire of Realistic Theatre (新劇樹立ui 烽火)." *KyungHayng Newspapers*, 25 Oct 1949.

Kim, MunHwan. "Oh Taeseok: A Sense of Reality in Unrealistic Play." Oh TaeSeok, *Collection of Oh TaeSeok's Play 2: Why did Simcheong Thrown Twice into the Indang Sea? (Oh Taeseok Higokjin 2)*. Seoul, PyeongMinSa, 1994.

———. "The 1st Young Theater Festival." *Seoul Daily Newspaper*, 15 Jun 1973.

Kim, SeongHee. *Art World (藝術世界)*, Nov 1987.

———. *The Comtemporary Korean playwrights (韓國現代 劇作家)*. Seoul, PakMunSa, 2014.

———. "A Painful Life and a Vision of Overcoming it." *Young Lady*, Aug 1992.
Kim, UiGyeong, "The 20 Hard Years of the Women Theatre." The Program Book of *Across the River to NeoBuSil*, Mar 1986.
———. "Start and Re-start of the Experimental Theatre." *10 Years of the Experimental Theater (劇團 實驗劇場 10年史)*, 1970.
Kim, UiGyeong, and Yu Ingyeong. *The Selection of Lee JinSun*. Seoul, 演劇 gwa 人間, 2010,
Kim, Ujin. "About the So-called Modern Theatre." *Hakgigwang*, Oct 1921.
Kim, WooOk. *P'ansori: An Indigenous Theatre of Korea, 1980*. New York University, Ph.D. dissertation.
Kim, YoungPal. "Novel No Novel (小說非小說)." *Joseon Daily Newspaper*, 13 Apr 1928.
Kim, YuMi. "A Study on the Continuity of Sinapgeuk or Melodrama (新派劇 hokeun Melodrama ui 持續性研究)." *Journal of Korean Theatre Studies Association (韓國演劇學) V. 28*, 2006.
Kim, YunSik, and Kim Hyun. *Korean Literary History (韓國文學史)*. Seoul: Minumsa, 1973.
Kirby, E. T. *Ur-Drama: The Origin of Theatre*. New York, New York University Press, 1975.
Korean Modern Korean Drama: An Anthology. Richard Nichols, ed. New York, Columbia University Press, 2009.
Lee, Duhyun. *The Collection of Korean Mask-dance Theatre (韓國假面劇選)*. Seoul, Geyomunsa, 1997.
———. *Korean Mask-Dance Theatre (韓國假面劇)*. Seoul, The Association of Korean Mask-Dance Theatre, 1969.
———. *Korean Theatre History (韓國演劇史)*. Seoul, Hankyeonsa. 1985.
———. *A Study of Korean Modern Theatre History (韓國新劇史研究)*. Seoul, Seoul National University Press, 1966.
Lee, GeuSam. "Biggest Harvent of the Year-National Theatre Comapny's Burning Mountain." *Hanguk Daily Newspapers*, 29 Dec 1962.
———, "Young Company." *The 10 Years of the Experimental Theatre (劇團 實驗劇場 10年史)*, 1970.
Lee, GiBaek. *HangukSa Sango (韓國史散稿)*. Seoul, Iljogak, 2005.
Lee, GwangRin. *A Study on Korean History of Englightenment Period (韓國開化史研究)*. Seoul, Iljogak, 1984.
Lee, Heongu. "After Attending the New Construction's First Performance." *Joseon Daily Newspapers*, 26 Nov 1933.
Lee, JaeSeon. *A History of Modern Korean Novels (韓國現代小說史)*. Seoul, Hongseungsa, 1979.
———. *Literature of the Enlightenment Period (開化期文學論)*. Seoul, Hanguk Haksul Jeongbo, 2002.
Lee, JinSun. "The History of Korean Theater." *The Korean Theatre Review* Vol.6, Jun 1978.
Lee, Meewon. *Age of Globalization/Theatre in Deconstruction (世界化 時代/解體化 演劇)*. Seoul, Yeongeuk gwa Ingan, 2001.
———. *Contemporary Korean Playwrights (韓國 現代 劇作家 研究)*. Seoul, Yeongguek gwa Ingan, 2003.
———. *Kamyonguk: The Mask-Dance Theatre of Korea*. 1983. University of Pittsburgh, PhD dissertation.

———. *Korean Theatre in Postmodern Period (Postmodern 時代의 韓國演劇).* Seoul, Hyundae Mihaksa, 1996.

———. *Korean Traditions and Performances in Postmodern Era (Postmodern時代 ui 韓國傳統gwa Performances).* Seoul, Seoul National University Press, 2016.

———. *A Study on the Modern Korean Theatre (韓國近代劇研究).* Seoul, HyundaeMihaksa, 1994.

Lee, Meewon, and Kim Bangok. "The History of Korean Theater in 50 Years of Liberation." 50th Anniversary of Liberation, Articles (光復50周年 紀念論文集), Korean Academic Research Foundation ed., Korea AcademicResearch Foundation, 1995.

Lee, SangIl. "Ritual or Theatre." *The Korean Theatre Review,* July 1990.

Lee, SangRan. *A Study on Oh TaeSeok's Theatre (Oh TaeSeok 演劇 研究).* Seoul, Seogang University Press, 2011.

Lee SangWu. "Violence and Sacredness." *Theory of Korean Playwrights (韓國劇作家論),* Korean Theater Critics Association, ed. Seoul, Pyeongminsa, 1998.

Lee, SeoGu. *The Early Unoffical History of Korean Modern Theatre (韓國演劇運動 ui 胎兒期野史).* Seoul, Sinsajo (新思潮), 1964.

Lee, SeokMan. *A Theatre Study of the Liberation Period (解放期 演劇 研究).* Seoul, TaeHakSa, 1996.

Lee, SeungGyu. "Theatrical Company Bridge, 10 Years of Touring." *The Korean Theatre Review*, Jan 1976.

Lee, TaeJu. "Contemporary Korean Theater and Criticism." *The Korean Theatre Review*, Mar 2000.

Lee, YeongMi. *Madangguk, Realism, and National Theatre (Madangguk, Realism, 民族劇).* Seoul, Hyundae Mihaksa, 1997.

———. *The Principles and Characteristics of Madanghuk (Madangguk 様式의 原理와 特性).* Seoul, Korean National Research Center for the Arts, 1996.

Lee, YunTaek, "To Change the Perception of *Gut* and Theatre." *The Korean Theatre Review,* Aug 1990.

———. "The Writer's Handbook." *Laughs, Beat the drum, and Die (Utta, Buk chida, Jugtta).* Seoul, Pyeongminsa, 1993.

Lehmann, Hans-Thies. *Postdramatisches Theater (Postdrama 演劇*). Kim Giran, trans. Seoul, Hyundae Mihaksa, 2013.

Lim, Hwa. "Towrad the *Muddy Stream* (濁流e Dehayeo)." *JoseonGwang,* Aug 1929.

Lukács, George. *The Realism of Our Time*, Munhal Yeosul Yeongguhoe, trans. Seoul, Ingansa, 1986.

MacDonald, Eric. *Theater at the Margins.* Ann Arbor, University of Michigan Press, 1993.

Madanggeuk(Minjeokgeuk) Scripts (民族劇 臺本選). vol. 1 & 2, People's Drama Research Society, ed. Seoul, Pulbit, 1988.

Madanggut Script Collection of Jeonlado (全羅道 Madang-gut 臺本集), Shin Myung Players, ed. Gwangju, DeulPul, 1989

Min, YoungHwan. *The Posthumous Work of Patriot Min (Min Chungjunggong Yugo*). Lee Minsu, trans. Seoul, Ilsogak, 2000.

Myong, InSeo. "A Comparative Study of Korean and Japanese *Sinpa* Theatre and Western Melodrama(韓日 新派劇gwa 西歐 Melodrama 比較研究)." *Journal of Korean Theatre Studies Association (韓國演劇學) V.18*, 2002.

Myong, InSeo, and Choi JunHo ed., *Oh TaeSeok' Theatrical World (Oh TaeSeok ui 演劇世界).* Seoul, Hyundae Mihaksa, 1995.

Oh TaeSeok (Oh TaeSeok), Hanguk GeukYesul Hakhoe, ed. Seoul, Yeongeuk gwa Ingan, 2010.

Oh, TaeSeok. *Why did Simchong Throw Herself Twice in Indang Sea? (Wae Simchongieun Dubeon Indangsu ui momeul Deonjotneunga)*. Seoul, Pyongminsa, 1994.

Oh, TaeSeok, and Seo YeonHo. *Oh TaeSeok's Theatre: 40 Years of Experimentations and Challenges (實驗 gwa 挑戰 ui 40 年)*. Seoul, Yeonguek gwa Ingan, 2002.

Park, Hwang. *A Study of Changgeuk History (唱劇史研究)*. Seoul, Peknoksa, 1976.

Park, Jin. *Years and Years (歲歲年年)*. Seoul, Gyonghwa Publishers, 1966.

Park, NoHong. "The Trend of Akguek." *The Movie Era (映畫時代)*, Apr 1964.

Park, SeungHee. "Tales of Towolhoe." *Sasanggae*, May 1963.

Park, YongChoel. "After Attending the Second Performances of The Experimental Stage." *Donga Daily Newspapers*, 2 Jul 1932.

Parry, Milman. "Studies in the Epic Technique of Oral Verse-Making 1: Homer and Homeric Style." *Harvard Studies in Classical Philology*, vol. 41, 1930.

People's Theatre in Korea (韓國ui 民衆劇). Chae HuiWan and Im JinTaek, eds. Seoul, Changjak gwa Bipyongsa, 1985.

"The Performances of Hyeongsulhoe." *Mail Daily Newspapers*, 26 Jul 1923.

The Record of Western Travelog (西遊見聞): *Comlete Texts*, Lee Hansup, ed. Seoul, Parkeejung, 2000.

The Report of Blacklist in the World of Arts and Culture: Committee of Fact Investigations and System Improvements. Blacklist Fact-Finding Committee ed., Seoul: Munhwa Cheyuk Gwangwanbu, Feb. 2019.

Seo, HangSeok. "The Korean War and My Theatre." *The Korean Theatre Review*, June. 1977.

Seo, YeonHo. *Korean Theatre History (韓國演劇前史)*. Seoul, Yeonguek gwa Ingan, 2006.

———. *Korean Theatre History: The Contempoary Period (韓國 演劇史: 現代編)*. Seoul, Yeongeuk kwa Ingan, 2005.

———. *Korean Theatre History: The Modern Period (韓國 演劇史: 近代編)*. Seoul, Yeongeuk kwa Ingan, 2004.

———. "Korean Theater and Realism: Recognition and Development." *The Korean Theatre Review*, April 1987.

———. *A Study of Korean Modern Drama (韓國近代戲曲史研究)*. Seoul, Korea University Press, 1982.

Seo, YeonHo, and Lee SangWu. *100 Years of Our Theatre (Uri 演劇 100 年)*. Seoul, Hyunamsa, 2000.

"Shakespeare's Hamlet, An Experimental Production with 70 Young People in Jean." *Josun Daily Newspapers*, 15 Apr 1981.

Shin, GoSong. "The Start of Theatre Movement, the Present Stage of Proletarian Theatre." *Joson Daily Newspapers*, 29 Jul–2 Aug 1931.

———. "Theatre Movement and its Organization." *People (人民)*, Dec 1945.

Shin, HyunSuk. "French Drama." *Western Theater in Korea 1900-1995 (韓國eseoui 西洋演劇:1900 年-1995 年ggagi)*. Shin JeongOk et al. ed., Seoul, Seowha, 1999.

———. *French Theater of the 20th Century*. Seoul, Munhak gwa Jiseongsa, 1997.

———. "A Study on the Acceptance of French Theater in Korea." *The Articles of Duksung Women's University*, vol. 25, 1996.

Sohn, JongMuk. *A Study on the Social and Economic Cities of the Enlightenment Period (韓國開港期都市社會經濟史研究)*. Seoul, Ilgisa, 1982.

Stampton, Owen. "Sorrows of the Inner Room." *Asian Theatre Journal*, Spring 2022.

A Study of KAPF's Literary Movement (KAPF 文學運動研究). Yeogsa Munjae Yeonguso, ed. Seoul, History Criticism, 1990.

A Study on Shin JaeHyo's Pansori (Shin JaeHyo Pansori 研究). The Association of Pansori Studies, ed. Seoul, The Association of Pansori Studies, 1990.

The Thirty Years of YeonWu (演友 30 年: 創作劇 開發ui 旅程). YeonWu, ed. Seoul, HanWul Publisher, 2008.

Um, Haekyung. *Korean Musical Drama: P'ansori and the Making of Tradition in Modernity*. London and New York, Routledge, 2013.

Wu, SuJin. *The Formation of Korean Modern Theatre (韓國近代劇ui 形成)*. Seoul, Peureun Sasangsa, 2011.

Yang, DongHyun. *The History of People's Enlightenment in the Enlightenment Period (開化期 民衆 開化史)*. Seoul: CahngJoGak, 1988.

Yeo, SeokGi. "Korean Theatre in the 1960s and the Experimental Theatre." *The Record of 40 Years of the Experimental Theatre (實驗劇場40年史)*, 2001.

———. "Some Problems in Translated Performances." *The Reality of Korean Theatre(韓國演劇ui 現實)*. Seoul, Donghwa Publishing Co., 1974.

———. "That Personality, That Conviction." The Egeotto Theatre's 41st performance *My Name is Hobby*.

———, "Panel Discussion: The Controversial Works of This Issue." *The Korean Theatre Journal*, Winter 1976.

———, "Panel Discussion: The Controversial Works of This Issue." *The Korean Theatre Journal*, Winter 1976.

Yu, ChiJin. "After Attending the Performances of Joseonyeongeuksa (朝鮮演劇舍)." *Joseon Daeily Newspapers*, 2 Jan 1933.

———. "The Drama Center is Not Privatized." *Korean Daily Newspaper*, 1 Sep 1966.

———. "To Promote Our Creative Drama." *Joseon Daily Newspaper*, 3–6 Aug 1935.

———. "The Road Ahead of the Joseon Theatre-about its Policy and Solutions." *JoGwang*, Jan 1935.

Yu, DeokHyung. "Notes for Directing *Grass Tomb*." *The Korean Theatre Journal*, Summer 1973.

Yu, InGyong. *"The Grotesque of Oh TaeSeok's Theatre" Oh TaeSeok*, Hanguk Geukyeosul Hakhoe, ed. Seoul, Yeongeuk gwa Ingan, 2010.

Yu, MinYoung. *The History of Drama Movement in Our Time (Uri 時代 演劇運動史)*. Seoul, Dankook University Press, 1990.

———. *A History of Modern Korean Drama (韓國現代戲曲史)*. Seoul, Hongsongsa, 1982.

———. *The History of Korean Theatre Movemnent (韓國演劇運動史)*. Seoul, TaehakSa, 2001.

———. *History of Modern Korean Theatre (韓國近代演劇史)*. Seoul: Danguk University Press, 1995.

———. "Lessons of the 1st Theater Festival and Prospects for the New Year's Theater." *Theatrical Culture of the Late 20th Century (20世紀 後半의 演劇文化)*. Seoul, Korean Academy of Education, 2000.

———. "Opening a New Field ⑧-The History of the Women Theater." *The Korean Theater Review*, Oct 1982.

———. *A Study on the Theatre of Enlightenment (開化期演劇 社會史)*. Seoul, Samoonsa, 1987.
———. "20 Years of the People Theater." *The Korean Theater Review*, Jan 1984.
Yun, Baknam. "Theatre and Society (演劇 gwa 社會)." *Donga Daily Newspapers*, 14 May 1920.

Index